ABOUT THI

Geoffrey Hindley worked in London publishing, then freelance as writer, lecturer and teacher in UK, Europe and the US. As visiting professor, he travelled pretty widely, seeing something of poorer neighbourhoods and riding railroad sleeping car from Chicago to New York.

BLACK DYNASTY

The saga of the Stone and Porter families of Kentucky as told to

Geoffrey Hindley

by

Loretta Stone

With a Prologue by John Carman, *roving reporter retired*

Matador
9 Priory Business Park,
Wistow Road, Kibworth Beauchamp,
Leicestershire. LE8 0RX
Tel: (+44) 116 279 2299
Fax: (+44) 116 279 2277
Email: books@troubador.co.uk
Web: www.troubador.co.uk/matador

ISBN 978 1780881 959

British Library Cataloguing in Publication Data.
A catalogue record for this book is available from the British Library.

Typeset in 11pt Book Antiqua by Troubador Publishing Ltd, Leicester, UK
Printed and bound in the UK by TJ International, Padstow, Cornwall

Matador is an imprint of Troubador Publishing Ltd

To Sophie Jane Hindley

Contents

Prologue

The Greyhound coach continued to lose speed from its legal 55 mph. Here and there, an abandoned oil donkey dipped a rusting hammer head into the parched Kentucky "pennyrile" mint grass. Ahead, through the smoked glass of the windshield, the highway hurried to the horizon towers of Warrensville, ten miles of glittering heat haze still to travel.

'Hey there, what's the problem?'

'We gotta stop here, Mister.'

'Stop where? There's no stop shown on my route schedule before Warrensville.'

The tetchy, white, East Coast voice from the front of the coach cut across the neighborly chat of the mostly African American, blue-collar family vacationers. The one or two more prosperous travelers from out of state were no doubt hoping for a nostalgic journey back to their sixties youth; the heckler was no part of this amiable minority, and the interior of the luxury Highway-Master was boringly conventional. The New York journalist, John "Johnny" Carman – commissioned to do a "Bus Stop" photo feature by his unimaginative magazine editor, Art Greeley – cringed at the all-too-familiar tones of outraged "whitey", and cursed his own skin color, which inevitably badged him with the speaker.

The driver, slowing still further, was swinging the vehicle off the main road toward an unusual building, standing alone in the landscape on its own access drive. Standing up in the aisle now, the East Coaster burst out again.

'But this is ridiculous: stopping for one house and nobody on the bus getting out.'

They were now drawing up to the long, low terrace of a house. Four wide steps led up from the side road to the central balustraded porch, which was flanked by American colonial-style windows, while set in the roof above the second floor windows, a wide dormer completed the air of restrained domestic opulence. White-railed meadowland, grazing half a dozen quality stallions, stretched away behind and to either side of the residence.

'Huh! A rich man's ranch-hands' bus stop?' sneered the trouble maker. 'And in this new age of transport deregulation and competition – the South doesn't change!'

The driver shrugged, but all he said was, 'Cool it, bud.'

A tall, burly, grizzle-haired African American rose from a seat a couple of rows back from the front of the coach. Carrying just an overnight briefcase, he moved past the East Coaster, who shrank back between the seats, tipping the driver a twenty dollar bill as the pneumatic doors hissed open.

'Be seeing you, Lute. Thanks for the ride.'

There was no warmth behind the friendly cliché.

'Thank *you*, Mister Stone, have a nice weekend, now!'

As the Greyhound eased away and continued along the slip road to rejoin the highway, the journalist twisted round just in time to see a very British butler open the porch door to the elegant figure. "Mystery mansion on the way to Blue Grass Country"; the place seemed made for a tabloid headline. It was certainly strange.

In fact, thought Johnny Carman, you could almost imagine it had once been a row of nineteenth-century drill hands' cabins, flanking an old-style general store before a large scale makeover had thrown them all together into a sizeable, though still not palatial, residence. With its front porch veranda fronting direct onto the slip road, with no dooryard and no ranch gate, the building's whole effect was distinctly eccentric but the well-manicured acreage (the bus was only now passing the boundary fencing) and the classic cut of the stranger's suiting both murmured "money".

The journalist turned to his fellow passenger.

'Interesting character... best part of a coupla thousand dollars on his back I'd say, but a house more like half a street in a one-horse town. What does he do for money and why, for god's sakes, does he ride Greyhound?!'

'You sure must be from out of state, mister. That was Mr Ralph Stone I, the richest man hereabouts and pretty dam near the richest African American in these United States of America – you really never heard of him? You really never heard of Stone's Kerosene Lamps?'

* * * * *

The year was 1985, the place on a state highway in southwest Kentucky and those the circumstances of my introduction to the S.K.L. story.

Of course, I'd heard of the company. Who hadn't? After all, it was one of the biggest in "these United States of America", like the man said. But five gets you ten, you never guessed that behind those initials lay the name of an African American, who could have paid off Kodak's debt to Polaroid without troubling his back pocket unduly.

I was into cameras in those days. Art Greeley's idea of a photo story would have made even Kodak's nineteenth century founder George Eastman weep, but I needed the money so there I was, riding Greyhound. To be fair to Greeley, if we have to be, it wasn't all bad. Without that job, I would never have heard of Ralph Stone and the Dan Porter Lamp Patent; never made the connection between them and the legendary Elsie Marre, friend of Mary Church Terrell and herself a crusader for Negro American women's rights, and never met many a good friend in Atlanta, Georgia. Nor, for that matter, would I ever have come to know Loretta Stone.

Anyway, that sunny day in 1985, scenting a real story, I pumped my neighbor about the Stone family. He didn't know much, but what he knew was what I needed. Old Ralph Stone "the First" never gave interviews, but his son Ralph Junior, my informant had heard, was a big-time lawyer who lived with his wife and daughter in New York but had a place in a plush condominium outside Warrensville. He guessed a guy like that would be pleased to get a bit of coverage in a New York paper.

I had a hunch that any story behind S.K.L. would be too big to waste on Greeley, but I needed something keyed to a Kentucky dateline to keep him happy. Something about racing, say; that would be neat. I was in luck. The hotel barkeep reckoned the local racing rumor mill was a bit more heated than usual and suggested I contact a friend of his, a retired jockey. Forty-eight hours on expenses produced a photo interview with the old guy, delighted at the idea of being paid to talk me through the Kentucky Derby and the horse doping latest. With my "Greeley" feature in the bag, I could get down to the serious story. Again I was in luck. Ralph Stone II's condominium residence was listed in the local 'phone directory. He was down for a summer break. He loved the idea of a "background piece" on *The Law and the Profits: a Black Perspective* and offered me dinner that evening. His wife, Emma, was away on a duty visit to her sick mother, but his cook was not and nor, most certainly, was his daughter, Loretta.

A breathtaking lady, then twenty-three and heading for her first university professorship, she seemed flatteringly attentive to this footloose journalist. But, as I soon learnt, she had ambitions as a writer. Her doctoral thesis had been a research project on black history, focused on the family's history. With the help of a visiting associate professor in the humanities, she had worked it up to a full-scale faction novel. The college principal was urging her to give the manuscript to the university press, but she had other ideas. Now, from out of nowhere, was the guy with the contacts in New York who would find her a publisher.

I left the Stone residence that evening having spent less time than perhaps *he* would have liked interviewing her father, but, because of a promise made to his daughter, with a typescript under my arm.

I am happy, Loretta and Geoffrey, to pen this little prologue to *Black Dynasty*, thank you for asking me.

CHAPTER ONE

1876 Centenaries and Beginnings

A whip crack and a clatter of harness from the businesslike pony trap of Wilberforce Johnstone, the black storekeeper to "Boss" Johnstone, cut through the drowsy afternoon on Main Street, Johnstoneville, Ky. Cursing, Daniel Porter, the store clerk, hurriedly slipped the half empty can of tepid beer under the counter.

'Devil take him! The man said he was going to be out by ten this morning, why don't he keep to his own schedules?!' But the pony kept on its way. The boss would not, in fact, be visiting the shop today. Dan Porter's features relaxed. The bottle came back on the counter.

Drinking at all was frowned upon in Johnstoneville; drinking on duty could cost him his job. But it was midday, damn near midsummer and the first customer, Ollie Bagman, who did the messages for old Miss Ruth, would not be around before three. On Thursdays, the day before pay day, nobody else came shopping unless Elsie Marre or one of the other school kids sneaked out with a lucky penny for a bag of cookies. Elsie always got a bumper bag and Miss Ruth, who reckoned herself on no evidence whatsoever "a shrewd ole bird", had her theories about that. Largely on account of size and laziness, Miss Ruth never left the rocking chair on her porch, barely a plank's width above the level of one of the mean, rammed-earth paths that did for a street, outside the peeling clapboard frontage of her two-room home. It was her belief that on Thursday the store knocked a percentage off its prices to encourage custom in the dead hours before the Friday-Saturday stampede. 'You tell me how else that Elsie girl get them bumper big cookie bags,' she sagely commented.

In fact, the sparkling Marre child, eight years come Thanksgiving, pigtailed and ribboned, a real "piccanin" in white folks' language had it not been for the old wire-framed eyeglasses, always got a few extra cookies. She was one of those kids everyone loves. She was intelligent and thoughtful and she was, above all, the only kid in town who would share time, let alone a cookie, with the rumbling, rambling Miss Ruth. Truth to tell, because she was so "shrewd" the old woman had few cronies – even helpful Ollie claimed a cut of the "Thursday savings" by way of payment – and, so far as it was possible in the neighborly world of Johnstoneville, Miss Ruth sometimes suspected she might be lonely.

The heat and the beer combined to their usual effect and Daniel jumped guiltily as the swinging street door knocked the shop bell. The bottle was once again below counter level, still he automatically reached for the mint balls.

'They'll catch you at it one of these days, Daniel, an' then you'll be out of a job and I'll be out of extra cookies so you take care.'

He grinned back at the owlish little figure, brandishing her penny.

'Lookee here, Miss Elsie, this fool fellah done gorn pu' his job on the line for yo greed' tummy moh oft' times than he do rightly care to think orn! So don' you come no hi'h tohk over liquor.'

The Uncle Tom routine was their standard opening

exchange. Sixteen, going on seventeen, and too intelligent for this rustic backwater, Daniel saw a kindred spirit in the Marre child and looked forward to their weekly chat. He weighed out just that too many cookies that made the store Elsie's favorite place on Main Street. Then, over the clatter of the scales, they heard the distant thud of hooves and rattle of the coach whose twice-weekly visit from the local railhead was the township's link with the outside world.

'Well, Daniel, you think there'll be anyone exciting come into town today?'

Cheeks bulging, eyes alight, Elsie dashed to the door. The horses had made good speed despite the heat; the young driver, dangerously applying the breaks, brought the coach to a skidding halt amid a swirling dust cloud and muffled oaths from passengers half visible through the drop sash windows.

'Johnstoneville, Johnstoneville. All change for Darky Town,' bawled Barney the coach guard, clearly a man of wit and of Christian principle too, insofar as he served on this route at all. The age of slavery was more than ten years past; in theory, blacks still had equal voting rights with whites; the first of the South's segregation Jim Crow laws had not yet been passed. But a town of black freedmen of some twenty years standing was surely laughable. However, Johnstoneville was also a company town, very small and on a private estate and virtually unknown to the world outside. Thus, miraculously as it seemed to Harmann Tengdahl, packman, who now opened the coach door, the little community had escaped the wave of white lynch mobs slaying and burning through scores of Kentucky towns only two years before.

Elsie had yet to learn of the horrors the outside world held for her and her like, but her face puckered on the verge of tears at the sneer in the guard's voice. However, as she watched the packman clamber down the narrow folding steps of the coach, traveling grip in one hand and a bulky box tied with red string

3

in the other, and then saw the guard sway down a massively bulging samples bag from the coach roof, all was forgotten in a bubble of anticipation.

'Hi there, Harmann, hi…' she kept up a stream of excited squeaks as, arms, legs and pigtails flailing, she bounced across the dusty road and fell on the samples bag. The somewhat lugubrious and pudgy features broke into a grin.

'Hi there to you too, little Miss Elsie, how you doing?'

Six foot four, blond hair and as broad as a shield, Harmann Tengdahl was a distinctly overweight kind of Viking. Son of pioneer Swedish parents from Minnesota territory, he had soon left farming in favor of the traveling life and had spent the last twenty of his forty-five years selling general stores all over "These Expanding States of America," as he liked to call them.

Even as he rescued his samples from the little raider and handed her instead his traveling bag, the coach was beginning to pull away from the depot by the hotel. Barney and his driver had a long drive ahead, and rather than eat in "Darky Town" and with horses watered, passenger delivered and brake once again off, they were ready to go. A few good-natured loungers waved them on their way. Everyone in Johnstoneville knew the coachmen's attitudes but, insulated as they were, they were prepared to live and let live.

Elsie was right to be surprised at the packman's visit. Nicknamed in the distant days when he had made his rounds on horseback, flanked by massive pannier packs hanging from the special saddle, Harmann had soon been able to afford a four-beast mule train. But mules had to be unloaded every night and loaded up the following morning. Over the years, Harmann graduated to a succession of ever more splendid and capacious wagons. Sturdily built and cunningly designed with storage lockers and hanging space to accommodate the infinite variety of supplies – from pins to Franklin stoves, from frocks to frying pans – the latest model had been, in Elsie's eyes, the finest vehicle this side of the heavenly chariot, which the church spiritual told her would "swing low". Sometimes she thought it had already touched earth: charioteer Harmann Tengdahl. She was puzzled to see him now reduced to riding stage coach.

'Where's your wagon, Harmann? What's in the box, why you come today? You're not due for another three weeks…'

'All in good time, honey. How's Daniel doing? How's Mr Wilberforce. How're you'all in this happy town?'

He spoke smilingly, easily. Most children Elsie's age he expected to address him as "Mr Tengdahl", but somehow nobody could keep Elsie disciplined to social niceties of that kind. Even so, she was still a child and he did not feel obliged to disclose to this pert little miss the innocent deception he was in fact practising on the General Store of Johnstoneville. The fact was that he knew full well that the proprietor had been away for a month and was due back this coming weekend. His strategy when introducing some expensive new product line to his larger customers was, if at all possible, to get the store clerk interested and committed to the innovation in the hope that his enthusiasm would win over the proprietor. For this, the absence of the proprietor was obviously essential.

With his wagon out of commission for a fortnight and still at the repair yard, Tengdahl had determined to get to Johnstoneville by rail and coach before the weekend, hoping to work his way with young Daniel.

Inside the store the traveler accepted the seemly glass of Sarsaparilla which Daniel proffered, all signs of beer hurriedly cleared away. He held his little audience fascinated as he narrated how his magnificent wagon had been dragged to its ruin by a stampeding team, scared by the careless whiplash of another driver cracking at the feet of the leading pair. Tears stood in the corner of Elsie's eye, Daniel thought with concern of the huge cost of repairing that superb vehicle.

'Now let me see,' said Harman Tengdahl, always a sure sign he was about to shift a conversation to serious, i.e. money, matters. 'Your line of stock in the night lamps is, what I call, my Ami standard, isn't it?'

He knew full well that this was indeed the case and Daniel knew he knew and so ad infinitum. Even Elsie, whose first memory of the packman was that glorious day two summers back when she helped unpack a dozen gleaming new lamps, knew that he knew. But none of them minded playing the game of master salesman and hicktown store clerk on a sweltering day like this.

'Sure thing, Harmann! You sure know your territory as a salesman.'

'That is nothing; it is all part of my job.'

The two men smiled conspiratorially and Daniel waited patiently, preparing his defenses against a salesman's spiel which could end dangerously expensive for his boss and so plain dangerous for his job. Harmann went over to the back wall of the shop and stood on folding steps to reach the high shelf which served as home for all lighting fitments at this summery time of year.

'Allow me to refresh our memory,' he went on, taking down a new lamp and placing it on the counter so that he and Elsie, "the customers", and Daniel, the shopkeeper could have it in full view as he prepared to reveal its short comings. At the same time he fished a rumpled, dog-eared catalogue out of a side pocket of his capacious bag.

'The Argand Standard Domestic Oil Lamp,' he read, 'patented in London, England by Monsieur Ami Argand of Paris, is acknowledged the leader in its field, both in economy and efficacy.'

'What's "efficacy"?' demanded Elsie of the two experts. Like every other inhabitant of Johnstoneville she knew only too well what "economy" meant.

6

'Eh,' said Harmann, not used to having his spiel interrupted this early in the piece and also irritated at having to think about what it actually meant. 'Well, I suppose you might say "efficiency".'

'It means it does its job well, honey.' Daniel smiled, 'But then every damn thing Mister Tengdahl sells is perfect, isn't it, Harmann?'

'Of course, of course,' responded Harman, mollified but in the singsong intonation of his native language. He went on, now exaggerating the Scandinavian lilt as he always did when discussing technical matters, feeling perhaps that serious topics should be properly presented like the stark Norse sagas of old, rather than with the casual accents of America.

'"The Argand Original consists of a tubular wick within two concentric tubes or cylinders whence…' (Elsie raised a pair of expressive eyebrows) 'whence,' continued Harmmann with emphasis, 'we derive its common name of the "double current burner".'

As Harmann paused for breath he found himself interrupted once more, this time by Daniel.

'Tell us something new. I've been selling the Argands more than three years, ever since I joined the shop in fact. And I can tell you that though it may be economic, it could surely be more efficacious.'

As soon as he spoke, Daniel knew he'd made a mistake and grinned ruefully as the giant Viking, chest swelling, prepared to seize the offered opening.

'Exactly, my young friend,' he smirked, 'just so… the design is more than eighty years out of date. Now old man Argand's invention's lost out to something entirely new.'

With this, he bent with as theatrical a flourish as his 240 pounds would allow, raised a gleaming new lamp, still dropping shavings from its packing case, and plonked it on the counter next to the sturdy, old-fashioned Argand with its solid brass pedestal, pot-bellied brass oil reservoir and simple glass cylinder chimney.

'Allow me, Lady and Gentleman, to present the Hinks Duplex – the "True Lamp of Today" and an absolutely new type of uniquely decorative BLUE parafeeeen.'

The newcomer was a real dude of a lamp, a prince charming of a lamp, a fairy tale of sapphire blue, of seeming gold and of crystal. Elsie, silenced for once, simply stared in wonder, her eyes as round as her eyeglasses. Daniel looked, he hoped, casually interested, but he too was very impressed. The first things to strike you were the fine globe round the glass chimney and the limpid blue fuel.

It was the first time that Daniel had ever thought about the delicate color of the ordinary kerosene he sold every winter from the tank out back of the store. But then why should you notice it? Once bought, it went straight into the brass tank of your Argand Standard and you thought no more about it. But here, in the "Hinks Special", as he had privately named the newcomer, the vivid blue was held in a thick, quality-glass, drum-shaped reservoir. The drum's "frame" was made up of twelve finely cut square facets and the top and bottom of the reservoir comprised shoulders and ridges that rose to the brass lamp-fitting at the top and narrowed to the brass pedestal at the bottom. The pedestal consisted of a deep fluted neck, flaring into an inverted bell shape, like the bell of his trombone, thought Daniel. This in turn was supported on a lustrous pottery base glazed to look like polished jet.

'She's a real beauty, isn't she then?' Harmann Tengdahl preened himself on the impression he had made. (Elsie was still incapable of speech.)

'But she's more than a beauty, Daniel, she's really got that magic ingredient "efficacy". Yessir! She's PROGRESS.' (And you could hear the capital letters). 'Let's just take a look at the burner.'

As he spoke, he carefully lifted the globe up from the brass gallery on which it rested, raising it gently clear of the inner chimney before he moved it to one side to lay it on the counter. Daniel went to shift it further away so that he could get a better look at the burner mechanism.

'Mind you treat that gently, boy...' Harmann broke off, blushing. In this centenary year, with America celebrating the Declaration of Independence, he was continually catching himself out in the attitudes and language of the slave owners who had framed its ringing phrases, and was ashamed. For Harmann Tengdahl was that rarity, a white American who not only believed it to be "self-evident" that all men were "created equal" but that the Revolutionaries should have lived up to their rhetoric. He knew his history and he knew that in 1830, Philadelphia had hosted another assembly concerned with liberty, the first Black National Convention, and that it had celebrated 4th July by fasting. He bit his tongue.

'Sorry about that, Daniel,' he went on, 'but I reckon that globe's a work of art... can't be too careful...' Frowning, Daniel, who was grudgingly admired even by Mr Wilberforce for the care he took of all the stock in the little store, leaned forward as if for a closer look at the finely worked glass object. Even in sleepy Johnstoneville humiliations came one's way: but from Harmann!

'It sure is beautiful,' he said at last, 'and practical. I suppose that band of clear glass round the middle is to give you a direct light if you want it and the frosted glass top and bottom diffuses a more even glow.'

'Sure thing,' agreed Harmann, 'and of course the engraved pattern round the middle throws some lovely shadows on the walls. Anywhere I can show you the full effect?'

Soon they were all set up in the little back room with the drapes drawn. The new lamp performed impressively. Although the wicks were of the flat rather than the tubular type, the duplex effect of the double wick plus the globe threw a more powerful light than the old lamp, while the shadows made the little room something of an Aladdin's cave.

'And the cost?' the businesslike Daniel wanted to know.

'I'll tell you what,' said Harmann, 'I'll leave this beautiful model, complete with globe and its reservoir full of this experimental tinted fuel, for Mr Wilberforce to see when he comes back next week. The basic cost is just five dollars. For such quality it surely is a bargain...'

'Don't tell me,' interrupted Daniel, 'globe and chimney come extra. I'll never understand how you get away with that one. A lamp doesn't work without a chimney – I suppose a globe might be called an extra, but a lamp without a chimney just doesn't work.'

Harmann smiled knowingly.

'Oh come, come, Mr Daniel, Sir,' he said with mock pomposity, 'the flame will burn even without a chimney, the way all lamps used to in ancient Rome and surely that gives a charming, historical light...'

They all laughed and Elsie helped Harmann to unpack the other stock he had brought – stuff Daniel could decide on, by way of reorders.

When Harmann had taken himself off to the hotel, to be sure of a good night's rest before the return coach passed by at first light in the morning, Elsie stayed on for a while with Daniel. He didn't shut shop before seven of an evening and Elsie's mom never minded her back late on a Thursday because she knew she'd be down with Dan at the store.

This evening, the two sat on in the dusky gloom of the back shop, musing over the eventful afternoon; Elsie from time to time peeking down into the packing case where the chimney of the Hinks Special poked out from a cluster of shavings. Daniel was certainly taking no chances with his valuable charge and Mr Wilberforce would not be back for three days.

'You think he'll order in some o' they lamps, Daniel?'

The wistful question was posed for the umpteenth time.

'Now see here, Elsie, that there Duplex'd cost a mint too much, for folks hereabouts.'

'I know you're right Daniel, but it sure did look pretty and it surely was "efficacious".'

As always, Elsie finding a new word practiced it in every possible way. It was a kind of game she played, and it had its rules. The new word had to be mastered by the end of the day in which she found it. It was then written along with its meaning into her "WORD BOOK" – an ancient invoice book she had wheedled out of Daniel and which she had, so to speak, recycled by using the blank backs of the pages. Every month, her uncle Cassius was dragooned into running a test on her vocabulary. A sad family history of child deaths and still births meant she was an only child, "a darling child". Other grown-ups unwise enough to voice a new word in Elsie's hearing were ruthlessly recruited to the game, and pestered to correct her if she used it wrong. Being a sharp child, she could detect the least hint of the too ready assent designed to fob off.

Truth to tell, Elsie was perhaps fortunate that not too many new words found their way to Johnstoneville. Popular as she might be with the worthy burgers, she sometimes tried their patience sore. As it was, the Reverend Walcott, thanks to whose help and encouragement she could write so well, was sometimes tempted to regret his deep reading in the Bible and the collected writings of President Abraham Lincoln. Though an oath or a swear word had never been known to pass his lips, he did his best to control his language in the presence of Elsie Marre.

Only the garrulous Miss Ruth, who had retired before the war to the Johnstone estates after a lifetime in service to a family of Southern gentry, played the game with any enthusiasm. Given the hardness of her hearing and her love of her own voice, the constant repetitions that it entailed matched well with her natural speech rhythms. She had no idea that she was assisting in anything so intellectual as a "vocabulary divertissement" (both words, creatively spelt, to be found in the WORD BOOK). Yet she, like the rest of the little community, largely unknowing, contributed to the cultivation of a young spirit that was to prove one of the brightest lights of Black consciousness in the next generation.

Daniel noted that Elsie was playing her game (the 'quotes' round the word were almost silent now). He often wondered what would happen to this brilliant kid. What could happen to her, what could happen to any of them in this backwater, this "Darky Town" – Oh yes, he bitterly admitted to himself that Barney had the right of it. Freed the slaves might be, but nobody who really thought about the world could suppose that things had changed all that much. When he looked into the future the wildest fancy that came to mind was of himself as full manager of the store, supposing Mr Wilberforce's son, Willard, should head for something out of town and be content to leave Daniel to run the shop with a free hand. As to Elsie, she would end up like all the women of Johnstoneville, old before her time, tired out with worry and childbearing, struggling to make ends meet and keeping a brave face to fool her family that the future held hope.

He shook himself. The blue mood was uncharacteristic, in fact since Harmann had left, he had been turning over in his mind an idea which he thought might actually make him some money, and also benefit the people of the town. It was obvious that no one he knew could afford the kind of money to buy one of the new lamps, but it was also true that the lamps he sold gave a pretty poor light for the fuel they consumed. As Harmann had dismantled the lamps, Daniel had noticed the care with which he handled the glass chimneys, fragile and pretty with their onion-shaped bulge towards the base. And yet, he thought, that bulge seemed somehow wasteful. His mind struggled with the thought. What was he trying to tell himself?

Then the idea came to him. The catalogue of the old Argand Standard spoke of "drawing a supply of atmospheric oxygen up the inner tube to aid the combustion of the wick". But surely, the more concentrated that supply, the more effective the combustion. And that bulge, far from concentrating the air supply, dissipated it. Instead of working like a blow pipe, it worked like a goldfish bowl, in which the air could swirl round and past the wick without delivering the full weight of the oxygen it brought with it. Did the idea make sense, was this really the way the thing worked? He'd never been to school and fully accepted that a learned man of science could probably pick holes in his theory. Even so, Daniel mused...

'I said I must be going now.'

His little companion broke in on his reverie.

'Uh huh! Oh, sure thing, Elsie. Guess I'd better shut up shop and get on my way too,' he replied, 'but see here, what you said about that lamp being "efficacious" - nice word huh? - was sure on the mark,' he grinned. 'What'd you say if I made it so that our "old-fashioneds" worked better?'

Elsie mused on the way the brass fittings on the desk in the darkened back room had glinted, somehow moistly, in the limpid glow cast by the "lamp of today". She dreamed of a great house lit entirely by such magic lamps - it would be marvelous if there was even just one in the town, in the reverend's window for example, so you could look at it in the evenings as you walked back from the store. But in her heart she knew Mr Wilberforce would not place any orders, she knew too that no one, not even the reverend, would buy one if he did.

So now, with a little sigh but an encouraging smile, she said, 'That sure would be a wonderful thing, Daniel, do you think you could do it?'

'We'll see, honey, we'll see. Now you be careful on the way home, d'ye hear? And don't forget to tell your mom that that new headscarf for your gran's birthday will be here in good time, like Mr Tengdahl said!'

As if she could forget that, thought Elsie as she bounced out of the shop and went singing home full of the dazzling colors Harmann had promised for the great day, all thoughts of an improved Argand lamp forgotten.

* * * * *

It was a month later. The packman had been and gone on his regular mission. The wagon, its renovation complete, was more splendid than before, Gran had gone crazy over her headscarf; and Elsie had got one of her lucky pennies. The store did not have a new lamp on display, but Daniel and Mr Wilberforce were in deep conference in the little back room, talking lamps and improved chimneys.

With his rather distinguished, somewhat grizzled hair of middle age, there was nothing of the yokel about Mr Wilberforce "Wilber" Johnstone, to give him his full name. Like most of his fellow townsmen, he had been emancipated sometime before the Civil War. "Boss" Johnstone, the plantation owner, had made him manager of the town store and given his own name to the new freedman. Hard-faced, even ruthless, Wilber had proved a natural businessman and had persuaded his enlightened master to advance him a loan to buy the little store. The neighbors conceded that he was the local success story. After all, for the first twenty-five years of his life, he, like them, had been a slave, a chattel who, in theory, could be sold as easily as the Argand lamp he sold now in his shop. The fact that Boss Johnstone had not been that kind of boss made no difference to the fact that he could have been. The locals were grudgingly proud, then, that one of their number in their lifetime had risen from being part of the stock, so to speak, to running the store. However, it did not make Wilberforce Johnstone any the more popular.

'Give it to me one more time, Daniel,' he was saying.

'Well, Mr Wilberforce,' Daniel explained, 'I came to thinking about that chimney. The whole idea seems to have been thought up about a hundred years ago to protect the flame of an ordinary lamp from being blown about in the draughts. Quite something, huh? After 3,000 years some bright guy finally gets around to the idea.'

Daniel was fascinated that such an obvious idea, as it now seemed, had taken so long to think up. But then, come to that, why should anyone have had the idea at all and where did ideas come from in the first place?

'Yes, yes, we haven't got all day.' The boss was no philosopher. 'Get on with it.'

'OK, Mr Wilberforce. Anyhow, the chimney worked. The flame burned more steady. In those days perhaps glass making wasn't so good as it is now, perhaps chimneys got cracked by the heat. One reason why chimneys still swell out in that onion bulge at the bottom might be to keep the glass well clear of the flame. But modern American glass being much better, I wonder, could you could get Mr Stoddard over in Warrensville to make up a couple of dozen chimneys along the lines I described?'

'By the trumpets of Joshua,' it was the nearest Mr Wilber ever got to an oath, and there were those in town who thought that even it was a bit racy, 'by the trumpets of Joshua, young man, what do I need with newfangled chimneys thought up by the help?!'

'Uh-huh Mr Wilber, sure Mr Wilber! Well, like I said, the original chimney was simply meant to shield the flame but of course, like the catalogue says, it encouraged the up-draught too.'

Daniel, who had only grasped the concept of up-draught himself a week back and knew that his boss was still struggling with the elementary science involved, was prepared to linger over the details – if only for the pleasure of observing how long it would take for irritation to develop into apoplexy. However, as the purple began to flush dangerously behind the smooth ebony of the boss's over-fed cheeks, he hurried on.

'So my idea was to see if we couldn't make a different shape of chimney which would improve the up-draught – so as to increase the flow of oxygen to the flame and thus increase the rate of combustion. I've done some drawings here for Mr Jaggard's foreman. Six of each would give us a chance to try them out and allow for breakages.'

From a double fold of old newspaper he produced a sheet of fine white cartridge with four bold charcoal designs on it. Wilber raised an eyebrow. Daniel prided himself as something of an artist and last year had won the modest perquisite of buying quality cartridge paper at a 10% discount on the shop price. This was, in fact, a far better deal for the shop's owner than for his employee because the cartridge, bought in two years previously when Boss Johnstone's daughter had been dabbling in watercolors, had proved quite unsalable when she took up horseback riding instead, and then got married and left the neighborhood. The paper had of course been of the very best quality and cost so much, even with the notional discount, that Daniel could only buy a few sheets at a time. If he used this precious resource for his chimney sketches, he obviously rated them very highly. Wilber decided to pay close attention to whatever might follow. He had, however, not the slightest intention of letting the lad guess at his real feelings. As his shop assistant ran through the merits of each, the wheels of profit began to hum sweet music in the mind of Wilberforce Johnstone.

'This is my favorite.' Daniel pointed to the fourth of his

diagrams. 'The bottom diameter is wide enough for it to fit the burner basket but, as you see, just two inches up the diameter reduces sharply by about half an inch to make a shoulder in the tube. If my calculations are right, the effect of this will be to throw the rising stream of air in towards the wick so that a lot more of that atmospheric oxygen gets burned up before the air escapes up the top of the chimney.'

Mr Wilberforce got down abruptly from the high clerk's stool, the only form of seating in the little room.

'All right as far as it goes,' he said. 'I'll get Jaggard's men to blow two of each model. I've got to be on my way now. Let you know when I've got them made.'

He was halfway across the main shop before Daniel could splutter out his protests. 'But Mr Wilberforce, I said six of each.'

'Whose dollars?' came the response: to which there was no answer!

Daniel stared glumly after the retreating form of his employer. He was not anything like as confident as he had seemed. Would the ideas work? Would the glass hold? Would people buy and if they didn't, what would happen to his job? Daniel did not like failure. With a sigh and a shrug he went out to put the shutters up. There had been storms and heavy rains over the past few days and the frames of the window frontage were dangerously rickety. As he pulled the door shut and headed for home, he mused that perhaps his ideas, with luck, might pay off.

Under the dynamic reign of young Willard Stone I, the Johnstone family (renamed "Stone" by him) were to build a fortune on the impetus given to their business by the *Stone Patent Chimney*. Daniel received a modest raise in his wages.

CHAPTER TWO

The Mammoth Cave

It was a bright Tuesday morning in the year 1880. Elsie Marre was driving her mother insane and turning the house upside down. Today was the 15th of July of a hot, hot summer. In two hours time it would be too hot to breathe let alone argue with the child. They were preparing for Elsie's great expedition to Kentucky's famous Mammoth Cave. For the third time the little travel bag had been unpacked and re-packed to accommodate the treasured pair of shoes – the great decision had been whether to wear them on the journey and risk getting them scuffed, or keep them safe to put on at arrival.

Mamie Marre – a stupid name for a grown woman she always thought, especially if she was a mother (Ma Mamie Marre!) – grinned with a cheerfulness verging on the manic. She was hunting once more for that pair of white socks, gone missing ten days back when Elsie had come home from the Gullie stream with muddy skirt and bare legs.

Now where'd she got to? Drat the child! Oh, well, tomorrow, for three glorious days she would be away from home on a trip with Daniel Porter and his new wife, Elizabeth "Bess" Baldwin. They were to visit with Bess's family in Cave City, with that rambunctious little pipsqueak Willard Johnstone tagging along. It was to be the lad's first birthday holiday away from home. Old Man Johnstone was funding the travel plans:

by carrier to Glasgow, the county seat, with a change at Glasgow Junction on the main line, a round trip of fifty-odd miles. In return the Baldwins would put the boy up (put up with the boy, more like!) and Elsie too.

She and young Willard were inseparable and her mother did not approve. The boy might be nice enough for a boss's son, but he was not Mamie's ideal for a son-in-law. *Steady on there, Ma*, she thought to herself, *ain't you getting ahead of yourself a bit?*

She plunged for the last time into the bedroom chest for those socks. And there they were! The little miss! Now when did she find time to wash them and slip them back on the quiet? Mamie Marre burst into that heavenly laugh of hers, which always seemed to start on the dance floor, whatever her feet were doing at the time, and filled a room with happiness. She and her girl knew each other inside out. Guiltily she remembered that those "three glorious days" had been penciled in on her private calendar as three glorious days of peace from daughter Elsie. She loved the child, all the world loved the child, but peace had its attractive side too!

Elsie was sitting on her favorite tree stump down by the Gullie Stream and reading a rather turgid letter. It had been sent, at her request, by Bess's brother, Moses Baldwin; it was a description of Cave City and neighborhood and was, she guessed, mostly copied from a local gazetteer. This was Elsie's first journey outside Johnstoneville in all her twelve years, and she was preparing for it. 'Always know the territory,' her father used to say.

Little good it had done him, though, when the drill bit on the Old Chipper Rig had snapped and embedded itself in his chest. Her eyes clouded. A lovely man who, like many another, had died before his time on the rigs. But she had learnt from him and she would do him proud.

She shook herself and turned her thoughts to Daniel Porter and Bess, his pretty new wife. They had met ten months ago when Bess had travelled down from Cave City with her brother Moses, who was hoping for a job as one of Mr Wilber's salesmen. But "Mo" was one of those men who needed hand-holding at every turn (apart from her pa, Elsie sometimes thought, what man didn't?) and nobody in Cave City had given him a prayer of a chance of getting that job and holding it down. As for Wilberforce Johnstone, pillar of the community but hardly noted for his sense of humor, it was said that the nearest he came to laughing in the year of Mo's visit was when he was told that this slow-witted daydreamer had come in hope of a job. Mo's sister, by contrast, had stayed on in Johnstoneville. "Miss Wilber", the boss's wife, was on the lookout for a housekeeper and knew she had found the proverbial treasure in Bess. It did not last long, for Daniel Porter soon whisked her lively help-companion off to the altar rail and married life.

Elsie was delighted for him. She reckoned Daniel had deserved a turn of luck ever since, four years back, he and Mr Wilber had had what she always called "the Great Chimney Row". At the time she had barely understood what it was she was so angry about. All she knew then was that Dan had been done down in some way. Now, four years on and a precocious twelve-year-old, having heard Harmann Tengdahl talk about the affair, she was convinced that Dan had been cheated out of, what we might call, his intellectual property rights in the lamp patent. Harmann insisted that things were not really that simple since Dan had probably done some of his development in the store's time. But Elsie's crusading spirit was up. Daniel was morally entitled to the patent, and she had marked down "Young Willard" to see justice done. Young Willard, it has been noted, was not quite ten.

Over supper that evening, Mamie Marre failed to discover

how and when the socks had been washed and secretly returned so innocently to the chest. But then, Elsie failed to discover what had caused the gales of laughter which she had heard, even down by the brook, ringing from the house. Each resisted the friendly questioning and, delighted to have kept their little secrets, mother and daughter kissed and went up to bed early, so as to be ready for the rickety farm cart that was to take them into Glasgow early next morning.

Every week, Miss Ruth's brother, Amos, took his old rattletrap into the little market town, perhaps on some errand Mr Wilber had overlooked, perhaps riding the reverend into a meeting or perhaps, as was the case this Wednesday, going by reservation to the rail station. The new Jim Crow legislation imposing the color line on transport in the southern states, introduced in Tennessee back in 1875, post Reconstruction, was not absolutely enforced as yet on road transport in these backwaters; but there was no point in enduring ten miles of hostile sneers from Barney the coach guard if you didn't have to.

There was of course plenty for Elsie and Willard to talk about – after all, it was the first time they had been on a journey without their parents. As for Bess and Daniel, they were happy to have some quality time together without the usual pressure of the day's chores.

At Glasgow train station the party faced the harsh reality awaiting black faces traveling public transportation in post-Reconstruction America. True, "Johnstone's Stores of Johnstoneville" was so long established that many had forgotten the black face that stood behind it. True too, Mr Polk the station master, who valued the long credit the Jo'ville store gave him on his lamps, oil and candles, treated the travelers decently enough. But the railroad company clerk grimaced as he handed over the tickets for Cave City and on the train the four travelers found themselves marooned at one end of a cheap, slat-seated railcar wagon, while the white passengers talked loudly among themselves in the next car.

'Suits me,' joked Daniel, 'more room to spread ourselves.'

But Bess's eyes clouded and, as the train pulled out of the station, Elsie looked miserably out of the window at white faces who were smiling goodbye to friends but went wooden when they caught sight of her. Yet, with Willard at the other window keeping up a bubbling commentary on the lumbermen clearing the hillside sloping down from the rail yard, it was impossible to be miserable for long.

Changing trains at Glasgow Junction meant more sneers and cold hostility; Bess was hurt, Daniel was angry and Young Willard was furious and had to be restrained from shouting insults back. But Elsie refused to be depressed – the adventure was too exciting to let mean-minded white folk spoil it. And the day ended perfectly for her; when they reached the Baldwins' home her shoes were duly admired and, keeping uncharacteristically quiet, she was able to listen in on the grown up chats long after supper was finished. Will was half asleep so that the adults seemed to have forgotten about the presence of the "juveniles", as "Grandpa B." insisted on calling them. It was not until well past nine o'clock that the two youngsters were packed off to their swing cots on the sleeping porch. Even then, it was the drone of voices that slowly lulled her into dreamland.

Next morning, bright and early, each with a tied bandana of picnic provisions, they set out on the two-mile walk up to the entrance of Mammoth Cave, Mo Baldwin in the lead, comically full of his own importance.

As they made their way up the forest ravine towards the mouth of the cave, he kept up a stream of chatter in a sing-song voice: 'warning and informing,' he said. '…and boring,' Willard, the birthday boy, added under his breath.

It appeared that they were more than 150 feet *above* Green River! It was, in part, fed by subterranean pools (Elsie proudly told Bess she knew the meaning of the word); and there were underground rivers too, wide enough and deep enough to float a full-sized barge!

'And what's the good of that?' grumbled Willard out loud.

'You hold your tongue, Will,' Elsie remonstrated in the prim tones of a school ma'am.

'But say!' objected the ten-year-old, determined to make his point, 'you got to get your barge down there in the first place and then you got to get the lading down there an' even then you cain't know for certain the goldarn river's goin' any place you got customers.'

'Will, if you ain't nice and p'lite to Mo, I'll tell your ma when we get home.'

'Tell her then, but Pa'll tell you river boats for sure ain't interesting if you cain't trade in 'em!'

Above the children's heads, Daniel and Bess exchanged happy, holiday grins – 'Kids!'

Mo, on the other hand, striding out in front "marking the way", was vexed to find his guidebook patter treated with less than proper respect. It had taken long evenings after long hard days of work (and no small expense in beer) to get word perfect with Stephen, the official guide employed by Mr Klett, the cave's proprietor. Mo, who was rather proud of his delivery, fondly supposed that Stephen would one day put him in charge of regular tourist parties – a belief that Stephen was perfectly content to foster for as long as the supply of free beer continued.

They were now approaching the great natural arch of rock marking the entrance to Mammoth Cave and, what with the awesome nature of the sight and the roar of the waterfall cascading from the ledge fifty feet further up, the little party fell silent. At the entrance a short man in his mid-fifties, his close cropped hair already thinning over his nut-brown scalp, was waiting for them by a half-open clumsy wooden barrier gate. Raising his voice to a rather self-conscious shout, Moses Baldwin shook the white man's reluctant hand.

'How*dee*, Mr Stephen!'

'Howdi, Baldwin,' the other responded with a frown.

'This here's my party,' Mo continued.

'Uh, huh,' came the reply.

'Now remember, everybody,' Moses turned to harangue his group, 'we are here thanks to Mr Stephen the guide. The caves are usually closed on a Thursday, but because today is young Willard's birthday, and because his pa supplies the caves with lamps on generous terms, Mr Klett the proprietor has asked Mr Stephen here to come special to open them for us – which he very kindly has consented to do…'

'Only an hour, mind!' interrupted the surly white guide. 'If you was paying, you might choose the four-hour tour. But you're not payin' and today is properly my day off, so just one hour is all I'm ready to agree to. I've lit a few hanging lamps in the first stretch, but you'd better take carry lanterns as well. And, Moses Baldwin, don't you forget you're the guy responsible, if there're any problems.' With that, Stephen sloped off to the billy can brewing on the open fire at the door of his cabin.

If the grudging tone of voice was intended to spoil his visitors' enjoyment of their trip, it failed completely. Daniel and Bess had heard so much about the fabulous caves from Mo that they were eager with anticipation. Elsie was simply awed by the prospect and even Willard seemed excited. As for Moses, he was delighted with his moment of authority and puffed himself out importantly as he prepared to do the honors.

'An hour will do fine to get an idea of the place and it would take weeks to see everything. They reckon there may be 150 mile of galleries under this hillside, with alleys and dead ends, sudden pit shafts and lofty domes, and grottos… and… sink holes!'

His voice fell dramatically.

'So y'all keep close, and, Dan, you hold on to your lamp. It's mighty dark in there.'

The two men took up the bull's-eye lanterns standing on the trestle table inside the barrier, the flames burning behind the thick glasses set in their metal cylinder cases. With Moses leading the way, and Dan bringing up the rear, the venturesome tourists began their descent into the Mammoth Cave. Elsie shivered in the cold draught of air that gusted up to meet them and even the well-protected flames of the lantern flickered.

Willard shuddered nervously despite himself, all he said was, 'Why is it so windy?'

The winding rock-cut staircase was giving way to a narrow sloping passage and in fact, as they penetrated deeper into the cave, the draught was losing force.

'Hot air rises,' Daniel smiled.

'That sure is right, Dan,' was Mo's comment. 'Down here – we've reached the beginning of the caves now – the air temperature stays a steady fifty degrees, or thereabouts, all year through. Well, it was more like seventy up on the surface today; so the hot air rising at the cave entrance drags colder air up to take its place – like a Wilber Johnstone Lamp Chimney, eh, Dan?'

'More like a Porter Lamp Chimney, if you was to ask me!' muttered Bess to herself, though loud enough for them all to hear.

'Now then, sugar,' Dan patted his wife's arm soothingly, 'I got my raise, didn't I? An' Mr Wilber is paying our transportation for this trip.'

'An' Mr Wilber, he gets his penny-a-piece till kingdom come, don' he? It ain't right, Dan, it ain't right!'

'Sure it's right, honey. It's legal right. The boss has promised me another raise come New Year's. And anyways, today it's holiday time for young Willard. So let's enjoy ourselves.' He spoke with a laugh but the tone of voice, which she recognized but rarely heard, was that of Daniel Porter laying down the family law.

As the travelers' eyes grew accustomed to the gloom, they saw they were entering a vast hall as wide and as high as a church, stretching, it truly seemed, to "kingdom come". In the remote distance, a shimmering shaft of light disappeared through the misty vault, like the wake left by Elija's fiery chariot. They stood in silence.

Guidebook Mo broke the spell.

'Ahead,' he announced, his voice strangely thin in the vast underground chamber, 'we can see the gallery known as "Gothic Avenue". It is illuminated by a vertical sink hole.'

With lanterns held aloft, the little group moved hesitantly off down a side gallery. They had long since left the zone half-lit by the three hanging lamps, grudgingly prepared by Stephen the guide. To Elsie it seemed as though the glistening walls of the great cave moved away and back, like waving water curtains. Here and there, crystal encrustations, some falling as stalactites, others rising as stalagmites, sparkled in blues and gold, and rainbow colors, like a mansion lit by the magical Hinks Duplex that still haunted her child's memory. Suddenly, as they advanced, the walls fell back entirely beyond the light of their lanterns and they stood under a darkling dome, where only the gleam of sky through a sink-hole funnel far above marked the immense size of the cavern.

'Tread careful, folks,' Mo warned. 'That skylight above means that there's likely a shaft-hole beneath it hereabouts that's been pierced by the dropping water of the ages. It may not be deep, but it'll be deep enough to mean trouble – of that you *can* be sure!'

Edging carefully towards the cave wall, Dan held up his lantern to show Bess a cluster of crystals, looking for all the world like a bunch of grapes; either side of it hung trumpet shapes swaying like flowers in a breeze.

'Oh my!' gasped Elsie, 'ain't that wonderful, Will? Let's go look.' Taking him in tow, she struck out boldly towards the magic garden.

Suddenly, the floor was not there any more…

'Daniel!'

' Bess!'

'Help!'

'No ooo oooh… Help!'

'Oh, my God; the kids… what's happening?'

The mingled cries of the children and Mo, moving as fast as he dared to their rescue, were followed by two heartrending screams, a crash and a thin, distant spattering like glass splinters. After a bruising, grazing tumble from rock edge to boulder and down the hidden shaft hole, the youngsters had come to a jolting stop on a brutal jagged rock, some twenty feet down. Sobbing with pain and fear as he felt the blood seeping from a gash on his leg, Willard clung to Elsie. Barely conscious, she too could feel blood streaming from a gash on her forehead that was already throbbing. Dimly, but thankfully, she was aware that her eyeglasses must have flown free from her face, before her head hit the rock edge.

Shaken and winded, the two of them could hear distraught cries above, but at first they were too stunned to answer. At last, Willard managed to croak out they were still alive but terribly hurt and would someone help. As Bess was to say later: 'That Willard has the luck of the devil.'

The cruel rock, which had arrested their fall, shelved into a drip pool just twenty feet below the gallery floor. The children huddled whimpering, bleeding, scared, and increasingly cold…

More than an hour had passed since the disaster. Dan had, of course, taken charge. First he had thrown down his jacket, in a vain attempt to keep them warm – it had snagged on an

27

unseen projecting rock. Then, with little faith in the navigating skills of the shocked Moses, and determined that Bess, his "number one person", should not come to harm, taking one of the lamps, he had set out with her to get help. Mo kept the other one but, left with the job of keeping up the spirits of the children, all he could think of to say was that he was sure that everything would work out for the best.

Shivering in the damp gloom, the light of Mo's lantern barely reached down to where they were; neither Will nor Elsie found this much help and they soon stopped listening. They hugged one another for comfort. Willard was "the man", but Elsie was older. And in any case, she was not really afraid. She was confident that Dan would get them out.

'You think a lot of Daniel, don't you Elsie?' Sometimes Willard read her thoughts like a twin brother.

'I certainly do, Will… He's the cleverest man I know!'

She gasped. Her whole body was one great throbbing scar and delayed effects of shock were beginning to set in.

'Oh, he ain't all that clever. He don't even know how to be sure and hide that beer bottle of his. I found it easy when I was rooting round for candy the other day.'

'Well, you be sure you don't tell your pa! Dan'll lose his job else. No, I mean real clever."

Elsie hesitated, was this the right time to tell young Willard some home truths about his father? Why not, there'd never be a better time and he ought to know sooner or later.

'… I mean, do you know who thought up your pa's patent chimney?'

'That's easy… my pa of course.'

'Well that he didn't, Willard Johnstone. That there chimney was invented by Daniel Nahum Porter!'

Before he could react, Elsie had let out a piercing scream. Something was crawling over her legs, something like a blind midget with two white sticks, methodically taking soundings.

'What is it Elsie?' squeaked Willard. 'What you scream for?' 'Y'all all right down there?' This was Mo.

'Ugh, it was something horrible, jus' horrible, climbing across me like some kind of blind thing feeling its way.'

'Is that so?' mused the thick-skinned Moses Baldwin in a detached tone of voice. 'I guess that might be what they call a wall-eyed hopper, a kinda blind cricket without wings. Never seen one myself – but I sure would like to. Sounds interesting.'

Good-natured but stupid was the general family assessment of Mo. This was his idea of keeping up the kids' morale. By now the thing had left Elsie and slithered down the rock face onto a little ledge. With no way back and with sheer drops ahead and to the side, it evidently decided to take advantage of this convenient launch platform, gathered its legs and projected itself into the dark void. It found Willard.

Shivering with cold, fear and shock, the ten-year-old screamed and clawed at his open shirt neck, where the scaly creature, all legs and feelers, was struggling to fight clear.

'No, no, no, no!' screamed the boy, as he squirmed to get rid of the foul presence until, without at all meaning to, he crushed the cricket against the rocks – and in the process smeared his hand with its oozing body parts. He almost fell into the pool, straining to wash his hands clean. Elsie's thin arms encircled him and minutes passed into silence. Mo, after checking that nothing "serious" was wrong, to use his word, mercifully had the sense to hold his tongue. Terrified, Willard was also ashamed of his outburst. Shuddering, he pulled away in the dark and sat up.

'I… I'm sorry about that Elsie, I guess you're scared too. But do you think Daniel'll really save us? You're always saying how clever he is. But if he is so clever and if he invented the chimney and my pa didn't, how come he's not rich and my pa is?'

'Because, Willard, your pa took the patent off of him.'

'You saying my pa's a thief?! What is a patent anyway?'

'It's a kind a paper that says you've invented something.'

'And you're saying my pa stole a paper like that from Daniel?!'

'Well, not stole exactly. But you heard what Bess said this afternoon. You see, Daniel invented the new chimney but your dad gets most of the profits. He gave Dan a raise in salary but he told him that because he made the invention in the company's time, when he was being paid anyway, he cain't expect more.'

'Well that was a fair deal, wasn't it? He got a raise for work done in the shop.'

'Willard Johnstone, that's pure whitey talk and I'm ashamed of you, and you should be ashamed of yourself. That invention was more than just work, and of course a lot of the thinkin' and tryin' things out happened when Dan was back in his home. The result was a chimney improvement that made big money in its own right and even bigger money because having its own patent makes a company big on the high street.

Willard, I want you to promise me that if Daniel does get us out of this hole and you live to become boss of the shop, you'll do right by Daniel Porter and his family!'

The dropping, damp noise of the caves and the scuttle of the cricket had been partly forgotten as the two children talked patent law as best they could understand it at their age. But now, Elsie's talk of the hoped-for rescue reminded Willard that it might never come! Nearly two hours of an eternity had crawled by, the rock overhang was still there and no hope could surely be expected from Mo. At ten years old, dark, cold and shock can have powerful effects. Willard fervently hoped that the wonderful Daniel Porter could somehow come to their rescue.

For this, he would swear anything.

'All right Elsie: cross my heart and hope to die. I promise that I'll do right by Daniel and his family if I ever get the chance.'

CHAPTER THREE

A Death and New Departures

This is to certify that Wilberforce X, now called Johnstone, born in or about the year 1830; purchased by me, Owen Warren Johnstone, in the year 1850 and granted his freedom by me in the year 1855, is hereby appointed by me, the said Owen Warren Johnstone, as sole manager and responsible agent of the oilman and general stores in my town of Johnstoneville, in Barren County in the state of Kentucky. Written with my own hand and dated this first day of July 1861.

'… And three weeks later came the First Battle of Bull Run… And with it the end of the history of mah life part one.'

Laughing at his own feeble joke, Wilberforce Johnstone, now mellowed by advancing years and illness, broke into such a fit of coughing the watchers by the bedside worried for his safety. At last the fit died away in a series of spluttering, choking hiccups. Petulantly he waved away the glass of patent medicine being handed to him by his weeping wife.

'Oh, Wilber, dear, have a care, have a care. Don't trouble yourself so. Young Willard here ain't going back to college before a week and Doctor Monroe told you to rest and take your medicine when the fit seized. I'm sure it would soothe you. When doctor said he had it special over from England I tried it mahself and I sure believe it would cure any cough o'mine. Try a sip jes for my sakes, dearest heart!'

Weakened by his convulsions, old Wilberforce steadied himself with a visible effort to soften the irritation he now felt and reached out a soothing hand to his wife's arm. Standing back a little from the immediate circle round the bed, Elsie Marre, by now an adopted member of the family, let flow her tears without shame, to see this once hard man of business gentle himself towards the sweet and trusting woman, whose innocence and strength had never once betrayed their loyalty to him.

'Honey! Honey! If it's the last thing I hear you say, promise never again to touch that stuff.'

'But, Wilber…'

'Sweet Ella… honey… I know as well as the doctor that that limey quack Browne's "Chlorodyne" is no more an' no less than good ole alcohol with a dash of molasses and quinine water to lend a medicinal quality. I never yet took alcohol knowingly and nor have you and we's ain't about to start at our time of life, is we? I don' know if Doc Monroe thinks he's doin' me a favor, to dull my pain by alcohol without my knowledge. I wouldn't sell that stuff even to make a profit so I certainly won't have my wife drinking it for free! Now you jes get me some water.'

He smiled weakly. Ella smiled back through her sobs.

'I promise, Wilber! I promise. And I'll see young Willard here don't stock the stuff when you're gone.'

Finding herself caught unawares by the realities of the sickbed scene, she turned, her shoulders shaking, to take the glass of water proffered by Elsie and pass it on to her husband. He took three steady sips and, closing his eyes, three long, deep breaths with his hand to his diaphragm. With a long, slow out-breath he slowly opened his eyes. The face cleared, the eyes had found a new sparkle. The breathing was slow and regular. Wilberforce Johnstone smiled almost smugly at the group round the bed, like a veteran circus juggler who has just pulled off a difficult trick.

'Learnt that from a Chickasaw redman when I wasn't but a no good slave boy, recuperatin' me from a thrashing. "Air and water, wind and river, fire the clay and cool the fever". That's what he said as best I can remember. Never rightly knew what he meant. But it sure works in times of trial. Body more like alive again, head cool and clear… Now, Ella,' he went on, 'I got a new lease on life, I can promise you. I'll be keeping a check on Main Street a few days yet. So jes' you an' Elsie go see to the supper. I got business talk with Willard here.'

Convinced by the remarkable transformation she had seen, and confident as always in her husband's authority, Ella meekly accepted the instruction and led Elsie from the room.

'Right, Willard my son. You are the son of a slave, as you well know. But that's nothing remarkable for men of our color in this God's own Land of the Free. You've no cause for shame, so long as you is true to your family and true to your name. Your name…' He coughed and paused as if for breath, but in reality for thought.

What was the name of his family? What kind of names did men have in Africa, the home of their ancestors? For generations the men of his seed had been shamefully made to breed in a foreign land under foreign skies for foreign masters, often for foreign owners, like so many stud cattle.

He silenced the whisper of a new cough at the back of this throat. Redman's magic and black man's pride united to check a cry of weakness in the face of white man's oppression. The life he had lived was *his* life: here he had made his destiny. To the medicine men of his distant tribe these were foreign skies, but they were *his* skies. Neither he nor young Willard here could hope to change that. But the name… the name, that was something different.

The pause was so long that Willard began to wonder

whether his father had suffered some kind of stroke; the staring eyes, the breathing so low as to be almost inaudible, but then Old Wilberforce blinked, shook his head briskly, reached out for the water glass on the bedside table and turned his serious eyes on his son.

'When Boss Johnstone made me a free man under white man's law, I was happy to take his name to repay, as best I could with a token of gratitude, what he had given with some generosity. As a man, freedom sure was my right, but Willard, you'll find that in the real world, liberties under law are more use than rights of man. When he "emancipated" me Mr Johnstone surrendered rights at law which, howsoever unjust they were, had money value. You'll understand that as a businessman, whatever you think about it as a slave's son!'

'But you paid the debt, Pa. And it's my right to start the family on a clean sheet. Is that what you're sayin'?'

'That's exactly it. You owes no one nothin', but you owes the family everything... But there is one thing as you might like to consider. Your pa carried the name Johnstone for twenty some years and he sure would take it friendly to be memorialized in some way. Ah've sometimes toyed with the thought of taking "Stone" as a name. It's got a sort of proverbial ring, don' you think?'

His father smiled faintly and Willard flashed a grin. 'Sure thing, Pa. Good foundation material, and hard to get blood out of, they say!'

'That's it, boy. Act legal but keep close and business will take care of itself.'

He paused for a sip at the water glass. The illness was more advanced than he had admitted to Ella. If his new lease on life could last him through this day then he would be ready to cross Jordan whenever the Good Lord called. He winced a rueful grin. Wasn't it a bit late in life to talk religion, even to yourself?

'You all right, Pa?'

'Just a thought , Willard, just a thought.' He settled himself further up on his pillows and breathed deeply. 'And now for the history lesson. You're holding part one in your hand. There's nothing about the life of a slave or a freedman before the war you need hear from me. There'll be plenty others to tell you of that humiliation. But I want for you to remember from your father a message to be proud of, a record you can build on, something positive. Back in '61, start of the Civil War, Kentucky was a heavy slave tradin' state. But she was border territory between South and North... perhaps she hoped to wait and then declare on the winning side. Anyways, Kentucky declared for neutral.'

He paused.

'Never forget, Willard, white folks oft'times think more like children than like grown men. For twenty years this war had been a-makin' but Kentucky thought it could stand neutral in the front line!

Others thought different. That summer, an army of Confederates came up from Tennessee and occupied Kentucky from Bowling Green west all along to Columbus in Hickman County on the Miss'sippi. Their recruiting gangs came right up to the edge of Warren County. They set me a'thinking. Ah was set up well and at the store, but I didn't fancy the chances for me or the Mr Johnstones of this world if the slaveholders won the war. So about Christmastime, I went to join the Yankee army, jus' in time for the battle of Mill Springs, over in Wayne County, January '62.

Ah served in the Chattanooga campaign of '63 all the way through to September. Our division held out along the cricks of the Chickamauga, long enough for the main army to regroup. Our stand gave the North time to fight another day. It certainly finished my days as a soldier. Ah was damn near killed.' He paused and winced with remembered pain.

'Damn near killed on the battlefield and damn near died of

gangrene in the hospital when they dug the bullet out o' mah leg. Ah didn't get back to Johnstoneville till early '64, ah di'n't recover mah full strength for another year and di'n't get round to marrying your mawh for a year after that. Four years lost. Lucky for me, Mr Johnstone put ole Hyram Porter in to look after the store while I was away.' The old man paused, he seemed puzzled. 'Why did he let me get back in? If ah'd had a head start like that, no limping veteran back from the wars would have got a second chance.'

'Perhaps Mr Johnstone didn't want him in.'

'Don' you believe it. The Boss was good to me sure, but he wasn't no charity. Hyram ran a good store. He was agein' a bit, but he made good profits and could've lasted easy long enough to hand the place over to young Daniel.'

He paused for another drink of water, thinking back to the day when Hyram had handed over the store keys. "Guess mah days o' stewardship have run their course, Wilber," he had said. "Perhaps you won't take unkindly to a word in season. Play fair by the townsfolk, like ah played fair with you, young fellah. There's many in hardship can do with' a helpin hand." Wilber found that Hyram had in fact helped some of the poorer local families keep afloat, by dipping generously into his own pocket. It was a policy he quickly discontinued.

'Hyram kep' my place warm and that's why ah gave Daniel the job as store clerk when he was old enough. He's a bright fellah, Porter. His ideas can mean money.'

'Already have, eh, Pa?

'You mean the chimney? Ah was comin' to that. That is a tricky situation altogether. No doubt that young Dan made the invention. Difficulty was to get the patent, him and me being Negroes an' all. Boss Johnstone arranged things, paid the fees. Ah'm too tired to explain the legalities.'

'But you get the royalties, don' you, Pa?'

'Who told you that?'

Now, Willard told his father about the accusations Elsie had made on that historic day in the Mammoth Cave seven years back, and the promise she had extracted from him. The old man gave a thin smile.

'She could be mighty hot on righteousness in them days, young Elsie Marre, for all her pretty ways. One Sunday afternoon she found me in the counting house and preached me good an' long 'bout workin' on the Lord's day, and then she went on to lecture me on robbin' Daniel of his birthright.

In fact, the patent hadn't come through at that time and anyways I'd given Dan a fair raise on his salary. So I told her not to meddle in things she din' understan'.'

'And you give him a share in the royalties when that patent did come through, Pa?'

'Well,' he dragged the word out uneasily, 'Dan got a good raise in his wages, which the lawyer says is more than ah'm obligated to.'

'Still an' all, I reckon I needn't concern myself unduly much over the arrangements.'

'O' course, that'll be up to you, boy. Ah don' suppose a man can be held to a ten-year-ole's "cross mah heart an' hope to die". But ah will say mah conscience come to question me now an' then... The papers are in mah desk in the counting house, all drawn up on lawyers' parchment an' tied up in lawyers' fancy pink ribbon. Perhaps you better read them, when we're through here.'

He leaned laboriously over to his bedside locker and took from a drawer the old key that controlled the secrets of "the Desk". The key with its scrollwork head had fascinated Willard ever since that historic tenth birthday when his father had shown it to him.

'This you get when I'm gone. For now jus' bring those papers: you'll find them on the top of the pile.'

When Willard returned, documents in hand, he found his father breathing lightly, relaxed against the pillows, arms parallel to his body outside the covers. The old man opened his eyes. 'Best leave me now, son. Perhaps your mah was right. Ah could do with some rest. Just put that key back in mah drawer, an' you go read some.'

Back at his own desk in the counting house, Willard weighed the roll of documents pensively. Given his father's condition, as reported by the doctor, it could hardly be long before he was sole director of the store. Untying the ribbon would be his first act towards independence of decision and action in business. Opening the documents and spreading them out on the desk before him, he decided that the actual patent itself, with its legal implications, would have to wait until he could consult a lawyer. But a letter from Boss Johnstone to his father summed up the general situation clearly enough. Dated May 1877, it read in part:

Wilberforce, having now had the chance to examine thoroughly young Porter's chimney improvements as modelled to your commission by Stoddard's of Glasgow , I agree with you that it should yield considerable economies in the consumption of kerosene and give a corresponding increase in candle power. Accordingly I have lodged notice of the appliance at the patent department with notification that the intention is to proceed with a patent application.

I am advised that as the invention was made on the store premises and in time paid for in the form of wages to Porter, and as the model chimneys were built at your expense, Porter himself probably has no legal claim on royalties. However, so as to comply with the Patent law of 1874, the actual patent application must be made in his name as inventor. To safeguard the interests of the store he should then be required, in legal terms, "to execute" an assignment to the Johnstoneville Store Company. The patent itself will then be assigned to the company as assignee. You may think it only fair to recompense Porter in some way. As to any rights in the profits of the invention

that may or may not accrue to me as landlord, these I waive in your
favor, having now no close family.

(At this point his father had written in his large school book
hand in the margin of the document: *No such rights. And I just*
bought the store outright from Boss Johnstone, this glorious 14 June
1883.)

The application will take time, the more so, I am sorry to have to
say in that the applicants are Negroes. Feeling runs high in Kentucky
against the Federal government. Patent applications also cost money.
In this regard I will cheerfully meet all necessary expenses on the
understanding that the company will reimburse me from the expected
profits. I should add that during the application period the invention
is provisionally protected by the wording "patent applied for", to be
engraved on the chimney. Once the patent is granted, the patentee
enjoys exclusive use and exploitation of his invention for seventeen
years...

Willard laid down the letter thoughtfully. The patent grant
was dated March 1882. It was now 1887, which gave the patent
another twelve years to run. It would be tough going for a
Negro to maintain his rights on such a money earner. In the
immediate post-war years the Kentucky state legislature had
refused to ratify the thirteenth and fourteenth amendments to
the Federal Constitution, abolishing slavery and guaranteeing
civil rights to all citizens. The Federal authorities had
thereupon assumed direct control and proclaimed
emancipation of slaves without compensation to their former
owners.

Boss Johnstone's people, long liberated, were of course
lucky. Sure, he had tended to emancipate only those of his
slaves he reckoned would remain loyal and respond with hard
work. But the terrible leather punishment lash, in daily use by
overseers on other plantations, was wielded only to penalize
violent assaults on masters or on fellow slaves. As the 1850s
progressed, Johnstone had brought in labor from outside and

liberated more and more of his work force. The discovery of oil in the Barren County estates had called for an increasing number of artisans – carpenters, smiths, cartwrights, coopers – to prepare installations for the drilling equipment, maintain and replace parts and then to make barrels and build dedicated transport wagons to cart the product to Glasgow railhead. Such skills were scarce, and Johnstone needed manpower fast. He found it on the docks and quaysides of Louisville. A sizeable minority of Johnstoneville's inhabitants had been brought in originally to train local men in their skills. Some of them, like Elsie Marre's father and uncle, had been freedmen.

So, by 1860, "the Boss" had had comparatively few slaves among his people. When the war came he had, of course, supported the North and afterwards stoically accepted the loss of compensation for his few remaining slaves. Other slaveholders loyal to the North during the conflict had been furious. Sometimes the Reconstruction and readjustment period of the late 1860s and the 1870s had sometimes seemed as bitter as the war itself. Small wonder if the state officials, through whom application had to be made in the first place, had done what they could to slow down paperwork which testified to the ingenuity of one black and would result in large profits for another!

In a note attached to the patent document his father had written: *All agreed expenses repaid to Mr Johnstone from royalty proceeds, May 1883*. Rolling all the documents together with Boss Johnstone's receipt, and tying them once more in the pink ribbon, Willard reflected that there was rather more than a decade in which to exploit for all it was worth the Stone's Patent Chimney. He frowned. But what else, if anything, should he do about Dan Porter?

* * * * *

40

It was a week later. A faint smell of wood varnish still lingered in the front parlor, where the casket had lain. Ella remembered the decent grave clothes the funeral director had dressed the body in. The dead man himself had firmly instructed that his own clothes be distributed among the poor (the one act of charity in his will) and that he be buried in a simple winding sheet: what had been good enough for his ancestors in slavery was good enough for their descendant in freedom. But Ella could not bear to think of that beloved body stretched unprotected in the cold earth, while Willard had no intention of laying the family open to the sneers of the poor whites of Johnstoneville.

The casket had been trundled to the burial ground in the glass-walled hearse brought specially over from Glasgow. The rigid horsehair "brush" plumes pointing skywards from the four corners were matched by the nodding black feather plumes on the horses' head harness. And the coachman, with his switch and stovepipe hat, had looked like the devil in gentleman's suiting. Ella shivered at the memory.

She remembered too how the funeral director had broken in upon her vigil, early in the morning of the ceremony. Creeping into the room, hat in hand, he was apparently as surprised by her presence as she was disturbed by his intrusion. He was followed by Willard, who explained that the time had come to seal the coffin in time for the journey to the church. The man worked fast, screwing down the lid, slipping round on tiptoe. He turned to her, deferentially, with a polite question about the inscription upon the brass plate, rubbing it with his coat cuff. She could say nothing but gestured to Willard. His query answered, the man had taken up his hat and glided out, stealthy as a cat.

Now Ella looked round the familiar room, somehow suddenly strange in the knowledge that the hard but honest presence of its one-time master would never return. *Oh! Wilber,* she thought, *never properly sure of yourself. Proud of a freedom earned on your own merits and owing nothing to politicians, but ashamed that any man was once able to call you "slave". Proud of your part in the War of Freedom, but shy to talk of it for fear of comparison with those braggart "ribbon heroes" who came South with the corrupt carpetbaggers. Hard on your family and your workers but no less hard on yourself. Wanting to be honest but sometimes slipping into doubtful dealings. Like any human being, a mixture of virtues and failings, but like all black folk in America, condemned to earn that title of "human". Why can't blacks, like whites, enjoy the right to be bad without being branded "damn nigger"?*

'Oh, am I intruding Mother?' Her reverie was interrupted by her son. A Willard she had not known before; stilted, polite and a little nervous. Feeling her grief and grieving too in his own way, seeking to fill out into his new role of head of the family. 'I think you said Elsie was coming round this morning to take you out walking. I'd like to have some moments talk with her alone first, if that's all right by you?'

The sad, tired, beautiful eyes lit up with pleasure. She had long set her heart on Elsie for a daughter-in-law. She knew the girl had ambitious plans for an education. Ella did not see what use that could be to a woman even if a black woman could overcome the practical difficulties of getting placed. But Willard was only just seventeen and four or five years should find Elsie, with or without education, as sweet as ever on the boy and ready to make him a good wife.

'Sure it's all right, son. See, she's comin' along Main Street this minute. You have your talk while I go see to mah hat an' things.'

Elsie Marre had grown into a tall, well-formed young woman. She still needed glasses, but the owlish looks of the round-faced child had subtly changed their proportion to the classic, full-cheeked, slightly broad-nosed beauty of a Benin queen. Sadly, the effect was disfigured by the weal of the scar from her fall in the Mammoth Cave, running from over her left eye to cross the hairline directly above the bridge of her nose. The doctor that Wilberforce had summoned when she and Willard at last returned home had done the least amount possible, compatible with his exorbitant fee, before rattling off in his fashionable horse gig back to Glasgow. A cheap proprietary ointment preparation and a carelessly applied plaster in place of the sutures that had been called for meant that the fearful gash suffered by the twelve-year-old had become dangerously inflamed, had opened and even threatened gangrene before Wilberforce fell back on the Reverend Walcott and his traditional herbal remedies. Over the years the puckered edges of the scar had quietened but even now, depending on the weather and Elsie's general state of health, it could flair an ugly gray-white.

This morning she seemed under the weather. Willard had rarely seen the scar so bad and he felt sorry for her. His young but calculating heart had a soft spot for Elsie. Sure, at times she could be something of a school miss, sure she was a bit older than he. Sure, at seventeen romance and marriage were very definitely two different things. Even so, insofar as love came into his life, he loved Elsie Marre – perhaps more than he realized.

'Hi, Willard. Your ma feeling all right this morning? We'd planned to walk down along the Gullie Stream a ways an' if she has a mind I want to go down to the Old Quarters for ole time's sakes and check out a few things.'

She gave a cheerful smile. *Always put a brave face on things, that's Elsie for you*, thought Willard. The Old Quarters comprised a number of now derelict cabins run up some thirty years ago to accommodate the artisans on the new oil workings. It was here that Elsie's family had put down their first roots in the "Ville". When their contracts were finished most of the men had returned to Louisville. The hired slaves had had to be returned to their masters, of course. These went with a heavy heart, for Johnstoneville, with its easy punishment regime, had seemed like some kind of paradise. By contrast, the white craftsmen were pleased to get back to the normality of town life where blacks "knew their place".

For them, Boss Johnstone's system had seemed stupid, even dangerous, nonsense. Working side by side with blacks whose skill, they grudgingly acknowledged, had been unsettling. The slaves, of course, did not receive wages, instead the Boss paid their owners a weekly hire charge. No one could reasonably quarrel with that even if it was a far cry from the days when slave labor competed only with unskilled men. But in this strange township – one of them dubbed it "Darkyville" and the name had stuck – the black freedmen negotiated their own contracts with the employer and were paid a regular weekly wage into their own pockets. And, although the whites' "Quarters" were set apart and were a little more spacious, they were still "Quarters" with all the overtones that word carried in the Old South. The white craftsmen were happy to leave when the job was finished and few in Johnstoneville, even among the poor whites, had been sorry to see them go, with their sneering, would-be superior ways.

Freedmen both, Elsie's blacksmith father, Henry, and her uncle Cassius "Beau" Marre, a cartwright, had decided to stay on in Johnstoneville. They had reckoned there would be enough maintenance work at the wellhead and in the town to keep them both. Within a few years they had been able to move into the more comfortable house on Main Street that had become the family home. By that time Henry was married to Mamie, beyond question the prettiest girl in town and a fine seamstress. Beau, it was said, had once remarked he could see no reason to get hitched, and was in his early thirties before he did the deed. Sadly, his wife, Josephine, was unable to have babies and, as a result, when Elsie came along she was center of attention for four doting adults. It said much for her strength of character that she'd emerged unspoilt from her pampered childhood.

The death of her father when she was only five was a foundation experience for her. Into Elsie's young life it brought a grief which, even when the pain dulled, remained a touchstone of reality. A cool, quiet man with a dry wit and seemingly studious eyes prone to an unexpected and wicked twinkle, Henry Marre was adored by his "two women folk", as he called Elsie and her mother. Killed by a fracturing stay-bar as he was engaged in running repairs on a pumping engine, his death was the result of, what a later age would call, metal fatigue. For his wife it seemed the act of a vindictive God angered that three of his black creation could be so happy as they had been. She survived thanks to the love and fellow grieving of Beau and Josephine and the need to support her child through the period of trial. Even so, it was more than a good year before her natural ebullience began to resurface. The house knew that she had come through, one sunny Sunday morning, when a burst of laughter brought them out into the yard, where the family cat had played once too often with its prey and a diminutive field mouse could be seen hightailing it through a hole in the fence.

Henry's death naturally impacted on the family economy. Beau was making good money and happily contributed what he could to the upkeep of his sister-in-law and niece. As always, Josephine's vegetable garden was a mainstay of the family diet. But Mamie was not aiming to live on charity for the rest of her life and looked for ways to expand her dressmaking. She already had Ella Johnstone among her clients, now she asked Ella if she would, perhaps, mention her name among her wider circle of friends. Some new orders resulted. A breakthrough came when Mrs Lafayette Pearson, one of the leading lights of Glasgow's merchant society, saw one of her creations

From time to time, Wilberforce Johnstone would take his Ella into Glasgow to consult on some new line in household goods he was thinking of stocking for the store. These trips were partly for interest, partly for the prestige of doing business on an equal footing with the white community, but largely to let Harmann Tengdahl know that he was not the only supplier in "these United States of America". For Ella the visits meant her best clothes, the ones made for her by Mamie Marre.

One morning, as Ella and Wilber were inspecting a range of hanging lamps in Harley Pearson's warehouse, Mrs Pearson had put her head round the door to remind her husband that they were running late for a luncheon appointment, and Ella's dress caught her eye. Never too proud to learn "even from our colored sisters", as she put it, the merchant's wife asked her who had made it. Before she hurried off with her husband, she had asked if Ella could perhaps arrange, if it was possible, for "the black seamstress of Johnstoneville" to call at the servant's entrance of her mansion with her samples book at her convenience.

Accordingly, the next time the Johnstones ran down into Glasgow, Mamie was squeezed into the back of the gig. The Pearson connection brought Mamie so much work that she was able to put a few jobs out to neighbors.

Mrs Pearson also opened new horizons for Elsie. By fourteen she was helping her mother with deliveries and so came to the lady's attention. Impressed by the girl's bright intelligence, she decided to adopt her as a protégée. There was something of a fashion in ostentatious philanthropy at the time and Mrs Pearson was able to make much of her "little Negress" among the ladies of the Missionary Society coffee circle. It was largely thanks to a modest loan from the Pearsons that Elsie had been able to embark on a year's studies at the Fisk College in Nashville.

The college ethos was progressive in the conventional sense of that term. The academic body as a whole considered it undesirable and morbid for their young charges to dwell on the injustices of the past. Students were encouraged in a forward-looking philosophy of self-improvement befitting pioneers of a new future for the colored people of America. But one professor, frowned on by the college establishment, ran an off-curriculum study group committed to the records of the slave past. Elsie's account and drawings of the ambivalent status of Johnstoneville and in particular the mixed white artisan-freedman-slave community of the Quarters had fascinated him.

'Fill it out with facts and figures, Miss Marre, facts and figures,' he had said. 'The drawings are workmanlike, but wouldn't it make a better archive if we had measurements, inside and out? Just how much bigger were the white accommodations? Exactly how much bigger was the gap between two white cabins and that between two freedmen's cabins? Just how many windows and air vents in the slaves' dormitory long house? That sort of thing.' He had lent her a surveyor's measure and this morning she was hoping to persuade Ella Johnstone to give her a hand as she made a start on the work.

'If your ma ain't feelin' too good, Willard, don't trouble her now. I understand. Perhaps it is too soon after the funeral.'

'Oh no, Elsie. It ain't that. She's looking forward to gettin' out the house. She reckons Pa would approve. "Doin' somethin' practical" always rated pretty high with him. She's jus' fixing her hat. But there's somethin' I'd like to ask you meanwhiles.'

'Sure thing, Willard dear. What would that be?' She smiled happily. Over the years the childhood friendship had flourished into young romance. For all she was his senior in age by two years and by experience, with a year at college

47

behind her, yet more, Elsie often thought dreamily about a future when she and young Will would team up. One day, she hoped, he would ask the question; this morning, she supposed he had some trip in mind.

'I've been looking through Pa's documents this past week,' said Willard, unexpectedly, 'an' I found the lamp patent. You remember, the chimney improvement you told me "belonged" to Dan Porter.'

'Sure, I remember. And I remember how you promised me way back when that you would see to it that he got a fair crack of the whip when you became boss of the store. And now you're boss, aren't you Willard? So where's the problem?'

She smiled, but she was genuinely puzzled. Why all this talk about a subject she thought had been settled seven years back?

'Awh, c'm on now, Elsie. I wasn't but a kid in them days. Nobody could hold a grown man to a promise made when he was a kid. And anyways, like I said, I been looking in those documents an' according to the law, that chimney patent don't belong to Daniel and never did. Sure, his name is listed as inventor, but he assigned over the rights to the store, not even to my pa.'

Elsie glowered, her scar seemed to flare still more livid. Her knuckles tightened on the back of a chair and, leaning tautly towards Willard across the table from her, she spoke in the low, controlled voice of a very angry woman indeed.

'Now see you here, Willard Johnstone. Don' you come that white man's legal talk with me. Dan Porter invented that gadget, no questions asked, pure and simple. Even your pa gave him a raise and, what's more, once said he might have to rethink the possibility of royalties. He never got round to it, so now you can put things straight. Now you're the boss and you've got a promise to live up to, and a mighty angry woman to sweeten.'

The young man's eyes took on a steely glint which she had never seen before. He pulled a chair out from the table between them, sat on it and spread his arms, hands clasped with the two forefingers pointing up like a chin rest. Looking up into the furious eyes opposite, he spoke coldy.

'It is not simple, like you seem to think. That improvement was made in company time on company premises and with company materials. The store paid to have the samples made. Dan Porter assigned away all claims in the patent, knowing full well what he was doing. I don' say as I absolutely won't give him some kind of a share in the profits – maybe at that I do owe you somethin' on that promise. Meanwhile I got a store to run and Dan Porter's got a job to watch. For a start he'd better check back on that beer drinking…'

'Drinking… drinking! I can't have heard you right! You calculating young varmint. You sure have grown up some since I was last here in Johnstoneville. Don't you think we can stay friends if Dan Porter don't get his deserts.'

The eyes were ablaze and her body was shaking as Elsie swung away towards the open window, as if for air.

'You heard me right and, sure, Dan will get his deserts, and now,' Willard pushed back the chair and got up, 'I'll go call mother.'

* * * * *

It was Sunday morning, three weeks since the break-up. Elsie was playing host to a college friend, Judith Lear, and Judith's kid sister, Sarah. Her little party walked into the church to take her normal place across the aisle from where Willard, back home after a business trip, was seated next to his mother. The church was packed, as usual, and all heads turned towards them in the hope of some confrontation. In fact they ignored one another. As far as Elsie was concerned, he might as well be in the infernal regions where, in her view, he so richly deserved to be. The reason for the breach remained a secret between them. However, this did not prevent Jo'ville gossip dividing into two schools of thought, both of which "happened to know the facts". Hopelessly wide of the mark as to the real issue, both assumed it revolved around a proposal of marriage. According to one version, Elsie had refused because Willard was "not well-schooled enough for a college girl"; according to the other, she had been insulted because he expected her to spend the rest of her days as a store clerk. Either way, the town was impressed with the cool way in which Elsie behaved.

First Purchase African M.E. Church lay between Main Street and the Quarters. It was a sturdy enough clapboard clad frame building with a high-pitched roof and a bell. Here and there the cheap single coat of white paint was beginning to flake under a succession of burning summers, but the place still presented a bright, confident exterior to visitors. Construction had begun in 1871, paid for from the savings made on the first wages earned by the community as a whole after emancipation, hence the name. Formerly, Reverend Walcott and his predecessor had held services in the Quarters Warehouse, run up to take the materials and equipment of the artisan team. The preacher had conducted the proceedings from a portable lectern-pulpit which now held pride of place in the new church, set on a dais between two reading desks.

Inside, the church was somewhat dimly lit by four frosted windows, two in each wall. It was unpainted and rose without ceiling to the steep rafters; along its walls, kerosene hanging lamps were suspended from brass brackets. On the wall behind the central pulpit a silvery white banner, embroidered in blue under the supervision of Mamie Marre, proclaimed the message "God is Love". A move from older members for a panel painted with the Ten Commandments had been vetoed by Reverend Walcott, on the grounds that most of his flock were only now beginning to learn to read and he had no desire for them to be disheartened every Sunday with a barrage of "Thou Shalt Nots". Strange ideas from a God-fearing man, opined Miss Ruth and for once she was supported by the aged Joshua Tubman, the community's oldest member. Joshua generally resented her claims as rival sage and had done ever since her retirement to Johnstoneville – this time he could only agree with her.

Pine benches flanking the central aisle served as pews but these did not fill the whole body of the church and latecomers had to stand at the back. At the aisle end of each bench lay a little pile of cheap cardboard fans bearing a somewhat wooden image of "Jesus The Light of the World" and below this the words "Compliments Johnstoneville Stores". It had clearly been copied by the Glasgow printer's artist from an oleograph of a famous painting then very much in vogue, but the storm lantern of the original had been replaced with something suspiciously like the basic model of lamp on sale at the stores in Main Street.

Noting that Willard was leaning forward for a glimpse of the glamorous Judith, Elsie leant forward too, her head dramatically bowed in prayer. Reverend Walcott, staring the congregation to silence from the pulpit, repressed a smile. Stockily built, he was of middling height with graying hair turning to white at the temples and in his black frock coat, dazzling white shirt front and black tie presented a figure of great distinction. At the reading desk to his left stood Amos Tubman, son of Joshua but himself a venerable figure of some sixty years, and opposite him, to Judith's surprise, a man in his thirties, with a smile behind his eyes and, on the desk in front of him, a big brass musical instrument that seemed to be all tubes and pistons.

'That's Dan Porter,' whispered Elsie, 'with his trombone. Reverend Walcott lets him give the melody, though the old-timers think it's a lot of newfangled nonsense.'

'Trombone?' Judith whispered back, puzzled. 'I thought I knew what they looked like and it wasn't like that.'

'Dan'll tell us all about it after church.' Elsie flashed a quick grin as, raising his eyes, Reverend Walcott cleared his throat with pointed emphasis.

'Brethren and sisters, we welcome company with us this morning, Miss Judith Lear and her little sister Sarah, all the way from Louisville, stayin' a few days at the Marre house.' He paused and Judith looked down with embarrassment as Willard peered once again in her direction, this time with success. 'Now,' continued the reverend, 'I'll call on the music superintendent to lead us in the first hymn, in memory of brother Johnstone departed from this life but surely received among the saints upon the further bank of Jordan.'

Amos Tubman reached down to his reading desk, opened a battered old hymn book and said, 'We'll sing number one twenty-two.' At the same time Dan Porter raised the trombone, blowing gently into the mouthpiece as if to warm it up. Clearing his throat, Amos read in a harsh gravely voice, "There's a land beyond the river."

Led in the familiar tune by the warm, strong tones of the trombone, some 200 voices sang out the words. The last syllable, held on a throbbing hum, was followed by Amos with "That we call the sweet forever."

The voices swelled again, and again the last note hummed, to be met this time with "And we all can reach that shore by Faith's decrees."

Again came the vibrant singing, with groups of voices leading the melody into simple, moving harmonies. Amos followed with 'In that far-off sweet forever, Just beyond the shining river, We shall join the saints in singing Jubilees.'

Over three more verses, the rows of worshippers swayed alternately left and right, clapping the rhythmic beat, the voices followed line for line while Daniel Porter, feeling the confidence of the singers, sometimes left the melody to them while he embellished the surging harmonies with a descanting tenor line. He was careful to curb his more florid inventions under the austere glance of the music superintendent, who shared his old father's view on all modern trends in worship.

As usual at the height of the summer, the reverend curtailed his sermon and the services were over in little more than hour. Through the milling crowd, chatting and jostling outside the little building, Willard strode dourly towards Judith Lear. He had no wish to speak with Elsie but he was determined to at least make himself known to this slender, soft-eyed beauty before she return to Louisville, which he had heard was only a matter of days away.

For her part, Elsie angrily realized that she would have to make the introductions or else betray her feelings in the matter: feelings which even now had not cooled to indifference. In any case the whole question of Dan Porter's future would have to come out once she started to explain and at this moment Dan, with Bess on his arm and the trombone bag over his shoulder, was making a slow, chatting progress towards them through the crowd worshippers.

'Good day, Willard,' she took the initiative with cool detachment. 'May I introduce you to my friend Miss Judith Lear and, of course, her sister, Sarah. Judith, this is Mr Willard Stone, proprietor of the town store and, according to his own lights at least, a gentleman of a very inventive turn of min'.'

Ignoring the implied sneer, Willard nodded briefly to the awestruck figure of Sarah, for whom this was her first formal introduction, and turning to Judith raised his Derby hat with all the charm of which he was capable – considerable it must be said, when he had a mind.

'Delighted to make your acquaintance, Miss Judith. I hear you're leaving shortly and I'm mighty sorry not to have had the pleasure before this time. I myself am off traveling about business tomorrow. I trust we may meet at greater length should you pass this way again.'

Sensing her friend's hostility but flattered nevertherless by the attention of someone who was clearly the most distinguished man present after the minister, Judith looked modestly down with a slight smile on her lips.

'Why, I'm flattered I'm sure, Mr Stone.'

With a curt 'Good day, Elsie' and a civil nod of the head to Judith, Willard turned on his heel and made his way deliberately back to his mother, her eyes sad with unhappiness at the break between the two childhood sweethearts.

Sarah had stared wide-eyed throughout the exchange. She had never seen such a handsome man and was enthralled by the strange minuet of formalities with which he had surrounded the meeting. They would certainly be this way again if she had anything to do with the matter. If Judith did her part, there seemed to be every likelihood that this hat-wielding giant would become part of the Lear family circle. And if Judith didn't, she, Sarah, would have to grow up mighty fast to make sure he didn't get away!

Her musings were dispelled as "the trombone man", her hero of the services that morning, came up to introduce his wife and to be introduced himself. Bess Porter was the kind of woman to whom children take an instant liking and who was never happier than when in their company. The town as a whole reckoned it a shame that she and Dan seemed to have no luck with kids. She and Sarah were to become "best friends", if only for a tragically short time. But this morning they were all absorbed by the mystery of the trombone. Like Judith, Sarah had always thought of the instrument as a "slide horn".

As the little party strolled back for their Sunday meal, Dan kept them all in peals of laughter as he explained how slide horns were all well and good but they might bruise the, how should he put it, the "backsides" of the man in front in a marching band. In fact the valve trombone, something like a big trumpet to look at, had been generally adopted by the federal army as a more workmanlike, compact instrument than the slide model. With the ending of the Civil War, hundreds had been sold off cheap as army surplus and many an enthusiastic but cash-hungry musician had taken advantage of the bargain time. 'Anyways,' joked Dan, 'it *must* be technically superior with all them extra pipes and pistons!'

He loved the instrument; he loved its music; he even loved the old timers who objected to it! Johnstoneville seemed a very good place to be on a sunshine Sunday morning. Even mean-minded Willard could not cloud Daniel's sense of well-being just now. Who could tell; he might one day even offer terms over the chimney patent.

But the store clerk's optimism was sadly out of place. Barely two years later, he and Bess would be forced to quit, pack their bags and leave their comfortable Kentuckian backwater for ever.

CHAPTER FOUR

Matters of Business

'Ten years to run on that patent, eh Willard? It seems only yesterday I first brought that Hinks Duplex to show young Dan Porter.'

Harmann Tengdahl, his blond hair now growing sandy-gray at the temples and showing a little more forehead, was still a towering figure. He smiled in reminiscence.

'"The True Lamp of Today", I seem to remember they called it, yet Johnstone's store managed to make improvements: isn't that so?'

He shot Willard, the young store proprietor, a shrewd glance. Elsie had given him her account of "the great patent battle" and Johnstoneville was still talking about the recent departure of the Porter family. Wilberforce had given Dan a raise in salary, while the latter, confident in Elsie's assurance that Willard would either persuade his father to disgorge a share in the patent or himself square matters after the old man's death, had stayed on at Johnstoneville.

Early in 1890, two years after the death of Wilberforce and still with no sign of any change in the arrangements, Dan, now in his early thirties, forced the issue. The only result was a bitter confrontation, during the course of which young Willard accused his store clerk of secret drinking during shop hours and fired him.

Harmann Tengdahl reckoned the real issue was age and community standing. Dan Porter was twelve years senior to the store's twenty-year-old proprietor, and had been keeping the shop for sixteen years. To the younger generation Dan Porter simply *was* the town store and a Johnstoneville institution. Willard, by contrast, on the road most of the year looking for business in the surrounding counties and building foundations for future expansion, was an increasingly remote figure, losing the prestige in the community once accorded to the senior member of the family (now renamed "Stone" by him). Having removed Dan, he had put his own mother in charge of the shop and found another eager young sixteen-year-old as trainee clerk.

Harmann could sympathize with Dan and he understood young Elsie's outrage at the turn of events, but himself a businessman he privately approved Willard's attitude and had no intention of disturbing a valuable commercial connection with pointless expressions of indignation.

Truth to tell, what with the growth in the store's turnover, Willard's youthful vigor and ever-increasing mobility thanks to the continuing advances in railroad communications, Harmann was a little surprised to still have the account as general supplies wholesaler. But he had a plan in mind that would strengthen his ties with Willard and at the same time help finance an extension of his own business. It was a plan that very much depended on Stone's patent lamp chimney. He listened with secret amusement as young Willard replied with a brusqueness he no doubt hoped sounded businesslike but which, to older, more experienced ears, indicated lingering embarrassment.

'Improvements were certainly made,' said Willard. 'Now, the question for Stone's is how to make as much profit as possible before November 1899, that is to say over the next nine years and six months. Joe Taggart of Glasgow is making the chimneys under license and doing good business in Barren and Warren. It earns me good royalties, but I'm looking for a market I can supply direct.' He paused, and then went on half to himself.

'Thanks to whitey and his color line, I couldn't trade direct with most of Taggart's customers.'

'Hold on there a moment, young Mr Willard Stone. Some of us are happy to cross that there color line and you shouldn't forget it.'

Harmann spoke in mock seriousness. He had suddenly understood why he still had the account. The answer was obvious when you thought about it. For Willard, to have a white wholesaler he could trust was a bonus. Harmann had been doing business in Jo' ville for so long, better than twenty-five years since he opened the account with Boss Johnstone himself, that he had entirely forgotten the color line. He realized he was in such good standing with the Jo'ville stores that his plans had every chance of success. He waited for Willard to continue.

'Sure, sure, Harmann. It never crossed my mind for a moment that you were part of the whitey color line.' The younger man was clearly startled at the other's intervention. He valued Harmann's solid support, indeed friendship, for the family firm and, insofar as business was the be-all and end-all of Willard's life, he counted him among his friends. With Dan Porter gone, Elsie Marre barely on speaking terms and even his mother obviously unhappy about the Porter affair, he needed allies – he also wanted to discuss an important new departure for the company which he had been thinking over for some time.

'Trouble is, I'm all tied up with the business these days. Big new ideas, Harmann – I'd sure appreciate to hear your thinking on them. First thing, I want to be selling my own lamps, "Stone's Patent Kerosene Lamps" sounds a good name to me, if I could find me a market: 'n I reckon I've found one at that.' He paused. 'Religion, Harmann! Religion! That's where the money is for the modern man of color.'

'Religion, Willard, religion? How, for land's sakes, do you reckon that? There is surely plenty of money in religion for the preachers, white as well as colored... but for businessmen?'

'How long since you been in a church, Harmann?' Willard broke into one of his rare smiles. 'There's no need to answer, you old pagan. But take the time to put your head round the door of the First Purchase here in Jo'ville 'n you'll see eleven hanging lamps, five down each side and one over the pulpits and desks. They were bought from the store and they're all fitted now with Stone's patent chimneys, and come winter the store supplies a handsome order of kerosene. Can you imagine the profit if Stone's supplied all the churches in the county, or half the churches in the state of Kentucky, or just one in five of all the African Methodist churches between here and Chicago and Philadelphia?'

Harmann was not smiling now. He was impressed. He'd had no idea that young Willard had ambitions on this scale. To be honest he had doubted the boy had it in him.

'That sure is mighty big thinking. Reckon you can do it?'

'Bigger than you know, and yeah, sure, I can do it. Reverend Walcott last year attended an assembly of colored pastors 'n preachers, some place in Virginia, forget where. He told me the church where they held the meetings was an ordinary small town First Baptist. Built of good brick, according to him it could accommodate a good 500 congregation. The inside was furnished in Georgia pine, it had stain-glass windows, an organ an' even carpets. The reverend sure was mighty taken with the place. Think he hoped I'd lay out for a stain-glass window or some such, here in Jo'ville!'

Again Willard grinned, this time at the improbable hopes churchmen could indulge in.

'He didn't say anything about lamps but it was a summer meeting and maybe they didn't have cause to light 'em. What he did say was that according to some report they discussed at the assembly, there were nigh on twenty-four thousand Negro American churches in the country with a total enrolled membership of two and a half million and financial assets amounting to $26 million and income to match.'

'Real money,' Harmann let out a low whistle.

It was midday. Sweltering in the heat, the two men were surveying the store from the center of a deserted Main Street. A faint, clean scent of new-carpentered timber freshened the sultry air. Just two months before, Joad Lynch, "Master Carpenter, Johnstoneville" (all reasonable commissions furnished at standard rates), had finished the porch that now shaded the frontage. Atop it ran a boldly painted nameboard: "STONE'S DRUG AND GENERAL STORES" and below that "Willard Stone # Successor to Wilberforce Johnstone # Prop.". For all it was so new, the structure was liberally cluttered with posters, boards and hanging banners promoting such proprietary brands as "Keiffler Fine Shoes", "Dr Vane Druetta's Renowned Embrocation" and "Beekman's Cigars Best for Chewing or Smoking".

But the men's attention was focused on two ornate boards which flanked the steps from the street and thereby obscured the handsome balustrade, lovingly finished only weeks before by the master carpenter. The board on the left read "STONE'S" and that on the right "LAMPS". The heavy, over-florid script was clearly the work of a city sign writing company and the boards, ordered by Willard some months ago from Harmann's catalogue, had arrived that very morning. Helped by his supplier, the "Prop." had himself just completed the installation. ("A crime against art" was the comment of old Joad Lynch, depressed to find that the flash black businessman who had commissioned him to make the porch had no more aesthetic sense than the slaveholder of the Tennessee plantation where he had served his apprenticeship forty years before.)

'Awkward sort of name for a Negro,' Willard said unexpectedly, as he led the way through the shop to the sanctum at the back. It was little changed since the day Daniel and Elsie had speculated on improvements to the "True Lamp of Today", except that now it was reserved to Willard and his mother. Daniel's somewhat rickety table had been replaced by a workmanlike writing desk, but the old office chair and armchair were still in service, while a fly grille over the window now darkened the shady little room still further. Willard settled himself in the armchair and the older man perched, rather less comfortably, on the office chair.

'Odd name, Lynch.'

'Come again?' asked a puzzled Harmann. They seemed to have strayed from the subject in hand for no reason that he could detect. For Willard, the train of thought was just now almost inevitable. For weeks he had been unable to see the new front to the shop without remembering what it had cost him. Joad had stubbornly refused to hurry the job, had insisted on the better of the two timber qualities and had in general made so many footling conditions, "Jes to make a top rating job", that the young proprietor's thoughts had flickered towards summary justice more than once!

'Lynch,' repeated Willard, 'awkward name for a black man, don't you think!'

'Uncomfortable, I grant you,' replied Harmann, his face darkened by an angry frown, as he caught the drift of his young friend's thoughts. He was recalling how years back he had cowered in a hotel bedroom in a small southern town, while a lynch mob bayed for blood in the street below, and he had never forgiven himself his cowardice. 'But it's an odd fact that one of the most powerful state representatives in Mississippi is John R. Lynch, a Negro – smart mustache too. I wouldn't be surprised to see him in Congress in Washington one of these days."

'You see much of Mississippi, Harmann? Uh shoot, course you do. I was forgetting, you got quite a sales beat down thataways. 'Fraid my mind's up north mostly these days.'

Willard paused again, marshalling his thoughts. Harmann waited. He had his own piece to say, but he was not so stupid as to interrupt the flow of one of his major customers who was in the middle of outlining long-term plans.

'It seems,' Willard continued at last, 'leastways, according to Reverend Walcott, that those bigger churches up north ain't just churches but more like clubhouses for the community. Seems the Virginia First Baptist had the church on the first floor and a big assembly room below it. Some of the pastors' committees were held there of an evening, each with its own area in the big hall and each with its own lamp – the reverend actually mentioned that and said they would have done much better with a few of Stone's patent chimneys.'

'Willard, I'm beginning to think you really are on to something big – if you can find salesmen. And,' he paused, 'if you can afford their travel bills.'

'I'm working on that very thing, Harmann. An' I may, just may, have found an answer.'

'Have you come into money then?' The question was put jokingly, but seriously meant all the same. Tengdahl had watched the store's growing prosperity over the past few years with fascination. He knew of no other Negro establishment to equal it for size, professional management or apparent profitability.

The peculiar situation of Johnstoneville itself, with a sizeable waged and free black population for some thirty years, had given the shop a head start. But the foundation of its success was laid back in the very early days when Boss Johnstone himself ran the stores with the young Wilberforce,

Willard's father, as his assistant. From the start, Johnstone decided, for the convenience of his bookkeeping, to funnel retail sales of kerosene from the oil workings through the Jo'ville stores. In this way he could keep bulk sales and the day-to-day retail trade business separate. The speed and efficiency with which Wilberforce mastered the procedures involved soon meant his employer could concentrate his attention on developing the main operations of the oil plant. When eventually he handed the store over to Wilberforce as sole manager, he left the now flourishing retail business with him and loaded the rent on the shop accordingly.

Kerosene sales to the working population of Jo'ville as such were not large, few could afford any but the simplest of lamps and those that could burned the fuel sparingly. However, on the Boss's system "retail sales" also included the lamp and heating oil sold to the small farmers, and share croppers, even the occasional drum of lubrication oil for the carts and the slowly increasing numbers of simple farm machines finding their way on to the land.

Since Johnstone's shop was the only supplier in the locality of general stores – oil, chandlery, groceries and whatnot else – and since he sold at very fair prices, his white neighbors stayed loyal even when the place was quite obviously being run by an ex-slave. Those who objected to dealing with "a nigger", and they were a majority, had slaves, later freedmen, collect their supplies. Payment was made by means of sealed purses given in charge of the farmhand agent with strict instructions "to leave it for collection by Mr Johnstone".

For years, Wilberforce had a small, sturdily made chest on the store counter under a notice reading "For the Boss". When a farmer's agent presented such a purse, a note of the payer's name was attached to the draw strings, the chest was unlocked and the payment was solemnly deposited. At the end of the day's business, Wilberforce matched payments received against the actual cost of goods supplied to each "purse payer", as he called his prejudiced customers. From time to time they would receive, as if from Boss Johnstone, notice of any balance outstanding. The system, so far as anyone knew, was unique in its complexity but all concerned accepted the fiction.

The years went by and Wilberforce got richer. He was careful not to spend ostentatiously but his account with the bank in Bowling Green, some forty miles further away than Glasgow and with a less gabby bank manager, was building a useful capital reserve. Willard was determined to delay touching it for as long as possible. What he would use it for was not clear as yet, but it would be something important, something decisive.

For his part, every time he passed through Jo'ville, Harmann puzzled over just how much the Stones were worth. Young Willard's apparent plans for setting up a major sales force suggested that the sum was a great deal larger than he had supposed. In fact, Willard's answer to his bantering inquiry did not support the speculation.

'Come into money?! No I have not. No. I have a plan for salesmen who stay in the field while I do any traveling that's necessary.'

'How you reckon that, Willard? I've never heard of a sales force that don't travel: unless you call store clerks a sales force.'

'One of the pastors at that assembly up in Virginia was from Philadelphia, an' he told the reverend something that's had me thinking on and off these six months. The big Bethel there has various boards of administrators, separate groups led by class leaders and more than twenty societies meeting on its premises. Even that little town has two insurance societies, a woman's association and a lecture association, that hold regular meetings on the church premises. All of them have secretaries and other officials, all of them touch dozens of families, Harmann. I'm off on the road next week to see if I can't recruit me a few resident salesmen in societies nearer home. If I can find me an agent in each church willing and able to talk up S.P.K.L. with friends and neighbors, I reckon I can look to increase my sales next time I travel that way.'

'I reckon you could Willard, I reckon you could.' Harmann was truly impressed by the idea. He wondered whether the young man before him could carry it off. But Willard was speaking again.

'There's another trouble, Harmann,' he said. 'What you heard 'bout this newfangled electricity they got up North? Mr Alvar Edison ain't it? You think it's going to catch on?'

'Bound to Willard, bound to. I heard the Carpenter mansion outside Louisville already got it a coupla years back and other gentry families will surely follow suit. I'm a thinking of running a novelty line in "electrical fitments" myself. Fifty years from now it'll be everywhere in "These Expanding United States".' The old slogan, thought Willard. 'Sure thing, it's going to catch on.' Tengdahl paused, with a hint of drama. 'But that's a long ways in the future. You got a few years trading in your church societies before that will change any. An' me, I'm here today to talk about the prospects for Stone's Lamps, Stone's Kerosene Lamps, Stone's Patent Kerosene Lamps, however you call the company in this last decade of the nineteenth century.' He paused with a touch of drama before continuing.

'You asked me if I do much business on the Mississippi, I sure do and I'll soon be doing more if you an' I can make a deal. I don't know about your churches for sure, but I do know about steamboats. If you get yourself sold on them, it'll be the making of your fortune. Let me just tell you about the steamboat *James Howard*.'

The evening was darkening. Willard lit the one Duplex Hinks Special the company had ever bought and, knowing his visitor's likings, pulled out the bottle of good bourbon kept for occasions such as this.

'It was three years back I first saw the great river,' said Harmann, sipping appreciatively from the glass Willard pushed towards him. 'Took the railroad from Louisville, Kentucky, to Memphis, Tennessee, and there went aboard the *James Howard*. That boat was everything they say, Willard – a floating palace, a floating palace.' He paused. 'Back in '72 it was chartered to take Grand Duke Alexis of Russia and his party down to New Orleans for Mardi Gras. The grand saloon, more than 100 feet long I reckon, had a great centerpiece carrying potted ferns and so forth, and atop it the most magnificent clock I ever did see. The base was inscribed "A Gift from His Serene Highness, Alexis Grand Duke of Russia" or some such flowery language. It was cased in green-black malachite with gold mountings and it had two dials facing fore and aft, so big you could easy read the time from either end the saloon.

The tablecloths were dazzling white, the silver sparkling clean and the dinner plates richly painted; the ceiling was shiny white picked out in gold leaf. Of an evening that saloon was a-glinting and a-glittering like the Mammoth Cave lit by a hundred Duplex Specials. Willard, that boat had lamps of every kind and description you could ever wish to see; simple pedestals in the crew's quarters up to triple pendants in the great saloon.'

He paused, as if dazzled by his own descriptive powers.

'Imagine, if you will, a hanging brass fitment suspended on a brass frame with a glass bowl reservoir held in a brass hoop and above it a down-turned mushroom shade with the chimney projecting up through it. Now add two "S" shaped brackets swaying out either side from that brass frame: each carrying a milky glass-bowl reservoir, with a dished bowl-shade throwing the light from that lamp up to the ceiling. The lamps in the smoking saloon were different yet again, with green shades; in the ladies' drawing room the lamps had glass drops like reflectors for a chandelier. There were other types too. There must have been a good 200 lamps on that boat. An' d' y' know sumpthin', Willard?' Harmann paused. 'Not a one but had a standard "onion bulb" chimney. Imagine the economies in kerosene if they'd fitted Stone's patents, imagine the impact on your sales. And, Willard, imagine this. We don't stop with the *James Howard* steamboat. There's the *St Joseph*, the *Lula Prince* and many, many more.'

For all he prided himself a calculating businessman, Willard Stone was not yet twenty and ambitious: the bourbon may have helped, too. Before the evening was over he had decided to reshape his commercial policy to accommodate Tengdahl's proposal of a partnership. In exchange for a share of the profits, Harmann was to sell lamps and chimneys the length of the river from Memphis, Tennessee, to New Orleans, on the paddle steamers and, where time allowed, in the wharf-side bars and hotels. Both men knew that on that stretch of river a black face would do no trade whatsoever. Willard was indifferent to principle when it came to profit, there he was single-minded. Five years later, when Harmann finally retired, Stone's Kerosene Lamps had warehousing facilities in Memphis and a white manager recruited by Harmann in Ohio.

That warehouse was the first to carry the logo S.K.L.

CHAPTER FIVE

Ambition is Dangerous

A flash of sunlight on the locomotive piston under his oiling can dazzled Dan Porter back to the present and now he heard the voice. Cheerful, male and insistent, it seemed to be hailing him from the blacks–only Jim Crow car of the Chicago "Indi" Flyer held up by the stop signal on the main through-line, two tracks away.

'Hey, you there: Oiler! Come over here a moment.'

It was a baking day in early June. Dotted here and there, the hoses swaying from the inverted funnels of the cylindrical water tanks gave the Union Depot, Indianapolis, the air of some ancient menagerie of mammoths. The matt blacks and rusts and yellows of the contraptions were the only elements for as far as the eye could reach that did not flash back in the midsummer glare. Away in the distance, rising on the city's central mound, the State Capitol, completed just a couple of years earlier, shone white-domed and proud above the spreading roofs. Here in the marshalling yards the light glinted off the metal fittings and paintwork of passenger coaches and liveried locomotives, and even the coal wagons flashed highlights from their glistening cargoes. Everywhere, the railroad tracks, burnished by the daily transits of a thousand vehicles, burned up from the glinting granite ballast.

Squinting against the glare and shading his eyes from the

sky, Dan saw the speaker to be a colorfully dressed city-type about his own age. Having caught his attention, the man now beckoned unmistakably to the overalled figure, oil-can in hand, who, until that moment, had been musing on ideas for mechanical improvements to the loco under his care.

'Happy in your work, Mister Oilman?' The tone was bantering, the eyes laughing, but behind it all, Dan, who was now standing on the track below the open carriage window, sensed something more.

'Yes, Sir!'

'Really. But hopin' for somethin' better.' It was a statement rather than a question.

'Yes, Sir, I am!' Dan replied in all honesty.

'Really!' The falling tone suggested that some half-formulated suspicion had been confirmed. 'Well, it seems as though we may be held on this signal a few minutes yet, so permit me to introduce myself: Oliver "Rainbow" Williams, formerly of Louisville, Kentucky, now of Chicago, Illinois.'

The flamboyant flourish of the language squared with the bravura of the clothes: a frock coat of light olive green, a flowered vest and matching beige-brown Derby hat and cotton gloves.

'Happy to meet you, Sir! Daniel Porter at your service: formerly of Johnstoneville, Kentucky and presently of Indianapolis, Indiana.'

'Really!' This time the word in the two-tone pitch signaled heightened interest. 'Another Kentucky man. Cain't rightly say I ever heard of Johnstoneville, but I'm more interested in you. Consider yourself an engineer?'

'Not sure I'll be allowed to go that far, Mister… '

Williams slapped his hand impatiently against the frame of the drop sash window and frowned slightly. The hostility of white skilled workers was a terrible obstacle to black Americans' ambitions since the end of the decade of

Reconstruction. But evidently Rainbow Williams was not a man to accept defeat without a battle. Dan hurriedly pressed on with an air of confidence he almost felt in this man's presence.

'But I'm learning all I can. A mainline depot like this – more'n a hundred locos in an' out every day, traveling nationwide and almost every type built in the States, that's what I call an engineer's university for a guy as keeps his eyes open.'

'An' you do, I guess.'

'I like to think so, Sir. Right now I'm working on an improvement I reckon they could make to the connectin'-rod-crank-pin assembly on that Baldwin-Mallet combination you saw me working on over there.'

'Really?' This time the favorite word indicated polite puzzlement. A sigh and hiss of steam from the Flyer's locomotive indicated the engineer, in anticipation of a signal change, was readying his locomotive to pull into the main passenger station. Williams rapidly extracted a card from his vest pocket, scribbled something on the back and handed it down to Dan, together with a dollar bill.

'Well Mr Porter, I'm staying in Indianapolis a coupla days and I'd be mighty obliged if you could drop by at my hotel this evenin' after you've had a bite to eat. The money should compensate you for your time an' trouble,' he coughed with unexpected delicacy, 'and, perhaps, you may be able to change out of your working clothes?'

The rising tone indicated that the speaker appreciated that this might not mean any great change for the better but hoped that his new acquaintance might be able to present a somewhat less grimy aspect. As the train pulled slowly away, Dan, whose wedding day suit was kept carefully laid away for just such rare eventualities, gave a half-military salute with a reassuring 'Sure thing, Sir,' and then glanced at the card. The written address was the smartest hotel in town to accommodate blacks. He was intrigued and excited.

Late that evening, nearer eleven than ten o'clock, he eased back the catch of the door to his one-room apartment so as not to disturb Baby Jim. Bess, too, was asleep and as he crept gently into the warm bed and eased his arm round her, he found himself worrying about how tired she was getting these days. She had never fully recovered from what had been a difficult delivery, he knew. But he sometimes wondered whether there might be something else. Maybe the doctors in Chicago would have the answer. If Mr Williams meant what he had said then, for the first time in his life, Dan should soon have the kind of money it took to get decent medical service.

His mind was still spinning from the meeting at the hotel. The wedding suit had won warm praise from the elegant Williams, who had launched into a cross between an interview, an offer of work and the establishment of his own standing. A studio photograph had shown him soberly suited with four discretely clad "business advisers" and, together with an impressive bill fold, had established him as a man of substance. A few well-informed questions had shown that he had a serious interest in steam power, with special expertise in marine engines. The groundwork had thus been laid for a job proposal which Daniel was still finding it difficult to credit.

It appeared that Mr Williams, by means unspecified, had recently come into money on a scale that would enable him to fulfill a boyhood dream – the running of an all-black steamboat company. He was negotiating for the purchase of a boat on the Chicago waterfront. Chicago, where he had moved some years back, rather than his native Louisville because he reckoned a black at least had a chance up there. Would Daniel like to become his engineer? He was sure he would grow into the job given his intelligence and experience of steam. As a symbol of good will, he had handed over sufficient money to pay for the family rail fare to Chicago and a cab to the address where he had arranged for them to live. If Dan had any difficulty in persuading his wife he could bring the money back to the hotel tomorrow, Sunday. Otherwise, Williams would expect them in Chicago on Saturday week, which would give Dan time to work out any notice that might be owing to his present employers and to arrange his move. When Dan had expressed his surprise and thanks at being entrusted with the rail fare even before he had agreed to take the job, the remarkable Mr Williams had replied: 'Mr Porter, as company engineer you will rank as a business partner. In the sincere hope that you will respond to the gesture I propose to treat and trust you as such from the outset – and now, perhaps, it is time for you to return to the bosom of your family.'

The next morning being Sunday, the little family had a half hour longer in bed before they went to the morning services. As they ate their midday meal, Dan gradually unfolded the course of his meeting, checking the irritation he had felt the night before on returning home from such an errand only to find his wife asleep. But when he had finished and her only response was to say that Chicago was a long way to go and cold into the bargain, he protested.

'Aw c'm'on, Bess. Chicago's the North, where a black man can breathe like emancipation ain't just a forgotten chapter in the history books. Chicago's got history worth hearin' an' tomorrows worth sharin'. Chicago's the future I'd say. Always dreamt about Chicago ever since Elsie Marre came visitin' to Cave City that time back in January. You remember, when we'd quitted Johnstoneville and headed for your folks' place to rest up and figure through what we and young boy James should do with our future...'

As always when he spoke of the boy, Dan's face lit up.

'... wonderin' whether we even had such a thing as a future

after kid Willard Stone'd thrown me out for a drunk… me, me the man who's made his family's future single-handed… '

He paused for another pull at his beer and then intoned, like a bishop reading the bible, what was in fact paragraphs from a lovingly memorized encyclopedia article.

'Chicago, which, though 1,000 miles from the eastern seaboard of the United States, cleared more than 12,000 vessels from its harbor in the year 1883; which, with population of more than half a million souls, has more than 200 churches. And two of them Colored Methodist, Bess…' he added, trying to josh her out of her negative mood.

He looked dreamily out at the sunlit shanty dwelling across the shabby, rammed-earth street. He saw not the crazy lean-to boards of the rail hand's "cottage", with its straggling vegetation to serve as a garden, but a decent, if modest, stone-built family house befitting the engineer partner in an up and coming steamboat transportation company.

'… I've been wanting to go to Chicago ever since Elsie told us what she'd found in the encyclopedia… '

He stopped, startled.

'Say hon', why you cryin'?'

'Sure, Dan, I reckon you've always been sweet on anything Elsie said.'

Daniel laughed, disbelievingly, 'You serious, hon'? Elsie's still a kid.'

'She ain't so still a kid, Dan. That "kid" was twenty-one last year… or have you forgotten the fool sight you made o' yohself at that "kid's" birthday party! You seem to think time stands still for you and she… you seem to think we're all like we were when you was foolin' round with kerosene lamps an' rescuin' little kiddies in distress. The world's moved on, an' you an' Elsie Marre with it.'

Bess dried her eyes and tidied herself up with characteristic economy of movement. Tears were a rare event with her and they were to be dried up with commonsense efficiency. But, although she had shown something of herself she would rather have kept hidden, she did not try to deny the emotion or pretend that nothing had happened.

'Well there's nothing to be done about it. I knows you loves me, dear. But I know too you got a soft spot in your heart for Elsie ever since she was a chil', an' I cain't help but be a bit jealous. I guess it'll be for the best if we do go on up to Chicago. That should be far enough from Kentucky. An' now I'd best start sortin' things if we're to be changin' homes again.

It was a sore point with Bess that Boy Jim was still not a year old and they had already moved twice. She would have been happy to settle in Cave City near her folks and her dear old brother, Moses. But Dan wanted more independence and more possibilities, more distance between him and Willard Stone, "the man who cheated me of my future".

On that subject, Bess had long come to think that things might not after all be quite so straightforward, but she never let slip the disloyal thought. That day at the Mammoth Cave – was it really fourteen years ago! – she had been so indignant. The idea was Dan's and he should have the money, the issue was clear-cut. But was it? Without the job Dan would never have had the idea, and without Willard's father it would never have been patented. Over the years, where Dan's good nature had begun to sour, Bess had mellowed and saddened. Boy Jim was her fourth child; one had been still-born, the two others had died in infancy. Deepened personal awareness of the tragedy of life had made her more tolerant of other people's maneuvers to fill in the time before death.

But she had gone along with Dan's decision to move to Louisville, where he had found work in the stoke hole of a steamer. The engineer was an easy-going old-timer, more interested in the mysteries of his trade than he was concerned with the demands of prejudice. It was rare for him to find anyone below decks with this black's intuitive engineering sense and he was generally quite happy to chat with the young fellow during his breaks from the stoke hole, and to answer his questions about the old-fashioned beam-engine that powered the *Ohio Rapide*.

For her part, Bess was delighted that a new obsession with marine engine technology was distracting her husband, at least to some extent, from his grievance over the patent. But in his cups, a too common state in her opinion, Dan was all too liable to hold forth on the great injustice done to him by his former employer. The steamboat crew became hostile and when the steamer's master came to hear of it he was outraged that a mere black should use such language about a boss, no matter how unjust the man might have been. Naturally, it never crossed his mind that the boss in question might have been black.

So Dan was sacked as a troublemaker and once more the Porter family were on the move. The thought of another new start, plus the fact that she had convinced herself that Dan's crush on Elsie Marre was a large part of the motivation, was a depressing combination. However, she could not oppose her husband's decision.

As things turned out, the adventure of the long rail journey and the novelty (for the outraged white cab driver as much as for the Porter family) of the cab ride, brought her to Railway Cottages, South Side Chicago, in a more optimistic frame of mind than she had felt for a long time.

They had started early that Saturday morning to make the rendezvous and, as promised, the affable Rainbow Williams was there to welcome them into their new home. He had paid the first month's rent in advance: 'After that,' he commented, 'on the terms we agreed for his pay as chief engineer, I reckon your husband should be able to take care of that himself.' All this was said with an expansive gesture and almost patronizing wink in the direction of Bess. *Talks big, only hope he can deliver,* was her private assessment, for the accommodations, though clean and quite solidly built, were not overly elegant.

They somehow reminded her of the Quarters at Johnstoneville, though the surroundings here were much bleaker. Half a dozen long wooden dormitory huts stood on the fringes of a rail-freight marshalling yard. Here Bess supposed the black labor force, recruited to build the large rail complex, had pitched their bedrolls – on bunks if they were lucky. At the head of the line, rather like a shunting loco at the head of a train of coal wagons, stood a semi-detached house no doubt for the black ganger and his assistant and their families. The white gangers and foremen would surely have been housed (*like decent white folk should be,* Bess thought bitterly), in town. Whatever they had been intended for, the "dormitory blocks" were little better than the shed-like rail-side shacks which were to be settled by the great influx of black immigrants to arrive in Chicago at the turn of the century.

The house, which she immediately dubbed "Ganger's Hall", comprised two dwellings, each with a largish first floor bedroom and, downstairs, a general living room with kitchenette adjacent and an outside earth closet. Lighting was provided by two oil lamps – not, she was relieved to see, S.K.L specials! All things considered, it was comfortable for two adults and a one-year-old baby, but if the family should get any bigger, they would soon be cramped. The rent was high but could be afforded on Dan's expected salary. The second of the semi-detached dwellings was not yet occupied but would be, they were told, by the crew members of the Rainbow Williams one-ship fleet.

'And now,' announced the flamboyant owner of the line, 'it is surely time to visit the flagship!' He laughed at his own sally. 'OK. OK it's the only ship, I know, but from small beginnings...'

With a flourish he opened the door of the rockaway carriage he had hired for the day and handed Bess up into the four-seater with Boy Jim. Dan climbed in after them and they were at Chicago's Outer Harbor gates within the half hour Rainbow providing a running commentary on such sights as they passed and performing very capably as his own coachman. Leaving his outfit in the care of a burly out-of-work docker, whom he tipped generously with promise of more to come, he led them proudly to a quay where a tug boat (built 1875 at the latest, Dan reckoned), painted out in a smart chocolate brown and gold livery, lay at the moorings.

'Permit me to make the introductions,' said Rainbow in a sing-song voice meant to mimic a flunky at a City Hall social occasion. 'Steam tug *Spokane,* meet the family Porter, Porters meet *Spokane.* You like the name? I started my ride to fortune with the Kentucky Derby last year. Put all I had and more than I should on Spokane and he came home a beauty. So there she is, my pride and joy, the Spokane-to-be, called the *Charlotte* just now, but we'll rename her all right.'

'You sure that's a good idea?' queried Dan. 'That old engineer at Louisville reckoned it brought bad luck to rename a boat. 'Sides, *Charlotte's* a good name for a tug. According to my student friend, Elsie Marre...'

'*Our* student friend,' Bess interjected with a tired smile. Rainbow Williams raised an eyebrow.

'Sure, sure,' said Dan hurriedly. 'Well, anyways, seems the very first steamboat was some British canal tug called the *Charlotte Dundas.'*

'Well, your friend was surely wrong there, fellah. Everybody knows the first steamboat was Fulton's *Clermont* on the Hudson.'

'There yuh are, Dan, I told you Elsie got it wrong but you wouldn't have it.' Bess triumphantly backed up Rainbow.

Dan laid a conciliatory hand on his wife's arm. 'Sure, honey, Fulton was the first to make a successful business out of steamboats – and come to think of it that Britisher had to give

77

up steam towin' after a year or two. So I guess, on second thoughts, *Charlotte* ain't such a good name for a tug after all.'

He grinned disarmingly and was relieved to see Bess relax the grim set of her mouth. It was true that Elsie Marre had a special place in his affections but he would have to watch his tongue. He loved his dear wife more than he could ever tell her and nothing nor nobody rated higher than she did. He gave her a kiss and then, perhaps just a little too businesslike in his switch of interest, he turned to Rainbow Williams.

'Say, Mr Williams…'

'…Call me Rainbow, fellah; call me Rainbow.'

'Think I'll keep it formal, if it's all the same to you, Sir, more professional that way. But, would you mind if we spent a bit of time here?'

'Sure thing, you stay as long as you like…well, half an hour or so let's say. Me, I'll show Mrs Porter here some of the sights of Chicago's waterfront. Shall we commence our tour with old Skipper White's famous clapboard house, Ma'am?' Rainbow Williams swept off his brown Derby in an exaggerated courtly bow, much to Bess Porter's confusion.

She was not overly concerned about Dan's feelings for Elsie Marre, she just wished he wouldn't talk about the girl so often. After four confinements, the last really heavy, and with her good looks wilting under the life of hard work and worry common to most of her impoverished black sisters, she did not relish rivalry from younger women and especially ones so pretty and alive as Elsie. However, that did not mean she was open to offers from flash city dudes like Rainbow here. *There again,* she thought to herself, *I ain't dead yet and perhaps that Dan Porter's due for a shake-up.* So, with a dazzling smile of the kind Dan himself rarely got these uxorious days, she gave her arm to be helped back up the gang plank and so to the quay.

Unfortunately for Bess's little display of coquetry, her husband was already heading back towards the engine housing. It had struck Dan that since the *Charlotte* was not as yet his property, Rainbow Williams was making rather free with the run of the ship. Himself, he was determined to make the most of this opportunity to extend his education in the knowledge of marine engine technology. He had already spotted a number of points where the machinery of this sturdy little workhorse differed from the monster contraption of the Louisville riverboat.

He was content to examine the mechanism by eye and careful to touch nothing. He had brought his drawing materials and in half an hour was able to make a number of workmanlike sketches to be studied at greater leisure back at his new home. As he tucked the carefully folded documents into the capacious inside jacket pocket of the famous wedding suit, the full realization of what he was doing struck him. Authorized only by the friendly Mr Williams, he was in fact trespassing on private property.

It being fairly late on a Saturday afternoon, not very many people were about on the harbor quay. However, the time had definitely come to leave... just one quick look at "the bridge": daydreaming, he already saw himself as a fully fledged skipper. Looking out ahead through the wheelhouse window and across the little ship's bows, his eye leapt to the outer harbor wall and the horizon line of Lake Michigan beyond. Automatically, his hands dropped to the spokes of the tiller wheel then to the lever of the throttle control.

'An' who might you be?' The rasp of authority turned to a hoarse but terrifying whisper of incredulity as Dan, his hands slumped to his sides, swung guiltily round.

'... a goldarn Nigger, by god and damnation...'

Glowering at Dan, feet confidently spread on the little boat's deck-planking, his insignia glinting in the declining afternoon sun, stood a one-star admiral in the United States navy. Technically an officer of the line, Admiral Robert

Gottschalk was in fact a senior figure in the bureau of yards and docks. He was also that rare type, a Southern officer who had made his personal peace after the Civil War and joined the Yankees. 'But if I'll wear their braid,' he would quip, 'I'm damned if I'll wear their principles.' The braid he in fact wore on every possible occasion, just now to a Chicago chamber of commerce reception. The "joke" bored even such friends as he had. At this moment, however, it was no joke.

Gottschalk was on leave, visiting his friend Paul Delaware, owner of a small fleet of tugs, among them the *Charlotte*, and on the point of retirement. Officially Delaware's guest, the admiral was exploiting his official credentials for a little private snooping along the waterfront before the reception began, in quest of any information that might be useful to his wife's family's shipyard in Annapolis, Maryland. Thus it was that he had spotted an intruder on the *Charlotte* and he was consumed with rage.

Admiral Gottschalk liked to boast that he had "come to terms with the "disaster" represented by the defeat of the Confederacy". In fact he was neurotically sensitive to signs of what he called the "degeneracy of national life caused by the advance of the colored race". Only last year, his wife had returned from an expedition to Baltimore with a barely credible story.

The objective had been the purchase of a piano for their granddaughter, Mamie. Desiring to test the Babcock iron frame deluxe model, the child had just commenced her showpiece, Beethoven's "Für Elise", when "a jingle of showboat music", to use his wife's words, broke out from the back of the shop. The culprit was a black infant, not more than five years old, son of the cleaning woman and, astonishingly, encouraged by the proprietors to "entertain" the clientele. The fact that the child rejoiced in the soubriquet "Eubie" Blake, and thus besmirched the name of one of the heroes in the history of naval warfare, compounded the offence. Now here was another "upstart black" preening himself in Delaware's boat.

Clown he might be, but the admiral was dangerous. The menace in the voice made the hairs on the back of one's neck prickle. Only once before had Dan, cosseted child of Johnstoneville, heard the sound. It was the authentic voice of a Southern gentleman with the bloodlust of indignation rising in his gorge. Boss Johnstone had never used the tone: indeed it was the general view of his grateful slaves and freedmen that he did not have the correct vocal equipment. But once, when a boy, Dan had been helping serve table up at the big house when the Boss was entertaining three neighboring landowners to Sunday lunch to talk farm politics. As was often his way, when dining alone, the Boss had Reverend Walcott to say the grace.

Old "Squire" Pendleton, who had endured the ignominy of being blessed by a Negro in silence, delivered such a tongue-lashing when the reverend prepared to sit down at the table that even that good and dignified man slunk out like a whipped animal. Boss Johnstone ordered Pendleton from his house and the two never spoke again. Now it was Dan in the firing line.

'On the quay at the double, boy!'

There was no room for argument. For once a white man was in the right. Dan wondered exactly how he was going to extricate himself from an extremely unpleasant situation. Then in the distance he saw Rainbow and Bess returning from their walk. Confronted with the evidence of a letter from Delaware to Rainbow Williams, concerning the terms of the proposed sale of the *Charlotte*, the admiral was obliged to concede that criminal trespass was not necessarily involved. Equally, he thundered his intention to see Williams "disciplined" for allowing unsupervised access to the vessel by an unauthorized person.

It was the vocabulary of the plantation. In the circumstances it would be difficult to bring any serious charge against Dan.

But it was obvious that Gottschalk could sabotage the friends' plans for the *Charlotte*. Rainbow was not the only buyer in the market, and Delaware would not press ahead with a deal if the admiral stirred up opinion along the waterfront. The Southerner left the little group uttering angry threats, which they knew were not empty.

It was a crestfallen party that trotted out from the harbor gates. Even the effervescent Rainbow had lost much of his fizz. Even he realized his folly in authorizing a third party to look over property of which he was not yet the owner. As for Dan, he kicked himself for allowing eagerness to extend his engineering experience to persuade him to fall in with the idea.

They were riding down the dingier purlieus of State Street when the rockaway was slewed on a right along Twenty-Second Street and brought to a halt outside an ill-maintained and rickety three-story tenement block.

'I'd like for you to meet my good friends Ben and Martha Church before you finish your first day in Chicago.' Chastened but still cheerful, Rainbow had jumped down from the driver's box to help Bess out of the carriage. But the door had already been opened and a little voice was pertly adding: 'And not to forget their good, good daughter little Harriet.'

The welcome extended to Rainbow and his friends by the Church family lightened their gloomy spirits. Ben and Martha, Chicagoans by birth, had good reason to look upon the man from Louisville as a benefactor. Until last year, Rainbow, like Ben, had been working in Chicago's notorious stockyards. Indeed Ben had helped him find the job on his arrival in the northern city. But ever since the rise in his fortunes begun by the sensational racehorse win and continued by more obscure means, Rainbow had repaid the favor several times over, helping the family with the high rent for their cramped two-room apartment and paying for an expensive course of medication for young Harriet.

When they returned to their own comfortable quarters in Railway Cottages, Dan and Bess agreed that of all the events of that dramatic but unsettling day, the best news was the making of three new friends: 'Not forgetting the good little Harriet,' added Bess, with a happy smile of reminiscence.

In the coming months it would be a friendship they would have cause to value. Admiral Gottschalk left Chicago but not before he had "brought Delaware back to his senses". The *Charlotte* was withdrawn from the market and as soon sold on to a white buyer. One night, returning home from an evening on the town, the debonair, generous and elegant Rainbow Williams was set upon by a gang of hooded attackers who, it was said, scarred him for life and left him for dead at the gates of his own house. The outrage ruffled the pages of the liberal press, but no attempt was made to find the assailants and Rainbow himself was heard no more of. The general, if unexpressed, view among Chicago's small black middle class was that an overly conceited fellow had been taught a lesson and that an unfortunate episode was best left to fade into obscurity.

Thanks to Ben Church, Dan got work in the stockyards. But he lasted barely a month. The long hours and hard work, even the clamor, blood and stench that surrounded him for most of his waking hours were, paradoxically, a relief. Ever since the "Spokane" fiasco he had been cursing himself for abandoning the comparative security of the humdrum life in Indianapolis and dragging Bess and the baby to the cold uncertainties of Chicago. But the new job at least paid well and the pandemonium of the slaughterhouse made almost all thought impossible.

The problem was what Dan was coming to see as "the curse of Johnstoneville": passing the first thirty years of his life in a community where blacks had lived the lives of ordinary people had given him the idea, which he would never lose, that blacks were as much citizens of the Republic as were whites. The result was that he could not adjust to the daily humiliations handed out by the white ganger. The man, a Southerner who had come north in search of better pay, was hated by the black workforce. But they shrugged, pocketed a comfortable wage each week and kept their heads down. Absurdly, as it seemed to the ganger, the black who caused the most trouble was the one who should have been docile – that damn Kentucky darky. When, in the course of one of their regular confrontations, Dan angrily brandished his meat hook, the murderous-looking work tool of the Chicago stockyard worker, his dismissal was inevitable.

As Christmas approached, Dan was reduced to casual stevedoring jobs along the docks and water slips of the South Branch of the Chicago River. The modest comforts of Railway Cottages became impossible luxuries. The hopes of September withered in the whistling winter of the windy city. The dapper brown Derby of Rainbow Williams seemed like a memory from a summer's vaudeville show. With only three days left before the bailiffs would arrive to throw them onto the streets, there was a knock at the door.

With Bess cowering in the bed against the cold and cuddling young Jim close to her, Dan went to answer. Outside was Ben Church. Pushing the door a six-inch welcome wider and pulling it shut the moment the visitor was inside, Dan showed him silently into the empty front room. As the two men took the two chairs facing one another at the cheap pinewood table, the insistent whimpering of the unseen child was suddenly masked by a long shattering cough from his suffering mother.

'You got plans for the future, Daniel?' Ben paused. 'Reckon you can hold your pride in check come spring? Or do you figure on them starving with cold and empty bellies, rather'n you should knuckle down like a black man must in "God's own country" if he aims to live?'

Ben spoke little and generally cheerfully, but in the two months since he had come to know Dan Porter, his outlook on the world had sharpened in focus. Where Bess indulgently saw an able man fighting the outrage of prejudice to keep his dignity, Ben saw a husband and father behaving like a hurt and touchy child.

'I hear they need an oiler on the Pittsburg, Fort Wayne and Chicago. Ain't paying well,' he paused and his eyes darkened angrily, 'damn it, they ain't paying proper for a skilled man… but they're paying. Your girl ain't going to see the end of this winter if you ain't careful. I know you ain't got no place to go come Monday… '

This time the pause was so long, Dan wondered whether he would leave without completing his message. But he waited and said nothing.

'Well, me and Martha have talked this over, Dan Porter. I ain't happy but she's over-persuaded me. Usually does,' he laughed abruptly at the comment which generally evoked a contented smile. 'If you swear your bible oath to hold this job through April next, which is as long as they're offering, then you and the family can share along with us on Twenty-Second Street.'

Dan had not spoken a word since the other's arrival, first out of curiosity then out of anger. Now he paused to gather himself.

'So! They're not paying right money for a skilled oiler? You think that bothers me any, Ben Church? You think I ever aimed to spend my life as a railway man?… Me! I'm an inventor, a guy who feels for machinery, a guy with the ability to become a true engineer AND… A GUY WITH THE AMBITION TO BECOME ONE!'

The words gushed in a rising yell. Across the table his friend watched sad and silent, staring as if through the wall into the next room to the poor woman racked with pain, fearful for her child and now harassed by her husband's anger. Did this fellah Porter think? Did he think about his wife? Did he think about what this offer of accommodations meant to the Church family. The apartment had two rooms, just enough for decency for him and Martha and fourteen-year-old Harriet. If the Porters came in, and he was already regretting the promise he had given to Martha, then he and she would have to share their sleeping with the child. Sure, he knew plenty lived like that and worse, but not the Church family.

Only this summer Ben reckoned he'd licked the problem of how to live decently, though black. Twenty Second Street was mean, it was cramped. The plumbing was... well it was outside. But with the two rooms he could afford he had secured, for his little tribe at least, the basic need of decent modesty. The Porter's arrival would change all that. And here was the man sounding off about ambition.

As if he had heard some unspoken cry from Bess, Dan slumped forward, cradling his head on his arms and sobbing quietly. 'What is to be done?' he murmured half to himself. 'Ambition to do well in life is a terrible thing in a black, ain't that so? But I'm afraid it is the fatal flaw of all us Johnstoneville darkies. "Beggin' yoh pardon, sir."' He smiled a secret smile, remembering the Uncle Tom routines with Elsie Marre all those years ago... But he was interrupted.

'Daniel Porter, you ain't the only man in black Chicago to have ambition. And you ain't the only man to have been forced to put that ambition on permanent hold in the interest of food for his wife and children. But you is the only man I knows to beg folks should all the time be thoughtful of him and his troubles. Just now you have a good offer, thanks to Martha Church. Either you takes it or you leaves it. Either way, we need to know tomorrow. If you ain't round by midday, you needn't come round at all.'

For him a veritable oration, these words had been delivered

standing. Now, without waiting for a response, Ben Church let himself out of the house, seething with rage.

Dan, who had not moved from his chair, sat staring at the door for what seemed like minutes. In fact it was barely fifteen seconds before Bess, her coughing fit ended, called to him in a frightened voice to come in and explain what had been going on. It was a conversation that changed the dealings between husband and wife. For the first time he saw the blood on her handkerchief. For the first time she truly saw the hurt in his mind.

'Seems they didn't make us free, Bess: they only called us free... Free to do what they want from us. Back in Johnstoneville, where Mr Wilberforce and the reverend seemed as good men as Boss Johnstone, and even young Willard was a man to be reckoned with, I never thought black was different from white more than you could change with belief in yourself. Now I ain't so sure.'

She clung to him tearfully, the coughing stilled as if in sympathy, and promised him all her strength. He held her to him lovingly and silently pledged himself to her. The two sobbed quietly in each other's arms. The baby, as if sensing the renewed bond of solidarity behind the tears, dropped off into a peaceful sleep.

The next day, having hired a handcart for their few belongings, Daniel and Elizabeth Porter, with their baby, James Owen Porter, moved house. That evening, with Baby Jim snuggled down in a boxcot away from the faint glow of the kerosene lamp, they ate their evening meal with Benjamin and Martha Church and their daughter, Harriet. Soon after supper, young Miss Harriet retired to the inner room, where the former sitting room sofa had been made up as a spare bed behind a blanket rigged up as a curtain.

It was part of a pattern that was to last for nearly two years. Ben and Martha did their loving when they could at weekends, when Harriet walked out with the Porters, in charge of Baby Jim. Dan Porter held to his oath. His resurgent love for Bess made the humiliations at the railroad depot easier to bear. Those five months, too, deepened his understanding of the steam engine and all its workings. When the job ended he was out of work for only a week before he began to pick up occasional and quite well-paid stevedoring work on the quays served by the railroad off the Chicago River.

Dan had made a second vow, to himself, and that was never to work in the stockyards again. The white ganger had left but Dan did not try his luck with the new setter-on. Even if the man should offer work, Dan felt he could never again trust himself armed with a meat hook and in argument with a white man. He refused to consider the question of what to do if the time ever came when he could no longer afford the modest medications prescribed by Dr Sugden for Bess.

A new stage in her decline was marked when she decided she must give up Sunday church services, until then one of the fixed points of the family calendar. As she grew steadily worse, spending days in bed coughing and spitting blood, Dan knew in his heart what the doctor had known from the start: short of a long stay in some sanatorium far from the South Side, there was no cure. The good doctor was merely prescribing the simple and inexpensive drugs to ease some of the pain and discomfort and to reassure the patient that she was not abandoned.

In October 1892, with Baby Jim approaching his third birthday, a double problem threatened the little community at Twenty-Second Street. Bess Porter was finally confined to her bed on Dr Sugden's orders and Martha Church announced she was expecting her third child. Since Harriet had already lost one little brother, Ben Church was determined that no risks should be run with the new arrival. He ordered his wife to rest as much as possible and encouraged Harriet, now able and happy to help mind the demanding toddler, to search for part-time work. A new mouth to feed would mean more expense.

By this time, Dan had found a regular job as assistant store clerk to a lakeside ship's suppliers and chandlery. After three years, which had begun in hope for the future, he found a job almost identical to the one he had left. But he could afford to pay Harriet to help look after Baby Jim. Bess, who was now failing fast, spent her days weeping for her husband's lost dreams and her nights fighting the tears to keep up a brave face.

Outside, the world seemed perversely indifferent to her plight. After years of depressed conditions of labor in Chicago, hope was in the air as the city prepared for the Columbia World's Fair, to be held in 1893. Building was proceeding apace on the exhibition site known as the White City. Transportation companies and ships' suppliers like the one Dan worked for were certain of orders, but the increased activity in the docks also meant more openings for seamen and ships' engineers. Just when he should have been a free agent to follow up such opportunities, Dan found himself in a safe berth he could not afford to jeopardize. The irony of the situation merely emphasized the disappointment. During these sad days, paradoxically, it was a white face that brightened Dan Porter's outlook.

His job as assistant store clerk was to fetch the parts and supplies ordered at the counter from his senior colleague, Harry Formby, a good-natured Chicagoan. Harry kept the customers happy, Dan kept them supplied. Within a few weeks he had learnt the inventory and it was obvious that when it came to engine parts he was far more expert than the senior clerk. For his part, Harry was quite content to let Dan do the work while he passed the time of day with the customers. Nor was he much bothered when they began to ask directly for his black assistant. He knew perfectly well that no company on the

Chicago waterfront would even consider putting a black in charge of the front of shop service counter. But while Harry's presence kept up the appearances, skippers and ships' engineers who used the store found their business went much more smoothly once they had accepted the idea of discussing complex technical problems with his black help.

In fact one of the store's regular customers, Skipper Thomas White, owner of the tug *Titan*, positively enjoyed Dan's conversation. A veteran of the Federal Navy, Skipper White liked talking to one of the former slaves for whom he, at least, had fought his war back in the '60s. He also appreciated Dan's solid good sense, absolutely reliable advice and trustworthiness. Dan warmed to the old salt, with his rambling fragments of history and proverbial wisdom – if only because they provided entertainment for Bess of an evening and reminded her of that happy afternoon spent with the gallant Rainbow Williams, sightseeing outside Skipper White's famous clapboard house.

'You realize, boy,' the skipper would say – and Dan did not object to the term from the old man, who called anyone under the age of fifty "boy" – 'you realize that this 'ere city gets its name from the river an' *that* gets its name from the local Indian thunder god? It's a marvel the place is still standing. Chacaqua's river used to empty into the great Lake Michigan until white man's engineering turned it back on itself. Maybe he's biding his time to take his vengeance. The arrangement suits me well enough. They connected the main branch of the river to the Illinois-Michigan canal, which they deepened, so that the water flows down from the lake to the canal wharves and docks. Most of *Titan's* business consists of hauling the big ships into those docks.'

'So the canal flows into the Illinois River... '

'Sure does!'

'And the Illinois flows into the Mississippi...'

'Sure does!'

'And the Mississippi flows down to the South?'

'It surely does! So if you got yourself a canoe and started out from this quay right here, you could get down to New Orleans without once touching dry land, if you had a mind to!'

As usual their business talk ended with a joke and a laugh, a mighty *un*usual thing in Dan's dealings with the white race.

One December day, about a week before Christmas, he went to work worried and unwilling. Bess had woken them both in the small hours with a desperate attack of coughing and, left to himself, he would have stayed with her. But to have done so would have made her yet more worried about the state of her health and about the prospects of his staying in work. A wise man did not take sick leave if he himself were not sick. Dan decided to follow Harry Formby's example for once and to leave work at the set time rather than stay on after closing to tidy up unfinished business. Accordingly it was with a sinking heart that, as he was preparing to put up the shutters, he saw Skipper White approaching with a purposeful stride.

Despite his good resolution, Dan returned behind the counter. It was difficult to say no to the skipper, who was, in any case, a favored, if garrulous, customer. This evening, however, he seemed uncertain how to begin... almost embarrassed, Dan thought. He cursed his own soft-heartedness. There again, if the store's best customer wanted to chat of an evening it was hardly the place for an assistant store clerk to cold shoulder him in the name of domestic problems. But White was pulling himself together, with an almost visible effort, for what was clearly to be a serious talk. Though about what, Dan could not for a moment imagine.

'Let me get to the point at once, Mr Porter. I've been to this store many times since you joined them and every time I've come away with exactly what I needed for the job in hand. All the skippers on the waterfront privately acknowledge that you know most engines backwards, though it pains them to have to admit as much about a Negro. Hiram Halliday tells me that you're practical too.

Now Hiram's a fine guy in his way but he'll never raise you any higher in the outfit than you are now. So he's agreeable to my making you a proposition. I'm looking for a ship's engineer who's a quick learner and who can be trusted. How would you like to sign up from next January as ship's engineer on the *Titan*, with salary and perquisites proportional and, who knows, interesting prospects? I'll be retiring as skipper in a couple of years – no reason why I shouldn't break with tradition and promote the chief in the engine room to be chief altogether. In other words young man, you might get to be the first engineer in the history of the Chicago waterfront to become skipper and the first black to hold such a position on any waterfront. Now what do you say?'

With a grin that buckled his beard, the old captain thrust forward his hand. Since Dan could think of nothing to say and probably could not have spoken if he had had the words, he shook the hand with a vigor that offered physical injury to his employer-to-be. He made his way home later than he had intended, but for the first time in years, with a bounce in his step. Here was something like a Christmas present to cheer Bess. They could begin looking for a place of their own again. Come January, he might, he dreamed, get a loan against future wages out of Captain White, for a month's sanatorium care for her.

From the moment he opened the door on Twenty-Second Street, Dan sensed that his dear wife was gone. He broke into a howl of despair, stumbling toward the bed; he collapsed beside it, clawing the sheets, desperate to hold her to him as if to give her his life. For minutes he was alone with his grief.

Ben Church came in from the back room; he had sent the others to stay with neighbors. With firm hands on the heaving shoulders, he began a slow, methodical account of what he had heard from Martha and had himself seen of the last hours of Bess Porter, beloved wife of Daniel.

She had died that afternoon, about half past two they reckoned. She had died alone, Jim Boy had been causing trouble and his mother had asked Harriet to walk him out in the air for an hour or so. The girl had been uneasy, but Bess had been unusually insistent, bright eyed, more lively than usual of late. Her coughing seemed to have eased up. Puffing up the pillow and standing a glass of water by the bedside, Harriet took up the baby urging Bess to get some sleep before the men returned with their chatter. A gentle snore from the other bed behind the partition indicated that Martha was setting the example. With a quiet laugh and a wave to Harriet, Bess had settled back into her bed.

Soon afterwards, it must have been, her frame had been shattered by a retching cough. Martha was to tell how she had been dreaming of the abattoir which she had once visited with her husband, the animals roaring horribly. In her dream it seemed that blood was everywhere. The sense of violence in the air woke her up and she supposed she must have heard barking in the street. She dozed off again.

When Ben returned home he found the body of Bess on the floor, contorted in a last rictus of pain, the bed and the sheets the color of the killing floors. Strong man as he was, he had vomited convulsively. Then, working with brisk efficiency, the tears flooding down his cheeks, he restored the room to present the tragic scene of a decent death, only moments before Harriet and Jim Boy returned from their walk.

* * * * *

Three weeks elapsed before Daniel Porter could bring himself to speak of what had happened. During that time he entered on his duties as engineer on the *Titan*: cold, efficient and distant – a mystery to friendly Tom White.

Miserable and bitter, Dan found he was not only lamenting the death of Bess, but also cursing the world that had contrived it. First, and above all, he cursed Willard Stone with deep and measured hatred for robbing him of the revenue from his invention. With money that would have been his own had he received a fraction of his due from the patent, dear Bess would now, he was convinced to the edge of madness, be recuperating from her consumption in a Vermont sanatorium, enjoying the best health treatment money could buy.

Bess herself would have told him that such ideas were fantasy. But then Bess had seen the calm and sunny spirit of her adored husband cloud over and sour through the long, blighted years of ambition denied.

CHAPTER SIX

Mississippi Night

It was a balmy evening fast falling to a warm night in late spring. As the last glow of sun faded, a strengthening shimmer of starlight spangled the sky, like tiny diamonds on a jeweller's velvet. The churn-clapper-splash of the great stern paddle wheel of the Riverboat *Vidalia* thudded away in the distance, as Harmann Tengdahl, S.K.L.'s senior representative on his first major river sales campaign, leant over the rail of the upper forward deck, savoring the soft breeze of twilight. It offered a pleasantly murmuring hiss of a background to the monotonous call of the leadsman in the bows. The large, ungainly vessel edged gingerly in toward the bank and the scattered lights of Natchez-under-the-Hill, just beginning to wake up for the night.

Partner Tengdahl (Harmann liked the sound of that) reckoned it might be worth exploring. Business had been slower than he'd hoped. The Vidalia Line management had agreed to trial S.K.L. specials in the small saloon and the steamer's captain had provisionally, and grudgingly, approved their performance; but this was not a done deal. If the Line actually did adopt the lamps, it would surely boost sales in the shore bars and hotels. Ever the optimist, Harmann was confident this breakthrough would come somehow, though obviously not in the rundown river port they were now coming into.

Indeed, this was an unscheduled stop. No berth was open at Nachez itself. "Underhill" was now a rough and ready wharf for trading vessels and a fuelling quay for the steamboats, more often than not loaded by coal lighters, ferrying back and forth. The quay now comprised merely half an old steamboat hulk and Captain Dunleith was by no means certain that the pool could still take a vessel of the *Vidalia's* size. Much against his will he had yielded to the insistence of Congressman Lynch that his niece, Eliza Sterling, sick since that morning, be put ashore. The captain's reluctance had very little to do with professional reasons.

Descended from a junior branch of one of Mississippi's old plantation families, Dunleith did not take kindly to falling in with the wishes of a Negro, and particularly one who had served as Speaker of Mississippi's House of Representatives, and had been twice elected to Congress in Washington. Worse than all, this *"congressman"* – Dunleith sneered the word to himself – had had the captain sound the ship's horn to summon out the transport detail which the company had the use of at Natchez-under-the-Hill.

Set up long ago on the whim of a company director who had owned a property in Adams County, the outfit had declined from the grand equipage and immaculate team of horses once maintained by the company itself, to a trim little buggy and pert trotting pony run by "Bunker Revels – Carriage and buggy hire for all occasions". The company had prior call on Bunker's services at any time, day or night, as part of the deal agreed when he took over the detail as a commercial franchise, and the little horse-trap was painted in the Vidalia Line colors. But Bunker was, in reality, just another small town livery stable and outfit hire business, and Dunleith resented having to parade what he considered a fall from past splendors. A cheerful, deferential black who "knew his place", Bunker was, in the opinion of Captain Dunleith, the best kind of Negro one could hope for in these post-war, post-Reconstruction days. Tonight, however, he was going to be pressed into service and the fictions of the once gracious Vidalia Line were going to be exposed, on the orders of some upstart of his own race, so as to carry one of the fellow's womenfolk to the fellow's personal plantation! Thanks to the heroic exertions of the Ku Klux Klan and the ruthless policies of restored Southern democratic legislatures, the worst excesses of "Carpetbagging" Reconstruction had been undone but anomalies persisted. Dunleith spat over the side.

In fact he harbored a general contempt for the times in which he lived, so that he would have been suspicious of Miss Sterling's malady whatever her skin color. She had been taken violently sick that morning thanks, so the former congressman claimed, to the river crawfish chowder on last night's dinner menu, but of the three who had eaten the chowder only Miss Sterling had suffered ill effects. Dunleith reckoned there were other causes of sickness in the morning for a young woman. It was bad enough that the blacks were allowed in the dining room. But the company directive was explicit. For reasons undisclosed, Lynch was to be indulged. So now the pride of the fleet was tying up at a ramshackle mooring as crewmen and stewards fussed with gang planks and valises.

Harmann watched the bustle with amused detachment. Not for one moment did he suppose that the ailment of Miss Sterling was anything other than she had given out. A taffrail chat with the congressman two evenings back had left him pretty well informed on the Lynch family and their connection with the Sterlings, Eliza and her mother Deborah, so he had no reason to doubt the young woman, even if he felt the congressman was being over protective.

In fact, as Tengdahl was to learn, John Lynch had good reason for throwing something of a smokescreen round the true identity of the mother and daughter traveling in his company.

Yet he had been faithful to essentials. Eliza came from a strict African Methodist Episcopal background, Harmann had been told, and now he deduced she would have had neither inclination nor opportunity, whatever Dunleith might choose to suspect, for what a young Harvard business acquaintance had once described in Harmann's hearing as "extra-mural activities". Much more likely that Eliza Sterling was one of those people with a biological aversion to shellfish. Either way, it was gratifying to watch these Southern white folk inconveniencing themselves to please a black man and his women friends or relations.

Congressman Lynch, who, like a few other blacks, had made his mark and something of a fortune during the decade of Reconstruction following the Civil War, was on his way to the Republican Party National Convention for that year of 1892. Aiming to give the girl the holiday of a lifetime and also widen her intellectual horizons, he had gone considerably out of his way to board the *Vidalia* at Baton Rouge, Louisiana, where Eliza and her mother lived just outside the town. He had taken a protective interest in the twenty-two-year-old since her childhood on account of an old debt to her father, but had come to respect her on her own account and wanted, if possible, to promote her career.

No beauty, Eliza Sterling was highly intelligent and, though frail in health, very determined. She already had an appointment as an elementary school teacher. Given the swing of events in the Deep South since the end of Reconstruction, few blacks and very few black women indeed could hope to rise above that level. It was, in fact, a remarkable tribute to her abilities that she held any job at all since her father, Micah Sterling, had fallen foul of Southern conventions some years back.

At the moment, however, Harmann was a detached observer and pleased for a break in the journey: after all,

Natchez-under-the-Hill was once reputed the wildest stop on the river. He planned to explore after a quick evening meal. The "Barbary coast of the Mississippi" should, he reckoned, offer a challenge worthy of a man descended from the legendary Viking sea rovers of old Europe and whose modern countrymen were acknowledged master brewers and distillers – and master consumers of their products!

As he looked out over the murky shadows of the dilapidated quay-cum-landing stage, Harmann sensed, rather than saw, the crumbling outlines of decayed timber warehouses and stores, where the smoky lamps of some bar lightened the gloom. The noise level from the town had already risen since the *Vidalia* had come to its mooring. Natchez-under-the-Hill had never been part of the glamorous scene of the great riverboat era, always a sort of ruffianly hanger on, one of the trading stations where the real business of the river was conducted. But now, it seemed, even it had sunk a little lower.

The great days of the riverboats were in fact a fading memory. Harmann had not been absolutely frank when singing the praises of the Mississippi steamboat to Willard Stone in the little store on Main Street. In truth, the riverside ports he had passed on his way south and now on the northward journey were all a bit more dowdy, a bit less smartly painted, than they had been on his trip in the early 1880s. But if the glamour had gone, the great waterway was still a significant artery of commerce and the riverboats and riverside towns still needed lighting. That meant, he told himself, that this river trip venture had to pay off, big time.

The putter-ter-putt of hooves on the wooden planking of the landing stage, the rattle of harness and the startled curse of Bunker Revels, announced the arrival of the buggy, evidently the skittish little horse had dashed dangerously close to the quayside. A murmur of voices interrupted by words of command, and the muffled but unmistakable rustle of stiff silks and satins of well-to-do women on the move, told its story. Within a matter of minutes the vehicle, its horse now on a tight rein out of consideration for the invalid, pulled away into the dark. Congressman Lynch, acidly polite, could be heard thanking Captain Dunleith for so considerately disrupting the schedule, before clicking off with martial precision along the deck to his cabin. Dunleith's "Happy to be of service" floated up with equal lack of conviction.

Harmann grinned to himself. *What fools these mortals be*, he reflected. A white man thought an upstart black had a whore for a "niece". A successful but, truth to tell, somewhat pompous black, reckoned whitey was "making a monkey of him", while apparently meeting his wishes, was the story line. A riverboat captain, eager servant of his company, deferentially acknowledged the gracious thanks of a satisfied customer, was the dialogue.

Suddenly a square of yellow light opened, like the shutter of an advent calendar, halfway up the climbing roof line beyond the quay. A cacophony of screams and oaths scratched the velvet night. Below him, cabin windows banged shut. Harmann, no Christian on a night like this promised to be, hitched his belt another notch, patted the wallet with "this-night's-spending-money" of twenty dollars, settled his hat on his head and hustled down to catch Captain Dunleith. Best confirm that the steamer was indeed tied up for the night. At sixty-plus, even Vikings, if they knew their business, made sure of their line of retreat.

It was just after nine when Harmann tracked a careful way across the rickety planks of the landing up into the town. He stopped, puzzled. A sudden breeze brought the sound of distant shouting... or was it chanting? But the town itself now seemed, no definitely was, muted. Certainly it was not performing with the raucous abandon to be expected of a Saturday night waterfront. *Ah well*, he thought, *alcohol is still no doubt available*, and, as always when embarking solo on a night's drinking in a new town, he entered the first bar he came to.

A cigarette pluming from a charred table, a neckcloth over a slewed chair, half a hundred abandoned glasses and two well-used spittoons indicated an early start to exactly the kind of evening he was in search of. But where were the people? The place was empty except for two river pilots. Drink-stained uniforms and the trampled cap now half smothered in sawdust boded bad news. One of them slumped forward as Tengdahl navigated the fog of foetid tobacco smoke and kerosene fumes from two badly trimmed lamp wicks.

'What gives?' he asked the barman, knocking back a stiff whiskey and topping up his glass from the bottle on the bar. 'It looks as though those two've cleared the place.'

As he spoke the second of the two men lurched up in his seat, declaimed an incoherent sentence or two, failed to get to his feet and swung a belligerent bottle in the direction of the bar, where a litter of empty glasses was the only sign of his recent audience.

'… damned to hell…' was all Tengdahl was able to catch before the orator slumped down again.

'Laid off yesterday, bud. Reckon they've drunk their severance pay… an' most of it in here.' As he spoke, the barman, trawling empty glasses and bottles onto his tray as he went, crossed to the drunks' table. With clinical precision he extracted two greenbacks from the billfold projecting invitingly from the speaker's waistcoat. He then tucked the billfold safely into the man's inside pocket. Next he corked up the half-empty whiskey bottle and lodged that in another pocket, and finally he dusted down the tattered cap and slapped it onto the nearest head.

'Give a hand here, bud.' He heaved the man to his feet. Harmann, who had assisted more than once at such ceremonies, did as asked. With some difficulty the two drunks were dragged, feet trailing, out of the bar and across the planking sidewalk to be deposited on the rammed earth track of a road. To Harmann's surprise, the man tossed the two quids of chewing tobacco down onto the snoring forms.

'Good conduct prizes for missing the entertainment,' was the enigmatic response before Tengdahl could voice his question. 'I doubt they'll be troubled before dawn. Probably bed down under the sidewalk when they came to – it's early for a Saturday night under the hill.'

Mystified, Tengdahl returned to his drink until the laconic barkeep should offer a few explanations. The man continued his brisk tidy-up of the debris. At last he returned with a tray-load of empties, which he deposited out of sight on the draining board of the sink beneath the bar.

'Tomorrow will be soon enough for that lot. Right now I'm putting up the shutters. So mister, thanks for the help with the drunks but now it's drink-up time for you too. You wanna buy a fifth to take up to the show?'

'Show! Entertainment! What's going on in this burg? The night's not even started so far as I'm concerned.'

'Boat passenger, huh? Well, if I was you I'd be on my way back to my berth. Never could rightly relish a lynching mahself… So what's it to be, huh? One more fast slug or a bottle to take out?'

Tengdahl stiffened. Lynching? 1893, and the South was still lynching. He cursed himself for a naive fool. What did he expect? Then his mind switched from philosophy to reality. Lynchings were for blacks, and the friends of one black he himself was learning to rate as a friend had been ridden into this town only an hour earlier.

'What lynching. Where…?'

His voice was urgent but not with excitement.

'You got friends you're worried for, huh? Good for you, I

got nothin' against blacks mahself. But don' you go tell anyone I said so. I still got to trade here.' He corked up the whiskey bottle and put it back on the shelf behind him.

'Where they doin' their devil's work, you asked. That I cain't rightly say. All I know is, a bit before you showed up one of Jim Starkey's men strolled in, grinning from ear to ear. "Say boys!" he says. "We jes found us a darky, doin' like he shouldn't outside Miss Sadie's. An' we got us a couple of colored women folk to join the show. You'all's the last bar I brought the news to. Better hurry now 'fyuh don't want to miss the show." Cleared the place that did. But not before every manjack had packed him a fifth of bourbon or more. I did the best part of a night's takings in a matter of minutes I did and now I'm shutting up – want no more part of their "celebrations".'

The man expertly shot a gob of saliva against the further rim of a spittoon before continuing thoughtfully.

'Miss Sadie runs the local whore house, an' she wun't let a black touch one of her girls. The poor critter musta lost his way, noo to town I shouldn't wonder… found himself outside the window and stopped to admire what's on offer. Hereabouts they reckon it's harassment for a black to so much as look at a white woman. Don' much matter of course what he did. Long times since they had a decent lynchin' and if they've got two respectable black women corraled into the bargain they'll reckon the chance too good to miss…

… Hey bud, where you off to?'

The two men had reached the street. As the barman secured his premises, Tengdahl went striding off, apparently purposeful but in fact not sure of his direction.

'I know those two ladies… ' he shouted back over his shoulder.

'Hold it… White knighting can be dangerous, but if you're determined to risk your neck, better not head into the center of town, which is what you're doin'. I don' know for sure of course but they usually do their business at a lone tree in McClellan's Acre, half a mile out of town thataway. You take care now.'

The inappropriately homely phrase was accompanied with a sour grin in the gallows humor of a man out of temper with his community.

The barman's guess was soon confirmed by a distant roar of voices which swelled in volume with every step Harmann took. The road led up to a plateau-like field, spreading away into the darkness. Harmann found himself on the edge of a crowd surrounding an old gnarled tree, its branches spreading into the night like some monstrous, petrified insect. All eyes were riveted on the group at its base. The focus was provided by a rickety, flat-bed farm truck with a surprisingly sturdy little horse between the shafts, a horse which for some crazy reason Tengdahl was certain he recognized. The cart supported a group of three, two burly whites flanking a black.

Aged about twenty-five, the man wore a pair of farm-hand's levis and a collarless shirt, cuffs rolled up to the elbows. Once a creamy white, it was now badged with dark gouts of blood, discolored in the glow of smoking lanterns and torches that illuminated the grim scene, but still spreading as fresh wounds in the man's head bled freely down. It was obvious he could barely support himself, and equally obvious that he had to. The tail end of the noose encircling his neck was securely tied to a stout branch of the gallows tree. When the truck was driven from its position he would be left hanging, left for as long as it took him to die – perhaps an hour, perhaps more. Tengdahl remembered with shame that other Mississippi night twenty-five years ago, when he had stood cowardly by, spectator to another act of Southern "justice". Cost what it might, this time he would act.

One of the white men was supporting the victim: the moment had not yet come. The criminal must not hang until the grisly, ritual travesty of judgment was over. The other white, Jim Starkey, Tengdahl supposed, was coming to the peroration of his indictment. The "charge" had long since been forgotten. The words were a vomit of hatred delivered with the bland grin of the mentally unbalanced. Either side the farm truck, in mockery of an honor guard, stood four well-fed, well-dressed figures, clearly pillars of the community, each armed with a wooden bludgeon. Harmann saw similar weapons scattered liberally through the crowd and many a shot gun. Any attempt at rescue must surely be suicidal. Frustrated, he clenched his fists and looked for any opening. Then he froze. Across the circle he saw another vehicle, not a truck but a buggy and one without horse or driver. Two women cowered in each other's arms on the passenger seat, staring as if mesmerized at the horrid tableau in the circle. They were black. They were Eliza and Deborah Sterling. They had been abandoned by their driver. Their horse had been commandeered for the death truck. And when the "execution" was over, what would their fate be?

Driven by a new priority, Tengdahl began to edge round the perimeter of the crowd. People shuffled and muttered, irritated at the distraction. Even so, the crowd noise seemed unnaturally loud. When he was just five yards from the buggy and its terrified cargo, the noise swelled into the drumming of hooves and the clatter of a racing chaise driven at speed. Time accelerated.

The rescue triggered its own tragic logic. Tengdahl had time to register a flamboyant figure in a shovel hat hauling on reins, people scattering in alarm and a foam flecked stallion, when the little horse between the death wagon shafts plunged away in fright. The white "judges" were hurled to the ground, their victim, after one strangled scream, left swinging and kicking feebly. Over the pandemonium a ragged cheer went up from some distant spectators.

Tengdahl heard nothing. His target was the plunging little horse, its hooves flailing to beat a way through the crowd. Shoving for a position to approach the cart from behind, he shouldered a woman to the ground, perilously close to a churning cart wheel. *'The "gentler sex"! Some chance!* His mind raced in disbelief that women should be spectators at such a scene.) By a miracle he got a hand to the flapping reins. A life time's experience and "feel" for horses came to his aid. The animal sensed authority and, though the turmoil round it continued, began to settle while Tengdahl moved up alongside, shortening the rein and murmuring reassurance.

All the time he was looking across to the two women in the buggy. Thank god they were staying put. Grief stricken, their eyes signaled the tragedy of the lynch victim, but the older woman had the sense to see that nothing was to be gained by plunging into the melé, where two more deaths would be the inevitable outcome. At least for the moment, they were forgotten above the milling crowd.

Tengdahl's immediate problem was to get the horse out of the death truck shafts and hitched back to the buggy. Then he could think of getting the women the hell out of this mayhem. Just then, his neighbors' attention was distracted by renewed commotion round the gallows tree, and he worked feverishly to unhitch the traces.

The flamboyant "Shovel Hat" had edged his terrified horse up to the swinging man. Handing the reins to his black co-driver, whom Harmann only now noticed, he manhandled the swaying body so that the feet rested over the chaise. Then, drawing a great clasp knife from his belt, and flicking it open at the same time with a single sweeping slash, he severed the rope. The inert form slumped to the chaise beneath. The rescuer bent his head to the chest, loosening the slip knot round the neck as he did so.

His co-driver suddenly lunged at an attacking figure and made a savage cut with the stock of his whip. A deep-throated roar of pain followed. Tengdahl cursed as the little horse, now freed from the death wagon shafts but still jittery, bucked and reared. However, a glance back toward the chaise cheered him considerably. Jim Starkey was reeling back, clasping his right wrist in his left hand. He had been attempting to stop the removal of the noose – the only result was that his gun hand was now useless.

At this point Shovel Hat straightened up and took the reins from his co-driver, who immediately bent over the inert form, massaging the chest and chafing the skin of face and temples. Shovel Hat, whip brandished defiantly in his right hand, his left controlling the horse, rose to his full, considerable, height and roared out across the crowd.

'The Lord be praised, Jem Fisher here still breathes. You murderous pack of good-for-nothin' Underhill no-goods. Cain't not one of you even make a workmanlike hangman's knot that'll break a neck good and clean?' He spat contemptuously down at the glowering Starkey, struggling to raise his gun. 'And as for you, Jim Starkey, if you set this mob on one of my ranch hands ever again...' But he was stopped short by a lucky shot from the crowd which caught his up-raised arm and spun him round.

'Go join them darkies in their coontown god box, Will Schuster,' screamed a pinched and shaking voice close to Tengdahl. 'We don' need none o' your preachin' ways. You an' your old father never did know the meanin' of true white justice.' The speaker, for all the hysteria of his voice, was a well-set up, imposing figure of a man who now prepared to take a second, steadier aim.

Without pausing to consider the consequences, Harmann Tengdahl seized the heavy farm cart-whip from its rest by the driving bench of the death wagon and, wielding the butt hard and true, stunned the would be murderer to the ground. The gun flew from the man's nerveless fingers. Tengdahl's neighbors took a moment to register the presence of a second white troublemaker in their ranks. Shoving and pulling his horse like a clumsy battering ram, he swung a space clear to back the animal into the shafts of the buggy.

Methodically hitching the nearside shaft, he sensed a cloud of commotion across the animal's back. The older of the two black women had jumped down, skirts bundling and tearing on the trappings. She threw the reins up to her daughter and then, oblivious to the abuse of the crowd, completed the hitching on the far side. This done, she clambered unmolested back up into the buggy

'There're still some folks with a sense of shame, ma'am, even in this devil's armpit of a hell hole: if you'll pardon the language,' Tengdahl called up as he prepared to follow suit. The calculated insult to the "gracious world" of the Old South was, he immediately realized, stupid in the extreme. For whatever reason, the crowd surrounding the buggy had been holding back, perhaps truly unwilling to harass women, even black women. Now, two "Southern gentlemen", with the physique of bare-knuckle champions, shouldered their way forward and, turning, Tengdahl was just in time to evade a sledgehammer fist which crashed instead into the iron bracket holding the buggy's canopy support.

With a pistol crack of bone and a scream of pain, the man, no faint heart, retired, whimpering, to the crowd's fringe. His companion, one of the honor guard from the "ceremony" advanced like a trained infantry man and swung his nail-shod wooden club to Harmann's head. Throwing up an arm to protect himself, he swiveled on his left heel, his right leg making a short, vicious kick outward. He felt the heel of his boot connect with bone through crushed gristle, but not before the nail of the bludgeon tore through the summerweight coat sleeve deep into his upper arm. He grunted in pain but grinned too. With a cracked scream of agony, his assailant staggered back, both hands clutching at his pulverized groin. The club fell to the trampled grass and lay there.

The crowd fell back. Most of the men were overfed, all of them were overweight. They had left their bars at the promise of an evening's entertainment with someone else the victim. Now two of the toughest of Underhill's bad guys were writhing on the floor while the stranger, for all he was streaming blood, seemed set fair for all comers. Tengdahl gained the comparative safety of the buggy, where he curled down awkwardly out of sight. *Commonsense*, he was thinking, *is the better part of bravado*. The crowd parted. Seeing two well-dressed females in a buggy with the arrogant out-of-towner apparently thinking better of it and cowering in fear, they let the flimsy vehicle through their ranks.

'Don' you worry about Mr Schuster, Mr White Knight.' The soft voice teased Harmann awake from a haze of pain. 'He's the big man round these parts, my uncle says. Even Jim Starkey thought better of tangling with him any more. I can see them, Bunker Revels, our coachman who brought the rescue, Mr Schuster and even Jem Fisher, God heal his hurt. The chaise is being let go just like us. Now you best sleep some.' *There must be more to tell*, thought Harmann, *but for now he would...* Pain, shock and loss of blood drowned his thoughts in unconsciousness.

Eliza Sterling, feverish but suddenly alert with the demands of another's need, made a businesslike tourniqué, from lengths torn from her petticoat, and with Mrs Sterling at the reins, the impromptu hospital wagon rattled, briskly now, back down towards the quay it had left not quite three hours earlier. Settled as comfortably as could be expected in the Lynch suite, Harmann submitted with gritted teeth as Deborah Sterling cut round the shoulder hole of his shirt and then gently prised the material away from the wound on his right upper arm. It could now be seen that the makeshift weapon of his assailant had torn a deep and ragged scar in the flesh and, as the best part of an hour had elapsed since the rescue, the blood was beginning to dry hard so that fragments of the material were clotting into the scar forming over the wound.

Captain Dunleith, whose rudimentary medical knowledge and a copy of *Silver's Home Medical Help* did duty for a ship's doctor, had talked darkly of the dangers of lockjaw on hearing of the rusty nail. He promptly had a large pan of boiling water, complete with sponge and hand cloths and the medicine chest's bottle of iodine, sent aft to the cabins allotted to the congressman's party. Given the company's directives and the account he had been given of the night's doings on shore, it was clearly time for wise men to mend fences. With reluctance, the captain had stayed to hear the black women's account of their ordeal. As the story unfolded it had become obvious that the bills for this night's work were going to cost more than money for anyone like him with friends in Natchez-under-the-Hill.

Heading out of town for the Lynch plantation with his two passengers, Bunker Revels had caught up with a drunken procession escorting Jem Fisher on his farm cart-turned-tumbril. Four white "guards" on the cart were entertaining themselves and the crowd by trying to force their prisoner, hands bound behind his back, off the cart with vicious blows from fist or cudgel. Recognizing Jem as a new farm hand on the Schuster estate and hoping to get him released, Bunker warned the ruffians they would have young Mr Will Schuster (despised as a liberal but feared for his wealth) to reckon with. But as far as the crowd was concerned, Jem was a stranger in town who had been caught "messin'" with white women and would have to pay the price.

Then they spotted Bunker's passengers and, with whoops of sneering delight to have two "real society ladies" as their guests, forced the buggy to join the procession. At the execution ground they lined it up in pride of place on the arena. Willing to let Bunker, the "good black", off, they took his sturdy little pony as "price of admission for the ladies", unhitched the old cart horse from the shafts of the tumbril cart and, throwing Bunker across its back, drove him off into the night with a blow to the animal's rump. Knowing that alone he could do nothing to stop the building tragedy, he had ridden his protesting mount for the Schuster estate like he had never driven a horse before. Thanks to him, Jem Fisher was alive and the little party in the congressman's suite were now recovering their shattered spirits in some tranquility.

'Mr Tengdahl,' Lynch was saying, 'my friends and I are eternally in your debt. Like a gentleman, you have refused all talk of payment and indeed money does not really meet the case. Nevertheless, I am a man who likes to repay his debts and there may, perhaps, be some way in which I could assist you in your business ventures down here in the South. Unfortunately, I shall not be in a position to intervene in person: my plans will obviously have to be reshaped. Before I go onto the convention tomorrow I shall personally take the ladies back to my estate in Adams County… Fortunately perhaps in the light of tonight's events the railroad will serve for the greater part of the journey.'

He paused thoughtfully, 'though I doubt those ruffians would dare assault a traveling party of which Congressman Lynch was actually a member. I am of course marked down as a successful black in this state of Mississippi and like any politician I have my enemies but, Mr Tengdahl, I think I can say without excessive pride and fear of contradiction that I have a certain standing in the community.' He paused, 'I see you are in pain, Sir!'

'It's nothing the rest and the river cruise up to Memphis won't cure, Congressman.' Harmann smiled wryly and winced even as he spoke. 'I'm real sorry you can't continue with us.'

'There's nothing to be done in the matter.' Lynch cleared his throat with the practiced self-depreciating cough of the orator. 'My duty clearly lies with the ladies. But I was explaining, or rather,' the man clearly loved the sound of his own voice, 'rather, I was preparing to explain how I might be able to help you. A brief account of my personal career will, I believe, give weight to my offer, as well as distract you from your present discomfort.'

A salesman, Harmann Tengdahl made no comment on this improbable analysis of the needs of the sickbed. Long ago, he had learnt that simulated fascination with the life stories of potential customers was part of the job. The fact that Deborah Sterling had just about finished her ministrations and now protested that what her patient most needed was rest would, he guessed, not deflect the kind of bore which the congressman was now appearing to be. Gamely assuring her that he was really quite comfortable, he settled himself as best he could into that state and prepared to listen. Soon he was absorbed by the life story of an exceptional man, though one who, it had to be said, was himself fully aware of the fact.

'You see before you, Mr Tengdahl, that all too rare phenomenon in American life – the slave made good. My success I put down to a combination of factors: a certain natural "presence" as a man, certain God-given talents which I have made it my duty to deploy to the top of my bent and, one admits, a certain amount of luck. But before all, in the peculiar aspect of the human condition which is the lot of the large majority of black men in the United States, I claim for myself the unusual habit of mind, bred from conviction maintained by will power, which consists in the refusal to be ashamed of having been a slave.'

He was interrupted at this point by a smart rap on the door and the almost immediate intrusion of a ship's steward. Without acknowledging the presence of the owner of the suite in any way, he swiveled briefly to locate the white man on the bed before announcing: 'Captain Dunleith presents his compliments, Sir, but is Mr Tengdahl perfectly comfortable or, if he is sufficiently recovered, would he perhaps care to take a nightcap with the captain in his quarters?'

Although formally correct in the stilted terminology of company etiquette and although, by its wording, it could be understood to be addressed to Congressman Lynch, this seemingly deferential enquiry was delivered, both in tone and gesture, with all the studied insolence of a disciplined schoolboy aiming to score off a despised teacher.

'Mr Tengdahl, what is to be my reply?'

Lynch had paused long enough to see how the white man would react to the calculated insult delivered to his black host, and Harmann, ignoring the steward, had glanced enquiringly at Lynch, for his cue.

'Congressman, might I suggest: "No reply to any message unless and until delivered by a messenger who has learnt manners"?'

Smiling grimly, Lynch responded.

'I think we can do better than that, Mr Tengdahl. And you stay where you are young man, if you wish to keep your job!' The sudden bark of authority froze the steward in his tracks. 'Tell Captain Dunleith that Congressman Lynch acknowledges the captain's kind concern for the well-being of his guest but that Mr Harmann Tengdahl is comfortably accommodated and sends his thanks. Further, Congressman Lynch would remind Captain Dunleith that the company directive as to the welcome to be accorded to Congressman Lynch while on board the *Vidalia* is signed by the Chairman of the line himself and that its provisions extend even to cabin staff. Have you got all that?'

'Yes, yes, Sir,' the steward reluctantly replied.

'Repeat it then.' And to Harmann's astonishment the youth did so.

'And now, I think, you will apologize to me for your earlier discourtesy.'

Again, the order was complied with and, thoroughly chastened, the steward made good his escape.

Once the door was shut, Deborah Sterling, who had seemed to be in trouble for some minutes, burst out in gales of laughter. Tears in her eyes and coughs alternating with guffaws, she stuttered out: 'Jack Roy Lynch, you sure know how to put a boy in his place.'

'Part of the art of politics, my dear Deborah, part of the art.'

The grim smile cracked wide and Harmann found himself surprised once again by this man and his people. Two hours back, they had been recovering from a terrifying encounter with mob violence, two minutes back they had been subjected to sneering verbal harassment and now they were laughing like kids at a birthday party. The incident opened Tengdahl's eyes to a bond of solidarity, private from the world outside and strengthening to those inside the charmed circle. For what reason he knew not, it seemed that he had been admitted to that circle.

'That surprised you, didn't it, my friend? To see a black man reacting to insolence as though he was a man! Well, I said I might be able to help you and by the time I've finished my tale you may understand why. But perhaps it really is too late, like Deborah here suggested a while back.'

'Late… an hour past midnight late? Mr Congressman, when I set out this evening it was not until daybreak that I expected to be back on board. And with the throbbing in this arm I doubt I'll sleep much before then anyways. You did a fine job, Madam, in cleaning up that wound and I doubt I'll suffer many ill effects. But just now, short of a glass of laudanum, I reckon a glass of whiskey and the diversion of a well-told tale will surely keep the pain at bay.'

'Or perhaps send you off to sleep, eh?' John Lynch gave a vague but friendly smile as he gathered his thoughts.

'I was born on the tenth day of September in the year 1847 in Concordia Parish in the state of Louisiana,' the congressman began. 'They kept regular records on that plantation, Sir, you can be sure of that. I grew up to be a valuable item on the inventory, though perhaps I shouldn't boast!' The twinkle of humor in eye and voice was quite genuine and once again Tengdahl found himself marveling at a cast of mind which could joke over such humiliation. 'You see,' the narrator continued, 'I meant it when I said that I refused to be ashamed of having been a slave. A man cannot be ashamed of his birth and live, and from the first I intended to live!'

They were the words of a practiced orator but delivered with a passion that was almost frightening.

'Well anyways, I was a tall, well-set-up young fellow and, folk told me, good-looking. So when emancipation broke I upped and went my ways, like the good book says, 'til I found myself in Natchez, where I took up accommodations. In those times, blacks in the South had a chance to make them a life just like real people. Of course, it didn't last. But while times permitted, I got me a trade and a modern trade too. Became a middlin' good photographer and built me the beginnings of a reputation in the only currency of credit they reckon here in the United States: money!'

He laughed.

'Picture making was fun sure, it's still my hobby as a matter of fact. But politics was always my aim. I moved fast: was a justice of the peace by age twenty-two and elected to the Mississippi House of Representatives. Next, they made me Speaker of the House and the same year the voters sent me to Washington. So I made enemies. Success in politics means making enemies, but me, I had to do it double. Too far too fast and of course I was black. "To the injury of his color he adds the insult of his youth," wrote a liberal yankee journalist soon after I arrived in Washington. And he went on, "John R(oy)

115

Lynch is also good-looking, physically strong and intellectually capable. Such a combination, just about tolerable in a 'healthy young darky' working shoeless from dawn to dusk on the plantation (the congressman's lot for the first five years of his adult life) is, to the prejudiced Southern mind, insufferable in a gifted, black photographer who successfully ran his own business and now has run his own campaign to Washington".'

The congressman paused. 'To be honest, that last bit was not strictly true. Like any candidate, I had much help and without help from the Republican party I would never have made it to Congress at all, much less my second term in 1874. But most people in this life need luck and that was mine. It came to an end with the corrupt deals over the '76 election, and out I went. But four years later I was back. Thought I was, anyways.

Good friends helped me make a campaign second to none. But the local electoral authorities were having nothing of this Negro "blacklash!", as one of them termed it, and declared the result null. We campaigned day and night to get that decision reversed. The outlook was hopeless: no white was going to testify to "losing" ballot boxes and no black dare testify to what he had seen until a certain Micah Sterling came forward with evidence. The affidavit he swore was enough to turn the tide.

Soon after that Micah took his family South. A year later he died, reportedly dragged to his death, while riding coachman to one of these fine old Southern families. That left Deborah and Eliza in Baton Rouge. Me, I got back to Washington. You see, thanks to Micah they were forced to give me that third term.'

He stopped abruptly. Deborah Sterling, her merriment stilled, was sobbing quietly into her hands. And the loyal Tengdahl, interested and concerned though he was, was also now on the verge of sleep, fatigue having suddenly set in under the combined influence of stress, weakness and the effects of the medicinal alcohol. Lynch laid a consoling hand on his friend's shoulder and saw her to her sleeping quarters.

Returning to the main room of the suite, he leaned over the nodding Tengdahl and said quietly: 'So you see why I am loyal to the Sterling family. Over breakfast I will tell you how maybe I can help you. It being Sunday they will probably conduct the services here on board with a reverend from the shore. But we must be gone soon after. And now I wish you a good night and once more thank you for your help rendered this night.'

Sunday morning broke clear and Tengdahl surprised himself by waking well refreshed. Fatigue had brought deep sleep and, thanks to his dressings, the wound was healthy, if still throbbing painfully. He was ready for breakfast and intrigued to learn how Lynch would propose to help him swell his order book. But his benefactor was not to be rushed.

After his triumphant third term he had retired to his Adams County plantation in 1883. Harmann deduced that while not corrupt, beyond the accepted norms of a congressman, Lynch had feathered a modest nest for himself. In 1889, following the Republican triumph in the electoral college of November 1888, he had returned to public service with appointment to a senior position in the auditor's office of the Navy Department under President Benjamin Harrison.

'No better place to be if you want the lowdown on the Mississippi shipping fraternity, I can assure you, Mr Tengdahl. Why do you suppose I enjoy my favored treatment on the river when the tide has set against the Negro in every department of Southern life? I will explain.'

Clearly, thought Harmann, *this fellow is not to be stopped!*

'My official title was Fourth Auditor of the US Treasury for the Navy Department. However, President Harrison gave me a private briefing which sure filled out those dry-sounding words. He instructed that I make the closest possible scrutiny of all the navy's contracts on the river south from Memphis to the Delta. I had been selected because, as a Southern Republican of long standing and a plantation holder in a riverside county, I had the right background. The President added that his office had briefed all major companies concerned with dock works or navigation on the river to afford me all necessary assistance.

A month in the office persuaded me that a tour of the territory was necessary, another month sufficed to account for the deference with which I was received.'

He paused to refill his coffee cup, a smile of reminiscence on his face. The atmosphere was still friendly and intimate, but the congressman had relapsed into the formality of the bureaucrat. 'Mr Tengdahl, the records under my scrutiny go back to the Civil War, when control of the river was a vital element in the triumph of the Union. They come down to the present day, when government contracts are vital to many operations!

The waters of patronage do not always run clear and between the banks of the Mississippi the water is notoriously muddy. Information comes my way which could break many a prosperous career. But until last night I made no use of it. Like the rest of the tribe, as an active politician I took my pickings, modest though they were by the standards of modern white man's Washington. But on retiring I closed my account. I have not reopened it since.'

He paused once again, musing; rueful, perhaps, over his moderation when feeding at the trough that nourished pork barrel politics.

'I am a man to be reckoned with on this river, and there will be burghers in Natchez-under-the-Hill who will be regretting that their township offered violence to friends of John Lynch. As for you, Mr Tengdahl, if you are looking to confirm that lighting contract with the Vidalia Line, you need only apply to the manager of their Memphis headquarters with this letter of recommendation. You will see that the envelope bears my personal wax seal, which I require you not break.'

He handed over a rather bulky packet. Without comment, Tengdahl slid it into the inside pocket of his torn but capacious traveling jacket. The envelope certainly contained something more than a letter. Something, as he would discover, that had magical properties to ease difficult negotiations. And so Willard Stone and Partner of S.K.L. got that all important breakthrough for their Mississippi operation: and they got it at Natchez-under-the-Hill what's more.

'And now,' Lynch continued, 'I will be gathering the ladies for our journey to my Adams County plantation. I wish you a pleasant cruise and the joy of the state room, which is already paid for and which will be a last reminder of our gratitude.'

He made a slight bow and soon Harmann heard his martial step once more along the decking accompanied by the patter of ladies' pumps and the rustle of skirts.

CHAPTER SEVEN

The Port of Boston, the Sad and the Beautiful

If she was honest with herself, Elsie Marre had been bored. And by rights she shouldn't have been. Work had brought her to Boston, that beautiful and important city; she was making headway in her researches on the standing and achievements of the Negro clergy; she had been chosen as one of the delegates to the forthcoming conference on black women's rights in New York; and it had turned out that William DuBois, up and coming leader of her generation in the struggle and on a private mission to Boston, was lodging just a couple of streets away. Elsie knew him slightly and wanted to know him better. Even so, Elsie had been bored.

The minister she had come all this way to interview had been called out of town. DuBois, whom she had hoped to spend time with until the reverend returned, was "really too busy for the next couple of days". The weather had been awful and the family she was staying with were boring and had no interests outside the husband's job in the neighboring railroad depot.

On the plus side, her draft for a long-projected biographical note on Harriet Tubman, ex-slave and slaves' champion, was shaping up nicely and a recent news item concerning the great woman indicated that the time was opportune. For Elsie, work cleared the head and loosened the log jam of depressing circumstances; the weather had cleared and that morning DuBois's landlady's son had brought a note round to say that if Miss Marre was able to call that afternoon, he might have a moment to spare.

Elsie was there as soon after midday as seemed reasonable and settled with a rather obvious show of patience to wait until the great man should finish the reading he was engaged on, when she entered the room that served as his study. But she could not contain her impatience for long.

'I was wondering whether you would have time to look this over for me, Du.'

William Edward Burghardt DuBois, whose ancestry mixed a French Huguenot strain with the blood of African slaves, was a man who looked distinguished with his trim, pointed beard, aquiline nose and slightly receding hairline, and a man who anticipated a distinguished career once the University of Harvard had approved his doctorate of philosophy. He looked up with a puzzled smile at the young woman seeking his opinion on her writing.

DuBois allowed the use of the familiar diminutive only to the closest among his circle of friends and he was not quite clear how Elsie Marre had established herself in that elite body, even though at twenty-eight she was his exact age peer. No doubt it was in part because she claimed acquaintanceship with his colleague Mary Terrell and no doubt, he admitted to himself, his smile broadening into a grin, it was in large part because of her personal beauty.

He noticed again how her looks were set off by the line of that old scar across her forehead, which flared a livid gray-white when she was angry and which had led him to nickname her "Blaze", after the only race horse he had ever put money on. The animal had come home at very long odds, thereby making possible the purchase of an essential source book for his university thesis on the suppression of the African slave trade in the USA. But his best friend had lost a month's living allowance on a rival nag and DuBois had vowed never to bet again.

'Seems you already reckon I do have the time, Elsie! OK, OK,' he went on hurriedly, raising a hand mock defensively against the threatened protestations of apology as she made to withdraw the document. 'OK I will read it now and then we might stroll down to the docks.'

Although Elsie had been working for some months now on preliminary research to assemble material for a report on the Negro American church and clergy that DuBois hoped one day to publish with Terrell, it was the first time she had shown him any of her own written work.

'What is this then? Oh, I see,' and he smiled with pleasure as he read: *A preparatory article on the career of Harriet Tubman: by Elsie "Blaze" Marre.* So that nickname's by way of becoming official, is it?'

'I like it Du. Gives me a bit of a handle when I tell folks who thought it up. Kinda fiery, too, and I aim to start a few fires in my life.'

'Well let's see what that typewriting machine of yours is capable of.'

'*Harriet Tubman,*' he read, '*was born in the state of Maryland about the year 1819/20. Known to some as "General" Tubman, to others as "the Moses of her people", she is honored as a true beacon of liberty for the Negro American population of the United States.*'

'Florid stuff, we have here, florid stuff,' DuBois paused to interrupt his own reading, and then returned to the text. '*Given the quality of her service to the cause of Black Liberty, she is surely worthy of literary reverence.*

At the age of twenty-nine she managed to make good her escape from her native plantation and run to the North, which at that time seemed a haven of humanity. She surely was a pioneer of "underground railroad ethics". To the best of our knowledge, Harriet Tubman was the first Black Sister to return, yes praise God, to return, to the scene of her bondage while it was yet enslaved. Thence she "conducted", navigated, guided, escorted… ['and sometimes, at gunpoint, goddam drove!' DuBois expostulated, remembering one of the more down-to-earth traditions about the redoubtable Harriet] *'… no fewer than 300 people, it is claimed, from the South to the North. When the American War of the Union broke out President Lincoln may have seen it first of all as a struggle to save the Union. From the start, Harriet Tubman saw it as the conflict to decide, once and for all, the issue of slavery: perforce.'*

'"Perforce"!' DuBois exploded in protest

'Read on, dear Du, read on.'

'When the war ended she was honored, she was fêted but, in the one thing that for many signifies real worth, money, she was not paid! So this worthy woman remains worthy but poor, save for the most modest of pensions.'

'Well?' Elsie was expectant and eager.

'Weell, where are you hoping to place this little piece?'

'Don't rightly know, DuBois. That's what I was hoping for advice about from you.' He noticed that Elsie dropped the diminutive when important matters were under discussion.

'Hum. Well, it's sure got passion, Elsie. But to be frank with you, it seems to me it's neither one thing nor the other. It's too wordy for a popular paper, too heavy for a college journal, and not long enough for either. See if you can't work it up to about twice the length. Then come back to me with it and we'll see if we can't find a home for it.'

DuBois pushed back his chair with a decisive gesture.

'But now, let's take a stroll to look at the shipping down by the Navy Yard off Charlestown. Even in this age of steam there's many an old clipper and tall ship plying the ocean. I've a couple of points on tackle and rigging I want to check out by practical comparison against my reading on those hulks of death, the slavers.'

For reasons of finance, DuBois had cheap lodgings off Cambridge Street, where property values had fallen since the building of the Junction and the Fitchburg Railroads, close to the wharwes of the Charles River. Today, however, he wanted to visit Boston Harbor itself, the best part of a mile and a half away. As they left the house, a train came chugging along from the direction of Cambridgeport, its smoke stack belching clouds of smuts to add to the pollution and dirt already miring the buildings in the area.

'By the way, I'm hoping we might be able to recruit you as full-time researcher,' commented Dubois. 'It sure helps to have someone who knows their way around. Of course it all depends if Mary's father shows friendly to the project so we've got money to pay you – and if Mary offers enough to pay you properly!' '

Elsie smiled to herself; Mary Terrell, who travelled a good deal and boasted she could make a dollar go further abroad than most of her friends could at home, was reputed to be tight with money. At Wilberforce College, where she had taught Elsie German, Mary Church, as she then was, had the nickname, with some of the students, of Fräulein Pfennig. She was a great advocate of folk wisdom and above all proverbs in the teaching of languages, and her favorite German proverb was: *"Wer den Pfennig nicht ehrt, ist des Talers nicht wert"*, or "If you don't respect the pennies, you won't be worth a dollar". In fact, as her students well knew, she was generosity itself in cases of real need. It was just that she hated to see anything being squandered, whether money or opportunities.

Elsie approved of this attitude, as indeed of most of her German teacher's opinions. The two in fact had much in common. Like Terrell, Elsie was an alumna of the model school Antioch College in Yellow Springs, Ohio and, like Terrell she was an enthusiast for the ideal of political rights of women.

At a time when white women and most black men were excluded from the vote, commitment to black women's rights was idealism verging on the fantastical but, as Elsie's mother once remarked: "An idealism that may bring in a steady payin' job cain't be all that bad!" Thinking of her mother always made Elsie happy and her secret smile broadened into a grin.

But DuBois was anxious that people should get fair dealing and repeated the point on salary. He guessed that Mary's husband might resent the family resources going into what he would probably consider almost subversive work, the investigation of what might be revealed as dubious clergy dealings.

In many ways an excellent man, Robert Heberton Terrell, a Harvard-trained lawyer with ambitions, disapproved of hostility to one of the liberal professions. As for Robert Church himself, as a self-made man he was leery of being imposed on by "scroungers". The son of a black woman and a white riverboat captain from Memphis, Tennessee, he had built a solid fortune on shrewd real estate deals in the immediate post-emancipation decades. He had been able to give his daughter a fine education ending at Oberlin College, where she had been editor of the *Oberlin Review*.

The last thing Church senior wanted, it seemed, was for his daughter to join the teaching profession. He considered it belonged to a social class distinctly inferior to the level to which he had raised his own family. Nor was he at all happy to learn that, despite what he considered the advantage of a light skin color, Mary proposed to spend her life working, in his words, "behind the color line" and devoting herself to the advancement of the status and educational opportunities of colored people. He had pulled himself up by his own bootstraps; let everybody else do the same, was his view of the matter.

When, however, his daughter sounded him out on a project for a social study of the black church ministry, he relented a little. Men of the cloth ranked well below even teachers in his meticulous calibration of the scale of social worth, so he nourished the secret hope that her pursuit of such work could bring to light large and sensational evidence of, what he firmly believed was, a network of systemic moral malpractice and financial peculation.

Most people knew that there were church elders, even ministers, who were not ebony pure through and through when it came to cash inducements, but although "the girl", she was now thirty-two, had produced no evidence to match his hopes, Church hoped something "might turn up". DuBois feared that, anxious to stretch the money as far as possible, Mary might stint on the stipend of her assistant.

But Elsie, who so far had been living on expenses, treasured the opportunity of being paid to travel and to widen her experience of life outside the charmed world of Johnstoneville. She assured DuBois he need have no worries.

As the two walked on toward the port area, they discussed Mary's involvement in the planning for the launch of the National Association of Colored Women's Clubs. Glancing up as they turned the last corner leading to the Navy Yard wharf, Elsie let out a gasp of wonder.

'Oh Du, isn't that just beautiful?!'

Across the water, lying in a berth off the wharfs of East Boston, was a stately five-masted schooner. Top masts stepped but sails all furled down, in seamen's terms, so that the rigging and shrouds made a filigree against the eastern morning sky.

'Sure is beautiful,' agreed DuBois, 'and tomorrow when they raise sail she'll be still more so. Should interest you too, given you're from an oil town. She's no tea clipper, the *Rebecca*

Palmer, though she is registered here in Boston.'

He paused and a bitter smile twisted the handsome, distinguished features.

'Say, something has just occurred to me. We blacks are bitter about our history in this land, and with good reason. But the redman, too, surely has cause for grievance. Did you know that when the Bostonians rebelled against the English crown, asserting most high-sounding principles for their actions, these noble champions of liberty disguised themselves, of all things, as redmen. Claiming the right to live in freedom in their "new found land", they adopted the costume of the true owners of the territory their ancestors had dispossessed!'

In their brief acquaintance, Elsie had never seen DuBois so wrought up and so passionate.

The great ship, some 200 feet from bowsprit to stern, her masts towering more than a hundred feet above her deck, was ready for loading. As they watched, two thick, black cables stretching from the shore into the ship's hold began to throb.

'Look like mooring hawsers, don't they? In fact, those are the fuel lines and they're pumping the "black gold" aboard at this moment.' DuBois paused, a troubled frown on his face. 'Terrible turn of phrase that, isn't it, when you reflect on what it must have meant before the discovery of petroleum here in America.'

The friends, their eyes clouded with pain, looked out across the bay at the lovely vessel. Her sleek curve from stem to stern and the towering frame of masts and spars, with its filigree of ratlines and rigging, brought a lump to the throat with its beauty. And yet the associations were with horror and death.

Just such a ship in days not long past, sailing into a southern port under a pyramid of sail, would have bewitched a child; eyes straining against the morning sunlight with dreams of a life of glamour and adventure on the ocean wave. And yet, beneath those dazzling white billows of canvas had

127

seethed the stench and filth of ten weeks of human ordure, and of blood and decaying gangrened flesh; the groans of the dying and the screams and curses of the survivors. And behind all this lay the calculating accountancy of the slaver in the master's cabin, balancing his books of profit and loss, profit from the beauty and strength of the surviving people; loss from "dead stock" and "damaged goods", corpses dumped at sea and maimed and broken bodies to be driven dockside, half blind and emaciated, under the lash of blaspheming, mocking seamen.

'Is there nothing for us, for the black people of this beautiful earth, which will not be stained with evil or the memory of evil, Du? Is there nothing in which we can take pleasure without the fear of history?'

Although he sensed his companion's heaving shoulders, Dubois dared not look in her direction for fear that he too would burst out into sobbing. He cursed himself for voicing his thoughts so freely. There was a time and a place for lamentation for the lost centuries of black dignity in this baleful land, but a brisk, businesslike day like this was not it.

When she arrived at his room, Elsie Marre had been at the top of her creative, confident form. She was a strong and capable person on track of a career schedule of considerable promise, which she was surely able to meet. But she was also imaginative, and much more so than he had realized. There were surely few enough blacks with her potential without him, William DuBois, demoralizing those that there were. He shook himself and rubbed a salty tear from the corner of his eye, smarting from a sudden, sharp squall of wind.

'Of course there is, honey. The slave ships that brought our people over the ocean were ferries from hell. But for us history is populated, too, by an ancestry of black courage and endurance to make us strong.'

But already Elsie, with the resilience of her race and the

outgoing optimism of her personality, had tidied up her eyes and was obviously set to get back to the agenda of the day. With an occasional glance across at the workaday business of the tanker loading, and picking their way over the coils of rope and the usual detritus of a wharf, the two of them made their way along the waterfront.

CHAPTER EIGHT

Black Admiral Chicago Docks 1895-96

The fist smashed into Dan Porter's temple with the force of a steam pile driver. It was the last of a flurry of blows and off-balanced him so that his feet skidded on the spray-drenched timber quay. He crashed down, a rib cracked by a bollard in the fall, winded and concussed. Up till this moment he had given a good account of himself. But now the three white assailants, snarling like mastiffs, fell on their prey. The leader cut a length from the coil of rope dumped a few feet away with the men's jackets and bound the victim, hands and feet, so the knots cut into the flesh.

'Okey dokey, Peterson, let's be havin' that boulder.' A man built like a navvy, the ridge of an old scar disfiguring his nose and left cheek, did as asked, staggering slightly with the weight. The "boulder" was a sizeable block of white masonry, one of a pile of discarded builders' materials further up the quay. Its regular corners and edge-lines facilitated the work of the leading thug, who was now tying the rope round it as if to rig up a makeshift drag anchor. He measured two arm spans before cutting the rope, which he secured tightly to the bonds round Dan's ankles.

'Know what this is? Funny kind of rock they call "staff",

what they built the World's Fair "White City" from. Peterson here worked on that, worked on the harbor here too, years back. Knows a might of things 'bout buildings and harbor works, does Peterson. Like, for example, the dock hereabouts is sixteen foot deep, easy clearance for ships up to fourteen-foot draught. Two fathoms of rope gives you twelve feet to the bottom. You're a big boy, six foot two if you're an inch. That should give you a good ten inches clearance when you're rigged proper.' The man was now securing a single span's length of rope to the rope round Dan's wrists and chatting conversationally as he did so.

'But then you'd know about the depth of the harbor basin w'dn't yuh, Mister "Black Admiral" Porter, bein' as you're master of the tug *Titan*... wouldn't you, eh!'

He tightened the knot with a sudden vicious tug that wrenched Dan's aching shoulder sockets. He let out a sharp groan. The two bystanders laughed with the genuine pleasure of sadists. 'Make it again, Joe,' said the man called Peterson, seconded by his companion whose massive, broad boots somehow gave the impression that Wolf "the Door" Berliner, was as wide across the ankles as across his heavy, muscled shoulders.

Joe Macey, waterfront boss in this stretch of Chicago's dockland, ignored them and warped the free rope end round the bollard. Straightening up to his full six foot and lighting the stogey offered from Berliner's cigar pouch, he surveyed the varied ships at the moorings, with their yards and rigging, masts and funnels, rising against stars and a bright half moon.

It was 2.30 am on a crisp October morning in the year 1895. Daniel Porter, skipper of the tug *Titan*, had begun the day early. They had to clear the berth by 3.30 am latest to haul the *St Lawrence Trader*, a Canadian merchantman, one of the few vessels still willing to use the black crewed *Titan*. Waylaid by a gang of white harbor thugs led by union activist Joe

Macey, Dan lay trussed and helpless. He heard the distant shouts and occasional creaks of a cargo derrick in the sharp night air, from the Canadian. In two hours time her master would be hammering furiously at the door of Tom White's legendary clapboard house on the harbor side, demanding explanations. Tomorrow the four-man crew, just now dragging themselves out to meet the early morning sailing, would be asking White for their papers, so they could re-enlist as numbered deck hands on some anonymous white man's "monarch of the lakes". Tears of misery, mingled with the pain, streamed down Dan Porter's cheeks for the five black families whose timorous hopes of a human future had now been effectively sabotaged.

Macey had heard the same sounds of the Canadian readying for sea. He smiled a slow, malicious smile. Now there was not a single line operating out of the port of Chicago that would use the *Titan*.

'Fine night for a launchin', Admiral Porter, don't you think,' he sneered. 'But I's forgettin' you're by way of bein' a rookie on this waterfront. Long time since we had to discipline anybody, so maybe you's unfamiliar with the word. Sound's like lynching from down South, don'it? Well that's pretty near what it is, only we use water not fire and on the waterfront anyone as steps out o' line, black or white, is a candidate.' He paused with a sly grin, 'Though mostly I guess it's blacks!'

As he talked, he methodically tidied up, wiping the blade of his clasp knife, which he then carefully closed and packed in a holster at his belt, coiling down the remnant of rope. This he gave to Peterson, clearly the sherpa in the party. 'An' you and Thomas White sure have stepped out of line, Porter. You been told often enough – a black on a steamboat belongs in the stoke hole. But tellin' ain't good enough for Tom White, never was. Always reckoned himself above the other owners along of his popularity with the waterfront. Well, making a black master, even in a four-crew tug, sure dented that.' Macey spat venomously down into the moon's reflection in the sluggish water. 'We'll be visiting with him in an hour or so I guess, when, that is, we've finished our business with you, boy.'

Aged thirty-seven and a skilled ship's engineer, Dan Porter winced in fury at the contemptuous term. But he shivered too. The icy lake breeze cut through his wet clothing, through to the bone. Immobilized by the ropes, he had all but lost feeling in his hands and feet and now cramp seemed to be seizing up every other muscle in his body.

And he was frightened; for his good friend Tom White, to be sure, but for himself too. What was a launching? Could a man survive it? And if he did, what then, what future was there him for him and young James? *The Black Admiral,* he sneered at himself. So proud when his five-year-old son had given him the name six months back, proud too when the whites took it up, if only to mock him. Now, he was helpless to save the boy from anything these louts should decide.

They had gone into a huddle a few yards off. Twisting his head painfully, he could just see the great boots of "the Door". Their whispered conference was surely about him, the black who had dirtied the name of Chicago's water men by daring to boast the title of engineer. Macey was right. The white sailors had grudgingly accepted him, but only for Tom White's sake. The old salt, a veteran of the federal navy, was popular, he paid well and he would stand no nonsense. But six months back he had retired and made his black ship's engineer master of the *Titan.*

At once, the little tug became headline harbor news. The remaining three-man crew took their papers. Black replacements were signed on. But an all-black boat working as effectively as any other was too much for the waterfront. The skippers of visiting ships were briskly informed of local feeling and calls for the *Titan's* towing services fell off dramatically, until only the occasional Canadian vessel called for them and then only when all other boats were in commission. Tom White stayed loyal to his new team. 'Makes no odds to me, Dan,' he said. 'Made myself some good investments an' if it costs to keep principles alive, then who's complainin'?'

The answer to that was easy, as Dan could have told him. The entire white waterfront was complaining. After three months' harassment and victimization, the black engineer trained up by Dan himself had left to take work as a stoker on a lake steamer. Last week, his replacement had demanded a rise to compensate for the harassment he was suffering. Tomorrow, the entire crew would surely leave. And who could blame them? But now, *he* was to be "launched" – Dan shivered, what did the word mean?

'A penny for your thoughts, "Admiral".'

Now he was going to learn about launching, waterfront style. Pain, cold and fear convulsed his tortured body. The men laughed, Macey too. The evening was going well and he was looking forward to wrecking Tom White's house. There would be outrage from some of the dockers and most of the wives but no action. The old man had used up his goodwill credits over the past couple of years. Macey led the little group back to the prone figure. In an attempt to ease his cramps, Dan Porter had drawn up his knees on the slack which roped him to the boulder and rolled over onto his side.

'Good thinking, boy,' said Macey, 'best not be on your back for a launching, eh, fellahs?!'

'Sure thing, Joe.' Berliner frowned his agreement.

'Wolf here don't approve. He holds to the old saying: "Launch a ship and cheer the Jacks, launch a man and break a back". Well I reckon the Jack Tars on Chicago's wharfs will be cheering some tomorrow when the news spreads that the Black Admiral been cut loose from his moorings. But of course,' he laughed again with false friendliness, 'you still don't know what we're talking about so I'd better explain.

First, you gotta understand just how they built this stretch of wharf. Like I said, Peterson here was working on it some ten years back an' he tells me it's just a row of wooden boxes, about fourteen foot square and deep, filled with rocks and left to settle. Six months later they laid planking along the tops and bolted it home to cover the cribs, as they call 'em, and make the wharf we're standing on now. That right, Peterson?'

'That's right, Joe. 'Cept this particular stretch is a bit different. For the most part them cribs were made of timber baulks, 'bout a foot square an' planed to a rough finish. Along here they were runnin' late on the contract and jus' used barely trimmed tree trunks, bark and knots and here and there a branch stump sticking out. All under the waterline y'understand…'

'… and it's all very uncomfortable for a guy who happens to be strung up between a bollard on the wharf and a drag anchor on the bottom.' Macey finished the structural survey with brutal directness. 'So there you have it, Mister Porter, that's why we hold our launchings along this-a-way.'

'An' the broken back, you bastards?'

'You watch yuh tongue, boy, or yuh may end up with one at that. That's a full launch. Coupla guys hurl the rock out into the harbor as far as it'll go. The rope snakes out and yanks the victim over the edge of the timber decking into the water and hey presto, if he ain't ready and aint' crouched something like you is now so he can go over bent on his belly, then – bang goes his back. For you, I have in mind to make it a half launch. That way, we just drops the rock down the side here and you's left stretched with chin just above water for most of the time and your back grating along those logs with every movement of the currents and eddies.'

'An' how long you leave me like that?'

Macey looked genuinely surprised.

'Oh we don't come back boy. You gotta pray that some guy with a friendly attitude passes this way and hauls you up onto the wharf before he cuts the rope tying you to this bollard. There should be just enough slack below the waterline to get you back up to your waist. Won't be easy any of it, but that way you has a chance. If the guy ain't friendly and cuts the bollard rope first… well, work it out for yourself.'

The three of them laughed, cheerfully. Peterson and Berliner lobbed the anchor stone over the side and actually eased Dan's body over the edge as the rope jerked him downward. That was the limit of their consideration. The shock of the cold water stunned him, a slime of bilge and oil slopped against his face before the swell settled back to just above his shoulder height. The pull of his body weight on the rope above wrenched his arms and shoulders. He whimpered with the agony, staring helplessly at the clear night sky.

'Now don't you go away boy.' Macey's mocking voice was fainter and the receding footsteps told him they were indeed leaving him to his fate. 'We's just goin' to pay a visit to Tom White and we'll tell him where he can look for his admiral. Shouldn't take him but more than an hour from now. An don' you catch col' now.'

Dan barely heard the parting jeer. There was a roaring in his ears and his head slumped forwards. He jerked it back and wondered just how long he would be able to fight the tearing fatigue that wracked his body and mind. With the temperature just above zero, the moisture of his soaked sleeves was slowly able to evaporate to increase the chill factor. The rope cutting his wrists had choked the blood supply to his hands, threatening the probability of gangrene if help did not come soon, while the pull on his arms dragged up the diaphragm and constricted the action of his lungs to make breathing itself syncopated agony. The pounding in his head throbbed louder and a curtain of blood came down over his eyes. He jerked his head again. If he blacked out now, that would be the end.

Doggedly, he forced himself to concentrate on some rational line of thought. At once a question lurking behind his pain surged forward. How had Macey known he would be on the wharf so early in the morning? For weeks now, the *Titan* had lain idle with no commissions. Eight o'clock every morning, to the sneers of the wharf, the Black Admiral had been down to see all was shipshape on the mooring before making his way with other skippers out of commission to see what work might be on offer. Every day for weeks the answer had been "nothing for you, Mister Porter"; every day, that is, until yesterday, when the Canadian master broke the boycott.

Just then, the rigid mask of misery twitched in a rictus of… laughter?! Incredibly, painfully, Dan felt himself grin and try to laugh. Few fish swum near the surface of the oil-polluted water but, at this moment, some creature he could not see, no matter how he twisted his neck, had found the rip in the armpit of his shirt and was nibbling at the hairs and flesh beneath. "If you tickle us, do we not laugh?" The phrase floated up from some remote memory of Johnstoneville Sunday School with the Reverend Walcott. Depressingly aware that his Sunday classes for the inculcation of religious knowledge were the nearest many of his pupils would ever get to literature, Walcott had interlarded his readings from the King James Bible with brief passages not only from the speeches of Abraham Lincoln but also from his treasured copy of the *Memoir and Poems of Phyllis Wheatley: the Negro Poetess* and finally from the collected works of William Shakespeare. Just why these should have included a reference to tickling, the battered mind of Dan Porter could not now recall – he was only too relieved when the unseen visitant sculled off along the oily current, with the flick of a silvery tail fin.

He spat and sneezed at the miniature wash of scum stirred up under his nose. The drag on his ankles and the stretch at his arms tortured him almost beyond endurance, and all the time he had to struggle to maintain his breathing above every lapping wavelet on the docile waters of the inner dock. The word triggered a flash of memory. '… so ah guess we'll be leaving dock 'bout a quarter after three.' It was the hesitant, lazy drawl of Jethro Tulliver, overpaid engineer of the *Titan*. Just before swooning into semi-oblivion, Porter identified in his mind's eye the shadowy figure the seaman had been talking to the evening before when he broke off shiftily to get last-minute instructions as to the morning's sailing. A figure who normally would not on any account speak to a black, but one who, Porter now realized, had every reason to be interested in the doings of the *Titan*. A figure who went by the name of Wolf Berliner.

Throughout the misery and pain of his ordeal, the Black Admiral had never once thought of abandoning the struggle for survival. All his thoughts were for his little son, James Owen "Shout" Porter. Even now, in the half world of pain and pain-induced trance, the haloed head of the child, as caught by the vignette photographer for his fifth birthday, haunted the mist of his father's delirium like a reproach. Without father or mother, what hope would he have? But physical realities have their own laws. A draining combat with brutal assailants followed by some thirty minutes of icy crucifixion imposed its own moratorium on pain. Dan Porter was well past consciousness and barely this side of Jordan when the soft pad and flap of bare feet and shabby shoes announced the approach of Will and "Duke" Sidelaw, the *Titan*'s deckhands.

"A right pair of jokers," according to the Bethel choir, where their finely-matched voices buttressed the tenor line of a Sunday. They were, too, men of unswerving loyalty. Now, at 3.15 am, a good hour before the first hint of dawn would begin to gray the sky, they were on their way to join the *Titan*, kidding whether loyalty couldn't be bought too high. Their wives would have agreed, though for different reasons. 'A bit more consideration for your family and a bit less for the admiral,' Belle Sidelaw had grumbled of late. Will's daily rate was little better than on the steamers, where a black could get by reasonable enough if he knuckled down. 'Don' know but she got a point there, Duke,' Will commented with a cheerful grin into the dark. 'Leastways we'd be having another coupla hours in bed this mornin'… aw shit, some goldarn fool's hitched a mooring line to this…' The indignant yell was cut short by a splash as the speaker, having tripped on the rope of Dan Porter's calvary, hit the water headfirst.

'Lucky for the skipper I gave a final twist to his torture,' Will joked later, as the two families took a belated midday meal together in Duke Sidelaw's apartment. The four adults, along with Jim Porter and the two older Sidelaw children, were packed round the square deal kitchen table on spindle back chairs and stools. Drafts blew through cracks in the uncarpeted boards, flaking plaster had fallen away to reveal the laths round door and window frame, the fog and smoke of the city conspired to darken the early afternoon to early evening, yet the single primitive oil lamp remained unlit and the small, black-leaded coal burning stove was economically stoked just sufficient to keep the skillet of soup warm.

It was a mean, impoverished room but the atmosphere was warm and loving. It was a good soup and, with the doorstep slices of bread, made a substantial meal. The friends were happy to have escaped the morning's terror without tragedy. In the adjacent room, one of the two family beds was occupied by the sleeping form of Dan Porter, his bleeding, pulverised body nursed and bandaged with all possible love and care by the two women. Mr White had been visiting to satisfy himself that all was as well as could be with the *Titan's* skipper. But he had cares of his own, having been roused from his bed by the smell of fire and smoke and having barely escaped with his life from the charred ruins of his house. 'Tell him to come and see me soon as he feels up to it and we'll talk plans. And tell him not to worry,' he had added as he hurried away.

'Yuh know,' Will finished his soup with a flourish of the spoon, 'first thing, I thought it was a lubberly-tied mooring rope of some rowboat I'd overshot in my divin' practice! If the captain had'n't holla'ed, I'd've heaved myself back on the quay with a hand from Duke here, gone on to the *Titan* and come back to mah bed double quick, soon's we found skipper and engineer weren't turning up.'

'He's jes lucky you and Duke paid no heed to Jethro and went along to the quay this mornin'. 'Fyou'd stayed in yuh beds Dear Dan would've been dead 'fore Mr White got there, no blame to him either.' Belle Sidelaw shook her head in sorrow for the pain their friend had suffered and the mortal danger he had been in, and laid a motherly arm round young Jim Porter's shoulders. Slightly-built, but with clear eyes and the strong sensitive hands that promised the gift of music, the five-year-old slid down off his stool.

'Can I go in an' see him now, Aunt Belle? I know he's bad, but he is my pa an' if he should wake up he'd sure be glad to see me.'

She glanced round the table; the nods of assent confirmed her instinct. 'OK, hon'. But you be quiet now, you be reel quiet!'

* * * * *

It was Sunday morning two days later. Jim Porter and his father were once more in their own apartment. A modest two-room affair, like those of the Sidelaw brothers, it was that bit more comfortable thanks to Dan's superior pay scale and the fact that man and boy had the place to themselves. Yet they would willingly have traded the space if only Bess, beloved mother and wife, could have been returned to them.

Sunday morning was the time Dan missed her most. The visit to church prepared with meticulous care, the services themselves when he and she, with the toddler standing on the bench, brought him up in the traditional harmonies and rhythms, while Bess from time to time introduced one of the "Shouts" that were her special pride. Jim in fact had only faint memories of these times of family participation in the worship, for his mother had taken to her bed when he was just three and died some four months later. That the beat was in his blood, however, was due as much to her as his trombonist father, who dubbed him James "Shout" Porter in honour of that dear lady.

This Sunday was quite unlike any that Jim had known before and as such was exciting. First of all they were obviously not going to church, second of all Mr White – 'not such a good Christian as he should be,' Bess used to say – had invited himself round and was at this moment pottering about with pans and milk and coffee percolator on the well-stoked stove. while Jim's father stretched as comfortable as he could on the sleeping couch which served as Jim's bed in ordinary times.

'You see, Daniel,' Mr White was saying with the vague hint of Irish strengthening behind his Chicago accent as it always did in moments of self-satisfaction, 'it was the two together that clinched the deal. The fact that Macey's knife was found outside my place by patrolman Stibbins didn't prove anythin' one way or t'other. Macey claimed he could've dropped it anytime and since everyone knows Macey's been 'a visitin' me for weeks past there wasn't no real argument. The precinct captain hadn't been overly worried to see a bit of trouble going my way. Sure he reckons Macey means union and union means trouble and sure, he's never been able to get him. But there ain't much to choose between "nigger lovers" and union men in O'Donlan's book. But arson in Chicago – that's something else.'

He paused at a critical stage in the coffee-making sequence. 'You like sugar, don' you, Dan? Coffee for you, son? No? OK, go down the soda fountain an' see what you can find.' Mr White fished out a dime, to Jim's considerable satisfaction, and the boy disappeared through the door.

'So the captain has made a marker and Macey knows it. However, it's what I know about those lodge elections last year that's forced him to lay off and that makes it possible for me to propose what I'm just going to propose to you. "You cain't prove that vote was rigged" was his first reaction. But there's no call to prove anythin' on that one. "Knuckles" Bowdler's slow but he's not stupid. He's been muttering foul ever since the results were called. What I got would light him up so fast, Macey'd be blown out of the water afore he could even set a course for safety. Soon as I outlined what I do in fact know about that finaggle, he backed off like a steer from a branding iron.'

Dan smiled faintly. It was barely forty hours since he had been hauled, half drowned, starving with cold and bleeding from ears and nose, from the foetid waters of the Chicago "pool". His hands were like two bundles of frankfurters, two of his ribs were cracked, he had lost crew, command and career in half a day's mayhem and here was Tom White talking plans for the future. Of course, it might all sound good if only he'd come to a point. Right now, Dan thought to himself on his first Sunday morning out of church in years, a lecture by an old sea dog was barely fair trade for release from a sermon by a dog collar.

'How you like to run a ship's stores?'

The question seemed to surge up from nowhere.

'Come again?'

'OK, Dan, what I meant to say was: Dan Porter, how would you like to run, own and pass on to your son and heir a ship's chandlery on the waterfront here in Chicago? And don't tell me a black wouldn't be allowed, after I've spent twenty minutes explaining why Joe Macey will lead the Civil Rights brigades if anyone tries to bust us up.'

'Mr White… Mr White…'

'Call me Tom, boy, call me Tom, it's my hope we' going to be partners.'

Dan smiled weakly and raised a hand, turning painfully on his couch to look the other directly in the face.

'Mr White, for until we are partners that's what I'll be callin' you, what you say sounds fine and dandy, but we've gotta do business, businesslike. Jes now I'm real weary.'

'Course you are Dan, course you are; don' know what I'm thinkin' about rattlin' on like this. But you think things over, cool and easy, and we'll be havin' us a serious business conference as soon as you're ready, jes as soon as you're ready, boy.'

And without any awareness of his gauche misuse of language, the good-natured Tom White bustled out of the little room into the apartment house hallway, nearly knocking Jim Porter down as he did so. As his young son quietly pulled the door to, mindful of his father's need for sleep and rest, Dan smiled once more. Tact had never been one of White's qualities and maybe at his age, the man was pushing seventy, he called all sorts of folk "boy". And yet, Dan thought to himself as he drowsed off into a mildly feverish sleep, and yet it would be wise to keep everything on a clearly business footing if the two of them were to continue in business together.

CHAPTER NINE

New York Daytime

'Willard, for heaven's sakes, what you doin' here?'

The ringing, confident voice surprised the muted bustle of New York's Dubose Hotel entrance lobby. Even the bellhop lowered his tone here in the plushly carpeted domain of the reception clerk. Elsie Maare had no such inhibitions.

'Ain't seen you in a whiles,' she continued breezily.

Willard Stone, having completed the formalities of the check-in desk, turned toward the imperious young woman bearing down on him with outspread arms.

'And what brings you to New York, Elsie?'

He had the advantage of her. There were few places in the great city that took colored folk and the modest but comfortable Dubose, on 27th Street, between 6th and 7th, was one of the more popular; Willard had just been told he was lucky to find a room since the place was nearly booked out with delegates in town for the inaugural sessions of the National Association of Colored Women. Moreover, the growing reputation of Elsie Maare in the movement for black women's rights had filtered down even to Johnstoneville. So Willard was not particularly surprised to encounter Elsie here. He was, however, taken rather off balance by the warmth of her welcoming embrace. A hand on each shoulder, she held him away from her as if for inspection, her eyes dancing with pleasure and amusement.

'Gettin' on for six years, ain't it? And we hardly parted best friends did we? Now, boy, I got business down at The Richard Allen Center, down by Madison Square, not more than five minutes' walk from here, and that should just give us time to start and catch up on old times. Then this afternoon you can give me a real nice luncheon. You look rich enough and it's so long since we met.'

This was a far cry from the bitter atmosphere of their last encounter and a bit forward for "a nice young lady". But Elsie had always been much more than a nice young lady and Willard, who had recently decided it was time for a family firm worth the name to acquire a wife, did not argue. However, while six years in the business world had taught him many hard lessons, not one had led him to second guess his decision in the Porter case. If Elsie thought she could sweet talk him round after all this time, she would have to think again. In fact, with some three years still to run on the patent, he was in New York to get the best legal advice as to whether anything could be done to extend his exclusive use of the invention. However, he had no objection to a walk: indeed he still cherished a soft spot in his heart for the woman who, arm linked in his, was now steering him out onto the jostling, sun-drenched sidewalk.

'Your doin', Elsie, not mine,' he said. 'Your doin', not mine, we ain't met for six years. But how's life been working out with you? Lovely as ever but something seems to have changed.'

The tall, elegant figure, in its tight-waisted, full-skirted, ankle-length dress set off by matching auburn-red hat, was taut with energy and with an air of mature authority. In the black women's movement, Elsie was generally tipped to become one of four regional fundraisers for the new organization. It was recognition of her success after six years as senior class leader and as campaigner. And she meant to go farther yet.

'Some things certainly have changed since those distant days in Johnstoneville,' she smiled quickly. 'For one, I've learnt a thing or two about the ways of the world and I've come to understand, Willard, that if you didn't treat Daniel Porter as a friend, you did treat him like a businessman would and, Willard dear, a businessman is certainly what you are!'

The two walked amicably along down 6th Avenue, reminiscing about the good times and by tacit consent skirting round the bad. At the Masonic Temple on W 23rd, they took a left and walked the block to the three-way junction with 5th Avenue and Broadway. Private carriages, one-horse cabs, commercial drays and here and there a smartly-turned-out horseman congested the thoroughfares skirting the railings of Madison Square Gardens. 'A lovely park for those as can get in,' commented Elsie. As they paused by the National Academy of Design at the corner of 23rd and 4th, she pointed up the avenue at the vista of fine houses and great mansions, entirely free of the garbage cans and piles of rubbish that garnished most other properties in New York, thanks to the original city planners' failure to allow for back entrances. 'Rich man's country!' she said tartly, 'They can pay for private garbage collection and need I tell you who provides the labor?'

Suddenly, Willard felt dirty, ashamed and out of place. Who was he to walk tall down a city street, in a fine suit and an immaculate brown Derby hat. Who was he to be making a mental note to explore the exhibits in the academy of design? Who was he to claim the normal freedoms of a citizen? Instead, he should be leading the dray horse, he should be tipping trash cans into the garbage wagon along with a team of black brothers; sweating for a pittance to clean up after whitey. By what right did he, Willard Stone, a black man with half a white man's name, live like a human being? Who was he to shake free of the chains of three centuries when, daily, thousands of his soul brothers drudged in slavery's shadowy after-world?

For an extraordinary, seemingly endless, moment, the sensation of guilt was intense, terrifying and implacable. His body seemed to be cowering within his clothes. He began to sweat. He began to shiver. He began to fear…

'Shit! Damnation! And hellfire!'

The stupid, angry words broke unbidden in a slow growl, like the boiling fury of a volcanic lava outflow. Immediately he felt a surge of empowering anger welling up. Welling up as though from depths beyond his own being. His whole body was shaking as if in a fever. The passionate anger for himself and for his oppressed people swelled. He too would do battle with the world of white in solidarity with the black race. Yet even in the heat of emotion, so powerful were the social conventions that Willard saw thankfully that his outburst had passed unnoticed by his companion. Elsie, happy and unaware of her friend's trouble, had moved on and was examining a notice of forthcoming events at the academy.

Thus did Willard Stone stand isolated, virtually unobserved, on the thronging sidewalk of the metropolis. The urgent stream of pedestrians noted the quivering, and no doubt contagious, black only to part either side of him like a shoal of jolly boats and fishing sloops giving a wide berth to a dangerous rock. After an eternity of seconds, Willard felt his old self returning. It shook him angrily at displaying, even acknowledging, such emotions. Instinctively it felt threatened by any sense of solidarity with the black condition. Since the declaration of emancipation of 1863 he, like every other colored person, had been a full citizen of "These Expanding United States of America" and entitled by the founding fathers to follow and enjoy the provisions of the Constitution. And he, Willard Stone, would make himself a power in the land no matter how much his fellows were held back. If company success was seen as a vindication of color against white, so be it: if not, not. Grimly amused that his memory had fished up Harmann Tengdahl's slogan, and invigorated by the knowledge that he and "the Viking" had already quadrupled the turnover of S.K.L., he shook himself. The fit was past. 'Hi there!' he called and hurried up to join Elsie.

Together they crossed the road to the Y.M.C.A. building opposite, headed down for 21st Street, took another left and finally reached their destination.

'Five minutes from the Dubose, huh?' commented Willard with a grin.

'Do you good,' came the amused retort. 'I saw you take that breather back on the corner of W 23rd. You outa condition, young Master Stone. Grunting like a grampus you were.' Again Willard grinned but said nothing and turned his attention to the building they were about to enter.

The Richard Allen Center, named for the founder of the African Methodist Episcopal Church, turned out to be a neat, copper-plate name board slotted into the postings panel of a medium sized apartment block, whose first three stories were given over to office accommodations. The board immediately above it announced A.M.E. Church Class meeting room, 3rd Floor. Elsie pushed open the street door and they were met with the musty, dusty smell of iron stair banisters, old wood polish and the background presence of piled-high paperwork common to such places.

'New York has seven A.M.E.s with regular churches and paid-up ministers and you'd 've thought one of them could have given us house room, now wouldn't you?' said Elsie. 'But some of the reverends aren't so enthusiastic for women to break out of the kitchen, and two of 'em have have suspicions that sister Mary Church Terrell is researching a project on the history of the black churches and the ministry since the end of slavery. I'm sorry to have to say that Jo'ville's Reverend Walcott is not a model followed by all of them. There are some real bad brothers out there and the churches are getting mighty worried about what such a report might reveal.'

While speaking, Elsie had been riffling through the letters

posted in the meeting room's mail slot. Selecting three items apparently addressed to her, she turned to Willard, one foot already on the stairs.

'In fact I'm involved in such a project and I can tell you it'd be dynamite if they published some of the answers I've been gettin'.' She brandished the letters. 'Now Willard, you coming up to say howdee to the folks, or shall we fix our evening rendezvous right here and now?'

Willard, with an hour still to go before the meeting with his lawyer, suggested a fairly late lunch hour and named a restaurant in William Street, not too far from the law firm and near to the original site of Delmonico's. 'Similar in quality but not in price,' Harmann had told him, 'and surprisingly friendly to colored clients.' With a swish of skirts, Elsie pattered up the stairs and Willard pulled a folded paper from an inside pocket. It was a list of addresses of New York's black churches, among them the seven A.M.E.'s Elsie had spoken about. It had been his first request to the desk clerk on arriving at the Dubose off the overnight "Chieftain" that morning. On his first visit to any city he checked as far as time would allow on the lighting arrangements of the faithful. An hour was time enough to tick off one address on his list. He might come up with something unexpected, something to please Elsie. With a feeling of the joy of life quite rare with him, he swung out into the sunshine to do battle with the first cab driver to object to a colored fare.

Arriving a little early for his lunch date, Willard found himself shown to a table in one of the private alcoves, much in demand of an evening but generally shunned at lunchtime when diners liked to see and be seen doing business, or passing the time of day in the better known hostelries. He shrugged off the obvious slight, thankful for small mercies, and left word with the maître d' to expect a lady asking for a Mr Stone. The man was civil if cold. The cut and quality of his customer's clothes clearly spoke of money and, after all, the place did not follow the color line.

A glance at the menu confirmed Harmann's judgment on the food, if the chef could do what he claimed, just as the correct behavior of the waiter backed his comment as to its "social policy". Willard gave himself up to thoughts on his morning's work and his plans for the coming meeting with Elsie. The first was quickly disposed of. The lawyer had confirmed his fears. Nothing could be done to keep the patent after 1899. As to the little church he had dropped in on, if it was typical of New York, the market was going to be a hard nut to crack. The lamp fittings were good quality and the supplier clearly looked after his customers. Willard had the information from a young and very pretty deaconess, whose exact standing with the minister might merit a footnote in Elsie's black book.

As to Elsie herself, his mind was made up to raise the question of marriage with her. He realized that he had never really got her out of his mind and the unexpected meeting today was forcing the issue. A true businessman, as she had said, Willard hated risks that he could not calculate. But the more he thought it over, the more sure he was of his ground. She had admitted a change of attitude. She was clearly more sensible about business now and she too seemed to have kept a place in her heart for her childhood sweetheart. As she sailed through the sea of tables, turning every male head in the room, he rose to greet her, confident that if not this afternoon then after a suitable period of maidenly consideration, he would receive the hoped for "yes".

As she glanced through the menu, Willard suggested that in the evening they should meet again at the hotel, where he supposed she was staying, take in a show and then perhaps share a nightcap in the hotel's bar. He had no thoughts of anything further than that. He did not see Elsie as that kind of woman. Indeed he hoped she wasn't. That was no kind of wife for a respectable man.

'No no, Willard. Nice idea, but I've got work to do tonight. I'm expecting to be called on to speak at the assembly tomorrow and I want to prepare my thoughts and re-read some of the notes I made on that great speech *The Progress of Colored Women* by Mary Church, now, sadly, Mary Terrell.'

Noting Willard's surprise, she went on, 'No! I'm not stayin' at the Dubose. Nice enough hotel, don't get me wrong, but not the kind of area after dark for a young girl. No, I'm stayin with the Hardings, a respectable family worth a hundred thousand dollars I'd say, with a comfortable house out Brooklyn way. There's a few coloreds that way well set up like them and can boast a free ancestry back a half dozen generations. And,' she smiled, 'they're already getting the electricity laid in, I'm afraid!'

'But you ain't a young girl any longer, Elsie Marre, well not what I take to mean by "young".' He saw how clumsy it was to talk to a woman like this but he was genuinely astonished by what she had said. Whatever else could be said about her, the Maare girl had never been known as a shrinking violet back in Johnstoneville. 'How come you's worried about the "area"?'

Elsie looked back at him blank for a moment and then burst into a roar of laughter.

'Not me, Willard, not me. I've brought a young friend along to learn something of the movement. Judith Lear's kid sister, Sarah – perhaps you remember her. I'm sure you remember Judith; sweet on her, weren't you?' She grinned mockingly.

At this point the waiter arrived with the first course and Willard hid his embarrassment with an elaborate show of consulting her over the seasoning of the dish. But Elsie was not to be deflected and wickedly kept to the subject.

'Perhaps, though, you ought to meet her sister. Judith got married a-whiles back, but Sarah... Now Sarah's a lovely young girl likely to do as she's told. Make a fine wife in a few years, Willard!' Her serious mood returned as quickly as it had lifted. 'But you're wondering why I should bring a young person along to the assembly. Well, to tell the truth, I believe in catching 'em young! Mary Terrell is an inspiration and this association she's a-minded to set up will do a power of good for colored women. Young Sarah's as bright as she's pretty and she could make a campaigner for the cause to be proud of. Excellent fish this by the way. I congratulate you on your choice of restaurant.'

For a time the two ate in silence: Willard mulling over what he had heard; Elsie thinking how single-minded Willard seemed to have become and wondering whether he ever would get married.

'What brought you into the movement, Elsie?'

Willard was feeling that for all her flippancy and independence of mind, this was a woman a man could be proud to make his wife and he had decided that if the question was to be put, it should be put today. Marriage, like any other move in a businessman's life, needed planning and there were only so many minutes in a day. But before he committed himself beyond recall, he wanted to make a few further soundings on the subject of the new Elsie Maare.

'Didn't you have ideas for journalism once?'

'Sure I did. Still do! But Mary Church's example showed me the way there. I met her at college when Judith and I were trying to launch our own journal. Mary Church showed us a few tricks and then I went into her class for German. Got to know her real well and it turned out she and I had a lot of background in common. Seems her father was a white riverboat captain based on Memphis.'

'Wait a moment. Something's coming back to me.' Willard had seen the waiter advancing with the sweet course and had no wish for Elsie to develop her present theme in the presence of a third party. When they had made their selection and the man had left, Willard continued.

'Hold it right there. Don' I remember somethin' in the Jo'ville gossip about river water running through the Maare house?'

'So that's the way they put it, eh!' Elsie gave a thin smile. 'Well, they was about right at that. When she was hardly but a girl, Grandma Beth was "favored" by a skipper on the Louisville waterfront, she told me when she was a very old woman. I never could think of it as anything other than a shameful rape. But it seems she loved this white man... and he may have loved her in his way. The important thing was that "Jo Boy" Maare loved Gran'ma Beth so much he took on her little love chil', Henry, when they married. An' Henry Maare, of course, became my father. Wonderful man– only hope I'll live up to them.'

'And your mother, Elsie, and your mother. Don' you want her to be proud of you?' Willard remembered how close the two had been and he always supposed a girl would want to match her mother.

'Oh Ma!' The sparkle came back to the eyes, which had clouded over seriously for a moment. 'She still the same as ever, ain't she? Came up to see me last year when I was teaching high school in Washington D.C. Saw everythin' there was to see, I reckon, and never once stopped talking excep' to laugh!'

The talk ambled on, hither and thither. The table was cleared, the coffee ordered and brought. The afternoon was advancing and the tables in the main dining room were beginning to empty one by one. The time was hardly ideal but Willard had set a schedule and meant to fill it. He cleared his throat and, catching a moment where Elsie had paused to marshal her thoughts in mid-anecdote, broke in crassly.

'Now see here, Elsie. It sure is nice to converse over old times like this, an' you mus' know how real pleased I am to see

153

you again. But there's somethin' more to say, for I find you've been takin' more room in my heart than' I rightly reckoned on.' He stumbled, embarrassed and surprised himself to find that what he was saying really was the truth. 'More than I even thought of until today, truth to tell. I know you've got big plans for the next year or two. But what I want to say is this. When the time comes to settle down I'd be real honored if you chose my home.' He cleared his throat in an absurdly businesslike manner that even he saw was out of place. But there was no help for it so he pressed on.

'Miss Elsie Maare, I haven't as yet had time to ask your mother's permission for what I'm about to say but, if she have no objections… an' I don't see why she should have objections, certainly I'm as good as the next man, better than many when it comes to giving you a future… ' This was getting ridiculous, she knew what he was meaning to say and why should he apologize.

'Elsie, will you marry me?'

'That's mighty civil of you, Willard.'

The dancing eyes quietened to a serious, companionable gaze. She was touched and not a little flattered. Six years back he had left her with a petulant contempt that the mature man must look back on with embarrassment. For no doubt Willard, just twenty-six to her twenty-eight years, had matured impressively. It was no insult for a man like this to ask one to share his life. Elsie was well aware of the impact made by her fine figure and the classic African beauty of her features, 'the face of a Benin queen,' DuBois had murmured reverentially.

But she also knew that this other Will, leaning across the coffee cups as their waiter rather officiously busied himself with laying the evening's place settings two tables away, would be looking for more than beauty in a wife. A businessman before all else, he clearly saw those qualities that he most prized in herself: intelligence and determination. And, too, no doubt, he, like her, still felt something of the childhood love that had garlanded their lives in those far-off Jo'ville days. But there was a raft of reasons why they could never wed. Most important of all was the realization of six years back that a black who could flout, as Willard had done, the ideals of solidarity which guided her life could never be for her.

'It couldn't be, Willard, my dear. Too much is happening in the movement for me to pull out now.'

With a look that sent the waiter scurrying from the dining room with a nervous bob of the head, Willard frowned in concentration. He'd heard talk of "the New Woman" but mostly in the anecdotes of the vaudeville stage. It was obvious that, despite their old quarrel, Elsie still felt something for him as he did for her. He knew that "the movement", as she called it, was, at the moment, the center of her life. He supposed he would have to resign himself to a few years for her to get it out of her system. He could agree to such an unconventional lifestyle if she agreed to mother their children, essentially their son. Plenty of white society women barely saw their children and he had the money to pay for the best quality domestic staff. In five or six years of course, when S.K.L. was a power to be reckoned with and its chairman among the top figures in black society, she would take her share in the company decision-making as well as in the running of the New York mansion. That was in the future. Now he needed a wife; as soon as may be a son; and then just the assurance that the mother was a suitable candidate for chairman's consort. He explained his thinking and put the question a second time.

'Willard, no. There is no way to combine a girl's career with the conventions of wifehood, even wife to a tycoon who values her opinion. Oh, I know girls ain't supposed to have careers. But, you may laugh, my life is for the cause and nothing, but nothing, must get in the way. You know my respect for Mary Church. But since her marriage to Robert Terrell she's been finding "reasons of policy" to guard her tongue.'

For a moment, Elsie's brow puckered in irritation as she recalled Mary's last mealy mouthed "humorous critique" of Jim Crow legislatures. Merciless criticism and condemnation not "critiques", whatever they might be, was what was needed.

'Sure, Robert's a clever man. A Harvard Law graduate, no less and he aims to become the first black on Washington D.C.'s municipal court. That's some honor for a nigger. But that nigger, whomsoever he may be, had better be Uncle Tom in nature if not in name, with a deaf mute as his ideal wife. No, Willard. Me as Mrs Willard would not work out. How can a businessman have a wife who believes in equal opportunities for women?'

'But Elsie, you'll grow out of that kind of thing. You'll come to see the importance of helping shape America's first major Negro corporation. You'll become a businesswoman to outshine all the men.'

'Willard Stone!' The eyes were blazing and the old scar from the Mammoth Cave adventure had turned the ugly gray that marked her rare outbursts of anger. 'I trust I'll never "grow out" of my convictions. As to becoming a businesswoman, that is something I would not wish on my worst enemy. Your dealin' with Dan Porter shows what bein' a businessman made of you. Such a man as that can never share my life. Today, I flattered myself the cause would be better off by a handsome donation from S.K.L. thanks to my charm and sophistication and the good nature of an ol' friend. Well, I guess I've blown that, but if the cause has lost a cheque, I've still got my self-respect.'

With an imperious gesture she swept back her chair. In the same movement, she turned on her heel and stormed out through the hushed restaurant. Such was the danger of her rage that not a single voice broke the silence.

CHAPTER TEN

New York Nineties Nightlife

Willard felt flat. Ten o'clock on a bright night in New York; the lunchtime company of a beautiful woman; respectful looks from the local big men on her account and him "only a Kentucky hick"; the knowledge that he could buy out the lot without giving it a thought; a swaggering cigar and evening champagne at the hotel bar, with the lady delegates of this association-to-be fluttering at him like moths. But nothing could alter the fact. He felt like a boy from the Jo'ville Quarters who'd lost his only penny the day Johnstone's announced a new range of candy

Elsie, wearing her Mammoth Cave scar like a battle honor, had fought him to a standstill over the old terrain of the Porter patent. She had shown feelings of generous sympathy as remote for him as the days of childhood, when the two of them would watch from the Johnstone parlor window as ragamuffins came wistfully up to stare at the sugar cookies in the store. Elsie, who always refused the nickels and dimes proffered by Willard, had, perversely, always wanted to give the barefoot boys something from her own modest coffers. Willard, who even then only gave when he could see the possibility of a return, had restrained her spontaneous generosity.

Twenty years older and his only feeling was that he had

been cheated by her refusal of marriage. True, there was no shortage of girls to fill the role. But Elsie had been marked in the plan and now the sugar cookie jar had been finally locked away. He decided he needed a diversion. He went on a bender once or twice a year, as much to keep in touch with the world of his colleagues and rivals as for any pleasure he derived. Tonight seemed a proper occasion.

* * * * *

It was about half past midnight. He was on the town with James "call-me-Hartley" Dixon, encountered at one bar and now leading him to the next. A good-natured, barrel-chested figure of a man, husband of one of the lady delegates, he had attached himself to Willard in the hotel lobby at the hotel bar. 'Thought I'd take the young hick under my wing,' would be his explanation. 'Any excuse for a night on the booze,' would be his wife's comment.

Used only to the occasional heavy drinking bout, Willard was a newcomer to metropolitan nightlife. Thus, when, a few blocks west of 6th Avenue his companion dived under a red lamp and down a steep stone staircase into a basement area, he was taken unawares. Doubling back unsteadily, Willard identified his friend's upturned face and followed him down into a pool of frying smells and wavering light (provided, he noted, by a couple of very cheap oil lamps).

'Don't worry, don't worry,' his companion reassured an imminently bilious Willard. 'It's a chop suey restaurant. Ask anybody – Chinese chop suey mops up alcohol like Sherman mopped up in Georgia.' The guffaw died on the man's lips. Like most Southern blacks, Willard was grateful to Sherman's army for the decisive part his Georgia campaign had played in the Civil War. But, although a black, he did not care to dwell on the bloodthirsty mayhem by which it had been accomplished. Still, he followed advice to take a large bowl of chop suey and noodles and found that, by some absorbent magic, it certainly cleared the head.

So with heads clear and stomachs settled, the two revelers went up to the first floor of the building, bent on their constitutional right and duty to pursue happiness. They were in luck. Passing through a small vestibule, they entered a reception hallway, beyond which could be heard the mingled sounds of music and laughter, the clink of glasses and the pop of "wine" corks (by common convention, Willard was to discover, among the faster segment of New York's black club set, "wine" meant only champagne). Heedless of the beer-with-whiskey chasers already lapping against his stomach wall, he followed fashion and downed his first quick champagne before holding out his glass for a refill to be taken at greater leisure.

The room in which he found himself was a long first floor saloon, approached from the street by a flight of stone steps under a covered stoop or, from the basement restaurant, the internal stairs used by himself and his companion. Some eight feet above the sidewalk the shuttered windows had presented a gloomy aspect to the street. Within, everything was adazzle. Drop crystal chandelier lamps and conventional, if immense, hanging lamps hung down the center of the ceiling. Along the walls, centered between the long window casements and between cheval mirrors on the wall opposite, wall-bracket electric lamps proclaimed by their garish light the ambition of the proprietors of the "Club" to keep abreast of the latest trends by all possible means.

Festooned, or so it seemed, in scarf pins, diamond finger rings and cabochon stick pins in their flowing cravats, the male clientele seemed determined to outshine the women they were escorting. The settlement of the smallest drinks bill called for a flourish of bank rolls that would have impressed a Rockefeller, while more than one waiter could be seen plowing between the tables with a high denomination bill poking precariously from a waistcoat pocket, where it had been thrust by some generous patron. Willard saw that none of the staff were anxious as to the safety of this largesse. He himself would never make such donations to the help but, equally, he could see how impressive it could appear to a certain type of person, presumably female, if one did so.

'Excuse me, Sir.' His musings were interrupted by one of these very waiters, simpering expectantly as he proffered a tall glass of champagne. 'The lady hopes you will be pleased to drink her health.' The bobbing head bobbed more emphatically towards a table fenced in behind a curving rail on a little scalloped dais opposite Willard's table. He glanced across, blinked with surprise and looked again. The only lady seated at the table indicated was a startlingly beautiful redhead, in her early thirties he calculated, with lustrous gray eyes and very white skin. At the table next to her was a large party of white socialites. Such fashionable tourists were a familiar sight at the top nightclubs in New York's colored quarter.

But the woman who was sending Willard this, exceptionally good, glass of champagne was clearly different. The only other person at her table was a handsome young black man in his late twenties. Short, and slightly built, he was wearing evening dress in the height of fashion and on the middle finger of his left hand a heavy gold ring set with a single diamond of great size. At the moment he was leaning forward and subjecting Willard to intense and hostile scrutiny.

'Uh, huh!' slurred Hartley. 'Looks like "the Dowager" is out recruiting.' Strong as an ox, and more intelligent than he looked, Hartley was, unfortunately for him, weak in the head in the one faculty he valued most. Such is the injustice of life that Willard, for whom drink was little more than an occasional business necessity, had an impressive tolerance of alcohol. Hartley hadn't.

Raising his glass with a bow of the head in the direction of the lady, Willard noticed a disturbance at the table next to hers. One of the diners was pushing back his chair and glaring across the dance floor at the polite Negro stranger with raised glass. The man's companions held him back and were obviously arguing with him. 'Remember it's his home territory, Jack. God knows what these people do when they own the place.' The youngest of the women was pleading in almost hysterical tones with the choleric, but elegant, Jack. Older than the rest of the party and, from his voice, a "Southern gentleman", he subsided, protesting, into his chair. Nevertheless, in the sudden hush of the room his comments could be clearly heard.

'Who the darn does that nigger think he is, *bowing* to a white woman, just as if he thought he was her equal!'

The young man-about-town hosting the party turned languidly to him.

'You really shouldn't go "slumming" in the first place, Major, if you aren't prepared to encounter from time to time what you no doubt consider "slummy behavior". The "Dowager" can certainly look after herself.'

'Ah came under protest,' retorted the Major, glowering accusingly at the young woman at his side. 'That kind of behavior would be a lynching offence where ah come from.' With a final stare in Willard's direction, he pointedly turned his chair on the redhead. Throughout the exchange, she had continued to gaze calmly across at Willard with the flicker of a smile on her beautiful lips.

Willard, who generally prided himself as a man of the world, felt distinctly out of his depth.

'The Dowager?' he questioned Hartley.

'Okay, she says she just a simple widow, but she have the sort of a name that has to be some kind of old world European aristo, so some classy dude thought up "Dowager" – "dowager duchess", you get the idea? Sure, sure,' Hartley hurried on, seeing Willard's raised eyebrows, 'Wha's a lady duchess or some such doing drinking in a joint like this? Tha's wha' we all wanna know. Bu' she always have some hansum yung nigra boy with her. "Tap" Dawson tonight. She dress 'im real well bu' it don' laas', an' she always lookin' out for new escorts... spear carriers. "Reeecrutin'" I calls it and yoh better look real careful if you' thinkin' of enlistin'.'

Hartley's advance through a night's drinking was marked by the progressive collapse of his powers of speech. This lengthy oration had evidently overtaxed those powers so that now he slumped forwards, head on arms, planning to recover himself after a brief rest, but falling at once into a noisy sleep.

Finding himself deprived of company, Willard pondered what to do. He had no mind to play gigolo to the Dowager. She was beautiful indeed. But temptation always was. And for him, any distraction from business was temptation. True, with the lawyer's meeting behind him he did not have a particularly heavy program ahead of him. But a rich and libidinous white woman was no part of such a program. He had no need of her money and no liking for her color. Color-blind in matters of business, willing to chisel or cheat both black and white when it came to a profit, Willard had his code. And according to that code, sexual congress with a white woman demeaned a man of his race.

However, she had definitely issued an intriguing challenge with that champagne. Moreover, Major Jack needed a lesson. Willard called over a waiter, tipping him handsomely to see that Hartley came to no harm. Then he drained the glass, set it on his table and, having instructed the waiter to take a bottle of the house finest over to the lady's table, crossed the floor to join her.

'You don't trouble yourself over much with the conventions of racial discrimination, do you Mr... ?' The rising intonation of her voice asked the question and signaled him to take a seat.

As he did so, she glanced mischievously towards the eloquent back at the next table.

'Johnstone, Mr Willard Johnstone…' he replied, 'and I could say the same about you I should think.'

Dora Baroney Marlowe broke into a startling burst of laughter, like a shrapnel bomb that had the Major on his feet on the instant. Still with his back to the woman who was the actual cause of his anger, behaving indeed as if she did not exist, he snapped to attention like the Confederate Army officer he once had been and, his entire frame shaking with fury, he delivered an ultimatum to his host.

'Theodore, ah'm in New York strictly on business. Ah appreciate the deal your father has offered. Indeed ah hope that we may still close upon it. But if the loss of that deal is the price for leaving your table this instant, ah shall gladly pay it. Ah cannot for a moment longer assist at the degenerate conduct which prevails at what you are pleased to call your "Club".'

He spat the word out contemptuously.

'That is your right, Major. I'm sure Father will not hold anything you may do here against you. His own views don't entirely square with mine on these matters. But I must ask you to restrain your language among people whom I consider my friends and whose friendship I do not wish to lose.'

Without more ado, the Major stormed towards the door, followed by the young woman and a fluttering of comment and gestures from the rest of the room. Before his angry guest had reached the door, the man called Theodore summoned a waiter and said clearly for all to hear. 'My compliments to the management, and could you perhaps bring me and my party another bottle of this excellent "wine".' The whole room got the nuance of the use of the word and Theodore was, for himself, still in favor. However, it was noticed that he made no move of apology for his guest's outburst to the beautiful redhead or her party at the adjacent table.

'There's a touch of the Southern gentleman about young Theodore himself it would seem,' observed Dora. 'There is a very distinct code among certain society types on these "slumming expeditions" of theirs. Very much a matter of separate tables, you know. What I like to call spectator not participation events, if you follow my meaning. ' She smiled conspiratorially at Willard. 'I think, perhaps, the atmosphere might be more congenial in the next room, don't you?'

Wooden-faced, Willard responded with a noncommittal grunt. Like Theodore and the Major, his preference was towards a separation of the races. That way everyone knew where they were. He seemed to be being drawn into a liaison he wanted no part of and did not at all like the way things were developing. He had been a fool to come over. But he would look a greater fool if he bashfully withdrew at this point. He followed on into the room where, thanks to Tap's having a word with the management, they were all ushered to a table close to the buffet near the center of the room.

Willard found himself in a carpeted parlour, furnished with elegant little wrought iron tables and chairs and lace curtains at the windows. This, the club's inner sanctum, was a shrine to black American achievement. Anyone who had "done anything" seemed to be there, from Frederick Douglass, the author of *The Narrative Life of Frederick Douglass, an American Slave Written By Himself*, to the current star of the prize fighting ring and the latest song and dance team. With a mild frisson of interest, Willard noticed they were at this moment providing the evening's entertainment on the dais that served as cabaret stage.

Dora pointed to the Douglass portrait, with its shock of hair, its intent, frowning eyes, its firm set mouth and fashionably trimmed whiskers.

'A handsome man, wasn't he? Died only three years back.' She paused. 'Of course, you know, the real shocker about that book was the title.'

'How so?' pouted Tap Dawson. He was distinctly bored with the proceedings. His tenure as the Dowager's escort was barely three months old. On average, his predecessors had lasted a six-month before being expected to share the considerable fringe benefits conferred by the position with a rival. Why she had taken a sudden fancy to this sour-faced Southern hick he could not begin to guess. He had no time for literary debate.

'Because, dear Tap, no white American likes the ring of the words "American slave". Like Britons they think they "never, never will be slaves", point one. Point two, by that book title our black hero Mr Douglass was claiming outright to be an American. And the idea that Negroes are true Americans is still unacceptable in our white hearts, even liberal white hearts. And when are you going to have your picture on the wall, Willard?' Dora turned her attention with a flash of a smile. 'Tap here reckons he should be up already for his dancing. What's your specialty?'

'Like Major Jack,' replied Willard with an uncharacteristic attempt at humor, ' my specialty is business.'

'And you're not the only businessman here tonight,' Tap sneered, indicating with a wave of his arm a group of whites sitting at a table near the little stage. Glancing across at the table, Willard dimly realized that there was something rather odd about the set up. The five men ranged in age from the mid-twenties up, the oldest being nearer fifty than forty and the least smartly dressed of the group. The others were snappy and modish in the style of their garments but none of them had the kind of quality on their back he had seen at Theodore's party. A bottle of what, as a Kentuckian he could see, was cheap bourbon, stood at the center of the table. The drinking was steady and serious. Now and again, the oldest member of the party jotted something on the starched expanse of shirt cuff protruding from the too short sleeve of his evening swallow-tailed coat, as though taking notes on the performance. His companions were equally intent and their reactions to the entertainers' sallies, while as quick as any, lacked the element of jovial delight of the other members of the audience.

'Take a good look, Mr Stone,' Tap spat the words out venomously. 'White as ghosts aren't they. But back in white man's territory they black up minstrel style. "Darky character acts" they call themselves,' he sneered. 'Not actors, not artists, no sir! Them thah gentry are *character* acts,' he laid sarcastic stress on the word. 'Items ready made and offered for sale to white show managers to fit into any program slot those managers happen to have vacant. You'll find two or more here most evenings, coming to get their imitations first-hand from the real artists, the entertainers at The Club. The white clubs call them "variety performers". I call them businessmen.'

'There, there, Tap,' the Dowager was suddenly genuinely concerned for her young lover. 'There's no one can match you at the taps. Tap here, is the champion of the tap dance in New York and I dare say anywhere in the Eastern States. But now there's a group of white men learning the steps and putting shows on at Reisenweber's I think, or is it some other such smart restaurant, claiming to be "original Dixieland Tap Men" and earning the kind of money a black can never hope to see, simply by imitating black men's dance.'

Willard offered a noncommittal grunt which could perhaps be construed as sympathy. In fact he said: 'It don't seem Tap here has much time for businessmen whether white or black. But we're the ones that make the world go round.'

'Now there you're wrong, Mister,' came the rapid response. 'Don't you know, it's love that makes the world go round?'

'Hey there, hey there, you two,' the Dowager intervened with a quick laugh. 'No wrangling. I aim to enjoy myself when I go out on the town, not fight with friends. What do you think, Willard? Tell me what business you're into and what you're doing up here from the South.' She gave him a radiant smile and closed a hand over his.

'Now you watch it, Dora, I don't aim to be no patsy,' said Tap.

He turned on Willard.

'And you watch it, Mister Willard Stone, this ain't no territory of yours, JUST YOU KEEP OFF THE GRASS.' And to emphasize the point, he thumped the table at each drunken word.

The Dowager raised her voice slightly above the hubbub of the room.

'Tap Dawson, your behavior is tedious. If you intend to continue drinking this evening, please find somewhere else to do it.'

'B-b-but,' he choked incoherently on his words, 'you cain't...'

She waved a dismissive hand and turned toward Willard. A waiter had materialized at her elbow. His face was blank of expression, his attitude was deferential, and his size was immense.

'Causin' you trouble, lady?'

She said nothing, merely raised an eyebrow enquiringly in Willard's direction. He, also without a word, glanced at the waiter with a short tilt of his chin. The latter signaled to a colleague, equally tall, and the two, each gripping an elbow, raised the little man bodily out of his chair. 'Not a word, Tap!' whispered the first waiter while the other expertly flicked the chair out of the way with his free hand. 'Not a word!' And with that the two of them, still supporting their victim by his elbows, carried him, his shoes just clear of the floor, toward the swing doors leading to the kitchen from which he would be ejected in due course.

'So, my dear,' she caressed his hand more strongly than before and leant forward, 'would you care to show me home

167

when we have finished your excellent champagne?' Leaning over still further so as to expose the full cleavage of her breasts, she gently clinked her glass against his where it stood, almost full, in front of him. A saint would have been under trial and Willard was not a saint. He drained his glass and then refilled them both.

A little later, the bill settled, he allowed himself to be led down the stairs to street level, where the doorman had called up the private carriage from its waiting place down a side street. 'So much more satisfactory than a public cab,' observed the Dowager, and the coachman had barely pulled away when she drew down the blinds and smothered Willard with her body.

Fumblingly, she opened her bodice and brought his hand up to her right breast and awkwardly crushed against him. Her mouth against his, she gently teased his lips into opening with flickering caresses of her tongue. It thrust into his mouth. His member pulsed in his groin, pressing hard and big beneath layers of clothing against her belly. Unable to help himself, he began gently at first and then with ever firmer motions to knead the sweet soft flesh of her breast. What with the clatter of horses hooves and the rattle of iron tires on cobblestones, nothing could be heard of their encounter outside of the carriage compartment. But now, with an almost harsh moan of pleasure, Dora pulled back sufficiently to ease her hand down to find the ridge of his member, hard beneath his trouser front, and with a rhythmic grunting redoubled her attack. Willard, who knew nothing of the concept of woman rape on man, felt himself humiliated by the assault. Rather than climax in this squalid embrace, he pushed the woman away from him roughly, so that she slithered ungainly to the floor of the carriage.

'You make me ashamed of myself,' he growled, and hauled her unceremoniously back onto the seat beside him, before swinging himself onto the other seat so that they faced one another.

'Are not you ashamed? Have your coachman stop and let me get down.'

Hair disheveled, bosom heaving and eyes ablaze, she swung herself towards him with a sweeping blow of her flat hand which came so unexpectedly that his head banged painfully against the wooden carriage wall through the pleated felt of the lining. She recovered herself sufficiently to sit back on her banquette. Fingers working at the drawstrings and buttons of her bodice, she feverishly restored herself to some degree of decency.

'No one of your race nor of mine, Mr Stone, has ever dared speak to me like that. Nor will you ever again. Carlo!' She called out with authority and rattled her silver mail-link reticule on the exposed area of the carriage wall behind her.

'Carlo!'

The vehicle pulled up short at an intersection. Willard threw back the door and jumped down onto the sidewalk. Disdaining to descend, Carlo sat bolt upright on his box, whip across his body ready to flick the horses into movement, waiting until the black passenger, more fitting in the role of footman, should close the door. But Willard, his chest heaving with anger and shame, strode off down the cross street. He heard the carriage door crashed shut behind him; Carlo had obviously clambered down from the driving box. A moment later came the skittering flurry of hooves on cobbles as Carlo, once more at the reins, angrily whipped up his team.

Willard walked at speed, his eyes checking the street numbers, his brain whirring aimlessly on business matters, his mind trying to recover its self-identity and self-respect. About the middle of a block between 6th and 7th Avenue he abandoned the struggle in favor of distraction. Ahead, on the stoop of what appeared to be a private residence, a group of young, sharply dressed black men were chaffing one another, apparently waiting for the door to open. When it did they shuffled and skipped, laughing, up the steps. Willard followed.

Just as he reached the top of the steps, the door began to swing shut. Unthinking, he advanced his foot to block the closure, exactly as the boy Willard had enforced entry to the storeroom on Main Street against a too-conscientious Dan Porter, worried about his inventory of cookies.

'You a member, Mister?'

With one mystery solved (how come so many young fellows were allowed entry to a "private" residence at this hour?), Willard had no difficulty with the remaining minor problem. After being relieved of a folded bill of rather higher denomination than he might have wished, he was obsequiously waved through via the hallway to the front parlor, which had been converted into a bar.

Arriving in time to pay for the first round of beers ordered by the party of revelers, he established himself not merely as a member but as a member in good standing. In due course he eased away from his new friends, bribed a bourbon out of the barman and walked through into the back parlor where a high-level game of billiards pool was in progress, with sizeable bets placed among the spectators as to the outcome.

By the time Willard, a few dollars ahead of the game, at last found himself once more in sight of the Tubman Hotel, it was approaching breakfast time. Coffee and waffles in a cab man's cafe seemed preferable to troubling the kitchen staff and by half past seven he was in bed, just three hours before he was due at a meeting with the African Methodist Episcopalian Church board.

The meeting did not go well. Back at the hotel, he paused before the pier mirror at the entrance to the dining room, to survey his appearance. The bags under the bloodshot eyes told their tale. No wonder the meeting had not produced business.

Next time he would prepare himself more sensibly. For he was determined there would be a next time. Throughout the turmoil of the previous night, he had been dogged by self-contempt. This morning he reaffirmed his determination to build S.K.L. to a power in US business on a par with the best. There could be no more time for the untidy excesses of last night: excesses of emotion as well as alcohol. It was clear that he needed women's company; so, he needed a wife. The one woman he had ever really cared for in his short life had definitively turned him down. It was unlikely that he would find another to combine beauty, intelligence and business acumen to equal Elsie Marre. And, on reflection, it could be unwise to have a wife with such high-powered qualities. The world of business was a world of men. Given beauty and quick wits, business expertise was perhaps superfluous to requirements. More important were a sound childbearing physique in a woman who was younger than he was and who admired him and should therefore be biddable.

As he assembled this mental specification, it dawned on Willard that the ideal candidate was actually in New York at the moment and easy to come at. He decided to track down Elsie at the conference hall and have her introduce him to Sarah Lear with due formality. Elsie would object, and Sarah would not be able to make her final commitment without parental consent. But, as Willard well knew, Lear Senior was a prosperous Louisville funeral director with a lively sense of the value of money and of the excellent prospects for S.K.L. And, in an unguarded moment, Elsie herself had told him of Sarah's feelings in the matter. His mind made up, Willard Stone acted with his usually prompt efficiency in matters of business and headed for the conference hall, where the first afternoon session would, he guessed, shortly be drawing to a close.

A surge of applause from the lecture hall was followed by a businesslike patter of leather-soled boots crescendo-ing behind the linenfold panelled doors which now burst open under a flood of skirts, hats, fluttering hands and female talk. Willard stood his ground. Somewhere behind this advancing frontline, he figured, was Elsie Marre and with her, presumably, the object of his search. In fact he was nearly brought to the ground by an eager Sarah Lear dashing towards some unseen friend and waving excitedly at the same time.

'Oh, Mr Stone, I do beg your pardon.' She halted, eyes dancing, apparently embarrassed and confused but with sufficient presence of mind, he noticed, to warn off the friend advancing towards her behind his back. It was the kind of opportunity the Willard Stones of this world do not let slip.

By the time Elsie Marre did make her way out of the hall, deep in conversation with one of Mary Terrell's lieutenants, the businessman and the delegate from Louisville, Kentucky, were taking a decorous cup of tea in a quiet little cafe adjacent to the conference hall.

Willard was explaining to Sarah that he had had the deepest interest in her ever since they had met at Johnstoneville all those years ago and that now, if she was willing, he would be honored and delighted to make her the partner in his life. She listened with long black eyelashes fluttering over high rounded cheeks, and eyes glistening with excitement. She said that of course she could not reply without the knowledge of Aunt Elsie here in New York and the approval of her father in Louisville. But, she added, she had always had the greatest admiration for Mr Stone. He apologized, as a businessman, if she should find the setting a little unromantic but begged her to believe that he was in earnest and would in due time, with her permission, seek her hand in marriage from her father. With a heaving bosom, elbows on the table, chin on her hands, face leaning towards his, she said that she gave her permission.

At this moment Elsie Marre opened the tea room door for the lieutenant, glanced up from under the wide brim of her smart black straw hat and saw the engrossed twosome in the distant alcove. She shrugged with an inner smile and the mental note – "romance by agenda… any other business?"

CHAPTER ELEVEN

The Chandler and the Mogul

"PORTER'S CHANDLERY": the name board over the shop
front was elegant but distinctly eye-catching. Willard Stone,
recently arrived in Chicago, studied the effect. Humph! Damn
the man, Daniel Porter certainly had style. The young woman
fixing a display of tackle blocks in the shop window noted the
scowl on the face of the tall, lean, handsomely dressed stranger
across the street. Harriet Church, twenty years old, part-time
kitchen staff at the Chicago Bible Institute, part-time store clerk,
part-time trainee bookkeeper at the chandlery and full-time
admirer of its proprietor, stepped down from the display
window into the body of the shop and thus missed the grim
smile that had replaced the frown as the stranger crossed over
the street.

Willard had just recalled the day he ordered Daniel off the
store premises back on Main Street, Johnstoneville. Himself
behind the counter, Daniel, canvas bag in hand with its assorted
odds and ends – personal day book, cuff protectors, mob cap
for use in the musty store room – lingering by the door, eyes like
a mournful bloodhound. Between them, solemnly situated on
the counter, "the evidence of your unreliability" as Willard had
termed it, stood the half empty bottle of tepid beer.

He congratulated himself now that he had got rid of the
fellow and the smile faded, Dan Porter clearly had reserves of

determination and would have proved a troublemaker if he'd kept him on. Now Willard was in Chicago because he wanted an agency on South Side; he had been advised that the chandlery was the obvious choice. Pity about its proprietor, but he reckoned he could handle the situation and force him out of business if necessary. With a firm shove that clashed the shop bell, America's 110th most prosperous black businessman entered the store as if he owned the place already.

More on his back than my father earned in a year, Harriet thought to herself, instinctively hostile before the newcomer spoke. For his part, Willard checked his stride as if brought up by some invisible partition dividing the shop. Give this girl a pair of eyeglasses and a scar on the forehead and she could have been Elsie Marre keeping store on Main Street fifteen years back. He shook himself, the illusion faded somewhat and he was once more able to function like a man of business.

'Is Mr Daniel Porter on the premises this morning?' he enquired.

'Who shall I say is asking for him… Sir?'

'Tell him it is Mr Willard Stone, come to talk business.'

'THE HELL IT IS!' The words exploded from the back of the shop as the glass paned door behind the counter crashed hazardously on its hinges. With his prematurely grizzled hair, the once familiar Dan looked older than his thirty-six years – he also looked dangerous.

'YOU!!'

The monosyllable yelled contempt and a declaration of combat. Willard almost staggered under the emotional charge. This was a Daniel Porter he did not know.

In fact, it was a Daniel Porter he had helped create. Had he not driven them out of Jo'ville, the Porter family would never have trekked northwards. Bess Porter's frail health would not have collapsed in the icy winter winds of Chicago and she would not have died for want of money to pay for her treatment. Hardly a day went past when Daniel did not curse these facts and with them the Stone family. And here was the author of his misery standing coolly before him.

He jerked back the counter flap and strode into the shop, seized a capstan spoke from a rack on the wall and raised it, preparing to strike. Willard fell back towards the door, calculating times and angles: first to turn the handle, next to edge round the door still facing the enemy, then to run!

'No, Mr Porter! No, Sir !'

It was a cool, firm, feminine voice. The men had forgotten Harriet. She broke the spell. Roused from the emotional coma he had been in since his wife's death, Daniel at the same time returned to his senses. Killing Stone would do no good to anyone and would finish all hope of a happy life for his six-year-old son. Carefully almost, he laid the heavy stave of wood on the counter top, from which it was promptly removed by Harriet.

Daniel looked at her with a dawning of new interest. *The girl obviously keeps her wits about her*, he thought, *soon be old enough for new responsibilities.*

'Thank you, my dear, thank you… kinda forgot myself, I guess.'

And thank you, kind sir, thought Harriet, *for a glimpse of the blindingly obvious*. But she said nothing and meekly retired into the back room as ordered by the boss, while he and Mr Stone talked business.

'And what may the business be that brings you here, Willard Stone? In need of a new invention?'

The sneer was almost dangerous; the interview did not last long. So far as Dan was concerned it had nowhere to go. Willard spelt out his expansion plans, his need for a Chicago-based agent and outlet; how his original choice had been Farmerson's Hardware but how, hearing of Dan's success, he had come straight to him and how he reckoned if they could let bygones be bygones, they could work profitably together. If not, he had little doubt that Dan would soon find conditions of trade in the neighborhood hardening against him. He smiled. Willard did not hold grudges; on the other hand, he did not take prisoners.

'So! You steal my livelihood, you drive me an' mine from our home town; you as good as kill my dear Bess, and now you come along aiming to put me out of business. Well, don't try and snow me out of South Side, *Mr* Stone. In six years I've got myself well fixed up hereabouts. Even whitey looks after Daniel Porter. 'N if you do take over Farmerson's, it'll do you no good. Like I said, I got friends in these parts.

Maybe not exactly what I call buddies, for a start they call the chandlery "a dinge joint", but they got reason to treat me with care an' sure wouldn't let any other black move in. Maybe not friends you or I would chose. But then friendship don't come into business, do it, Mr Stone?'

Dan said nothing about Boss White and his capital and nothing about his own dream of taking over Farmerson's. The only effect of Willard's bullying had been to confirm the enmity of the one man in South Side that could, perhaps, have helped him. All that was left for him was to bluster his way out of his defeat the best way he could.

'I have been in this city three weeks, Daniel Porter, and I think you will find I have not wasted my time in South Side, either. I'll be here another ten days and when I leave we will see who is having the more success.'

In fact, his stay in Chicago had so far produced some useful contracts with existing church authorities and prepared the way for what could be a valuable business coup in a new Baptist temple in this very neighborhood. But he had yet to find that vital ingredient to long-term success, a resident agent. There was only a limited number of possibilities open to a black entrepreneur and, much as he hated to admit it to himself,

Porter's chandlery had been one of the most hopeful. However, what really rankled was that he had been routed on an issue of business by Porter of all people. And behind *that* was the knowledge that Elsie Marre, should she ever get to hear of it, would be deeply satisfied.

* * * * *

The Stones' dinner that evening, in the restaurant of Chicago's stylish Tubman Hotel, was a glum meal. Sarah Stone, née Lear, and bride of three weeks, was rapidly adjusting to the idea that this might become a fairly normal state of affairs. The triumph she had felt when Willard put the question in that New York tea room had already tarnished a little. He had been as good as his word in that he had solemnly petitioned her father for her hand. Pa had been delighted at such a rich son-in-law but he had warned his daughter that she would find the man was a bigamist – being already married to his business.

But Sarah was buoyed up by winning the husband she had wanted since a girl, and the thought of honeymooning in the great city of Chicago and the cruise on Lake Michigan had brought a sparkle to her eyes that would have dazzled another man. Willard, however, left her mostly to her own devices in the hotel lounge or on occasional and modest shopping trips in company with another "business widow"; while the "cruise" turned out to be a paltry one-day outing. The fact that her shopping companion's favorite topic of conversation was the honeymoon her husband had treated them to in Jamaica made her a less sympathetic companion than Sarah could have wished for.

However, she was determined to make her marriage as happy as possible and even Willard finished the dinner on a more cheerful mood as he remembered the given reason for their stay in the windy city. There were few evenings when the exploration of Sarah's beautiful body did not work its magic. This would be the case for years to come, so the union was less of a disaster than many.

In addition to finding an agent for S.K.L., Willard's principal business was to secure heating and lighting contracts with black churches and institutions. Third on his priorities list was prospection for real estate investment. Under him, Stone's had grown dramatically. Uptown S.K.L. Stores and agencies were to be found in town after town, in Kentucky and the states to the north. The basic business was retail hardware but this was backed up by highly profitable contracts in lamps and kerosene with the local churches. It had been Willard's fortunate experience (which would not have surprised W.E.B. DuBois) that many God-fearing pastors were gratifyingly eager to welcome the stranger should he offer suitable, and discrete, inducements. It was rare that Willard Stone left town without a sheaf of new customers.

However, he was increasingly aware of the long-term threat posed by the fashionable craze for electrification. Oil lamps had a future perhaps in the poorer city quarters and country districts like the Tennessee Valley, but he reckoned oil lighting would be finished in all but a few backwaters within thirty years, if not before, and his aim was to found a great family business dynasty. Diversification was essential, if he was to establish a new financial basis for S.K.L.

Landed real estate seemed the obvious choice. As Mark Twain had recently remarked, they'd stopped making it! Not given to jokes about business, Willard Stone appreciated that one. Wherever he went, he first checked out the local real estate office. So he knew that while Farmerson's hardware store was for sale, the rest of its block was tied up in other hands. The shop itself was not a serious real estate investment. Accordingly he would offer an agency on terms no proprietor could possibly refuse and in due course undercut and finally destroy Dan Porter. Next morning he directed the driver of his day-hire cab to the offices of a leading neighborhood temple. Had he known about Tom White's offer to finance Dan's buy out of Joe Farmerson, Willard would surely have acted differently.

About the same time as Willard was being driven to the church offices, Dan Porter, his best hat jammed on his head, the store left in the competent charge of Harriet, headed with all possible speed to Farmerson's. The arrangement, which still had one week to run, was that he should have first refusal on the store. Old Joe Farmerson, a member of the same Masonic lodge as Tom White, was quite willing to sell out, effectively to the black ironmonger, on the understanding that White would front the actual purchase. He himself was retiring to the suburbs and owed White a favor or two. If the man chose to make this odd gesture of help to a black, that was his business. The price was good and all that was needed was young Porter's formal decision. That morning, he had it.

When Tom White had first suggested he expand his business, Dan had thought the idea fanciful. Now he would be damned if young Willard Stone would get the better of him in Chicago as he had back in Johnstoneville. He hardly noticed the wince in Farmerson's rheumy old eyes as they shook hands on the deal. An hour later he was raising a glass of good rye whiskey with Tom White before hurrying back to work out the details of the future. Expansion of his chandlery's business, coupled with improvements in the operation he had just acquired, would secure the repayments on the loan. And then there were possibilities to explore at a new neighborhood Baptist temple that was looking to improve its old lighting system.

Apparently the board of elders had reversed a decision for electrification in favor of updating their oil lamps and had asked for tenders. Dan was not to know that the machinations of Willard Stone lay behind this puzzling change of policy; that by dint of a promised bribe he had already secured the contract for S.K.L. and that the competitive tendering was to be a charade.

Harriet and Dan worked day and night contacting suppliers, calculating costs and, of course, keeping the chandlery open as normal. In addition to her work for Dan, Harriet, at his insistence, kept up her part-time commitment to the Bible Institute. There, too, the small staff was badly overstretched, preparing for a forthcoming visit from the founder Dr Moody. She could hardly plead work overload and expect them to welcome her back if she deserted them in their crisis. So Dan took on more of the extra work than a boss need have, so that his young protégée could keep up her contacts with the dynamic Mary Bethune, leading light of the student body. Seemingly unaware of Harriet's similarity in appearance to the young Elsie Marre, he had become both protective about her and concerned that she have the happiest and most fulfilled life possible. In short, to make no further mystery of the matter, Dan Porter, unknown to himself, was in love with the young Harriet Church.

All of which explains why Harriet was so grateful to the unlovely Willard Stone. For three and a half years, afflicted by the grim nature of his wife's death and subconscious guilt for his suppressed love of Elsie Marre, Dan had been in mourning for his wife. He had immersed himself in the routine of business. But there was no fire, no life, no enjoyment, above all no true response to the world and the people around him. Only his son, James "Shout" Owen Porter, could bring laughter back into those kind eyes. Now, in twenty brisk and acrimonious minutes, the flint of Willard Stone's ambition and hostility had struck the spark needed to rekindle Dan's attention to living; and with it the realization that the "girl" who had been working at his side over the past four years was an attractive young woman.

It was eleven o'clock on the evening before the tender was due to be handed in at the office of the Baptist temple, when the boss and his lady assistant came at last to the end of the laborious business of writing out the fair copies of the tenders for lamps, kerosene supply and general hardware materials. Dan wiped a perspiring brow.

'A typewriter machinist will be my first addition to our staff if we win this contract, Harriet!'

'But won't that be rather extravagant, Mr Porter? The contract is not that big and I'm sure you'll need to save wherever you can to fund the repayment of Mr White's loan.'

Dan looked at her appraisingly. Cynics had been heard to whisper that the real reason Dan Porter wanted "his girl" to stay on with the Institute was the fact that elementary bookkeeping had been added to her course work there, thanks to the intervention of a friendly bursar. It was true enough so far as it went. But over the past days of close working with her he had come to confront his true feelings for Harriet Church. All he said was, 'I guess you're right at that, Harriet.'

He spoke with businesslike deliberation and with a thrill Harriet saw that at last this man she had loved for the past six years was registering her as an adult person to be reckoned with. 'I guess you're right. When we've got this behind us we'd better talk about expansion plans for the business and your future with the store... that is if you want a future with the store. For now, you'd best start calling me "Dan" as I'd like to think we might be business partners soon.' It was not much, but it was a start.

'Yes, Sir!' Harriet told Mary Bethune a few days later. 'It was a start!'

The two friends were window shopping for bicycles. Mary identified herself with the "New Woman" generation and the bicycle was very much the thing. Whether she would ever be able to afford the money – or the time – for such a luxury pastime was quite another question. For Mary had found a lifetime vocation for herself when still only ten years old – the cause of black woman's suffrage.

It had all begun when a friend of her mother's left a copy of the *Woman's Journal* in the house. She worked for a white family and one day had seen the magazine among the trash to be thrown out. Barely able to read beyond the title, she had taken it round to her friend Mrs Bethune. Most of the articles, it turned out, were concerned with the rights of women (white women of course) and, in particular, the vote. The ladies agreed it had little relevance for them and it was headed once more for the trash can – this time to be rescued by the precocious ten-year-old, Mary.

The tattered periodical had pride of place in the child's treasure box. She already had a reading age far in advance of the elementary tuition offered at the public school. The articles could be hard going, but Mary reveled in the challenge and by her eleventh birthday she could read all of them and follow most of the argument. She resolved there and then that if white ladies could have an organization campaigning for the vote, then she, Mary McCleod Bethune, would found such an organization for black ladies. A few years older, she discovered others in Chicago active in such a movement so decided she might permit herself Saturday afternoons off from the cause. Half a day did not seem too self-indulgent.

This particular Saturday, then, she and Harriet were engrossed in bicycle talk, in particular they were debating the rival merits of a two-wheeler and a tricycle displayed in the shop window and coming down in favor of the former. More stylish with its slightly dropped handlebars, it was also more maneuverable. To give the rider more control, a right-hand lever brake depressed a curved metal "shoe" down on to the tire of the front wheel. This was clearly a ladies' model with a diagonal "cross bar" and a skirt guard comprising strings running from the rear mudguard to the hub, so as to mask the upper half of the rear wheel. The oily drive chain was enclosed in a metal casing. The entire machine was painted in a handsome olive green picked out with gold.

'Land's sakes,' squeaked Harriet, throwing up her hands, fingers splayed to shoulder height in mock delight as practiced by the most elegant Southern belles when inspecting a new trotting buggy. 'Ah do decleah,' she mimicked, 'ah haeyave neeever seen such an eaelegant conveyance in all mah born daeeyes.'

Laughing, Mary Bethune clapped her hands in delight.

'Sure thing,' she agreed, 'that's the one for me one day perhaps. What about you, Harriet?'

'Me! I ain't got no money!'

'Well then, what about your husband to be?"

'Oh, Mary! And do you think any man you know or I know would let either of us ride a machine that expects you to wear clothes like that!'

She pointed to an apparition sailing down the street towards them. A young white woman, seated on the very model they had been ogling, was clad in garments the like of which neither could believe they were seeing. The fashionable street sloped a little so that the cyclist did not, for the moment, need to pedal. Instead, her feet were resting on little bars that projected either side of the front wheel fork, leaving the wheels to revolve freely (obviously, the model was not fitted with the new patent freewheel mechanism) and revealing a pair of neat ankles rising to charming, shapely calves. This was the friends' first sight of a woman wearing knickerbockers – the baggy pantaloon-like garment caught in at the knees. To complete the apparition, on her close-cropped blonde curls the girl wore a strange, flat, helmet-like little hat with two silvery bird wings projecting up either side of her head to suggest Mercury the messenger of the gods.

Rather to her surprise, Mary felt a rising sense of puritanical disapproval. For her part, Harriet reckoned that if for one moment, she thought her parents would allow her to wear such a garment she would be displaying her own shapely legs to Mr Daniel Porter the next day. He might be shocked but he would never again have difficulty in assigning her to the age group to which she in fact belonged!

The cyclist was approaching an intersection where a smart young gentleman twirling his cane had just rounded the corner. At the same time, a horse-drawn omnibus was pulling across the girl's line of travel. At once, she applied the handbrake to the front wheel. The gadget worked all too well. The front wheel came to a juddering halt, the rear wheel attempted to continue in line ahead, the little vehicle jack-knifed and the young man instantly dropped his cane to catch the tumble of knickerbockers, blonde curls and palpitating bosom that fell his way. Fortunately, the arms of the beautiful bundle locked unerringly around his neck, the bicycle rolled on a little way before toppling over undamaged into the gutter, and no harm was done.

'Hum!' gurgled Harriet, as she rubbed the tears of laughter from her eyes. 'So that's what they call an "accident" in smart circles down town.'

'You really think she did it on purpose? But why?' Mary was puzzled.

'Why, Mary honey? Why? Why, to get herself a man of course, perhaps a husband.'

Preoccupied with her life's work, Mary had never yet made a set at a man. *Do women really go to such lengths for such a very unnecessary result?* she wondered. She certainly had no intention of marrying, but to learn that other women could still look upon it as a career substitute shocked her. There was so much to be done in the world. She consoled herself with the thought that the girl in question here was white and probably had nothing else to do in life except get a husband. If so, the plan seemed to be succeeding: the young man was at this moment taking off his white suede gloves, the better to right the bicycle and apparently oblivious of the fact that it was depositing oil spatters on an immaculate trouser leg.

'Would you go to such lengths?'

'Hon, I'd go to any lengths to get Dan Porter!'

'But Harriet, he's so much older than you are and once you're married you'll never be able to do anything with your life.'

'Mary dear, everyone knows that age has nothing to do with love. And as to me doing nothing – that's nonsense. He's already as good as offered me a business partnership an' I don' see him canceling the contract when he finds he's got a wife in the bargain as well.'

She laughed happily. Daniel Porter, she reckoned, was on the verge of coming back into the real world and as soon as he did so, he would find Harriet Church waiting, there, ready for action.

Mary sighed in resignation. Though she was barely two years older she looked upon Harriet very much as her protégée to be recruited to the movement. The two walked on in companionable silence. Harriet was watching the white couple now walking arm in arm, the man pushing the bike along the street gutter, while Mary ruminated on the cause of human weakness and other such matters. At last she came to a conclusion which at least satisfied her. *Come to think of it*, she reflected, *there aren't that many black female store clerks who also keep company books!*

Aloud she said: 'Well, if you really love him, I suppose you'll marry him – once he's caught up with the situation. And if he really does make you a full partner in the business, I suppose we can rescue something from the disaster!'

'Reckon as how those two already knew one another.'

Harriet had been working things out and come to the conclusion that the white girl had sized up the possibilities of an entirely unpredictable situation and acted with admirable improvisation to achieve a most promising result.

'I should hope so indeed!' responded Mary with mock pomposity. They linked arms laughing and, courtesy of the next omnibus, made their way back to the chandlery. After drinking a cup of tea with the Porters, father and son, they returned to their homes.

That night Daniel retired to his bed a very happy, if a very tired man. He had been delighted with the outcome of the contract battle and also, truth to tell, puzzled. He had known in his heart of hearts that whatever he said, or Tom White's blackmail might threaten, Willard had the big money and money was the language that talked.

What Dan did not know was that Willard had overplayed his hand. Determined to leave nothing to chance in his negotiations with the board of elders, he had followed his standard practice of fixing a private deal with the board's "St Nickle Ass", his private term for any corruptible official. He plied the man with promises and finally dollars to such effect that not only could he not refuse, he could not refrain from boasting to his wife, even though he knew her to be a virtuous woman. She pleaded with him not to accept the promised bribes. When the man she had married for his spiritual charisma assured her that this way they could really be *rich*, and when she realized that he cared nothing for the values he preached, she went to the council. As the full council listened to her tearful denunciation, they saw it would be very difficult to go ahead with the Willard Stone fix, even if the corrupt negotiator were cut out in favor of another. Rather than risk public exposure and also because, be it said to their credit, there were a few men of principle among them, Willard was turned down and Daniel's honest estimate accepted. With this contract secured and the country as a whole emerging from the depression of the mid 1890s, the future for Porter's Chandlery seemed set fair.

The following weekend Dan, who had kept up a scrappy correspondence with Elsie Marre over the years, decided that now was the time to bring her up to date. His letters had been so infrequent, partly because writing made him feel guiltily disloyal to Bess, partly because he was not much of a pen man. So now it seemed to Dan natural to ask Harriet round to write the letter at his dictation. She did not think much of the idea.

'*Dearest Elsie,*' she grudgingly wrote, '*it is a long time since I wrote you a letter. In fact I'm not really writing you this one; that's being done by Harriet. I mean Harriet Church, the little girl of the people who gave dear Bess and me house room when we first came to Chi. I'm sure you remember.*' This is what Dan dictated, in fact Harriet wrote "daughter" for "little girl" and angrily bit back the protest that rose to her lips. The gaiety of last Saturday afternoon seemed much more than seven days ago.... Those knickerbockers! One day the great fool would really wake up – *by force if need be,* she thought. A grin took the place of the frown.

'Share the joke?' Dan found himself watching the changing expressions on his young assistant's face more than he used to.

'Oh it's nothing important, Dan, nothing important!' she replied and thought to herself, *Well, at least he's paying attention to me and, what's more, precious Elsie ain't anywhere nearby.*

'Well,' continued the letter, '*she has been helping me in the store.*'

'Does she know you've got a store?' Harriet intervened,

Then young Jim joined in. For him Sunday was a bore and he was hoping to persuade his father to take him out, but as soon as he saw their visitor he realized there would be no father–son walks that afternoon. Accordingly he had taken a seat at the parlour table and waited expectantly for whatever entertainment might be had from listening to someone else's mail. Now he interrupted.

'Does who know, Pa?'

'We're writing to your Aunt Elsie Marre.'

'Oh,' said Jim, disappointed. He had never met the lady, though he had heard enough about her and he slumped back in his chair. What *was* there to do on a Sunday afternoon? It was the eternal question, he reckoned.

'*Perhaps I should explain,*' continued the letter. '*Thanks to some good fortune I've been able to open my own small business as a chandler on the Chicago waterfront. Harriet is very helpful. She is studying bookkeeping. She reminds me of how you helped out in the Johnstoneville store as a matter of fact.*' Harriet gritted her teeth, So I do, do I, she thought, but said nothing. '*Though I don't think you ever got round to keeping books.*' Harriet brightened up. She vowed then and there to keep books better than any books had ever been kept in South Side Chicago. '*We're writing this on Sunday afternoon. Of course Jim and I went to church this morning.*' Jim stirred listlessly: *We sure did that*, he thought. But his father was a remorseless letter writer. '*But I must say I don't enjoy the services like I used to in Jo'ville. The reverend here ain't at all inspiring, an' I do miss my contribution on the trombone...*'

'The what?!' broke in Harriet.

'Yeah, Dad. What trombone?'

Dan Porter looked up, surprised. Had he really never told the boy? The instrument had only once come out of its case since they arrived in Chicago – and that was to be taken along to the first morning's church service. But the reverend had observed with pursed lips that he didn't have no horns playing in his church, and Dan had returned disconsolate and put the instrument away. It didn't occur to him to explore the possibilities of playing in a club. Bess would never have gone into such a place and after her death he would not leave Jim alone for a single night. Having lost children in their infancy and a wife, he was superstitious that if he did leave the boy alone for any length of time he would come home one night to find him dead too.

'You like to play trombone, Jim?'

'I never seen one, Miss Harriet.'

Harriet put down her pen and looked at Dan in astonishment. Then she broke out laughing and wagged her finger.

'Daniel Porter, aren't you just ashamed of yourself? Now you go find that horn this moment. Poor boy, who knows, you may have a music genius on your hands! And don' you argue none. I ain't writing no more of this letter till you show that son of yours this secret machine.'

'Din't know you liked music, Harriet!'

'But you know I love Dr Sankey's gospel hymn tunes we sing at the Institute… and don' you change the subject.'

She turned to the boy.

'What you think, Jim. You want to se that trombone?'

'Yessir, Miss Harriet! I sure do!'

The boy replied with confused emphasis and Dan joined in Harriet's laughter. Their eyes met in the collusion of adulthood and the moment of intimacy caught Harriet by the throat so that she had to take a hold on herself to keep the level of the exchange as light as it seemed. Still laughing, she got up from the table and went over to the door leading to the stairs and the upper floor of the premises. She swung the door wide and, holding the handle in one hand and waving Dan forward, said: 'Now let's have no more argument.'

Puzzled as to how he had got into a situation of being pressured by his son and his assistant into doing something he was really quite happy to do in the first place, Dan rose to his feet and went up to his bedroom, where the instrument lay in its box on the top of the closet. From the moment he ceremonially opened the case on the kitchen table to reveal the instrument, with its flaring bell, convoluted tubing and piston cylinders controlled by their finger buttons, he held the two of them enthralled.

First he buffed it up with some kitchen polish, next he checked the valves with the merest touch of light "engine" oil kept for the Singer sewing machine Bess and her neighbors had clubbed together to buy. This done, he tried what he called a "flicker" of the pistons.

In the early days of their move to Chicago, before the arrival of Owen Shout, this might lead into quiet improvisation on some spiritual melody. It was, in his wife's opinion, unfortunate that this could in turn lead into playful variations. She used to remind him that even in Johnstoneville the older members of the congregation had sometimes objected to what Joshua Tubman called "this steamboat stompin' music".

But now his boy's face lit up with wonder and Dan cursed himself for a fool that he had left it all this time to introduce him to the marvels of this one treasure in the house. It was a b flat model built by Boosey's of London, England and some thirty-five years old. Shout was delighted with the weird name of the maker, but had little interest in England. He listened wide-eyed as his father explained that tubes of different lengths made notes of different kinds, high and low. It was the best part of five years since Dan had blown a horn in earnest and his lip had more or less gone. Even so, he could make a note of some kind and when the boy produced a length of hose piping from the stock and challenged him "to make a note with that... any note", he had fitted the trombone mouthpiece into it and reduced them all to helpless laughter with what Harriet "considered to be a *very* unladylike noise".

Next, Daniel explained how the first kind of trombone could change the length of the tube and so the kind of notes it made with a kind of sliding arrangement. Then he held the instrument itself to his lips and gave a little demonstration of its capabilities from a flicker of melody to the very lowest possible "fundamental note". He was proud of himself for a very creditable effort here because these notes were the most difficult of all and if badly played sounded about as "unladylike" as it was possible to imagine. But instead of laughing, this time his little audience looked in awe at the contraption which had produced this solemn sonority. 'Like a steamship sounding through the fog from the other side of Jordan,' whispered Harriet. The boy said nothing, wide-eyed. The father bent down to the sparkling eyes in the little face full of wonder that was his child, while Harriet, now unobserved by either, her eyes filling with a mist of love, watched the birth of a new understanding between father and son.

Daniel returned to his lesson in elementary acoustics, just now the only important thing between the two of them. 'That's what we get if we use the whole length of the tube,' Dan was saying, 'but if I use these piston buttons properly, I can change the length of the tube to get all the notes I want.'

Gaining in confidence as his demonstration continued, Daniel blew a great blast of air down the instrument for what was to be an electrifying and joyful rendition of "Oh, when the Saints". He made it through the first line and then his lip gave out completely to produce a raspberry to end all raspberries. The little family was once more helpless with laughter, but as the horn blew up the door blew open and in came a storm of protest in the shape of a very large and irate Mrs Calpurnia, their next-door neighbor.

'Mr Porter!' she yelled, her voice carrying even above the screams of a suddenly active baby. 'Mr Porter, I have jes this moment cradled young Paul away to dreamlan' an' what do ah hear? For the first time in years ah hear you blowin' some of yoh heathen jass music. Let me hear one moh' sound like that an' ah'll call all the police in this city of CHI-CA-GO!' With which she roared out, heaving the door behind her with a crash that endangered the foundations of the entire building.

Baby Paul continued to squall, the decibels barely diminished by the thickness of a thin door. Mrs Calpurnia continued to shout, at the child now. Daniel, Harriet and Shout burst out laughing. The boy agreed it might be time to go to bed, if he could take the trombone with him for the night.

Dan looked at Harriet with a swell of gratitude in his heart that she had sparked this evening of revival and new directions in his life. Their eyes met, both of them aware of just how late it was and Daniel realized that here in his home was a young woman, whom he had once thought of as a girl, who would not be going home this night. He bent down to kiss her and she, without a qualm, lifted a radiant face to his. Pandemonium still reigned next door and tomorrow the neighbors would be off to work on the gossip mill, but who cared now? As Daniel's face came down on hers she thought to herself: *And to think, I did it without a bicycle, after all!*

CHAPTER TWELVE

Heroes and Heroines

The time was 4.53 on the afternoon of Monday 4th July 1910. The theater reverberated to a hubbub of voices, like waves drumming against a rocky shore. Robert Motts, proprietor of Chicago's Pekin Theater, the businesslike figure in the wings of the empty stage, estimated he had 2,000 plus, a super-full house. They were standing in the aisles; they had been kept waiting seventy minutes for the show to start; there was nothing to hear and nothing to see but the pianist in the pit who had stopped his interludes long since; yet they were delirious with enthusiasm. So was Mr Motts. He had made record ticket sales and there was nothing to pay out either.

Well, nothing except the telegraph company supplying the report. At that moment the background chatter of the ticker tape machine stopped. The telegrapher was at his elbow. 'I think you can read straight from the tape, Mr Motts.' The owner stepped out onto the floodlit stage, the ribbon of paper in one hand, a megaphone in the other.

Similar scenes were being enacted in bars, hotels, coliseums and private clubs all over America – Europe too. In London and Berlin, nightlife was on hold as crowds milled outside newspaper offices and smart hotels straining to hear round-by-round summaries of the action in the contest between James J. "Jim" Jeffries (thirty-five) at 230 pounds and John Arthur

"Jack" Johnson (thirty-two) at 200 pounds, presently being disputed in an open-air ring set up in Reno, Nevada.

This surely was "the Fight of the Century". Even Elsie Marre, on one of her biannual visits to Chicago and, against her better judgment, one of the crowd in the Pekin that night, thought that perhaps, for once, the headline writers had it right. When Jeffries had retired as unbeaten world heavyweight champion back in1905, even some white people had said that it was to avoid a meeting with the black champion. Johnson had harried the white successor, Tommy Burns, with challenges and headlines. He had tried to evade them but on December 26 1908 in Sydney Australia, pressured by public opinion and a declaration in favor of the contest by King Edward VII of England, Burns had been forced to stand. The police had stopped the fight in the fourteenth round for humanitarian reasons. For the first time in history, a black man was heavyweight champion of the world. (Hardly a civilized triumph in Elsie Marre's book, but then as she herself admitted, civilized values had only a small part in the war between the races.)

Now, five years on, Jeffries had come out of retirement, "the Great White Hope" who would vindicate his race in the noble art of self-defense. Just at the moment, however, it seemed that things were not going too well for him. Bob Motts raised his hand and a breathless silence fell in the Chicago auditorium.

'Round Two: ladies and gentlemen,' he announced with a flourish. When he cared to, the theater entrepreneur could display the panache of a true impresario. Reading from the tape in his hands, he continued:

'The round opened with Jeffries coming out of his corner in his famous crouch, left arm reaching forward as if to intimidate his opponent...' The reader paused to good effect, then went on: *'Johnson replied with a hard uppercut to the chin...'* The Pekin exploded in cheers and jeers. *'Jeffries countered with a left to the body...'* another pause, *'... and took another blow to his face.'* Again

195

the laughs and cheering. *'Jeffries crouched, waiting for his opponent. Johnson out-waited him. They sparred... there was a clinch... Jeffries emerged from it flailing forward... Johnson sidestepped coolly to land a wicked left hook to the eye... Seconds later, the round ended... Johnson threw his head back and laughed out loud as he retired to his corner.'*

As Motts returned backstage brandishing the megaphone above his head in a two-handed victory wave, the theater broke out in uproar – the boxer's mother, Ma'am Johnson as she was respectfully known, surrounded by a little group of local VIPs, was among the cheerleaders. Although born in Galveston, Texas, Johnson had made Chicago his adopted hometown some years back – so far as the Pekin was concerned, that made him a native son.

Elsie felt proud for the black brother in distant Nevada, and yet she was worried for him too. After all, Jim Jeffries had the advantage in weight, he was, they said, only an inch or two short of Johnson's six foot three inches and, if he was a few years older, he had been world champion for years and had never yet been knocked down. She had come to the Pekin with Dan Porter and some of his friends. They had assured her to expect a great victory for the Black Nation and, despite her objections to the sport, Elsie had decided she should be there to share the triumph with her brothers and sisters. Harriet, by contrast, had simply refused to join the party. 'Public bloodletting ain't no part of my amusement schedule,' had been her comment.

When they arrived at the theater Elsie was relieved to find she was by no means the only woman present. Indeed, as a celebrity in the black women's movement she was invited to join the party of VIPs with the boxer's mother. You go ahead Elsie,' Dan had said. 'I reckon my friends here may be using language less than right for a lady's ear by the time this night is out!' She had not said anything but she very much doubted whether anything Dan and his friends could think of could match the foul vocabulary familiar to a black woman who had had dealings with white police as long as she had. Now she turned to her neighbor to see a face ablaze with pride and joy.

'Many more rounds to go, Mrs Johnson?' Elsie shouted to make herself heard. The question sounded ridiculous. Why spoil the fun? Why worry the man's mother, who must surely be worried no matter how brave she appeared? But Elsie had heard that the contest was to last no fewer than forty-five rounds or until one of the combatants was beaten unconscious. Surely someone should stay level-headed, on that timescale celebrations seemed a bit premature. In fact, the cheering was abating somewhat, though only because, instead of yelling, 2,000 experts were now telling each other in which round the inevitable victory would come.

Tina Johnson turned to focus on her neighbor.

'Elsie "Blaze" Marre, ain't it? Well, Miss Elsie, we're surely honored to have you here. Jack's what they call a "rough diamond" I guess, what with his gold-topped walking cane and his blondes. Don' reckon much to women's votes, neither. But he do reckon a fighter, "an' those votes for women dames sure take whitey a round or two, Mama". His very words.' She paused to look at the beautiful gold pendant watch pinned to her bodice. 'Third round be ending soon, and after that another forty-two to go, according to the book! Land's sakes!' She threw back her head and laughed – surely the very gesture her son had just made. 'But don' you worry none. I don' reckon these good folk know much about boxin', but they's right to be confident. You wanna know why, hon?'

Elsie, who had decided that her concern for this lady's motherly sensibilities had been altogether too patronizing, nodded assent. Might as well learn something about boxing since she was at a boxing match.

'Well, I'll tell you!' continued the indefatigable lady. 'If that telegraph reporter's tellin' it how it happened an' Jack got that blow into the eye, then this fight's as good as over. Jack punch much harder even than he looks an' I guess Jeffries is seeing double already. Jack'll punish that eye and plunder hits as it suits him… an' when he's good an' ready he'll chose his time to drop the guy.'

If Elsie was startled by her neighbor's turn of phrase, she was utterly convinced by her analysis and decided that Jack Johnson could look after himself. In his press release after the fight, Jim Jeffries was to say: '*The blow to my right eye in the second round affected my vision and I could see two colored men in the ring before me.*'

Johnson "dropped his guy" in the fifteenthth round, though it could have been any time after the third. The Associated Press reported that after that he treated his opponent "*almost as a joke. He smiled and blocked playfully, warding off the rushes of Jeffries with a marvelous science*".

'Jus' playin' with him,' was the expert opinion of Elsie's neighbor. 'That Jeffries called Jack "a bad, gold-toothed goddam nigger" before the fight, and Jack don' like an insult.'

Mr Motts continued his commentary. Pacing his delivery to brilliant effect, using every device to give life to the words on the flimsy inked tape, he painted the scene in the distant sunlit stadium so vividly that many of his audience that day remembered the event like a movie picture. In the fifth round, the black hero joshed the faltering white man with the words: 'Let me see what you got. Do something man! This is for the cham-*peen*ship.' Many in the Pekin that day remembered the words as if in a bordered caption between the silent action shots of a movie.

As the fight developed its own murderous rhythm, they saw the bloodied white face bobbing at the end of the famous short-arm Johnson jabs, like a punch ball on a spring. At the beginning of the seventh, the right eye was closed, the nose bleeding; at the end of the eleventh a scything left to the jaw seemed to turn that head right around. In the twelfth, Johnson's dazzling display of speed and defensive mastery actually had the hostile white crowd cheering him. Jeffries was now coughing gouts of blood, bubbling as he tried to draw breath. One of his ringside friends fled the arena in tears. In faraway Chicago, the Pekin Theater hushed for a moment as if in a gesture of return sympathy for the earlier white cheers. But thoughts of sporting sympathy evaporated as the black triumph mounted to its climax…

'*Jeffries breaks from the clinch,*' ran the theater manager's report. '*Johnson pounces, shooting rights and lefts… Jeffries reels away… Johnson shoots a left from the hip straight to that jaw… Jeffries has hit the canvas for the first time in his career…*' A sigh broke from the theater, followed by a shout. When Motts came on stage with the report of the fifteenth round in his hand, his ear-to-ear grin said more than words. The theater erupted so that few ever heard the words '*FLASH / JOHNSON WINS IN THE FIFTEENTH…* '

Only seconds later, or so it seemed to her, Elsie Marre found herself in State Street. The local worthies had closed round Mama Johnson to see her to safety. Dan Porter and party, separated by twenty rows of packed seating in the auditorium, were nowhere to be seen. Over a stretch of ten blocks, triumphant blacks were surging and chanting, 'Jack, Jack, J-A-J: Jack. Jack, J-A-J.' Within the hour white gangs would be on the street to avenge the humiliation of their champion. But just now it was safe to move if one could avoid the reeling victory march of one's own people. Within thirty minutes, twice the time it would have taken her under normal conditions, Elsie was knocking at the Porters' front door.

* * * * *

The year following the great victory, Mrs Mary Church Terrell, honorary president of the National Association of Colored Women, was on a flying visit to Chicago.

'Long time since I been in Chicago but I can't say the place has changed that much. I sort of feel it should have now that I know it's the adopted hometown of Jack Johnson.' A distinguished woman of about fifty and once a notable beauty with her full, lightly parted lips, tawny skin and wavy black hair peeping from beneath an elegant broad-brimmed afternoon hat, she paused. Her eyes sparkled.

'What a fight that was!'

Elsie Marre, having had advance notice of the president's travel plans, had arranged her own 1911 visit to the city in the same time slot. She was anxious to introduce the celebrity to Harriet Porter and had persuaded her that she should make time to share her experience and advice with the young activist. The two women were seated at a table in one of the small committee rooms in the Methodist Church on 32nd Street. Elsie had just been describing the background to her own work in Chicago and Harriet's place in it and she looked up, startled, from her notebook. Mary Terrell's remark had opened a new perspective on the personality of a distinguished lady.

'Oh, don't get me wrong. I reckon boxing's a barbarous sport. They tell me Nevada's the only state in the Union where it's legal. But credit where credit is due. It was a notable triumph for our people. I was visiting in Indianapolis at the time and I cut the *Freeman's* editorial for my scrapbook: *"Perhaps no other event has held so universally the gaze of mankind"* is how it began, if my memory serves.'

'What event was that? Hope I'm not late, Elsie.'

Harriet Porter whirled into the committee room with her customary verve, documents case under one arm, walking parasol under the other. This meeting was a special occasion and as such it called for a bit of dressing up, even a hat, but no matter the occasion, she could not bear a hat on her head indoors, and this she took off before she sat down. After Elsie had made the introductions and Harriet had been suitably impressed with their distinguished colleague, she repeated her question. The explanation startled her even more than it had Elsie. She proceeded to make her views clear.

'Well, I must say with all respect, Mrs Terrell, that I personally do not reckon Mister Jack Arthur Johnson very highly. Elsie here'll tell you that even his mother is getting fed up with him and his fast cars and fast women; and me, I don't think it loyal to the sisterhood the way he goes with white women. An' as for that private railroad car with its phonograph and piano and buffet and man servant... I reckon it's just showin' off.'

'Isn't that being a bit of a puritan, Mrs Porter? It seems to me to be entirely excellent that a man of color is in a position to flaunt wealth on such a scale. I heard he took away a purse of $200,000 from that fight and that can only give our young men pride and hope.'

'And hope for what...? That if they beat one another senseless to entertain the white folk they'll be well paid for their trouble?'

Harriet pursed her lips angrily. Among her circle of friends her hatred of boxing, indeed violence of all kinds, was well known but she wished she could control herself better. Elsie Marre, nonplussed to see the meeting she had taken so much trouble to arrange heading apparently for a place in the record books as the shortest ever, moved into the unfamiliar role of mediator.

'Well, hold it there a moment, Harriet. It's true, most of the folks in the stadium were whites but I do assure you that the audience in the Pekin that night was one hundred per cent black, and you know yourself that this church we're meeting in today was just one of the churches all over the state where they prayed for a Johnson victory.'

Again, before she could stop herself, Harriet had to come back, almost sarcastically.

'Sure they prayed! You know how much money was riding on that man's gloves? Dan told me half our customers had pledged their pay packets for a month ahead on a Johnson-to-win wager!'

'Well that I *can* believe, young woman.' Mrs Terrell had returned to the debate, not, Elsie was relieved to see, in the least bit huffy about Harriet's straight talking.

'One of my husband's colleagues took out a mortgage on his home to put what he called "a real bet" on the outcome. Hardly a responsible way to behave but a very, very profitable one! No, I don't think it was only the white folks who were entertained by the outcome of that match. Indeed, when you consider that the federal government legislated to ban all public showings of the movie, you might think they were not entertained at all!'

The three women laughed easily together.

'But to business once more,' Mary Terrell took the meeting in hand. 'Before you arrived, Miss Elsie was telling me about your friendship with Mary Bethune and that you had had a letter from her. I can see that you're well on in the movement if you number such ladies as that among your acquaintanceship. Let us hear what she has to say!'

Laying her documents case on the table, Harriet took out one of the correspondence files, opened it and in her clear, confident voice began to read: '*Daytona Beach, Florida, September 1911, Dear Harriet, Wonderful to get your letter the other day. I often recall those mad days in Chicago and only wish I could see more of you. It would certainly be good to be at what you described as your "council of war" with Mary Terrell and Elsie Marre. My apologies and regards to both… and to Judge Robert T. as well.*

You ask me to suggest "useful" contacts and I know just what you

202

mean. The world's full of people wanting to know how they can help until you tell them! But really, you yourself must know all the useful women in Chicago; "Blaze" Marre knows everybody north of Kentucky and with Mrs Terrell visiting with you from Washington, it would seem you have a full hand. However, if you want historical back-up for any of your literature it might be worth writing to Carter Woodson. Just now, he's completing his PhD at Harvard. I don't know his present address but Mrs Terrell can surely get that from the judge or from DuBois. By the way, as well as my regards tell her: "No it is not all sun and sea-bathing here in Daytona." Some of us have to work even if others do see fit to spend their time gadding off to Europe.'

Mary Terrell laughed.

'I reckon she never will forgive me for taking up that place on the deputation to the Berlin Congress.'

'But that's seven years back!' protested Elsie Marre. 'And besides, I never heard that Mary Bethune could speak a word of any foreign language and you gave the address in German – real good German too, as I remember.'

'And in French at the committee stage… ' Good-natured though she was, Mary Terrell did not believe in being over modest. A stint teaching in the language department at Wilberforce University back in the 1880s and a European tour with her father had developed a natural linguistic talent of which she was, with reason, proud. But remembering she was with friends she went on.

'Sure, it's seven years back. But 1904 was also the first year of The Normal Industrial Institution for Girls, Daytona Beach founder Mary Mcleod Bethune.' The voice took on the stilted tones of brochure English and Harriet Porter, sitting opposite, hurriedly bent her head to the letter again, to a hide a frown. It seemed to her there was a hint of mockery behind the voice. Alert like any good committee woman to the mood of the meeting, Terrell leant across the table and put a friendly hand on the younger woman's arm.

'It's the tone she uses herself, honey. Too modest for her own good that one. That college of hers is a landmark institution and I reckon it'll be going long after they've all forgotten Mary Church Terrell.'

'Well they won't forget her in your family, will they, Harriet?'

Elsie Marre aimed to get the business of the meeting back on the road, but first she had to lighten the mood.

'Did you not know, Mrs Terrell, that Harriet here was born "Church" and she and her husband reckoned it was only proper to call their first born daughter Mary Terrell Porter.'

'Well, you don't say. I call that real flattering to Robert as well as me! But we got business here. Anything more in that letter we ought to hear, young Harriet? Carter Woodson was an inspired suggestion, should have thought of him myself.'

'Guess not, Mrs Terrell – rest of it's mostly private stuff. Mary wants to know if I have taken up bicycle riding yet, things like that...' Her eyes took on a dreamy look and a private smile hovered over the lips.

'Cycling, eh? Good exercise they tell me. Well, I'm certain DuBois will have Woodson's details. Was in correspondence with him myself , for my piece on lynching.'

'Didn't the *North American Review* publish that?' asked Elsie.

'They certainly did.' The reply was grim voiced. 'But they've not handled much else of mine. Too controversial they tell me! And still no law against lynching on the statute book.'

She lapsed into a brooding silence. Then, with a shrug of the shoulders, she came out of her reverie.

'When you next write, you tell Mary Bethune thanks. Carter Woodston certainly is your man for history – as he'd be the first to admit! Launching a journal they tell me. And tell Mary that Daytona Beach seems to have a few things to teach Washington D.C.'

'And Berlin?' Harriet prompted gently.

'Oh that! That was the Berlin Convocation of the International Council of Women. It might be worth reading up the reports in the back numbers of *Woman's Journal*. I suppose they got it in the library here in Chicago.'

'The *Woman's Journal*? That's mostly for white women isn't it?'

'Sure it's white. But it's the vote too. Started back about 1870. Same year as the Fifteenth Amendment anyway. That really offended our white sisters, you know. Many of them had been real enthusiastic for the black cause. But when the Fifteenth gave the vote to black men but not to women, not even white women, they decided they had their own battles after all! Funny really. The black sisters had been in the fight for women's rights 'bout as long as them. At least since the forties when Sojourner Truth got the call.' The businesslike voice faltered. The eyes misted over, with tears Harriet would have said if Mrs Mary Terrell was most definitely not the kind of lady to go weepy in public.

'Now there was a woman.'

'You met Sojourner Truth?' Elsie Marre spoke the name with awe. The famous apostle of blacks' and women's rights had been her chief heroine ever since her college days.

Terrell smiled suddenly and continued.

'Oh yes... I met Sojourner Truth – me just seventeen and she an old, old lady, eighty years and then some. I was in my first year at Oberlin College and one of the professors had friends near Elyria where the great teacher was visiting. The prof arranged a trip: I seized the chance and have never forgotten the radiant spirit I was privileged to meet that day. The weather was fine and we sat on the grass about the basket chair which had been set out for her in the orchard. As she spoke of the coming day of black women's emancipation, you could feel the passion and power of Sojourner Truth in the great days of her mission.

Those of us without benefit of divine inspiration can only do our best. We can work by writing. We can work by lecturing and speaking out, though there I shall have to leave the cause in your hands. Robert Heberton Terrell,' her voice took on a tone of exaggerated formality, 'is very conscious of his dignity as the first black magistrate on the Washington D.C. municipal court and has insisted that I curb my utterances so as not to jeopardize the chances of his reappointment.'

She sighed. 'It's a modest enough position in all conscience but it is an important black milestone I guess. Furthermore, Robert owes it to the personal intervention of that worthy man Booker Washington with President Roosevelt, "Teddy" as we members of the upper set call him.' She smiled a self-deprecating grin.

Harriet found herself wondering whether considerations like that would persuade her to keep silent on something she felt passionately about. She wondered whether Sojourner Truth ever in her life checked her work for the cause. She even wondered whether Mrs Terrell, for all her achievements and self-mockery, did not also have a pleasant awareness of the dignity that came from being wife of the first black magistrate in Washington D.C.

'Of course,' she was saying, 'my own position on the Washington School Board gives me a certain influence. I've just read a new book called *Meroë: City of the Ethiopians*. I am recommending it for college library purchases.'

Harriet said nothing, but a glance at the frowning face of Elsie Marre told her that she was not alone in thinking that if the cause of black liberation was to be advanced in the United States of America, it would be by more direct action than by reading books.

Again Terrell sensed the questioning mood.

'A small step perhaps, but in my view, education in the heritage of our black past is central. Africa is where our people

206

came from and Africa is where we should look to. Though like DuBois says, we American blacks have our own unique contribution to make to civilization.'

'You mean like Fenton Johnson here in Chicago with his electric automobile?' Harriet chimed in. The women laughed, they had all seen the young Chicago University graduate purring down State Street in his strange little vehicle which he said was the transportation of the future. Dan Porter had dubbed it "Fenton's Battery on Wheels", and if he laughed he also approved. The chandlery was preparing to open a new line in electric batteries when the time was right so the more ways of using them the better.

'Well,' said Mary Terrell, 'it's certainly something new and a perfect example of the Tuskegee principle of "learning supported by craftsmanship".'

'Craftsmanship?!' Harriet whooped with laughter. 'Have you ever seen it Mrs Terrell, have you ever *seen* it!'

'Sure I seen it and I reckon it's neat. Still an' all perhaps Mr Johnson had someone build it for him rather than do it himself and that is *not* Tuskegee I will say.'

'If Fenton built that thing himself,' burst in Elsie Maare, tears of laughter in her eyes, 'I'll eat my new hat, artificial fruit an' all, even though it cost me plenty. But seriously, Mary,' she continued as she mopped her eyes with an uncharacteristically elegant little handkerchief, 'seriously! Books about ancient cities, isn't it all rather a long way from Chicago!'

'But we got to get our children educated in pride in their past. And the great kings and queens of Benin, the emperors of Mali and Ethiopia, the rulers of Ghana and Kanem and scores of others, are part of our past. White children have history books with portraits of the great figures from their past, perhaps "African-American" artists should illustrate such books for our children. After all, no African history is taught in schools. Maybe it's up to us women to learn about the legends and the kingdoms of the ancestral continent and pass them on. It's for mothers to educate children in pride any way they can.'

'An' that makes sense,' Elsie Marre chimed in. '"You got to learn to stand tall in a country that most times aims to cut you off at the knees." Or so says Jack Johnson, according to his mother.'

Mary Terrell winced.

'Not my turn of phrase I guess but it sure makes the point. DuBois's family have been free for generations, but when he and his black and white friends convened at Niagara for discussions that were to lead to the founding of the National Association for the Advancement of Colored People, they met on the Canada side unsure, it is said, whether they would be offered accommodations on the States' side of the border. And that wasn't so long ago! Let us hope in years to come there won't be too many episodes like that. Meantime let us see to it that our children make the best use they can of the schooling they do receive, for with them lies the next generation of black heroes and black heroines.'

CHAPTER THIRTEEN

The Violent Death of a Matriarch

'Now you see here my girl, we send you to school to learn, but don't you forget you carry the family name. And don' ever again do anything to dirty that name.'

'But Ma,' whimpered a chastened Mary, 'I din' dirty the family name. I jes made a muddle on my writing book.'

It was a spring evening in the year 1915. Harriet Porter had just returned from the neighborhood school with her eight-year-old daughter in tow. She went along to the school two or three times a term, in part to assure the teachers that she would keep the child up to the mark, in part to reassure herself that the teachers knew their business. Mary was a bright child and, in her mother's opinion at least, merited the best attention the school system could give. However, this afternoon, the assiduous Mrs Porter (known in the staff room as "Harrier" Porter) had been met by an angry school mistress brandishing an exercise book "defaced by this naughty girl!"

The book was in its way a stylish little thing with a stiff paper cover in mottled red and gray and the name of the school printed across the center in a florid typeface. What was standard issue for the school had, in this case, been modified by a defiant slogan in a childish hand. "Lettering is boring," it read, "why can't I write stories? Signed, Mary Porter."

'Mrs Porter, if this is the way you encourage your children to respect the property of others, then I beg of you to think again! Mary is, I don't deny, a clever little girl but I'm afraid that she is not easily ruled in class and can be much too boisterous out of class as well. Pray *do* exercise stricter discipline in the home!'

Harriet was mortified and angry. The name of the family had been criticized, and if the teacher was a rather prim old school ma'am, she had a point. Mother and daughter walked home in a strained and tearful silence.

And yet, faced with the genuinely contrite expression on her daughter's face, Harriet, whose anger was already cooling, relaxed her grim expression. Maybe Mary was just too bright for her own good. Maybe the school was a little too eager to keep to the pace of the slowest in the class so as not to discourage them. Maybe Mary's outburst was understandable if not justifiable – and she had spelt "can't" correctly, not "cain't", the way she often pronounced it! Maybe Harriet would let the child off with a caution this time. She cheerfully gave up the struggle to scowl and her face broke into smiles: a far more natural state of affairs.

'OK honey, I guess doing your letters in that copperplate style can be a bit boring. But good handwriting sure will be useful when you leave school. You think up your stories while you're doin' your exercise and tell them to me when you get home. But be sure to heed what your teacher tells you to do. Is it a deal?' A nod of the little curly head, rather liberally spattered with mud from a playground confrontation earlier that day, indicated that the deal was struck.

'And like I said, don't you forget you represent this house when you're out at school; when you're at church with us; and even when you're playing in the park or in the street.' She emphasized the words with a wagging figure. 'Right, honey, that's behind us. Let's see what we can do about cleaning you up for bed. I don't know about the family name, but the family baby sure is dirty!'

Mary Terrell Porter was already eagerly pulling off her dress and socks. Things had changed a good deal with the Porters since the early days of the chandlery. Thanks to a lot of hard work by Dan and hard commercial sense by Harriet, the buy out of Old Joe Farmerson had produced a boost in profits. Boss White's loan had been paid off before his death in 1898. Daniel continued to concentrate on keeping his small staff happy and well provided for, while maximizing his profits. As a result, the business was well established in the increasingly black neighborhood and this evening, her scolding over, little Mary was excitedly bouncing up and down around the bathtub while her mother tested the temperature, adjusting the hot and cold taps as she did so.

Ten years back, the family had moved into a five-room house. Two years ago, Daniel had decided that further additions to the family were unlikely and that Shout, now in his mid twenties, should have left home by the time Mary needed a room of her own. Helped by a plumber friend, stage by stage, he had converted the third bedroom into, marvel of marvels, a bathroom, with its tub plumbed into hot and cold running water. Before that the family, like most in the street, had taken their baths in a zinc tub in the kitchen. From day one of the new regime, Ma had never had a problem with Mary and bath night. Even now, the child still reveled in a novelty the best part of twelve months old.

While the room conversion greatly boosted the family's reputation on the block, it inevitably attracted sneers from envious white neighbors and customers. Harriet had her own golden rule of life for proper self-esteem in such situations. 'Always remember two things, Shout,' she had once advised Mary's brother. 'First, you're no better than any one else; and second, no one else is any better than you.'

The boy got the nickname when he was barely three. At one of the last Sunday services she attended, Bess Porter, his beloved mother, a redoubtable singer in her young days but now failing in her powers, had been inspired to a last glorious "shout" that had held the congregation spellbound. All except for young Owen – who had joined her. It had been no childish wailing but a precociously skilled descant that had won the family much praise after the services. The episode had been formative for his musical life, but memories of his birth mother faded over the years. Harriet had established herself as a fixture in the shop and family: a true second mother in her wisdom and drive for life.

As for his father, life had been on the upswing for Dan ever since his marriage to Harriet Church back in '98. Sure she had lost her first child, the hoped for Daniel II, in childbed. Harriet had taken it hard. Dan had grieved bitterly. But he knew the statistics. When the dead child was followed by two miscarriages, he too began to worry. But with the birth of the little girl (in 1906), the sun came out again. From that moment, Harriet established herself as matriarch under Dan Porter's roof in a way that Bess had never done.

His second wife was a tower of strength to him, her self-assurance buttressed by the fact that she bore the same name as that great fighter for black women – Mary Church, now Terrell. For this reason she had named their daughter Mary Terrell Porter. Dan had no kind of objections. He had long since decided that whatever Harriet decided was fine.

That was why they were all getting ready to go out to the Moody Institute to hear a Mr Peter Ellington, from the National Association for the Advancement of Colored People, lead a discussion evening on *The Birth of a Nation*, the movie newly released by director D.W. Griffith.

Harriet and Shout were hoping the meeting would resolve

on some kind of protest demonstration along the lines of those held in New York. That made Dan uneasy. Tension had been growing between blacks and whites in Chicago over the past few years, as more and more black families came up from the South. Sometimes of an evening father and son would discuss the political outlook, when they were not talking music. Shout, a virtuoso on the cornet, was making his way in the clubs, and saw more of the world and was more aware of the growing racial tension. But, like most of his age group, he reckoned a man had to stand up for his rights and if this film was half as bad as they said, he was all for standing firm. Dan said 'Maybe.' He was wont to rehearse the favored motto of his sixth decade: "Praise the Lord; make profits; and don't make waves."

After that evening's meeting he was beginning to wonder. As described by young Mr Ellington, the film's depiction of the Southern Negro was a gross libel. It seemed that when he was not a simpleton he was a rogue, and when he was not cheating a benign, well-intentioned master class, he was oppressing gentle, tolerant and defeated Southern gentle folk, eagerly incited by vicious, wild-eyed Northerners. Dan's wife and son were on fire with indignation at the caricature of their black brothers and sisters, who in many states were barely better off than they had been under slavery. Harriet led the move for a protest. A group of the audience stayed behind with the speaker to lay plans. Dan took Mary home so that he had her ready for bed when, about a quarter past ten, the others returned.

With them was young Ellington. It seemed he had forgotten to fix his accommodations and Shout had offered him the Porters' sleeping couch for the night. What with the excitement of the meeting, the arrival of a guest and the fact that she, like the rest of them, had had no proper supper, Mary insisted on staying up. Harriet, remembering the school teacher's comments, raised her eyes to heaven with apologies to the Good Lord. 'Go ahead Harriet,' she could have sworn he said: 'indulge the child, after all tomorrow is a holiday.' With a grin she called Mary down to help her get the meal on the table.

They talked late into the night. Mary wilted with sleepiness and sadness. Why did that horrid man make people look so nasty? He pretended he was telling history how it was, but he was telling lies. It didn't seem her daddy understood.

'Well, I guess everybody knows it's just one man's idea like Mr Ellington had to admit,' he was saying, 'and a white man at that! As I see it, it's only a movie. An hour or so of show time down at the bioscope, that's all!'

'But, Pa, kids don't know that. I wouldn't of known that if I hadn't heard Mr Ellington explainin' things. I guess a lot of kids would be mighty unhappy if they saw that movie – an' a lot of other folks too.'

'That's right, hon'. Your father's bein' plumb stupid an' he knows it.'

Harriet Porter did not as a matter of habit talk like this about her husband. For many reasons: not least because he wasn't stupid. Also because she respected as well as loved him and knew, without any school mistress telling her, that if parents showed disrespect to each other before the family, the children grew up unruly and, more important, unhappy. But tonight she was on fire and Dan, for some reason she did not rightly follow, was being plain silly.

'Like you say,' she continued to her daughter, 'a lot of black folks, if they get to see the movie at all, will be unhappy and a lot of white people are going to be sneering. You know as well as I, Dan, that the man means no good to us and ours. Some whites are at last getting to grips with the idea of the black man as a citizen. Now this Southern movie maker is trying to put him back in a "coon show"! I thank the Lord our kids at least are schooled to think!'

' "Schooled to think"! That's something new, Harriet. You used to tell me a good education'd bring in good money – though me, I reckon black folk only get money by working.'

He was not bitter; he was not against education; but he was amused. Back in Jo'ville he had believed in education but life had taught him different. To please Harriet he had kept Shout on at school and to please her he had agreed that Mary should have a decent schooling and if possible get to college. This way, his wife had told him, both their children would improve their future financially and socially. Well, Shout had turned out to be a musician – no schooling there! – and Mary might get to be a teacher, and that was hardly a mine of gold. Compared with such "improvements" to be had through education, Dan often reflected that Willard Stone was now in the nation's top one hundred businessmen outside Texas and he, Daniel Porter, was the richest black in his neighborhood. Neither of them got above eighth grade.

'And where do you think your books would be without an educated book-keeper. Back when I was working at the Institute, Mary Bethune used to say to me: "Harriet Church, you be proud of your name and get the best education you can. One day the doors of opportunity will be opened wide to black children, and when that time arrives, better there be too many qualified people than too few..." '

Up till this point Peter Ellington, who had been so eloquent at the meeting, had had little to say, beyond commenting that he was just twenty-one, aimed one day to be a journalist on the *Pittsburgh Chronicle* and was really grateful for their hospitality. He had, in fact, been eating most of the time. He now leaned back, reached for an apple from the bowl – Harriet had ideas in advance of her time about fruit – and said: 'In my opinion, that Mary Bethune was one privileged lady. Mebbe there'll be opportunities one day for people of her kind but not, I guess, for most black folk. My father worked for thirty years at

Carnegie Steel and ended up as first assistant furnace man. He weren't allowed to go no higher, tho' he was sure good at his job. He trained white apprentices who went on to be his foundry bosses, in fact!'

'Foundry man... ?' Shout was impressed. 'That's skilled work!'

'Nice to meet someone who knows what I'm talking about outside a steel plant.' Ellington's eyes lit up with appreciation. 'I joined this N.A.A.C.P. outfit thinking they might do something for my pa and his mates. If he could have become a charge foreman he'd have reckoned he'd made an advance. Instead, he just got fed up waiting for the chance to run a furnace hearth and decided to open his own show, two years back he started a fish an' poultry shop.'

Dan Porter kept clear of the politics but he opened his ears at this.

'Say, that's real good. How's he making out?'

'Aw hell! – excuse me, Ma'am – I don' know, Mr Porter. I reckon he's too kind hearted to make a go as a businessman... Say... you know what I mean, Sir!... '

The Porters burst out laughing. The young man did not know where to look in his confusion. Bad language in front of a lady and now an implied insult to his host, a successful businessman, who owned two stores with talk of a third in prospect!

'Now don't you worry son. I guess I know what you have in mind,' Dan glanced at his wife with a wry smile, 'but I sure would like to hear even so.'

'Well, Sir! My pa started off with hopes he'd be able to set up something for me and my brother to inherit. And maybe he will. But we reckon he's too generous with credit to our friends. There's Hirom Walker, f'r instance. Never paid a penny since the place opened and with an account that's run into a second notebook!'

He stopped, puzzled. Harriet, Shout and even Mary were shaking with laughter, while the head of the household had a sheepish smile on his face.

'And your ma, Peter. What does she have to say?'

'Ma, Mr Porter?' The boy was astonished. 'Why, Ma don't have nothing to say about the business!'

'Well, you can tell Mr Ellington from me that if he aims to discipline bad debtors, there's no one better for the job than a woman – tough talking or sweet talking, whichever.'

'Keeps her under his thumb does he?' asked Harriet.

'Well wouldn't rightly say that, either. I reckon it's thanks to her I ever got to university. She had a decent education for a woman and decided I should have the best education possible. She used to say that her people can't have been very good slaves: "had ideas about the future you see and that was way above their *station in life*". She liked to talk with emphasis did Ma! Anyway, with Grandma expecting at the time, Grandpa put some money aside to start his son's education when the time came. Well, the "son" turned out to be my ma. Even so, grandpa stuck to the arrangement and Ma was sent to West Virginia Colored Institute as it then was, "Collegiate Institute" these days of course.'

'And your father…?'

'Oh, he never had any chance. Started in school at age eight and just three weeks later Grandpa Ellington took him away to help with the harvest – "Boy's too big to be wasting time in class." To be honest, Pa probably thinks the same way: a man should be bringing money into the house as soon as possible; though he keeps such thoughts to himself. I aim to get some more schooling before I join the *Chronicle*.'

The young man's hopes were destined never to be realized. Two years after this conversation the United States entered the European War. Peter Ellington, like many another young African American eager to demonstrate his patriotism as a citizen, enlisted. He lost his life fighting on the battlefields in France.

* * * * *

It was a hot night in July in the year 1919. Shout Porter, cornet case in hand, strode through the emptying streets for home. Two years back he had set up on his own. Usually he stayed on with the other members of the band unwinding after the evening session. This evening, he had left them in heated debate over the tactics of the Italian campaign against Austria, in which two of them had been involved. The Great War "to end all wars" had come to an end and soldiers were home from their campaigning to do battle in the labor market.

Among them were thousands of black soldiers, whose contribution to the victory was, it seemed to Shout Porter, being virtually ignored. Thanks to the Fourteen Principles of President Wilson, the little nations of Eastern Europe, liberated after centuries of imperial domination, were preparing for self-determination. *But*, thought Shout, *the black nation of America, which outnumbers any of them, live lives of second-class citizens, most of 'em afeared to vote.*

Shout was in savage mood. He recalled how his father had been forced to abandon a life's ambition because of his color. The Czechs and Lithuanians and the rest had no doubt known oppression but he doubted it had matched the sufferings of his people. *They* still had the fight for freedom to win and nobody was going to come across the ocean to their aid. He often recalled his stepmother's passionate plea for education in that family debate four years back. He was educated, but what good had it done him? He had a career because he had that rare thing, a black man's skill that was saleable in the white man's world.

Bitterness was not in Shout Porter's genes – but he was

bitter. Over these past eighteen months, hostility toward Chicago's blacks had turned ugly and violent. Many a black home had been bombed by white hooligans using grenades looted from army surplus stores. The police had, in most cases, done nothing. Two months back, one such bomb, hurled through the parlor window of Harriet's ageing parents, had gutted that friendly room, so full of family memories. Because the old people had gone early to bed that evening, the thugs had been deprived of the additional pleasure of murder. But a black was as liable these days to find death on the streets, and of course, there were a few black thugs who responded with matching violence. Porter was carrying his cornet case in his left hand, leaving his right free to snatch for the, non-lethal, blackjack in his deep trouser pocket.

With the grandparents' place restored and redecorated, the young Porters had set about organizing a local demonstration of protest against police inertia. Harriet had been the driving force. Her positive response to the outrage meant that neighborhood morale was higher than it had been for a long time past. Scheduled for late July, it was to take the form of a march on the neighboring precinct house. Following advice from the N.A.A.C.P. she had alerted the precinct captain, reporting that she had promises from 200 people and reckoned at least 150 were solid. In addition to the demonstration proper, she had been able to promise the marchers a bandwagon. Shout, who had been out of touch for months, made contact the day after news of the bombing broke in the Chicago black press and it was he who suggested recruiting a few musician friends to lead the procession.

He had been living in his own place across town for a year or more. Mary, thirteen years old and budding into beautiful adolescence, had taken over his room. Given that he was aged twenty-seven at the time, the move was hardly a shock, but his departure from the family home coincided with an important development in the fluid world of Chicago music, where James Owen Shout Porter was making something of a name for himself. About this time "King" Oliver, the renowned cornetist, had established himself in Chicago and made his club the radiation point for the New Orleans "Creole" style of jass music, or jazz, call it what you will. Young Porter was an instant convert, so when New Orleans-born clarinetist Ben Tatum offered him cornet in the line up of his new band at the Mich Much lakeside bar, he accepted without a second thought.

It soon became clear that the other musicians were looking more and more to the newcomer for inspiration. Ben had brought his New Orleans credentials to the waterfront bar, full name the *Lake Michigan and Much More,* and with the dazzling Shout Porter in the line up, the take at the bar continued its upward curve. Ben Tatum knew he was no virtuoso and rather than take second place to the rising star, he had let it be known he would "make a reconnaissance of the New York music scene"; Shout was in "temporary" control of the band. With Ben's departure he needed a new clarinet – a possible replacement had agreed to take his audition with the bandwagon at the march. Add "Wonder" Mason, the Mich Much trombonist, and Shout reckoned he had the musical component of the protest tied up.

On the morning of the march, Dan and Harriet set out for the assembly point in a sombre mood. The cause was just, but they were not expecting justice. She spoke confidently – at least, she said, there need be no violence given the precautions and advanced warning she had made. Even so, she had refused Mary permission to join them on the grounds that the thirteen-year-old had a terrible cold. Dan had made no comment, but he was uneasy. At the corner of the street they found old Elisha Mole waiting for them – for him, joining the march was an act of great daring. Now in his late seventies but about twenty years old at the time of emancipation, Elisha displayed the text book deference expected of blacks in the ante-bellum South. But the bombings had brought him out in solidarity, amazed at his own boldness. Harriet greeted him gravely. How *would* the police react to the coming demonstration? After all, it seemed, they had condoned the bombings. She said nothing about her misgivings to the others, but the little group walked on in silence.

At the rendezvous point, most of the pledged 150 volunteers had turned up. To Harriet's astonishment her stepson was there too, as promised, with a clarinetist and trombone in tow. Wonder Mason was notorious for being late so his presence was proof positive of the depth of feeling abroad. The banner carriers were spaced out, each surrounded by ten or fifteen people. More and more flocked to the growing procession pacing in step with the swinging music towards the precinct house.

By the time they came to the last block before the station, Harriet reckoned the crowd had reached 300, perhaps more. She was uneasy that it so much exceeded her estimate, and she was puzzled that, despite her advanced notice to the officials, no police were in sight to marshal the walkers. Then, directly ahead, some ten mounted police trotted round to block the gates and maneuver into position across the road. They were armed with long nightsticks and were flanked by a number of constables on foot.

Harriet's heart sank. She had stressed the absolute need for discipline. Each banner was accompanied by a marshal to see these instructions were observed. Would they be able to control a crowd some three times larger than her best guess? She saw that her question was already academic. At a word of command the police line began to advance.

As the horses came on, Dan seized Harriet's hand and prepared to hold on desperately. On the other side of her Elisha Mole took her other hand, and his frail figure straightened up.

Somehow the three of them seemed to be thinking that if the front line could only hold out, nothing really terrible could happen. About twenty yards behind them, its wheels locked in the gutter thanks to the pressure of the crowd, its horse team restive at the threatening advance of other animals, the brewer's dray that was serving as bandwagon was still blowing its music into the air, the street urchins delighted by the holiday atmosphere and the swing of Wonder Mason's trombone slide over the tailgate. Shout was deaf to it all – he played automatically while his mind was transfixed by the unfolding action sequence at the head of the blocked procession.

'Thank God our little Mary is safe home in bed,' Dan muttered to himself, gripping Harriet's hand more tightly. Another part of his brain was analyzing the music as showboat melodies "jassed up" like ragtime, but it was getting increasingly hard to hear as the crowd, now sensing trouble at last, shouted back and forth to friends in alarm. *Well, at least something can drown out Shout and his racket,* thought Dan in gallows humor that seemed to hint at the onset of hysteria. All this time, Harriet, desperate to rally the people, was struggling to free herself and shouting at him impatiently to "lay off" and give her freedom of movement. 'Cool it honey,' was his only comment for he had now seen that one of the mounted officers was heading purposefully towards their group. The rest of the line seemed at first to be leveling their nightsticks, like knights of old steadying themselves for a cavalry charge.

But these were no knights of old. It seemed their sights were set on anything that moved – women, children, sober-minded, grizzle-haired elders, as well as vigorous men. The constable riding down on the front line was wielding his baton with effective brutality and caught a woman who had edged in front of Dan a crushing blow. Without thinking, he moved to help her. Of course, Harriet immediately broke free and stepped out in front of the crowd, arms raised. Old Elisha stumbled bravely forward, as if to protect her from the curveting police horse. But his frail form was swept to the ground for the rider swung the creature round as if to give its back legs a clear field of fire into the people. Now Dan, who had left the woman he had aimed to help to fend for herself, cursing systematically, obscenely and quite unconsciously, was struggling in desperation to reach his darling wife.

He was not the only man aiming to rescue a loved one. At the very moment that Harriet turned her face once more inspiringly towards the crowd, and the police horse bucked, its rear hooves flailing, a massive door of a man pushed past Dan, swept up the injured woman Dan had abandoned in his concern for Harriet and returned through the milling bodies of the crowd as if through a wind-tossed bed of bull rushes.

Suddenly, it was as if the wind had dropped. The crowd went still; Dan watched, mouth stretched in a soundless scream, to see the bloodied hoof once more rise in a scything movement, to catch for a second time, as Harriet sagged to the earth, the disgusting crimson-gray mass of brains and bone that had once been her lovely head.

* * * * *

It was on the verge of his sixty-first birthday when death came violently to his dazzling and determined young wife, and Daniel Porter never recovered from the emotional blow. It was she who had brought him back to full life from the gray years following the death of Bess. Then he had still been in the prime of his manhood; now there could be no second savior. Harriet left memories of light and happiness, but without her at his side the sun would never again entirely burn the gloom from the midday sky. A once cheerful and equable Daniel, holding to the memory of her commitment to civil rights, now immersed himself in the life of politics and hardened his heart against all white society.

The matriarch's death and the manner of it had a radical effect also on James "Shout" Porter. He felt the loss of his second mother almost as profoundly as his father felt the loss of the second wife. The impact of her invigorating and optimistic spirit on the somewhat mournful one-parent family had been formative. Her daily presence in the store as shop assistant and book keeper had livened up his boyhood. As stepmother she had given his life direction. It was she, after all, who had persuaded Dan to reopen his trombone case and, in so doing, it was she who had, in effect, opened the ears of the ten-year-old to the world of brass that was to become his life. It was she who had persuaded the father to buy the boy a cornet of his own.

Her death marked the end of an era in Shout's life. It also marked a new departure. The good-natured dreamer was transformed into a passionate revolutionary. The words of old Elisha Mole on the day of that red summer atrocity kept running through his head. Elisha had been one of those lying among the untidy scatter of bodies, dead, dying or stunned, left when the mounted police withdrew. Shout, searching the wreck, had found the old man dazed and concussed, gasping for water. After a long draft from the flask he spluttered.

'Me! I trust nobody in future. Your ma tol' me not to worry about the future. We was all American folk now, she said, and could walk free, like citizens should.'

He shook himself with lethargic indignation, pointing to the bloody graze down the side of his head where he'd been dragged along in the confusion as the crowd cleared. Then he sat bolt upright. The moment of his life had come: that one moment when, for most men, what they say is what the world needs to hear.

'What you all need is a leader... What we black men need

224

is a leader. If we had a true leader, we could do something. We colored folk need a nation, a flag, an army. They say we all come from Africa... Well if that true, we need a leader to take us home... We needs our own Moses...'

Then the old face, so radiant for those last eternal seconds, went slack with fatigue. The bright eyes dulled, the firm features relaxed to an apologetic half-frightened smile as the weary mind trudged back through the plantation of memory to the time of childhood. Pain returned and the dying mind sent out messages demanding placatory gestures against further hurt. 'Thanks, th... thanks... Massah!'

'Massah... massah...' That this word of all words should be addressed to him, a fellow black, even in a delirium of death, scarred the young man's soul. The flask shook in his hand as he held it to the sagging lips, and he wept bitterly as the old life ebbed away in his arms.

Of the three of the family left, it was Mary who suffered least. She had not been present at the tragedy; she had the vigor of youth and in the aftermath she had to help to hold their father's shattered life together. Sometimes she would catch him watching her with tear-glistened eyes and she would know that he was seeing not her but "HARRIET CHURCH PORTER: HEROINE OF BLACK RIGHTS: BORN 1876 ROBBED OF THIS LIFE 1919: IN HER HOPE OF THE LIFE HEREAFTER: HER LOVING FAMILY". The wooden headboard in the cemetery, with its political undertone to the seemingly pious words, was the dirge of Dan Porter's once vibrant religion.

On the night of Harriet's death and those of her friends, over on the waterside a young man got involved in a violent brawl. Next day his body was found floating in the dock. In the heightened tension of neighborhoods rocked by rumors about the "precinct demonstration", five days of riot ensued.

For Dan Porter, those days of civic mayhem served like electric shock treatment to a sick mind. So much horror impinged even on his traumatized spirit. Set against the death of his beloved wife, numbers of dead meant little. But the volume of accumulated suffering, so many live souls weeping like his... that meant much. To him it seemed clear that violence was no answer, only a question inviting more of the same. He became a moving spirit behind the efforts to establish a Chicago branch of Asa Randolph's Elevator Operators Union and he sold Randolph's journal, *The Messenger*, from the shop counter. The slow slog of politics had to be better than the bloody road of violence, it seemed to him.

CHAPTER FOURTEEN

Easter 1924

It was a brisk spring day in lakeside Chicago. The kind of day when the wind rippled the vast expanse of southern Lake Michigan with the wavelets one expects of a municipal boating pond. But Willard (Will) Stone II, just eighteen years of age and already leading this month's sales figures in the family firm, felt a pang of disappointment. It had been his first visit to the windy city and, like many another, he had fallen in love with its superb seascape of a setting. He guessed there was plenty of bad as well as good behind the dazzling surface but he had had no time to find out about either. There was more business to be done and he had to leave.

'OK, son', his father had said, as he handed over the keys to the brand new black Model T Ford, standing in the dusty road outside the porch of the family house on Main Street, Johnstoneville.

'OK! So you're talented. But I'm not handing out any vacation tickets with these keys. Burnie Brock's paced out his itinerary up north over six weeks with hotel reservations in Indianapolis, Chicago, Detroit and Columbus. See what new customers you can find between stops but don't you miss any of those bed-nights. It's no game for a black to find accommodations. As I remember things, you'll know the inside of the back of this here limousine better than you'd like by the time you're home again. The firm's committed to those reservations... and besides, I've got eight men out on the road up there. At the moment there are at least eight places where they can be sure of a bed. Don't ruffle any hoteliers and don't drop on the sales figures.

He smiled his sour, almost contemptuous smile as the lithe young figure skipped off the porch. Sarah Stone, proud tears in her eyes, waved encouragement. She knew all too well the humiliations and bitterness suppressed over the years of business that had warped Willard's nature. The day they returned from their honeymoon he had spelt out to her the terms of their future life. She could rely on his love and on his support and rest assured for her security. But, whatever it took, the name of Willard Stone was going to rank with the greatest in American business and if this meant their both eating humble pie with a smile, then so be it. From that day to this, the iron resolve had broken only rarely in demonstrations of passionate affection and need. Willard could never know how she treasured these sunbursts of humanity and their assurance to her of his continuing love.

If only he could be warmer and more outgoing with the children. They had to content themselves with brief annual vacations when Willard played the part of father as convincingly as, for the rest of the year, he played the role of a black Rockefeller. Grasping, unforgiving and harsh and, because he was black, all too often humiliated. More than once dubbed "nigger" by outwitted white inferiors, he had begun by turning the "joke" sarcastically on his family circle, but the joke had long since worn thin. Sarah sometimes wondered whether he had forgotten that the respect of one's own flesh and blood had to be cherished.

Young Willard blew her a kiss before turning to check the interior of his little chariot with its cases of samples and his traveling overnight bag. Truth to tell, the Ford was not absolutely new. Burnie had made one local trip, just enough to run her in, and had been looking forward mightily to trying her paces on a real tour. Then he had come down with a crippling dose of typhoid. The doctor promised a full recovery but, meanwhile, the northern sales tour had to be filled and, rather than hire a new salesman (and also because he was secretly impressed by his son's capabilities), the harsh patriarch had, with proper reluctance, "ordered" the boy on the road.

That was three weeks ago and in the interim Will had made a score of new contacts, chivvied and encouraged the regional reps and outsold Burnie Brock by a respectable, though not embarrassing, amount. He liked Burnie and would be quite happy to hand him back his job when he was back on his feet. To judge from the way she was purring along the well-made road, his "ole Tin Lizzie" was feeling just about as smug as himself and Will let himself go in a chorus of one of the ragtime numbers he had heard in that jazz dive where he was dancing last night. Definitely not something to tell Dad about! Especially as it had meant delay on the road that would mean delay on his father and Burnie's sacred schedule.

His face fell as he remembered he would have to top up the tank at the next filling station. No problem as to gas, he was an efficient operator and running out of fuel, or even running at all low, was not his style. But a black behind the wheel of a car was an unusual sight even in the "liberal" north. His lip curled… Liberal! At least in the South you knew where you were, even if according to the theory you were Grade B human. Up here the inevitable discriminations were more humiliating because they were more awkward. Attempts to be "decent", and "not to notice", would be comical if they weren't so embarrassing. But they were comparatively rare anyhow, more general was the reaction he was getting at this moment at the "WELCOME TO BERKLEYVILLE FILLING STATION".

'Serve yourself, boy! If you know which hole to stick the pipe in!'

That same stiff breeze was rippling the grassland just as it had rippled the lake back in Chicago, cotton-wool clouds, as if from a kid's painting, were playing tag in a perfect sky, but Will could barely see to put back the filler cap for the fog of anger and unhappiness. Whizz-kid salesman and a natural on the dance floor he might be, and wearing more dollars in hopsack than this scruff would earn in a half year, but he was damn near crying as he drove off. Would it always be like this? Would whitey always be able to wash the colors out of the brightest day? And the guy had hardly been trying.

Nevertheless, Willard held to his resolve to overnight in Berkleyville. One-horse dump though it was. He needed to recover his poise before facing the important customers that awaited him that morning in Detroit. And that meant finding a room. He knew it was a dumb decision, given the reception he'd just had at the filling station and that an overnight stay here would mean he'd be a day late for that reserved room in Detroit.

But he was in luck. He found a modest rooming house off Main Street too worried about cash to worry about color and a bar with a public phone which they didn't actually rip off the wall before he could use it. Dad would have been outraged at the change of plan. He could not take the phone seriously as a way of doing business. In any case, appointments made should be kept, come hell or high water, and in his book, a hotel reservation counted as an appointment.

The older generation is always stupid. But they always have their reasons. Wilberforce Stone, Will's grandfather, had been a slave longer than Will had been alive. But he had built a business which Will's father had built into a turnover to match any other in the states of Kentucky, Ohio or Indiana. They had done this, in part at least, by recognizing that among the Christian white folks who had enslaved and now despised them, the household gods of Success, Greed and Punctuality were treated with a reverence accorded to very few carpenters' sons and certainly not one so foolish as to have got himself crucified before King Cotton was born.

Fortunately for Will, the reception clerk at Detroit's Downtown Roadhouse, where he was now arranging to change his booking, was only interested in paying customers. As soon as Will rang off the man immediately re-let the now one-night vacant room at double normal rates to a short, red-faced and overweight Ku Klux Klan member who had been besieging the desk for the past ten minutes.

This earnest small-town simpleton had come up from the sticks for the Klan's convention next day at nearby Annaton. He had taken the Klan's oath of secrecy so seriously that he had not dared ask his secretary to make a hotel booking .

Up the road in Berkleyville, having squared his new Detroit arrangements and with a surprisingly decent supper inside him, Will climbed into bed, his bruised self-esteem halfway to recovery.

* * * * *

The approach to Detroit was a long haul and the Lizzie was puffing a bit when she breasted the hilltop. But it had been worth the effort. Below them, yesterday's grays forgotten, was another of those eternal landscapes of prairie, lakes and wooded groves stretching to the horizon. Ahead, Will could just make out the smudge of Detroit, dirty but profitable.

Down to the right in the middle distance he noticed a crowd of oddly dressed people thronging into a vast meadow of a show ground. It lay at a crossroads off a side road from the highway he was traveling on and parked cars stretched along the verges of both roads back from the turnstiles. He turned his attention back to the road, none too wide at this point. A massive steam wagon was laboring up this side of the hill just as he had chugged up the other side. It made a dramatic sight with smoke and steam billowing up out of and round the chimney stack. The driver sat high up in the center of the forward end, arms stretched wide to manage the horizontal steering wheel, which in turn pulled on a heavy chain engaged on the geared wheel at the lower end of the vertical steering column to swing the heavy cast iron whipple tree, through which ran the axel of the huge front wheels. Will checked back and forth the width of the road and the narrowing distance between the two vehicles. He reckoned they could pass safely with a whisker to spare. At this point the verges of the highway fell away steeply to the fields below on either side.

The driver of the approaching juggernaut had made the same calculations and was edging as near as he dare to the verge to give the Ford as much passing space as possible. With just fifty yards to go he straightened his back and prepared to hold steady. Eased back in his driving seat he could take a closer look at the little car coming towards him. Now, slowly, the massive front wheels swung back towards the center of the road. With a sinking heart, Will realized the driver had decided to teach an upstart Black a lesson. That half foot adjustment of the monster's line of travel was just enough to tip the Tin Lizzie, with a long grazing scratch along her paintwork, over the edge and scatter his precious samples out of the open window along the muddy grass.

'Excuse muh Massah, ah'm shoh', came the jeering voice of the driver, 'but it never was mah intention to make no trouble for yoh pretty dolly wagon. Mise, mise, but ah muss be orn mah way.'

His guffaws faded on the wind and soon the wagon's smoke stack was disappearing down below the horizon of the hillcrest. Fuming, Will dusted himself down and surveyed the damage. The effect had been neatly achieved, he had to admit. The vehicle could have smashed the Model T to tin plate but that would have been difficult to cover, even against a Negro. The driver would have been called in and might, just might, have had to pay a fine. As it was, he had guessed that Will would not think of reporting this incident to the police without witnesses.

The sturdy little car, virtually unbreakable and known to be such by every driver in the States, was scratched and shabby but in full working order. By some adroit athleticism, Will had managed to stay in the vehicle and thus save his fine suit from any serious damage. He reached for his travel bag, changed into his second best shoes and, cursing solidly, began to gather up his samples from the damp verges.

This done, he took another look at the car. Somehow or another she had to be righted and hauled back onto the road; what sort of help could he expect? There was little point in walking back to the filling station. He had an hour and a half until his first fixed appointment. But could he even hope to get back on the road at all? He sat disconsolately on his haunches and watched as things developed on the showground, about half a mile below him in the valley.

Thousands of people, women as well as men, were flocking onto the place. The vast majority wore long, white, belted robes, some looked little better than clumsily stitched bed sheets. A few, still showing their everyday clothes, carried white bundles under their arms which here and there they were unwrapping and putting on so that they could join the uniform of the sheeted throng.

A few cars passed him and turned down the side road heading for the ground. The road on the other side of the valley was a creeping mass of cars. Many draped with flags and bunting, some displaying homemade flags and banners bearing such slogans as "The Pope will sit in the White House when Hell freezes over" and "America for the Americans". Willard was not a Catholic but he suspected he was not an American either as far as the milling crowds below him were concerned. A shiver ran down his spine. A voice behind him made him jump.

'The Klan's new to you, brother? Where've you been all your life, for heaven's sakes?'

Jerking round, he found himself looking up into the eyes of a dark-faced reverend, nearer sixty than fifty, with a twinkle glinting from time to time from a lined but friendly face, full of sad experience. Behind him, shabby but a solid six foot, was a Negro farm hand hovering uncertainly on the road verge, next to, heaven be praised, a muck-spattered but functioning farm lorry, shaking to the throb of an obviously serviceable engine. The reverend grinned as the young face below him lit up in expectation. Extending a hand he introduced himself:

'Taliaferro Washington, but not the famous one I'm afraid. Pleased to make your acquaintance young fellah.'

Will, who had no idea what a famous Taliaferro Washington might be, was fully alive to the beauties of that farm truck, in the back of which he had now identified a length of heavy duty rope. He took the proffered hand with the deference due to the age and calling of its owner.

'Willard Stone II, Sir, and honored to meet you.' And then rather more quickly than was strictly polite he started up the bank to make his own introductions to the farm hand.

Washington's grin broke into a roar of laughter.

'See here, Amos, our young friend has clearly identified you as the Samaritan in this team – anything you can do to help him?'

The lorry driver joined the laugh and Will accepted the joke on himself with a sheepish grin. 'Well,' he said, 'I sure would appreciate it if you could pull us back onto the road. I've checked out the engine and she'll run just fine.'

A relieved look came over the others' faces and while Amos hitched up the tow rope the Reverend Washington explained that they still had something of a journey ahead of them.

'I'm to preach the Easter sermon at the Jordan Bethel in Annaton this coming Sunday and my host, Farmer Chesnutt, sent Brother Amos here to pick me up at the rail station. It sure is your lucky day and you can thank those white folks down there, I suppose. The direct route to the Chesnutt farm lies along that lower road but Amos reckoned that it was looking for trouble for a couple of Negro men to run the gauntlet of 10,000 and more Klansmen on their annual outing, in a wagon that's not comfortable above fifteen miles an hour. The Klan may have begun to widen their attentions to Catholics and Jews, but better safe than sorry, as the saying goes.'

His face puckered and he leant forward a fraction as if to get a close look at the younger man's face.

'Well, I declare. You really have no idea what I'm talking about. Where *have* you been all your life… whereabouts do you come from?'

Will, who now dimly recalled childhood memories of family talk about some white man's clan, said truthfully enough that he knew it was probably best to steer clear of it, but what precisely *it* was he really did not know. That he thought it had more to do with history than with the modern world and that he came from Johnstoneville, in Kentucky. By this time the rope was fixed and, with the Reverend Washington lending a steadying hand on one side of the Lizzie and Will on the other, Amos climbed into his driver's cab and carefully eased the lorry into gear, so as to slowly take up the slack on the rope and haul the little car back onto the road. Will, anxious to be off but also anxious not to be discourteous, made his thanks and said he hoped one day he might be able to repay the kindness and succeeded in concealing his impatience with all the skill of a go-ahead eighteen-year-old. Washington burst out laughing once more. Even Amos smiled.

'Right you are, Willard, you've got things to do and we must be on our way. But let me ask, are you staying in Detroit over night? Because if you are, you might indeed be able to help me. This evening Amos is running me into town for a private meeting , but he's not best pleased at being out and about after dark, kicking his heels for a couple of hours or more and still have that drive back to Farmer Chesnutt's through all those Klansmen, eh, Amos?'

The old timer shrugged off the banter. Sure, this was one night he'd rather be at home with the wife.

'It's not more than ten miles, less than half an hour in your excellent little motor, Willard, so you could be back in your hotel by ten-thirty at the latest. What do you say? Could you run me out to the farm this evening?'

There was only one thing he could say and so, having agreed that the Reverend Washington could come round to his hotel as soon as his meeting was over and expect a lift, Willard stepped on the gas pedal and had soon left the farm wagon far behind.

The day went surprisingly well. His main customer placed an order for no fewer than eight dozen Stone lamps. Building developments out of town to accommodate the influx of automobile workers were on the verge of completion and while the electricity might one day be laid on, just now kerosene would have to do for the less favored citizenry. Will tried to feel sorry for these poor families but as he held out the order book for the dealer's counter-signature (something Pa always insisted on) he found sympathy coming a poor second to self-satisfaction.

As he took his seat that evening in the little four-table lobby that served as his hotel's dining room and began to choose a slap-up dinner from the bill of fare, he felt the bitterness of the morning at last draining away. To add to the pleasure of the evening the staff appeared to be genuinely color blind.

It was about seven o'clock and Will was waiting for his coffee to come through, when the Reverend Washington was shown into the dining room by a waiter quite willing, when asked, to fetch a second cup.

'Quite a civilized place you found here. I'd look after them, not too many like this around. Now,' the minister continued, 'tell me something about yourself and I'll trade it for something about the world you're about to grow into.' When Will had finished his account of Johnstoneville and its history, the older man pursed his lips.

'Weeell,' he said slowly, 'that sure sounds as near paradise in God's acre as a black is likely to find this side of Jordan. Now, let me tell you something about the Devil and all his works outside your little Eden.'

He lit up on a cigarette as he prepared to marshal his thoughts.

'Those crowds this morning were the beginning of a rally of America's filthiest organization. Just about now they will be listening to a hate-filled, screaming orator working them up to the closing ceremony of the day. Inside those sheeted robes you will find just the kind of white Americans, men and women, you might find any day of the week in any shop or office in any town in America. One expects rudeness, abuse or even occasional violence from such people. But once inside those robes, they may become positively murderous. Inside those robes they become the Ku Klux Klan.'

'It's certainly a weird name,' said Will somewhat impatiently, 'but where does it come from?'

'The Klan of today seems to be a rerun of a white secret society that terrorized the South fifty years back. After the Confederate troops got home after defeat in the Civil War, there were troublemakers with time on their hands. A group of officers in Tennessee got together to form an outfit on the lines of a college sophomore club with a title based on the old Greek word "cyclos", or "kuklos", meaning "circle". This became "Ku Klux" and then, because all six founders boasted Scottish ancestry, they added "Klan" for "clan".

Taken over by extremists it dedicated itself to reversing the reforms brought by the Reconstruction so as to defend "the American way of life".'

He smiled bleakly, nodded assent to another coffee and lit up a second cigarette.

'"The Grand Cyclops of one of the Dens" – to use their crazy terms – preached that the Reconstruction program was meant to start a black revolution in the South and the destruction of the white population.'

'How you know so much about it? Have you been down South?'

'Sure, I've been down South. But it's not something I talk about most times.'

'Sure, sure, Reverend Washington.' The eighteen-year-old paused, embarrassed to have touched so roughly on private depths. This was his first real conversation with a grown man. Dealings with the reverend back home had graduated from Sunday school talk to the technicalities of fishing, the good man's passion. With his father "conversation" seemed out of the question, "speak when you're spoken to" about summed it up. But now, it seemed, conversation was more than just words. More like a combination of intelligent understanding, sympathy and respect. He was not sure how to break the silence when, unbidden, a question that had been nagging at the back of his mind since their first encounter that morning broke surface.

'What you mean when you said you were Taliaferro Washington, but not the famous one, Reverend?'

Relieved, Willard saw the hint of a smile return to the lined face.

'Well, I guess that was a bit unfair. If I'd said I wasn't the famous Booker Taliaferro Washington it would have been a bit fairer.'

He peered astonished at the young face.

'Surely you know who Booker Washington was...? No...? 'Booker T. Washington, my half-brother, was, I promise you, really famous. Admirers called him "The giant of the first generation after slavery", enemies, and he had plenty, "that damned, jumped-up half-caste".'

He paused.

'But it's time we were on our way if you're to be back before half ten,' he said and pushed back his chair.

'But it's only just gone half seven,' objected Will, who had privately been looking forward to a nip of rye before setting out for Annaton, 'and according to you it's only a twenty mile round trip.'

'Time to leave, all the same,' said the older man with that hint of authority you always caught at the back of the voice of any minister half worth his calling.

Being merely the businessman, Will settled the bill and joined his companion under a sputtering street light where he'd parked the car for some kind of safety.

'Booker was none too sure of his own date of birth,' observed the reverend as Willard headed the Ford back along the road they'd traveled on into town that morning, '... he claimed 1858 or '59 in the story of his life.'

'Story of his life...?' queried Will. 'You mean he wrote a book?'

'Sure he wrote a book and more than one. *Up from Slavery* was the title he gave his life story and mighty interesting it is too. You'll find me in Chapter Two. He describes how, shortly after they moved to Malden, West Virginia his mother adopted an orphan boy into their family. He doesn't say it was thanks to him.

My father was long dead, my mother had died months

before, and I was scraping a living as best I could in the hellish world of the salt furnaces and coal pits that then surrounded our township. I worked as tubman for one of the hewers who, when I became homeless, gave me a bundle of rags on the floor of the cabin he shared with his family. That way he could keep his eye on me and cut my wage by half to pay for my keep – just about enough to keep me fit for the ten to twelve hour shifts in the mine.'

Will kept his eyes on the road. Many a time his father had bawled him out as a young good-for-nothing. 'Don' know y'r luck! At this moment thousands of children are scratching a living in the salt mines or worse.' He had supposed this was just one of his father's many colorful fictions. But the minister was continuing with his reminiscences.

'It was my job to haul the loose coal cut by my hewer clear of the face and load it into a tub for the wagon to transport to the mine's opening. I was determined to break out of that hell hole.

For some time hewers had been complaining of thefts from their lunchboxes – Jemmy Danford, the wagon man, was generally suspected. It gave me an idea. On the day in question Jemmy arrived just as my hewer was wedged in a working barely high enough for a man's prone body. As I loaded the wagon by the flickering light of our two candle lamps, I saw the lunchbox, unopened, tucked into a crevice. As soon as Jemmy trundled to the next hewer I sought the permission of my boss to relieve myself; even in those conditions the hewers expected to be free as far as possible of human excrements. Easing the box from its hiding place I hurried off with some madcap idea of making my escape clear of the mine altogether. A man-size lunch would, I supposed, see me safe to Charleston, where I would of course make my fortune.

It was fully a mile of winding shafts and alleys from the coal face to the opening of the mine. Before I had gone a hundred yards a sudden draft extinguished my candle lamp. There is no darkness to compare with the darkness of a coal mine. I had no light, no matches and, now, no idea of which direction to take. A sudden roar of anger told me my hewer had just broken work for his lunch. I dashed down an alley and, within moments, fell, and the lunchbox and its contents clattered out of reach. Picking myself up I could only stumble blindly on, in terror and considerable pain. God be praised, a glint of light down another branch of the tunneling led me to this boy, little older than myself but seemingly in full control of the situation. He it was who persuaded the family to take me in, though he does not mention the fact in his book.'

He paused, his eyes thinking.

'Booker was clever as well as kind, dead now, poor man, not quite sixty. From the start he was a worker. After a salt furnace, the coal mine; after that, night school, and after that a journey of 300 miles, begged and worked, to college in Hampton, Virginia. Thanks to his coaching I began my studies at that excellent institute.

I blotted my copy book with Booker when I got the call to the ministry. Hadn't much time for preachers, hadn't Booker T. Washington. "Too many, I'm afraid to say, see it as a magic ticket to the easy life." As to my taking the name Taliaferro, I told myself that it would be a way to honor the family that had adopted me but, if truth be told, I reckoned that with a name like that I would make my mark more easily.

Booker not only got himself and me into college but by the age of twenty-one he had founded his own... you never heard of the Tuskegee Institute? No? But surely you or your dad have heard tell of the National Negro Business League of Boston? Been going twenty odd years... and that was started by brother Booker too.'

They were on the open road under one of those clear spring skies, deep velvet but with a hint of frost as hard as iron behind

241

it. Willard glimpsed what seemed to be a shimmering on the not so distant horizon and idly wondered what it might be.

'By the time I was twenty-one I was at least teaching school.'

The glimmer on the horizon was resolving itself into what seemed a line of fires. The older man leant forward as if concentrating on the scene, a habit of his, Will noted. He sensed a grimmer set of the lantern jaw and somehow was not surprised when the monologue started up again, this time addressed, so it seemed, to the speaker himself.

'That was my big mistake. By now, in many of the Southern states white opinion was returning to the "good old days". Negroes were harassed from the polling booths, in most counties simply banned from them. Black children had only the most meager of education, except in Sunday schools. And that gave me an idea. There was a shortage of black teachers for these Sunday schools: I would teach there but use the lessons to teach the kind of thing they were denied in their day school. A more damn fool idea could hardly have been dreamed up... real education for blacks?!' He laughed bitterly. 'So, I set out one spring day, traveling pack on shoulder, to tramp and beg my way south to DO GOOD.

My moral crusade lasted all of four Sundays. On the fifth, the school room was broken into by a group of masked and white sheeted thugs. The Klan had been officially disbanded fifteen years back, but these were Klansmen alright. The kids knew it too. They just cowered silent while I was dragged out, tied over the back of a horse and galloped off to some remote farmstead.'

The Ford was now just a mile short of the site of the morning's accident. The curve of the road brought them nearer to the crowded showground. Willard slowed and pulled over on to the verge behind a scattered line of other cars, deserted by their curious passengers, who could be seen straggling down the hillside for a better view of the astonishing spectacle in the valley below. It was a moonless night, but the show ground blazed like a day in hell, with a thousand flaring, smoking torches. The inner zone comprised three concentric rings of counter-marching hooded figures, each bearing a torch and circling a rough-built stage. From it rose a massive cross, near forty foot high and made, so far as Willard could judge, of brushwood tied or nailed to a timber frame. At its base twelve figures, their hoods and robes scattered with crude cabalistic signs, stood in a shallow arc behind a thirteenth who was clothed in purple robes and hood.

'This is not play acting this is blasphemy,' hissed the reverend. 'They call the guy in purple "Grand Dragon of the Invisible Empire" the others have assorted titles such as Hydras, Kleagles, King Kleagles and I don't know what else. It's the same half-educated high school mentality of the old Klan but now they're mimicking Christ and the Apostles; twelve Judases more like!'

Towards the edges of the crowd the torches thinned out but here and there in the dusky fringes, groups of the weird witch-hooded figures could be seen patrolling the perimeter on horseback. The confused murmur of the huge throng floated up to the watchers. Then, at some signal from the stewards, the vast gathering fell silent. Now, the sounds of the night creatures and the distant hum of traffic, as if infected by the dark purpose stirring in the torch-lit assembly, seemed to throb with menace.

The Grand Dragon stepped forward a pace with a gesture of authority. A wide megaphone mounted on a tripod stand was wheeled up. The roar of cheering that greeted his every utterance reached Will and the reverend like the spreading rumble of distant thunder. What he said was, of course, quite inaudible.

'Citizens of the Invisible Empire of the Realm of Michigan, we are gathered this night by virtue of God's unchanging grace to pledge ourselves to obtain surcease from the tide of foreign elements that threat this fair land of ours. To commit ourselves, Klansmen and Klanswomen of America, to cleanse the   bosom of our motherland of the foul socialistical leeches that now besmirch it… to fight the scarlet whore of Babylon… to crush the Hebrew from the land… one hundred per cent Americanism…'

Willard turned in amazement. At his side, leaning forward in his characteristic pose of attention but with a face distorted with anger, the mild-mannered Reverend Taliaferro Washington was spitting out the overblown catchphrases as though they were expletives.

'I make it my business, as a Christian minister, to know my enemy. Unless I am much mistaken, that monkey in the purple night dress is vomiting the same anti-Catholic, anti-Jewish, anti-foreign, anti-liberal filth that Grand Dragon David C. Stephenson served up last 4th July to the Konklave in Kokomo, Indiana. They like their "K's" do the Klansmen.'

He paused, shook himself and smiled an ashamed apology.

'Forgive the outburst, young man. Whatever else may be proper to the Christian ministry, hatred is not. But it takes a deal of imagination to realize that there, below us, speaks one of God's children as open to His eternal grace as we ourselves.'

Will did not respond. It was not an act of imagination he was particularly interested in attempting.

'It's time to be going,' said his companion. 'Back to Farmer Chesnutt, just to be safe. Those characters down there are part of the new Klan started by a "Colonel" Simmons about ten years back. He and his team knew there was money in hatred and just then, it seems, "one hundred per cent Americans" were worried more about the Jews and the Catholics than about the blacks. But I guess it wouldn't take much to switch them to targeting black folk like the first Klan.'

They were heading back for the car when a roar rose from the valley so loud that it jerked them round. A pillar of fire shot from the central stage. At first like the streak of a giant rocket, thanks to the gallons of gasoline in which the brushwood had been steeped, it resolved itself before their eyes into the jagged, angry outline of a fiery cross.

Taliaferro Washington, his face gray, sank to his knees, his hands clasped, and turned to heaven. 'Father, forgive them,' he said, 'for they know not what they do so to profane the anniversary of thy Blessed Son Jesu's death.' He remained like this for what seemed an age to young Willard, awkwardly fingering the car keys. Then briskly he got to his feet, brushed down the knees of his trousers and wedged his tall frame into the passenger seat.

'Today,' he said in quite matter-of-fact tones. 'Today, Willard, you will not have forgotten, is Friday, that Friday we Christians celebrate as Good in memory of God's act of Redemption by the Crucifixion of his son, the Lord be praised. Down there men and women who also call themselves Christian have defaced that memory. For five years, back in the 1860s, the sign of the Fiery Cross proclaimed the Klan and terrorized the Negro people of the South. Maybe, this New Klan is not so different after all.'

Thanks to the cover of darkness, the two friends were able to get on their way unobserved. "Creeping about like criminals in your own country", as his father had once put it. The Reverend Washington continued with the saga of his experience down south as a young teacher.

'We'd just witnessed the young enthusiast being hauled off to a remote farmstead. "Shooting is too good for this fellow. What say we hang him good and slow, when we get through whipping him?" The suggestion was eagerly welcomed but fortunately for me, the speaker was not the leader.

'Not this time, Jed. This time, we agreed, we give him his notice. Next time he's for the high jump.'

'OK. Boss, OK, say that's good.' And they all laughed.

Soon after that, I was being tumbled out of the wagon, and dumped in the corner of a field formed by a couple of barns. The view was shielded from the road though I doubt whether anyone would have intervened. Two of them held me down and one of them took out a bundle of black-gum switches, a special kind of stick which stings and raises the flesh where it hits. "Fifty lashes each is what we agreed, black boy." And with that the leader stripped the shirt off my back. I asked what I had done to merit such treatment. "God damn you!" came the reply, "don't you know that this is a white man's country?" I pointed out, what was indeed the rather surprising truth, that some of the infants were white and their parents had no complaints about my work. "Yes, damn you, that is the worst thing about it, having a nigger teacher, or at least a half-nigger," he spat on my bare back, "teaching white kids." And then it began.... 200 lashes as promised. Three times they had to revive me with ice-cold water from the brook. Then they left me, blood soaking into my breeches and flesh hanging in ribbons. I lay under that hedge for eighteen hours. For the next three years I was racked with pneumonia every winter.'

Will slept badly that night. The first time he could remember having done so. But Saturday broke with a list of appointments longer even than the day before. It was late when he piled once more into bed. Sunday at least was a rest day. Since leaving home he had missed church, persuading himself that neither his father in heaven nor, more doubtfully, his father on earth would begrudge him the time off, considering how much work he put in on the other six days. As he was dropping off to sleep, an unwanted thought floated into the back of his mind. This Sunday it would be church as usual, after all – he had promised Reverend Washington he would go and hear him preach the Easter sermon at Annaton.

* * * * *

The church was full and, to Willard's surprise, boasted a pew of white faces at the back. Will supposed there had to be *some* Christian white folk, not that these particular specimens, notably the one in the pepper and salt suiting, looked very promising. The congregation was settling down, in that comfortable mood of expectancy, whether of a well-earned doze or of an uplifting homily, not unmixed with a modest awareness of personal piety. From the first words it was clear that little sleeping would be done this Sunday morning. The normally urbane preacher was obviously on fire with the Holy Spirit, there to make witness.

'Today,' the preacher spoke with a sonority of voice Willard would never have suspected him capable of, 'is Christ the Lord, our Lord, risen from the dead. Today, as always, his risen presence is with us in our daily lives. Three days ago we commemorated his death on the cross, the momentary horror of Golgotha. In Catholic Churches throughout this great city of Detroit this morning, priests and people are celebrating the ending of the Festival of Shadows – the *Tenebrae* they call it in Latin. It is not our way,' the Congregation responded with a sigh of satisfaction, 'but it is a good way.' Angry murmurings. 'It is a good way because through last night, in mournful memory of our Lord's sojourn in the nether world, vigil was kept with psalms and anthems, so that today, with the break of sun, the souls of the faithful might feel themselves revived by the glorious return of Jesus, of our Daystar.'

The transformation, wrought by the pulpit, in his wise and mild-mannered traveling companion of yesterday had Will enthralled. He could hear a passion behind the preacher's voice which had nothing to do with pulpit oratory and everything to do with flaming conviction.

He shifted uneasily in the pew. He was thinking of the day

247

he had come back from Sunday school, eyes glowing with the heroism of the Christians against the lions. 'Never be a martyr, son. It can mean a sticky end and there's sure no percentage in it,' his father had said. But the man in the pulpit was not looking for any percentage and had paid his tax on courage a long time back. Nothing was going to happen on this sunny Sunday, surely. Why should it?

'Today,' returned the ringing voice, 'we herald Christ the risen Lord in joy and love. But, my friends, three days back, not outside Jerusalem, not 1900 years ago, not by Jews and Romans but here and now, outside Detroit, by vile hands of hooded heathen Americans, the suffering son of God was profaned and defamed, blasphemed and cauterized in hellish flames with the emblem of the Fiery Cross and hymns of bitter hate.' Cries of 'Amen, Amen' and 'Praise the Lord', 'Hallelujah!' and 'Daniel to Judgement' drowned out the sermon now. The preacher held up his hands for silence. 'The Good Book tells us that all men and women are equal in the sight of God, all are loved. Remember as you leave the Lord's House on this Easter Sunday to pray, as Lord Jesus taught, for your enemies. Remember that beneath the sheets and hoods of Klandom move the limbs of human beings, God's children like yourselves. Pray that those souls find once more the love of God and those sheets become symbols of purity not shrouds of perdition.'

If he had any more to add, the preacher did not get the chance. The people swayed and clapped and the chanting swelled into a spontaneous hymn: 'Remember and Pray, Remember and Pray, Praise God and Bless thine enemy, Hallelujah!' Within moments the pianist had found a favorite hymn tune to fit the scansion. Will clapped with the rest until he saw the reverend descend the pulpit steps and start up the aisle, swaying to the dancing rhythm of the ecstatic worshippers. Will, near the back of the chapel, hurried out

248

ahead of the crowd. He was not the first to leave. The pew of white faces was now quite empty.

* * * * *

Willard had begun to wonder whether he would ever catch up on his schedule. The sermon at the Bethel was an event that would live with him always. But afterwards, the people would not let the minister go. He must join them in cakes and soda so they could tell him their troubles. His words had hit a nerve with the local black community. For more than a year, the local Klan associations had been striking fear into their hearts. Nobody had actually yet been killed, but many had been threatened, many had had mysterious fires at their homes or their businesses, or been abducted by hooded figures and beaten up or, for the women, worse. There was nothing, it seemed, the police could do without identification. Willard, having offered to drive the reverend to his next stop, down the road in Toledo, could also do nothing but wait. He was supposed to be in Columbus, Ohio for a morning appointment. That would have to be cancelled by phone first thing. But he was now beginning to wonder whether he would ever see a normal, suspicious, maneuvering, foxy-faced businessman again. Saints were all very well in their place but that place, Willard decided, would never again be in his Model T Ford.

By the time they finally got on the road, the evening was drawing in. He supposed they would have to find a roadhouse. His companion was silent and withdrawn. The traffic was slowing to a snail's pace for no obvious reason, and now the idiot behind was sounding his horn. Willard stamped on the brake pedal, and only just in time to avoid a shunt collision. The car crawling along ahead of him had stopped in its tracks. The horn-blowing joker behind rammed the Model T a

Willard, hands spread out on the steering wheel, prepared for a swearing match with old whitey.

At that moment a number of things happened. The front vehicle seemed to slip gears into reverse and rammed the front of the Ford, buckling the radiator grill and just denting its own rear bumper. The preacher was suddenly no longer in the Ford, having fallen through the passenger door, apparently loosened by the collision, and a masked face was pointing a workmanlike revolver through the driver's side.

'Hold steady, Mac.' It was a velvet, hard, white voice. 'You'll be having company.' And at the same moment, another masked and armed figure installed itself in the passenger seat in place of the reverend.

'Follow the car in front; don't try no funny business; and don't speak to me you dirt.' The passenger door slammed to. The front car pulled away. Willard obediently followed suit, "No percentage," he heard his father's voice saying from down a distant sunlit tunnel, and the car behind moved up. The incident was over in less than forty seconds. Your average Prohibition road cop could have blinked easy and not noticed any difference in the little convoy.

But there was a difference. The Reverend Washington was not in the Ford, Willard was under threat of his life, and the man with the gun was old pepper and salt from the "white" pew back at the Bethel.

CHAPTER FIFTEEN

Justice: Triple K

The convoy took a right off the highway and a hundred yards further on the lead car took a second right along a gravel drive. It pulled up in front of a clapboard mansion fronting the highway, with a gravel forecourt lit by a couple of standard lamps. Following orders, Will pulled up alongside and the third car drew up beside him. Light flooded out onto the gravel as the main door opened. The appearance was of a respectable residence with visitors for the evening. The reality was very different.

Stepping out of the Ford under the watchful eyes of the gunman, Will saw Washington bundled out of the third car's rear passenger door, stumbling and obviously in pain. In the light of the entrance hall, he could see one eye was already closing from a quick close encounter during the short drive. Their six captors were respectably but not well dressed. He was devoutly glad the hopsack was in his traveling case so that he did not present a target for envy as well as hatred. An impassive butler held open a door at the back of the mansion's entrance hall and the eight men passed through into a sparsely furnished reception room; there was an unseasonably hot log fire roaring in the hearth.

'I think you will find everything you need to hand, gentlemen.' The butler spoke with obvious distaste. 'Mr

Sanderson required me to inform you that he is not at home and that he hopes to have the use of this chamber in one hour's time.'

'If I know Sanderson, he'd willingly have a ringside seat at the little show we're about to stage but "See Nothing, Hear Nothing, Know Nothing" is his motto and so long as he gives us the premises and the protection, I'm not the one to complain.'

The speaker was the tallest of the masked figures and clearly their leader. The masks themselves were skimpy affairs. No attempt to hide a beard or one highly distinctive cauliflower ear. Like the pepper and salt suit, their owners had little expectation that any jury in the county would accept identifications. But the masks at least helped save the appearances in the unlikely event of any of them ever coming to court.

'Right, Reverend Heartache, take a pew.' The speaker, cauliflower ear, forced the reverend roughly down on to an upright chair draped with a brown dust sheet, legs astride so that he was sitting with his arms resting on the chair back. 'You ever heard of a gum switch?'

Will could not suppress a gasp. Nothing at all had changed. Forty years and a thousand miles lay between his friend and his last martyrdom and here he was facing a repeat of just that ordeal. 'No, no, you can't,' he blurted out. 'He's an old man and a good man, what did he ever do to you?' The backhand of a leather-gloved fist hammered his lips against his teeth, his nose crunched sickeningly and he staggered back into one of the fireside chairs.

'Not you! Dirt!' His gunman escort wrenched him back onto his feet and sent him lurching across the room, winded and doubled up with pain, so that his head butted the wall and he slumped, barely conscious, to the floor.

'I warned you, dirt... Don't talk to me, or anyone else in

this room. And DON'T,' he screamed, 'DON'T YOU FILTH UP DECENT FURNITURE WITH YOUR FILTHY BLACK CARCASS. What you think them dust sheets is for? And you thank God that bleeding nose didn't soil the wallpaper!

The man's body was shaking violently with the suppressed rage of a psychopath and he made a move towards the fallen figure of the young salesman. The leader of the group gripped his shoulder to hold him back.

'Not now, Billy, not now. You're quite right of course. But we are here on different business tonight and we do not have all the time in the world. You can discipline this young whelp any way you like later, when we've found some place to dump him and his saintly companion. Right now,' he continued, turning to the other members of the group, 'I think you'll agree with me, the boy's outburst is suggestive. Dean, strip the shirt off the old hypocrite's back.'

With obvious relish the burly figure addressed as Dean wrenched the reverend's arms out of his suit, tossed the jacket carelessly on the floor, removed the tie and with a grasp at the shirt collar tore it down in a ragged rip before laying back the two tattered remnants. The sight thus revealed made even the brutal onlookers stare. The ageing skin was scarred horribly. Not broken, but raised in a criss-cross of old welts like a strip of old coya matting.

'Well well, reverend Sir. It would appear that you are acquainted with the gum switch. I doubt whether the memory has much faded though it seems the introductions were made many years ago. Perhaps you would care to enlighten us on the circumstances that brought you this distinctive body ornament.'

There was, despite the cheap, desperado sarcasms, an air of sinister purpose about the man more frightening than the brutality of his subordinates. *But then*, thought Will, sick at heart, *he has them under his control and is going to make use of them in his own good time and to much more effect than those thick bruisers would be capable of.* After a moment during which the reverend had volunteered no response to the jeering invitation, the leader spoke again.

'The Klan, you see, does not die and I am sure you know why you have been brought to this place. Your punishment is of course assured, but due form must also be observed and that calls for a trial. Not by your peers, your equals, oh no! Something much better, a trial by your superiors. Morton, I call you to the witness stand.'

With smug pride, pepper and salt stepped forward and held up his right hand, preparing to take the oath.

'I, Ghoul Morton, of the Den of Annaton, do swear by all the Terrors of the Invisible World that the evidence I am about to give is true and not one wit faned.'

'The witness may proceed.'

'Your Dreadness, Lord Grand Cyclops, following the fiat of the konklave of the Den, I, together with five denizens, did this day attend Sunday service at the Annaton Bethel. We did not defile ourselves by participating in the activities, neither by prayer nor the singing of hymns. But we listened, Sir, we sure did listen and most especially to the words of this pretended preacherman. And the air was poisoned with words it grieves me sore to have to reiterate, Dread Cyclops.'

The horror of what he had to say made the witness lapse, farcically enough, into a more normal argot for a Detroit storekeeper.

'This 'ere black bolted nigger, goldarnit, Sir, called the burning of the Fiery Cross, the most high and Mystifient Ceremony of our glorified Klan, a blasphemy against God and Christ and several other such high falutin' nonsense, Mr Murdoch... er... Grand Cyclops... er... Your Dreadness.' Willard's stomach turned with the realization that such illiterate boobies could hold the fate of this noble minister in their hands.

'That will do, Ghoul Morton. Remember yourself. Never in the Klan do you use the family name of any member, and of the high officials of the Den you use no name from the Visible World at all...'

'But, Grand Cyclops there is something more important yet to report if you will only permit...'

The leader reflected then decided to allow the report to continue. 'You may proceed, but keep your report to the essentials.'

'On your order, Your Dreadness. What I must now say is beyond doubt true and will be confirmed by my five fellow Ghouls should you require corroboration. At the end of his sermonizing the accused called upon his congregation of niggers and nigger lovers to... to... f... f... forgive the Klan and to p... p... pray for the Klan!'

Pepper and salt ended his report in a splutter of indignation and retired to a couch by the wall to recover his composure without waiting to be dismissed. He obviously felt he had said all that was needed to close the case. From the reaction of Murdoch it seemed he was right. The stiffening of the body said as loud as words that the man's self-esteem had been struck a barely credible body blow. Nothing in his dealings with the world of whitey was ever to harm Will as deeply as this discovery, that for Murdoch and millions like him, the worst humiliation they could imagine was to receive the warm, tender and basic acts of human life, love and forgiveness from a black. Now, in this tawdry twenties' mansion, his first reaction was a youthful savage triumph that in some obscure way the reverend really had hit these bastards where it hurt. But the realities behind the events seeped slowly into his soul and over the years were to make him yet more bitter and yet more lost to the possibility of true happiness than even his father. A moment later he was sweating in fearful anticipation.

'I see; the final insolence. And you tell me that your fellows will corroborate this statement.' The infant school code language of the Klan had evaporated, leaving the elite, sophisticated and contemptuous vocabulary of the Grand Cyclops himself. *Surely*, pondered Willard, *he must wonder sometimes what he is doing, playing around with these moral hoodlums.* But this was to misunderstand the situation, theirs was the language of the psychopath seeking social camouflage.

'You, "Preacherman".' The sneer was audible to everyone in the room. But Washington smiled, his sardonic smile. It was a mistake, for it steadied his enemy.

'You have been arraigned before a duly constituted inquiry of the Ku Klux Klan, charged with offences against the values of the American Way of Life.' *I sure missed that one*, thought Washington. 'I have found you guilty with the assent of my colleagues here.' There was a murmur of approval. 'And I must, in due form, pronounce the sentence you shall undergo...' The speaker paused with effective drama. Then he continued as if quoting some manual of rhetoric.

'Punishment awaits you, and such horror as no man ever underwent and lived. The cusped moon is full of wrath and as its horns fill, the deadly mixture will fall on your unhallowed head. We that are of the dead undead are watching you, say the ancestral spirits! The far-seeing eye of the Grand Cyclops has rested upon you! YOU SHALL DIE!"

The silence was broken only by the heaving sobs of young Willard. The reverend, back bared, face bludgeoned, stared unmoving at the floor. *So, it has come again*, he thought, *after all these years; a second, final martyrdom... a true martyrdom. But Lord, oh Lord, I did not seek it.*

'Mr *Washington* – by God you blaspheme the All American way, you cringing half-caste, with your very name...'

'Not I, but you it is who should cringe, Murdoch, in your heart. A son of Belial, you are preparing the final sin, the sin against life itself, the killing of a fellow human to ease your own spiritual discomfort... '

The voice was silenced with a leather fist on a signal from Murdoch.

'Death will come soon to you. But not at once. First we must brand our steer before we send it to market. To switch you again would be superfluous. To mark you is essential, so that those who find the body will know which abattoir it came from. Dean, tie him to that chair.'

Washington began to struggle then, seeing it was useless, resigned himself to what fate had in store. Will screamed in the vain hope of raising some kind of assistance. His guard wrenched his hands behind his back and gagged him. At the same time the thug they called Dean, a glint in his eyes, had extricated a workmanlike iron poker from among the logs in the log basket and, on the order of Murdoch, lodged its point in the hottest part of the roaring fire. Washington had been positioned so that he faced away from the fire, but though he could not see the preparations he was fully aware of what was being prepared.

Murdoch moved round to face his victim.

'You well know that the Klan gives only one warning. You had yours the best part of half a century ago it would seem. Now you shall be branded with the mark of the Klan. It will then be time for us to leave. A conveniently short drive from here lies a quarry. There, you and your friend will each receive a bullet in the back of the head. Tomorrow being Monday, your bodies will be found by a worker on the site, a black laborer I presume, if things follow the usual pattern. He will be terrified and will think of his family. There will be indignant outcries from the liberal press, the police will announce a full-scale search for the culprits. Nothing will be done and it will be quite some time before Detroit is troubled by another slander of the name of the Klan... That iron red yet?'

'Two minutes, boss, and it'll be good and ready.'

'We generally like to use a branding iron, makes a more workmanlike job, you understand. My fault I'm afraid,' again the thin smile, 'never thought for a moment we were dealing with a second offender. Still, what is a slight inconvenience for you is something of a bonus for my lads. They find the smell of burning flesh adds a relish to the screams, which is all they get with a beating. And the dragging of the iron is undoubtedly more painful than the sharp clean stamp of a brand.'

While speaking he had moved round behind the trussed figure on the chair and taken the throbbing red hot iron from his henchman. Now he laid the poker on the scarred flesh. Taken unawares, Washington, in a rictus of pain, screamed, a tight choking scream. His tormentor leaned back in the parody of an artist judging his work.

'It is always the first stroke that determines the work, I find,' he said menacingly. Then he placed the point at the head of the upright and drew it down across the quivering flesh, then up to form a crude v for the top section of a stenciled letter K. Washington screamed again, the "artist" was dragging out his work as slowly as possible.

The "work" continued for five more terrible minutes. Will, sweating and shivering with fear for himself and sympathy for the reverend, could not, though he was ashamed, drag his eyes from the smoldering, quivering body on the chair. Washington manfully worked to suppress his screams. The blood was running from his bitten lips but more than once a wild, despairing cry broke from him. Murdoch had only one stroke to add to his handiwork when the door opened abruptly and the butler took a step into the room, no deference in his manner now.

'Mr Stannard requires that you cease forthwith. We have visitors. Three cars of county police are turning in to the drive. Mr Stannard has no wish to disrupt his normally amiable relations with the authorities. He will do his best to conceal your presence but do not expect too great an effort. Meanwhile, I must insist, Sir, that you interrupt your torment of the poor man – his screams will draw unwelcome attention.'

The artist had defiantly completed the last K with particular viciousness and forced a piercing cry from the contorted lips of his victim. Fascinated, Will realized that the supercilious Murdoch was trying to score off a butler! Fear yielded ground to contempt. Meanwhile, the Klansmen had thrown Washington's jacket over his brutalized back. Blacks tied up for "interrogation" could perhaps be explained but even in Klan country the official authorities would have to take notice of what had been done in this room tonight.

Silence fell. The crunch of tires on gravel heralded the arrival of the police. Voices and heavy footsteps in the entrance hall faded and muffled as the newcomers were shown into one of the front reception rooms, presumably to await the arrival of the owner of the mansion, at home to the authorities if not to his "friends" in the Klan. The hum of voices suddenly swelled as doors opened and the group in the back room realized that steps were heading their way. 'When this is over,' Murdoch hissed furiously at his subordinates, 'I'll find out which one of you is responsible for bringing down this intervention and have you stripped of your membership in full konklave.'

The door opened and once again the butler appeared. 'Mr Stannard has asked me to enquire whether there is a Negro here who drives the Model T Ford motor car presently standing on the forecourt, and if so that he will step out into the hall, where the police have questions to put to him.'

His hands hurriedly untied, Will, chafing his wrists, walked past the butler into the entrance hall.

In the hall he found a group comprising three policemen and a tall, impressive individual, clearly a pillar of the community but with an uncomfortable look in his eye. It was he who opened the interview.

'You, I suppose, are the driver of this car that the police are interesting themselves in.'

'It is my car, Sir.'

'I see, owner as well as driver?' The eyebrows went up.

'You got it, Sir.'

'You'd be advised not to take that tone, young man. It seems that you were involved in an accident on Friday and the police here want to put some questions to you back at their precinct house.'

Mystified by the turn of events, Willard could at least see that a visit to the precinct house was much to be preferred to his present situation. The question was how to extricate Reverend Washington and get him included in the party. Playing for time he coughed rather dramatically. 'I'm sorry, Sir, but could I have a glass of water?'

'I should think that might be arranged. Birchfield, perhaps you would be so kind as to bring a tray of drinks. The officers might care to join me in a soda.'

Deeply dissatisfied at the way the evening was turning out, Stannard's one idea was to clear his house of the unwanted visitors – police, Klansmen and their "clients", the term he always used – with as little fuss as possible. The young Negro seemed to be in genuine distress and water might well settle his throat. But the owner of the mansion also wanted to assess a little more precisely what this strange visitation was in fact about, and also to assess his current standing with the local force following the recent appointment of a new police chief. Up until January of this year, he had been treated with gratifying deference thanks to his close ties with the head of the force: a covert Klan member from across the county line who had owed his appointment largely to Stannard's influence. Under the old regime there would have been no Prohibition talk of "sodas". The fact that the new chief had not called round to make himself known, had Stannard worried.

His work for the Klan engaged his mental commitment as a good American and white supremacist. It also gave him gratifying respect within the community. But he had more important interests at stake and until he knew the chief's attitude to the new Klan – some Northern police were very hostile to the whole organization – he would keep a low profile. Besides, Murdoch was getting decidedly uppity in the way he seemed to take the availability of the Stannard mansion for granted. Take this evening for example; two blacks under his roof. It was absurd. However, there they were, and until he was sure of the new chief he'd better behave as though they were human.

Once Birchfield was off the field of play, so to speak, the door to the back room was unguarded. It was the best chance Will would get to rescue the reverend and he decided to risk the maneuver that had been half forming at the back of his mind when he forced the coughing fit.

'I sure did have an accident officer and I'd be happy to answer your questions.' He raised his voice so that it could be heard through the door to the back room left open by Birchfield. 'But I've got a friend, Reverend Washington, traveling with me and I would like to bring him along too as he witnessed the event.'

'A witness, eh? First I've heard of any witness,' said the police captain, suspiciously. 'I guess we'd like to have a look at him. The truck driver laying the charges said there was only the driver in the car so make sure your reverend friend doesn't perjure himself.'

Stifling a shocked reaction to this talk of charges being brought against him, Will hurried to the door, opened it and called through. 'You better come along, Reverend Washington, the police want to take us back to the station for questioning.' His eyes met a confused scene of activity, the masks had been removed and Dean and Morton were busying themselves loosening the ropes that bound the reverend. The group formed up round the sagging figure and Willard could see that desperate first-aid work was being carried out, not on the man himself, but on the two tattered halves of his shirt. With his tie once more round his neck, the shirt tails tucked back into the trousers and the jacket eased over his flinching back, he emerged as a desperately tired, down at heel and shabby traveling preacher. He was escorted through the door by a scowling Murdoch, while Morton and Dean and the fourth man hovered awkwardly in the background. It seemed that the Klan were not so confident of their standing hereabouts as they had boasted.

At this point, Birchfield returned with the tray of soft drinks, which he placed on the hall table. 'Would you like a drink of water, Reverend?' Willard moved over purposefully to the table and poured a tumbler of water for his friend before anyone could stop him.

'The old fellah don't look so good,' said the captain. Startled by the obvious physical distress of the old preacher, his suspicions turned to focus on the whole odd set-up in the house. What were the blacks doing on the premises at all and in the main residential quarters? And what about the white visitors, apart from the tall guy who seemed to be in charge, a prize bunch of rejects from some neighborhood fraternity, certainly not regulars on the local gentry circuit. Back at precinct headquarters rumor had it that Stannard was involved with the revived Klan and this, said the gossips, explained why he had enjoyed such a good ride from the ex-chief. Well, as the captain had reason to know, the new chief had his own cronies. Whether they too were Klan members station rumor had not yet pronounced. Three months was not long enough to decide as to whether the new man dabbled in illegality any more than for an occasional bootleg scotch.

If it came to that he was none too happy about the errand the chief had sent him on. In his opinion the lorry driver's story of being forced to swerve off the road by the reckless driving of a black in a Ford wasn't worth a hill of beans. He'd never yet heard of a Michigan truck driver taking avoiding action for a black. More likely the guy was drunk and needed some pretext for ditching his wagon off a road virtually clear of traffic to get the insurance. The fact that the owner of the trucking company was buddies with the county chief of police was sufficient cause to explain why he and his boys had been detailed off to find the Ford if at all possible. They'd been on the search for the past two and a half days and were coming back from their last fool's errand when young McCartney, stopping off for a roadside pee, had glimpsed the car standing all so innocent under the forecourt lights of the Stannard mansion.

The captain came to a decision. While preserving the decencies required when dealing at this level of the community, he would remove the two blacks back to the station and proceed with his case. He would also take names and addresses of all present. He did not consider himself particularly favorable to the black cause, but the law was the law and if this Stannard and Murdoch thought they could run their own "racial policing" on his territory, they'd best think again. Suspicious by nature, he was now distinctly dissatisfied with the whole set up in the Stannard mansion.

'Perhaps I should explain, Captain, my relations with Mr Murdoch and his guests. They are members of what I suppose you could call a patriotic discussion group but are temporarily without a meeting room. I have been happy to accommodate them for the time being, though I think this is their last meeting here.'

'Uh, huh. Well thank you Mr Stannard, that certainly helps my understanding.' Turning to the blacks. 'What would your names be?' Noting Willard's answers for both of them, he ordered his sergeant to escort them to the waiting cars outside and turned his attention to the four Klansmen.

Throughout the whole episode, Murdoch had been glowering thunder first at Stannard and then at the police, and on several occasions had been about to burst out but thought better of it.

'Well, gentleman,' said the captain with a cursory attempt at social grace. 'Perhaps I could take a note of your names and addresses, just in case I would need to come back to you on anything.'

'By what right, officer, do you think you can intrude on a private meeting in a private house. Mr Stannard may not be overly concerned but let me tell you, Captain, we see no reason why we should disclose any information to you. We are not, I suppose, on any charge – unlike those two niggers.' Now the dam had broken, Murdoch was nearly incoherent with anger.

'Mr Murdoch,' the captain spoke with dangerous coolness, 'I am in Mr Stannard's house following the orders of my chief of police to discover and bring in for questioning the driver of the black Ford which is presently parked outside. I find that driver associated with a group of other gentlemen, so far as I can make out, in close conversation with them. It is clear that, to carry through my chief's instructions, I gotta be able to check out any story he might feed me, with yourself and your colleagues if it seems advisable. My sergeant here will take the details.'

'And I advise you, Captain, that I have other colleagues with power in this community who will take a dim view if you press this matter.'

'Mr Murdoch, we've run out of time here. Either give the information I require to my sergeant or be prepared to be charged with obstructing a police officer in the pursuance of his duties.'

The "colleagues" were eager to volunteer the required

information and get out of this disaster of an evening as fast as might be. Eventually, blustering to the last, Murdoch capitulated. The captain rapidly wound up the proceedings and saw the four thugs off the premises. Detailing two of his officers to escort the two blacks in the Ford, he and the other officer led the way back into Detroit and a late session of questioning at the station.

CHAPTER SIXTEEN

Home Truths

It was three days later. The Ford, battered but sound of heart, was doing a cheerful forty miles an hour under a leaden sky. Will had crossed the Ohio-Kentucky state line at Cincinnati and they were approaching Louisville. The time was ten to five in the afternoon and the best part of 120 miles lay ahead to Johnstoneville; Willard would be lucky to make it home before nine. He felt as heavy as the sky. Between them, the driver of the steam wagon and Murdoch and his Klansmen had cost him, Willard estimated, four major orders. His father would be furious.

For three frustrating days, he and Reverend Washington had been at least secure in police hospitality, in a clean, if drafty, cell. Shattered by his tortures in the Stannard mansion, the old man had finally regained consciousness in a spell of unseasonably cold weather, shivering and on the verge of pneumonia. He had made a deposition against the Klansmen as a matter of form. The captain listened seriously and made copious notes. But they knew no action would be taken. 'Why should they make trouble for themselves on account of an out-of-state vagrant preacherman?' had been the reverend's weary comment.

On the credit side no action was taken either on the truck driver's deposition against Willard. In Kentucky and all points south, the black driver would have been fined, no question.Things were not quite so straightforward here it seemed. The captain clearly had difficulty in adjusting to the idea of a Detroit teamster going out of his way to accommodate a black. The two travelers found themselves leaving the precinct house by noon on the fourth day. Willard finally tracked down a doctor willing to give Reverend Washington a thorough examination and it was not until ten in the evening that they drove into the Chesnutt farm, both ready for a good night's rest.

Next day there were medicines to be bought on the doctor's prescription. Farmer Chesnutt had a stock sale to attend and, since his wife could not drive, Willard had to run the errand to the pharmacist. With the morning written off he nevertheless salvaged two of his appointments – one for that afternoon, the other for the following day. Neither client would confirm any follow-up orders; time for that when Mr Brock made his next visit. So, thanks to the murderous games of the K.K.K., an order book which ten days back had looked magnificent now looked ordinary. Willard reckoned he would be lucky to get another tour on the road this side of Christmas.

* * * * *

Making better time than he expected, Will found himself home around a quarter to nine, gently closing the car door outside the house on Main Street so as not to disturb his ten-year-old brother, Ralph. The precaution was of course pointless.

'Have a good trip?' The voice hissed from the attic window over the street door.

'So so, so so! Tell you in the morning. Now y'all get back to bed.'

'Huh?!' The rising tone in the voice derided the implication. 'I'm making a profit plan for Aunt Elsie.'

'A profit plan! What kind of a profit plan would she be wanting?'

'I told her she ought to be making money out of her soup kitchen work and she said, "Well, you make me a profit plan young Ralph, and we'll see what can be done." So I'm making her one.'

Willard grinned to himself. He could just hear the gently mocking banter in the voice of Aunt Elsie Marre as she tried to suggest to young Ralph that there were other things in life than money. But it was the kind of joke he would never get – you just didn't joke about money in Ralph's world. Perhaps, Willard thought, he should have been the eldest son.

'Aunt Elsie here then?'

'Sure, she been here a couple of days and she and Ma is going back up to her place in Louisville Tuesday, for Ma to have a break.'

Someone lit a lamp behind the mosquito blind on the open window to the right of the door.

'Anyone out there?' came the calm, unmistakable tones of Aunt Elsie.

'It's me, Aunty, I'm jes comin' right on in.'

'Willard, well I declare. We didn't expect you before tomorrow – who you talking to out there?'

'Can't you guess?' A laugh answered him as he ran up the porch steps, traveling bag in hand. His mother opened the door before he reached it and folded him in a great hug.

An hour later, with the big table in the family room at the back of the house cleared of the cold meat supper his mother had rustled up for him, Willard was recounting his travels and trouble to his two favorite ladies. His father was away a few days on business. This distinctly improved the quality of the homecoming. Willard Senior's relations with Elsie Marre had never really recovered from their teenage rift over Daniel Porter. He had no time for Elsie's social and political work, even though her high profile as a leading member of the National Association for the Advancement of Colored People was turning her into a celebrity.

The family of her old friend Sarah Stone, Lear as was, loved her and gave her the honorific title of "Aunty". But when she came visiting an awkward evening of welcome was usually followed by Willard remembering important business elsewhere. On this occasion, apparently, he had anticipated her arrival, but he was not going to welcome his son with open arms either when he had heard the account of his sales trip.

'Your pa will be real angered when he hears of this, son!'

His mother knew that husband Willard, though he would never admit it, had great hopes of the boy. Herself, she honored her son's motives in delaying his business to help the Reverend Washington, but she also knew Willard had no time for "meddling martyrs" of whatever race, color or creed. In his book, only money gave a black man hope of respect.

'Ah well now,' she said. 'I'll be off to bed. Young Ralph won't settle until one of us at least shows willin'... Don't let Aunt Elsie keep you up too long with her tales of "the struggle" for us women, now.'

The mildly amused emphasis of her last words was the nearest Sarah Stone ever came to political comment. Caught between her love for her strangely harsh husband and respect for her crusading friend, she had never seriously thought of joining the movement. But while the tone of voice might deprecate "the struggle", the smile blessed the fighter.

Willard thought his Aunt Elsie Marre was unusually quiet. In general she could be relied on for a racy account of some activists' meeting she'd been addressing, or some encounter with the police. Willard particularly relished the episode in which the forty-seven-year-old Miss Marre, Republican Party canvasser and law librarian, had, by a lucky fluke, caught thirty-eight-year-old Patrolman Kavanagh off balance outside the Bioscope on New York's Fifth Avenue, and floored him with a blow from her handbag. Seven days in the cells had been her reward, but Will guessed that that week had been the proudest of her life.

Tonight, she seemed in reflective mood.

Truth to tell, Elsie was alarmed at the reaction to be expected from Willard Senior. Sarah could not know the full depth of his aversion to do-gooders or the suppressed guilt that lay beneath it. He had never told his wife the full story of how the "Porter Patent" had come into his possession, nor of the childhood pledge in the Mammoth Cave – and Elsie had never mentioned it. Yet she had always considered it her duty, in due course, to brief the heir to the family fortune as to its origins.

From Chicago to Atlanta, from Nashville to New York, Willard's lamps and lanterns were standard lighting in the homes who put her up and the chapels and Bethels she spoke in. Everywhere, the little general stores carried the S.K.L. logo. Yet nothing seemed able to deflect even a mite of the man's profits from these modest communities into any form of charitable giving. She knew that the saga of young Willard's lost orders and philanthropic involvements would stir his father to fury. Nothing could be done to stop the storm breaking over the boy. But she could prepare him for what was in store.

The lamp on the center table suddenly began to putter, a sure sign that the fuel in the tank was running low. If it was not fixed it would soon run dry and the wick would char. In the excitement of the homecoming they had all forgotten to check the light. Young Will got up, lit a couple of stand-by candles and then extinguished the lamp wick. He would have to leave the chimney to cool before he could remove it and unscrew the burner. Then it would be a matter of refilling the reservoir, replacing the burner with the wick immersed in the paraffin and leaving that to soak for a few minutes.

'Leave it for now, dear. The candles will see us through this evening and I have something to say to you before your father gets home.'

Surprised, Will set the two candlesticks on the mantelpiece, where the flames, wavering occasionally in the draught from the half open door, shed a soft, secretive glow over the room.

'As you know,' Elsie Marre began, 'your father and I have known each other since we were children. My family used to live here in Johnstoneville and it was through me that your father first got to know your mother.' She sighed. 'Was a time when folks thought he and I would take the center aisle together and I shared the great expedition to the Mammoth Cave on his tenth birthday.'

'Say, that was some adventure for a couple of kids. I bet you was glad Pa was along!'

'Is that what he told you?! Well, perhaps I was at that. But I reckon we would both have been goners without Daniel Porter being there too.'

'You mean Porter, the drunk storekeep! I never heard Pa say he had much to do with the business, except pull y'all out of an itty-bitty hole… and take longer about it than he need to… guess he'd taken a bottle of liquor along for the ride.'

'He had not, Willard. And I sure hope your father never suggested such a thing!'

'No I guess not. I just supposed it must have been like that because of the time he took to help.'

'Let me tell you, Dan Porter had to run a mile from the cave's mouth to get help and then a mile back through those unlit passageways. And that "itty-bitty" hole was more than twenty feet of pitch dark, jagged rocks. When he got back, Dan scrambled down without a care to keep us in good cheer.'

The events were many years in the past, but the veteran lady, orator and political guru was seething with anger for the reputation of her childhood hero.

'OK, OK, I'm sorry, Aunt. Maybe I got that bit wrong, but that Dan Porter sure was a drunk – else why did Pa get rid of him?'

'And are you surprised he had a drink now and again?' The rising tone of indignation in the voice was pure Lady Blaze and carried well into the next room where Sarah, having as usual forgotten her night-time water jug, paused before entering the room on her little errand.

'Dan had good reason. Your pa robbed that man of his future as sure as if he'd stolen his soul.'

If she had wanted to go on now, Sarah could not. She was frozen with horror and fascination to hear what this fantastical accusation against her beloved Willard could possibly mean. She well knew that Elsie had been his first love. It had never mattered, she had told herself. Her love was big enough for both and Willard had been a good husband by any reasonable standard. And he had come to love her, she knew. She also knew that his love for Elsie had died the day the two had parted. She'd never known what had caused the break, but it seemed she was about to learn. Petrified with dread of what she might be about to hear, Sarah stayed silent in the shadows behind the half open door.

'Steady, Miss Marre, steady on. My pa never robbed any one and you've no right to suggest otherwise.' Young Will might respect this "Aunt" of theirs but she had no right to make such accusations.

'I'm right sorry, young Willard. Maybe I spoke too hasty. In lawyers' language he robbed no one. Yet he did steal that man's future. The fortune of the Stone family began with the Stone Patent Chimney, and that patent was invented back in '76 by Daniel Porter. Your grandpa gave him a wage rise and meant, he told me once, to see whether "royalties might go young Porter's way". But he was not legally obliged. He could say that the invention was made "in company time" so Dan had been paid for his work. But that was lawyers' talk an' I told your pa so. That fateful day in the Mammoth Cave I made him swear to do right by Daniel should he ever own the business.

Sure, he was only a child. But he had long been old enough to know his own mind. He promised me by everything that's solemn he would see Dan right. Nine years later, your grandpa died. Willard Stone Junior, your pa, took the business and the patent and Dan began to hit the bottle. Came the time he was fired and the Porters left Johnstoneville.'

She paused a moment to calm her heaving breast.

'If you don't believe me, ask your father yourself when he gets home. Oh! And don't expect any mercy for the trouble you've been to over Reverend Washington. Willard Stone is rightly known as "Stone by name and Stone by nature".'

Willard said nothing. What he had heard rang true. He barely nodded acknowledgement as Elsie Marre, with a half-apologetic 'Goodnight, chil'', took an unlit candle from the bureau in the corner of the room and walked over to light it from one of those on the mantelpiece. Sarah, her shoulders shaking silently, the tears trickling slowly down her cheeks, turned to the stairs and crept quietly up to her lonely bed. At the foot of the stairs, Elsie heard the rustle of a nightdress on the landing but in the glimmer of her candle flame it was of course too dark to see anything. She shrugged and made her way up to her room.

* * * * *

Next day the house was a sombre, moody place and young Ralph took off first thing, down to the Gullie Stream. Aunt Marre had shown no interest in his profit plan; Ma had returned to her bed after cooking breakfast, complaining of a headache and Willard, having stowed his rather numerous unsold samples in the storeroom, had shut himself away in the counting house as he labored to compose a cosmetic report of his three weeks on the road.

Ralph's present venture was retailing insect larvae to the local fishing fraternity, or "idle layabouts" to use his father's words. A week ago he had recovered the very promising remains of a water rat from the river bank. Lodged in a cunningly contrived biscuit tin "food safe", which allowed free movement to blow flies but excluded the local predators, it should by now be satisfactorily seething with stock in trade. He left the house carrying a tackle bag holding, optimistically, two cigar boxes.

He was able to fill one of them, but trade was slow and late that afternoon he traced despondently home, tackle bag and one inadequately sealed cigar box crawling with plump but uncontrollable maggots. For reasons of policy he approached the house via the back garden, leaving his bag in a private cache behind the outdoor privy. The house appeared to be empty, except for old Ruby Holder who was preparing the supper.

Ruby, who lived by herself in an old clapboard shanty at the end of town, had been "a comin' in to help out Miss Sarah on a temp'ry understandin'" ever since Willard Junior was born. She cooked the most divine chicken gumbo when she had a mind and never allowed Ralph in her kitchen. He dodged a flailing oven cloth to raid the cookie jar just within reach on the shelving by the back door.

'Where's everyone gone, Ruby?'

'Lady Blaze has taken herself off back to Louisville, your ma is still poorly in bed and Master Willard is working on his books… an' if you's hoping for any supper, young Ralph, you bes' stay out o' mah way now. You already made me forget ma' pepper sauce!'

As she swayed back into the pantry, Ralph heard the magic incantation 'Slow an' Steady Wins the Race.'. Like the rest of the family he had no idea how racing might relate to cooking, but like them too, he knew for a certainty that its utterance meant that Ruby reckoned she was on course for a super special gumbo. He walked round to the front of the house and Main Street to await the rattle of the old station cab from Glasgow that would herald his father's return, due in a matter of minutes.

Dinner was a glum affair for all the delights of Ruby's cooking. Mother, having unexpectedly cancelled her trip to Louisville, was quiet and serious, frowning Ralph into silence when he showed any sign of joking about. His father, always somewhat forbidding, was his usual taciturn self, though perhaps he should have been more cheerful. The last few days had been a gruelling schedule for Willard, but they had resulted in a massive nationwide deal. A man less constitutionally hostile to happiness would have been beaming – Willard Senior merely reckoned he had the right to feel exhausted. As for Willard Junior, from whom Ralph had been expecting a stream of stories about his first journey on the road – he was almost matching their father as a conversationalist.

The youngster was packed off to bed, even while Ruby was clearing the table. His mother, murmuring an apology for her poor head shepherded him up the stairs on her way to bed. With cutlery and table wear all taken through to the kitchen, Ruby carefully folded the fine white linen cloth and replaced it with a heavy brocaded table covering that draped in old-fashioned style over the handsome antique pedestal table. In the middle of it she placed a newly lit lamp. The two men of the family were left in awkward state around the re-dressed dining table, not yet used to this relationship of man to man. Then, to Will's complete surprise, his father got up and walked over to the handsome corner cupboard, reached out the fine old bottle of twelve-year Kentucky bourbon kept only for special occasions and said, 'What say we take a glass of something together, son?'

He measured out two respectable tots into finely engraved Libbey crystal glass and carried them over to the table. The style of the interior, which would have been elegant forty years before, was a world away from the chrome and leather, glass and light wood veneer in the fashionable bars and hotels of New York whence Willard Senior had just returned. But this was the South and the home of a self-made family. Every outdated piece was of the highest quality and proclaimed the cumulative achievement in wealth creation of the founding generations. Having set his glass in front of him, Willard took the chair to his left so that they were seated at two points on a quadrant of the table. The older man placed his own glass directly in front him and planted his hands palm down on the table either side of it. The pose had a rather awkward formality that portended weighty things to come.

'I've news as I'd like for you to hear first before I tell Mother. She has no real head for business, and this is real business.'

A wiser head than young Will's would have recognized that the heavily portentous moment had been contrived for effect and would have paused to await developments. Instead he blundered on to a collision that left a total wreck where only serious damage might have resulted.

'Fine, Sir. But first I have some news from my sales trip that I think you ought to hear.'

'Sure son, sure. Of course I ought to hear it, it was big time for you and I've no doubt of great profit to the business. But when you've heard the deal I was offered in New York jes forty-eight hours back, I'm mortal certain you'll agree your triumphs were small time in comparison.'

The heavy attempt at good-natured parental authority, so out of character with his usual style, was beginning to fracture; though it has to be doubted that young Willard was even aware of the mood. He knew full well his father's views on liquor; he knew he rarely offered drink even to a business partner, let alone his son; any other time he might have heeded the signs. This evening he pushed on to his Waterloo. The deal his father had cut with the Penny and Dime nationwide chain, to supply not only lamps and chimneys but also household soaps and cleansing agents, was set to transform S.K.L.'s marketing operation. And more than that, it should secure the future against the spread of electrification, which was revolutionizing lighting needs across the nation. For electrification meant more than lighting. He had seen modest suburban houses fitted up with electric-powered hot water systems. That meant hygiene and that meant soap and more soap. For decades vast fortunes had been built up on soap – S.K.L. was set to join in. Unaware of all this, unaware that in his own way his father was bursting to tell a good story, young Willard drove ahead.

'But please, Pa, I'd really like to say my piece and get it over with.'

'Get it over with! What's that you say? Get what over with?'

With the door ajar because of the heat, their voices had been carrying up the stairs in the undulating, indistinguishable murmur of conversation. But now the voices were raised and the words were becoming distinguishable. Willard Stone's career owed much to that rare quality needed by all successful men: a willingness to face problems as soon as they presented themselves. Clearly his son had a problem to present. The father's face tightened a notch.

As he listened, his rage at the boy's perversity mounted. At the very moment the business was facing its first great challenge the son and heir, boss next in line, was opening a sideline in amateur philanthropy bordering on agitation. He'd 've made a fine son for Elsie Marre perhaps but not for Willard Stone.

'Do you have any idea, son,' he broke in with menacing calm, 'do you have the slightest notion of the kind of work your grandfather and I put into this business? Do you suppose we had time for weak-minded do-gooding? You, your mother and your brother all owe your standing in the world and the luxury of this house to hard graft and money. Do you suppose the white world, "the Man" as folk say, is happy with Negroes as far "above their station" as we have risen? Given just one single chance and they'll be about our ears, to put us "back in our place". Let the preacher stick to his job and the businessman to his.'

'But, Father,' too late, Will had realized that diplomacy was in order, 'the Reverend Washington had helped me and it was for me to help him in return and stand by him... You got to understand...'

'No I ain't, boy. It's you's got to understand and understand one thing good and plain as long as you hope to work with S.K.L. Our money is made by working. And we are made by our money. I was always told it was the business of a Christian minister to show charity to a fellow being in distress. Well and good. It's *your* business to sell lamps and kerosene, sweet talk customers and build on a respectable order book. An' if you cain't outsell Burnie Brock, then at least see to it that he still has a sales territory when he's fit and well, for as sure as God made oil, you're not working that circuit this side you're twenty one.'

He paused for a response. But his son held his peace.

'An' another thing, if you should want to be part of "the struggle" then you might think on something that meddling Marre woman said to me a long time back, in the days when she had more sense than reputation. "Willard Stone, you know I can't approve of the way you came by all your money. Yet I do sometimes wonder if you ain't an unwitting tool of whatever fate guides the destiny of the Negro people. I've seen more respect for you in white folks' eyes than I ever saw them accord a preacher. I guess they reckon rich people are the only truly free people. Maybe we need fewer black crusaders and more black Rockefellers".'

Fighting a losing battle with his anger, Willard's rising voice had woken young Ralph, who decided to try a visit to the kitchen on the pretext of a glass of water. A family row was usually worth investigating.

'Now don't you get me wrong, son,' the tirade roared along its way, 'I'm not overly concerned what white folks think and not at all over what Elsie Marre might think. But I sure am concerned to see S.K.L. in the top one hundred US corporations before I die, and I'm not about to hand it on to a son who can't take it further.'

The storm seemed to have blown itself out. His chest heaving and fatigued by his late nights and exertion, Willard poured the untasted whiskeys back in the bottle, rammed down the cork and took the bottle back to its place on the sideboard. That done, he remained standing with the aid of a heavy club-handled stick he had taken from its rack in the corner, rather than sit in the face of his weakling son. Creeping down stairs, young Ralph paused, trying to weigh up the advisability or otherwise of heading on for the kitchen past the half open door. Those last words had hooked his attention. Now was not the time to break the flow of this intriguing bust-up between his father and his elder brother. Who was going to take the business further if not Will?

'And how did you come by your money?'

It seemed like Will was almost sneering.

'Like I said. By hard work. Harder than you've ever known and harder than any preacherman has ever done.'

'Hard work... and *fraud*,' came the astounding reply.

'You said WHAT?!' Their father was shouting now for the whole house to hear.

'You heard! I SAID FRAUD. Isn't it true that your whole career and this family's wealth rests on a simple act of theft and deception when you robbed Dan Porter of the fair return for his invention and then sacked him and drove him and his family out of town?' Will was shouting now. 'You despise preaching but you're one of the best preachers in town. Your text is hard work but in reality you're a cheat and a HYPOCRITE!' Will's rising voice ended in a scream of pain.

Terrified out of his wits now, young Ralph saw his father, swaying with fatigue though he was, bring the great stick, kept as a precaution against housebreakers, down about Will's shoulders in a fearful blow and raise it to strike again. The flickering shadows cast by the candles against the steady glow of the lamps made the room a shadow theatre of Hell, it seemed to Ralph, and he sobbed with fright and then stifled the sob lest he should be drawn into the terrible conflict.

But Will, younger by a generation and stronger despite his pain, wrenched the stick from his father – then caught him as he staggered in exhaustion towards the fireplace.

Nothing was said. Nothing need be said. A father was within his rights to chastise a refractory son. Nothing was said. Nothing need be said. Both knew it was the end of love and respect.

Nothing was said, nothing need be said, when the following morning it was found that Willard Stone Jnr had left the family home, his father's house.

For his part, too, Ralph said nothing about his hidden witness to the catastrophe. He need say nothing. But he remembered. He remembered that the one who received the blow was a brother who had offered Christian charity to a good man in need. He remembered that the one who had delivered the blow was a father who despised charity yet had money. He determined that when he grew to manhood he would have the money and he would wield the stick.

CHAPTER SEVENTEEN

Campaigns, Kingdoms and Crusaders

It was August 3rd 1923 and a cool summer evening in Vermont. Mr Calvin Coolidge, Vice President of the United States and Mrs Coolidge were, as usual, passing the vacation in the family farmhouse: the house in which Calvin had been born, and the house in which his father, the puritanical old John Coolidge, still lived. The clean mountain air was a welcome change from the steam and stench of corruption and tobacco in the White House drawing room, where President Gamaliel Harding was usually to be found playing poker with cronies from the "Ohio Gang", drinking their top-quality Scotch imported by their top-quality bootlegger. They were happy to keep the feckless President occupied while other cronies progressed the administration's main business of profiteering, from the Little Green House down at 1625 K Street.

In fact, just now, thinking members of the "gang" were apprehensive. In the spring, the easy-going President had begun to get wind of the scale of the malfeasance from which he had been cocooned. Hoping to distance himself from his cronies and perhaps to burnish up his image in time for the next election campaign, he was traveling the west coast by special train. Harding now did something that scuppered the Ohio Gang – he died.

As dusk fell, the telephone in the Coolidge parlor rang. The instrument was a grudged concession to the exalted position occupied in the nation's affairs by the son of the house. Calvin took the call. A distant voice crackled on the line.

'This is Secretary of Commerce Hoover, I am speaking from the Palace Hotel, San Francisco and it is my sad duty to inform you, Sir, that President Harding died some thirty minutes ago of acute indigestion brought on by crab meat served in the rail dining car – I quote the diagnosis of his personal physician, General Sawyer. May I be the first to wish you good fortune and God's guidance as you embark on your high office, Mr President. Do you have any instructions?'

'Thank you, Mr Secretary,' came the taciturn five-word reply. 'No!

The electrification of America was in full spate. And yet, like those of millions of poor Americans, the Coolidge family home was still lit by kerosene. Custom required that on the death of an incumbent president, his vice president be sworn in with as little delay as possible. So, as evening darkened into night, old John Coolidge handed his son the family Bible, swore him in as Thirtieth President of the United States, and then read a passage from the Bible, by the light of an oil lamp. The make of lamp was not specified in the newspaper reports.

Willard Stone Senior was to be intensely irritated by the omission. He was virtually certain that the Vermont residence had recently been supplied with S.K.L. Specials by one of his retailers in the state. The story of the folksy inauguration made all the headlines nationwide; the scandals had not yet begun to flood out and the Republican Party dared hope for victory in the 1924 elections with reliable "Silent Cal" on the ticket. Willard cursed a missed promotional bonanza. Even so, the decade of the Charleston and the Harlem Renaissance, the decade that for most of its run seemed buoyed up on a sea of money and optimism, saw Willard, with quiet calculation, achieve major corporation status for S.K.L. For other African Americans, that same decade had opened with an event of almost messianic inspiration.

On August 1st 1920, Marcus Garvey inaugurated in New York the International Convention of the Negro people of the World. Born thirty-three years before on the island of Jamaica, still a British colony and already free of slavery for the best part of a century, Garvey identified the problems of America's blacks with the problems of colonialism in Africa. Student time in London brought him into contact with students from Africa and with a book, *Up from Slavery* by Booker T. Washington. On his return to Jamaica he set up the Universal Negro Improvement Association: UNIA. Next, in New York, Garvey established a branch of UNIA to launch a crusade for the "redemption of Africa for Africans abroad and at home".

Many took him for a black Moses, dedicated to the return of his people to the home continent. He launched various businesses aimed at promoting his ideas and believed a Coolidge presidency would favour the black cause. Unfortunately, Garvey the businessman would later prove the hoodoo of Garvey the prophet. But as the 1924 elections approached, a list of Garveyite candidates backing the Coolidge campaign hit the streets.

* * * * *

In New Liberty Hall, Chicago, a heavy-jowled, somewhat lugubrious orator was briefing a team of campaigners. He shook with indignation as he brought news of the latest slander on the black race.

An angry murmur rolled through the audience. From the West Indies to Africa, from Latin America to the United States, the Garveyite organization claimed a membership running into millions. Here in Chicago some 9,000 were enrolled. Among them, James Owen "Shout" Porter, now in his mid-thirties, and his recently acquired friend, eighteen-year old Willard Stone II.

Shout took the occasional note. They had two hours canvassing ahead of them, before heading for the Tavern Club. Willard, who had little interest in politics, was there more as a gesture of solidarity. He couldn't envision a political strand in the career he was shaping for himself as a musician; but he reckoned Shout to be a friend.

In Chicago little more than a month, it seemed to Willard he had stumbled into the zone of some guardian angel and it was only common sense to follow the landmarks – Shout Porter being the most important so far. Willard had left home certain he would never again see his father, and the journey north had been depressing, though it had hardly been difficult: his mother had lent him good money and Burnie Brock, the salesman, had been happy to run him into the Glasgow railhead. Wishing him luck, he had put the puzzled query, 'But why Chicago?' Willard had simply flourished the cornet in its soft leather carry bag.

But Burnie knew nothing about King Oliver, nothing about his Creole Jazz Band; and nothing about the club where they performed – and where Willard had been dancing barely a couple of weeks before his memorable return home.

Truth to tell, Willard had known nothing about them either until that night on the town. Up till then the cornet, a boyhood hobby, had seen no more exciting company than the other members of the Johnstoneville Sunday Chorale – Morgan Ponders on base (an antique three-string bass fiddle) and old Jo "Stumble" Stacey on banjo. But under the impact of Oliver's music Willard had undergone a religious conversion. All he remembered of the girl was that she danced what she called "the flat foot floogie" in a way that explained what the cornet was for.

The cataclysmic confrontation that had terminated all prospects of a future career as chairman of Stone's Kerosene Lamps had forced a decision that, as soon as he had made it, seemed to have been there from the moment he picked up the horn at the age of twelve. He would be, he *was,* a musician. And since Chicago was the only place, so far as he knew, where they played real music, he would go there.

It took him no time at all to find the night life – rather longer to find a job. Vacancies at the club where Oliver played were never advertised. On the rare occasions when a barman or waiter left, his job was snapped up by some lucky friend. The idea that he, an unknown, might walk straight into a musician's job seemed pure fantasy. After three weeks in the Windy City, he faced penury.

In fact, one friendly manager at a place called the Mich Much had listened to his cornet and promised to mention his name to the bandleader. A couple of days later, for want of anything better to do, Willard was making his way back there. Yards away, the smell of paint was unmistakable. The ladder, just now being warily skirted by a superstitious trombonist with a limp, told the story. Above their heads the sign writer was swinging the final flourish on the "n" of "The Tavern", risking death on himself and a deluge of electric green paint on the passers-by, rather than get down to shift the ladder that necessary six inches to make the job rather less like a circus act. So the place was under new management, which presumably meant a new bandleader who had never heard his name. *Hey! Ho!* sighed Willard to himself – but at least they did have a band, he could hear a cornet-less rag was reaching the end of its warm up. Hoping they might still be in need of bar staff he followed the trombonist in through the main street entrance.

A few minutes later, following directions from a surly front of house man to "push off round the kitchen entrance", Willard found he had accepted work as a junior waiter – on a trial basis.

On trial for a job that meant doing everything a waiter might be expected to do, and then everything else that nobody else was prepared to consider. In a few weeks Willard had moved from the privileged position of a boss's son to the bottom of the ladder! But all this was the result of his own decision. In any case he would have money coming in and, best of all, he would be in company with a band.

Mid-thirties, pencil mustache lining his jet-black upper lip, just now the trumpet, with surprisingly long fingers for a horn player, was rapidly punching the piston valves of the instrument, so that only the patter of button corks on piston heads could be heard. Apparently the leader of the band, he was all the while in vigorous debate with the trombone.

This had nothing to do with the latter's timekeeping. Seemingly as old as Ole Man River, and certainly as liquid, the veteran's right to keep his own hours was clearly above challenge. As Willard discharged the duties of a junior waiter, setting up chairs and tables, distributing ash trays, supplying the surly doorkeep with a refill for his under the counter bottle of "water", he kept his ears open. The matter under dispute was the possibility of adding a pianist to the band's line-up.

'Meade Luxe Lewis! What kind of a name is that?! He dress fancy, or somethin'?' The trombone kept up a grumbling litany as he flicked the slide back and forth, or opened the water key to expel any drops of condensation before the real blowing of the evening began. A quick check on the fifth of bathtub bourbon tucked up in the wash leather, alongside the mute in the flip top compartment in the once resplendent lizard-skin instrument case, and he opened up again.

'Do we really need the guy? Where he from, anyway?'

'Born Kentucky, I reckon, but he's good. Sure we need him if he's looking to sit in at what we can afford to pay.'

'Hey man! He tol' me he came from Chicago. Only reason I'm goin' along with the whole idea.' A couple of warm-up riffs hadn't warmed up the trombone's temper. James Owen Shout Porter, trumpet player and bandleader, laughed to ease the tension.

'And did he also tell you he started into music, playin' the "vy-oh-lin"?'

'Hell, no! Whoever heard of a musician playin' the violin?' The trombonist paused; the smile was fading on his face. He saw no call for a piano. Never liked the instrument and never liked pianists. Always wanted star billing. Then he shrugged. No doubt who was the star in this band, whatever they called the joint. He grinned.

'Come to that, whoever heard of a musician coming from Kentucky?'

It was an old joke. Everybody knew where Shout Porter's pa hailed from and this ritual insult always signaled an end to hostilities. But this evening was different. This evening it triggered an unexpected response.

'Say guys, that ain't friendly, ain't even true. Where I come from, my Aunt Elsie told me we used to have one of the finest trombonists in these United States of America.'

It seemed a member of the table staff was putting in his two bits.

'You a Kentucky man y'self?' The trombone leaned back to shift the tuning slide a fraction, for the heat of the room was beginning to over warm his instrument.

'Sure am that, man; Johnstoneville, Barren County, Kentucky... er... er... Sir!'

Willard had suddenly realized his position which, in this company, was effectively nothing. It occurred to him that it was probably not the best policy, first night on a new job, for kitchen staff on trial to rile the bar's musicians.

Unaccountably, however, the trombone seemed highly

delighted with the way things were going. Having first refreshed himself with a "small half shot" from the bourbon compartment in the lizard skin, he leaned forward, face split from ear to ear in a huge grin.

'An' I bet,' he drawled, 'I bet this Kentuckyan master of the slide horn played a *valve* trombone?'

'Why yes, Sir, I do believe he did.'

'Waaaaell...' sighed the trombonist, now in the best of moods. 'I rest mah case...' And the entire band collapsed laughing.

* * * * *

'You see, young fellah,' Porter was explaining to Willard as they left the bar at the end of the evening, 'Old Wonder Mason makes a religion of the slide. Plenty of tailgate merchants reckon the valve is bad news, but hear Mason talk, you'd reckon my old pa was booked on a one-way ticket to hell for playing the thing at all. Well this is my place. Better look around if you're planning to move in.'

Willard's intervention in the musicians' debate had guaranteed him the job at the Tavern. Shout Porter, discovering he had a native of Jo'ville on the premises, told the management to keep him on and just then his word was law – changing the name was one thing, changing the band would have been quite another. Offering the eighteen-year-old newcomer a temporary flat share was typical of Porter's generosity. The next day, young Stone came round with his few belongings and installed himself. Despite the age difference, they soon became good friends.

A couple of days later they had snatched a coffee and sandwich before going on to the meeting and their stint of canvassing. For Shout that would be followed by a full night at the club. It was a murderous schedule. For the past three weeks, he'd spent no more than two hours in his bed of a night, what with blowing horn, pounding the streets on the campaign trail and hours in the committee room. Willard privately worried that the strain was sapping the power of his playing.

Old Dan Porter was worried too. but for a different reason. Active himself in mainline black politics, he looked on UNIA and its charismatic leader as simpletons led by a charlatan. He regularly predicted catastrophe round the corner. Had he known of Shout's friendship with the son of the old enemy, his forebodings would have been worse.

For Willard, the new world of Chicago looked ever brighter. Money of a kind was coming in; the world of music had taken to him and he was flat sharing with a great musician. Even so, he tended to share Wonder Mason's view when it came to the slide trombone. A scientist friend of Elsie's, with a passion for it, once told him in solemn tones, 'That, man, is the perfect instrument of music – acoustically speaking.' What he meant Willard did not know; but for him the word "perfect" uttered by serious people still meant something.

'It sure does seem weird,' he confided to Shout one lunchtime, over a coffee. 'Sort of cross between a trumpet and the real thing; how come your pa got into it?'

'Money!' Porter replied succinctly. 'Or, better, the shortage of it. That was the usual explanation for anything in our house. The army was selling them off cheap after the war. "Valvers" had been better for men on the march; when the marching stopped, they had a surplus.'

'Your dad fight in the war?'

'Naw, too young.'

'My granddad sure did.'

'And my granddad kept store for him. But why my dad left Jo'ville I never rightly figured. He don't much like yours, that I do know... I was hoping you might have a few answers.

Come to that, why are you here in Chi? Not on vacation for sure.'

He glanced shrewdly across the table and Willard felt the blood rising in his cheeks. The moment he had realized exactly who Shout Porter was, he had cursed his own impulsive intervention, expecting an explosion of anger from the trumpet player. But it seemed he did not know the history. Sooner or later he'd have to come clean about how Wilberforce Stone had treated Mr Dan Porter. Just now he'd play for time.

'Let's just say I had a difference over terms of employment with Father, never the most generous of men...'

'... so you just took off like my pa...' cut in Shout. 'Hum, could be...'

He paused reflectively then snapped back to the present.

'Time for another strong coffee I reckon, before we hit the campaign trail. Politics is demanding work.' He pottered about at the stove. 'Plenty of folks had grandpas fought in the war. Now most of them seem to wonder why the old men bothered. "What difference did it make?" That's the most regular question you get on the doorstep. Perhaps men thought the end of slavery in the South would bring freedom in the North.' Shout Porter laughed a short bitter laugh as he came over to the table with the two steaming mugs. 'You mean, like the fighting in Europe was going to make the world safe for democracy according to President Wilson.' He paused so long that Willard wondered whether he was supposed to say something.

But the older man followed his own train of thought.

'That was the Woodrow Wilson, you remember, who described the black people of America liberated from slavery by that Civil War as "a host of dusky children untimely put out of school". That was the President who decreed segregation for the eating and restroom arrangements for most federal employees.'

Now Willard did speak.

'Don't get heavy, man. Things surely are better than they used to be.'

'For the likes of Willard Stone Senior and his family, perhaps. Most African Americans are not so fortunate. But "The Man" don't distinguish between poor blacks and rich blacks. You think enough money will buy most things? Don't fool yourself. Money don't buy dignity. While our boys were out fighting for freedom and democracy halfway across the world, Congressman Frank Park of the state of Georgia introduced a bill to make it unlawful to make Negroes officers in the United States Army.'

Willard, who was quickly coming to understand that he knew very little about the real world, had not known this and was silenced.

'In the twelve months that followed the armistice which ended "the war to end all wars",' Porter was well into his campaigning stride now, 'the war that "marked the end of the threat to liberty in the United States", more than seventy blacks were lynched. Ten of them were soldiers and four of those soldiers were wearing their uniform... they had just been fighting for the land of the free and the home of the brave!'

'OK, OK, man! Don't get so *angry*!'

Willard decided he did not like Shout Porter in missionary mode. The grotesque injustices he was protesting had been real enough, but somehow there seemed an element of holier-than-thou in which resentment against "the likes of Willard Stone Senior and his family" seemed to feature rather strongly. Obscurely, he felt that being right so easily could lead to being righteous and from there it was a short step to being self-righteous. After all, he, Willard Stone II, had had first hand experience on his own body of the injustices suffered by their people – more, he guessed, than Shout Porter could claim. And he would never forget the torture of Reverend Washington.

Equally, he was sure that the reverend himself would preach a different sermon from this one by Shout. However, he was not to be let out of church just yet.

'But it isn't OK, man! Five years ago, Harriet Church Porter, soul sister, heroine and my mother, was kicked to death by a police horse on the streets of Chicago. She, and thousands more black folk, were following their constitutional right to demonstrate in protest against injustice. She was just one of hundreds who died that blood-red summer of 1919. Since then, the Ku Klux Klan have made more than 200 public appearances in twenty-seven states, North as well as South. We're part of the struggle just by being alive. Can you wonder I'm a follower of Garvey?'

He paused, his eyes blazing angrily. Suddenly he caught sight of the tinny old alarm clock, bell supported atop on its pillar, like a crash cymbal on a bass drum. His eyes came back to the present and he got up from the table with brisk economical movements.

'Still an' all, I'd better get me ready for this evening. Why not take a look through the old favorites over there.'

Willard did as instructed. Riffling through the pile of sheet music, with its faded studio portraits of legendary performers like Eubie Blake and Noble Sissle and many another he'd never hear of, he came to a heap of big brown envelopes, titles scribbled on them. Investigation showed them to contain song sheets in danger of falling apart from constant use. Putting the pile back on the shelf where it was stored, Willard glimpsed the one word "ABYSSINIA" carefully printed in large capitals on an envelope jutting out from the bottom. Intrigued, he found it to contain a collection of documents of the like he'd never seen before.

Among them was a flimsy pamphlet with the title "A Prophesy Relating to the Dark-Skinned People of Africa". A loose leaf engraving of a handsome face surrounded with, what looked like, royal emblems entitled "Prince of Abyssinia" fell out of its pages, with a vividly colored paper flag on a little stick. The proud figure of a black lion was emblazoned across three horizontal bands of green, yellow and red.

As the two hurried along for their meeting, Shout, music case in hand, explained how he had made contact with the Abyssinians of the Garveyite movement in that all important year of 1920 and had even thought of signing up for service in Africa.

'President General Garvey said we must send to Africa our scientists, our mechanics and our artisans and let them build the railroads and great institutions necessary for a great and powerful national homeland in Africa. Then, when these are constructed the order will go out to the "ebony-hued" sons of Ethiopia in the western hemisphere: "Come home". For 250 years we were a race of slaves. For fifty years we have been a race of parasites. Now the time has come to end all that.'

'And the Abyssinians?' queried Willard.' Where did they get their name?'

'Oh that's history for today. These guys consider "Negro" a white man's term to put us down; they call themselves "Ethiopians", the first name for the inhabitants of Abyssinia. In the Bible, Solomon dealt with kings of Ethiopia; the Roman empire fought Ethiopian armies. Back then the kingdom of Ethiopia made black a color to reckon with... But right now, here in Chicago, you an' I've got politics and rhythm to attend to – in that order... Not history.'

They were standing outside New Liberty Hall. Porter led the way into the committee room, a new spring in his weary body. Later that afternoon, as he knocked on his first ever door as a political canvasser, Willard felt he was living more than ever before in his life, like a full citizen of the republic to which history had consigned his people. Fighting for a black candidate here in the USA seemed more useful than anything that might happen in Africa; making his way as a brass player better by far than the treadmill awaiting the successor of Willard Stone Senior, Chairman of S.K.L. He had little realistic hope that his election candidate would get into Congress; but, remarkably for a son of his father, he had come to realize it was more important to be a warrior in the cause of justice than a victor in the cause of profit. As to being a musician; it didn't seem to him now that he had ever had a choice in the matter.

Chicago: Men, Women and Music

'Young Meade Lewis just talks for effect. Ain't no more than eighteen, arrived in this town but a year of two back. Like I said he's surely from out of town, though to hear him talk you'd suppose he's Chicago, born and bred. He's certainly a real sharp dresser.'

Shout and Willard were lounging in the Tavern, a glass of imported beer in front of each, courtesy of the barman. With the elections over they had time for a couple of quick drinks before the run through and Shout was briefing his cousin on the boogie piano Meade Luxe Lewis, debuting with the band this evening. If the boys, especially the cornet, liked his style, he'd be invited to join permanently.

'He had his violin with him in the early days too, on account his mother told him to try and find work with it. But he soon hocked that for ready money when he discovered that honky-tonk piano played better. Which... '

'Which is something, Willard, you ought to steer clear of... '

Shout's sister, Mary Terrel Porter, strode unceremoniously past the protesting bouncer into the room and, as was her habit, took charge of the proceedings. Just one year younger than Lewis, she had fallen for him the moment he showed up at the club some two years back, and while not daring to "reform" him, she did hope he might grow up to be a husband.

'Meade's got into bad company in the clubs, same as you could Willard Stone, if you plans to stay with this brother of mine.'

In Mary's somewhat puritanical mind, the exotic life of the Chicago clubs – born in New Orleans's red-light Storyville and migrating northward when the Navy closed the district down – was a threat to good men's morality. 'My idea of romance ain't no "jelly roll"', she was wont to observe contemptuously, if band members attempted to get fresh at the end of a session.

Willard, who was a waiter and should, by rights, have been getting the place ready, had started up guiltily when he heard the door swing and now eyed his drink with mock embarrassment.

Sure it was only beer but still it was an "illegal intoxicating beverage", containing alcohol well above the 0.5% by volume permitted in the Volstead Act to enforce Prohibition. This evening, however, Mary was more interested in the subject of the conversation than the rights or wrongs of the Eighteenth Amendment to the US Constitution. The new pianist and everything to do with him was of consuming interest to her.

'His mother had had ambitions herself, you see... A black woman with ambition... Well, there you go,' she gave a bitter little laugh. 'When she was a girl, she got into playing piano for the Sunday services. The local reverend was so convinced she had talent he tried to raise funds to send her to the Theodore Thomas College in Cincinnati. There was talk they would accept blacks, you see. But the reverend, he only ever raised enough to pay for the registration fee and to buy the test piece.'

'Test piece?' The saxophone player, head bent over his instrument as he carefully fitted the mouthpiece, seemed to be puzzled by the concept.

'Sure. Anyone wanting to sit the entrance exam had to be

able to perform a set piece of music or a song. But her family laughed at the idea of a girl going on to be a doctor of music…'

'Pretty damn silly idea *any*one going on to become a doctor of music if you ask me.' Wonder Mason, the trombonist, made his usual truculent entrance: late, of course. Mary ignored him, she always did.

'Without the reverend's help she never had a chance of raising the money for study, and she had to give up. But at least Bet Lewis kept that test piece. She kept it like a sheet of Holy Scripture in a folder with two newspaper cuttings about Dr Thomas, said to be setting up an orchestra in Chicago. Being a German like Beethoven, this Dr Theodore Thomas had to be the best kind of musician she reckoned…'

'Beethoven…?' Mason began again, one eyebrow raised in mock puzzlement. But seeing Shout's glare of warning he stopped in mid-sentence and instead blew noisily down the instrument, water key open, to clear the condensation. But even Shout grinned. Mary turned the corners of her mouth down more disapprovingly still and, to Willard's secret admiration, pressed on to make her point.

'When young Meade began to show talent she bought him a cheap fiddle that was something the family could afford. In any case she hoped one day he'd work under Theodore Thomas and made him learn the melody of her test piece.'

'So,' Shout Porter broke in impatiently, 'when Meade got to Chi last year, he was under instruction from his mom to find the Theodore Thomas orchestra. In fact he ended up being sent to me, me bein' known as Mr Music hereabouts. Well, I could have sent him on his way to the Chicago Symphony, once called the Theodore Thomas Orchestra.'

The band members were all on the premises now, though a couple were still at the bar. Shout paused with a grin, before going on.

'I don't reckon to know much about violins, or about

orchestras if it comes to that, but one listen to Meade Luxe Lewis told me he and they weren't going to be friends… so I suggested he stay with us.'

'You quite finished?' Mary Porter looked thunder at her brother.

'Maybe he ain't cut out for an orchestral musician,' she went on, 'but at least he did his best for his mother's ambition. Like most else about him, that middle name goes back to her. Dreams never filled a pot, so Bet Lewis never made the big time. All she had to remind her that she had once even been on thinking terms with it was that test piece. So, when she took Meade along to his first teacher, she had him play that melody, composer one Frederick Lux. The boy played the piano accompaniment as well, after just one hearing, without ever having been taught to read music. "Lux" seemed the natural nickname for the boy genius – he added the "e" himself because it looked like "deluxe" he said.' Turning on Shout she demanded: 'Where is he, anyways?'

'Gone down the Harlem Groceries Store.' Shout couldn't help grinning.

Willard was puzzled. 'What's the problem with the groceries?' he asked.

'Don't always get what you ask for, do you, Mary?' Shout was laughing now and gave his sister an affectionate bear hug on his way over to the bar to chivvy the latecomers . 'If you want a can of tomatoes, Willard, I advise you not go to the "Harlem".'

Everybody laughed. Mystified, Willard turned to Mary for help.

'So what would I get, Mary?'

'Death, as like as not!' she said huffily, with a sniff and an irritated stamp of the foot. Swinging round she called to her brother, 'It ain't funny. It's bad enough he should break the law in here, but at least the stuff's imported – certainly should be too,' she added indignantly to herself, 'price they charge for it. But that "Groceries" hooch would kill you as soon as look at you.'

At that moment, the clubroom door burst open to admit the doorman clutching his flask of strangely colored water and closely followed by a medium tall figure, no more than twenty. His baggy, large-check tartan jacket, of yellows, grays and browns, and a tip-tilted trilby hat made him an unmistakable mark for any pursuer. The doorman crashed his way clumsily on into the back of the premises, sounding the alarm of federal agents on a liquor swoop. For his part, Meade Luxe Lewis, welcomed with outraged concern by Mary Porter, came to a swaggering halt, and tipped the hat to a yet more extreme angle over his left eye. He raised the can in his right hand to his lips and took a prodigious pull at what, according to the label, was "Best Boston Baked Beans".

'Reckon I shook him off,' he announced smugly. 'Anyone care for a "bourbon".'

He grinned widely with an expansive flourish of the baked bean can. Shout Porter stared, open-mouthed and incredulous at the way he had brought the law to the door – he did not for one moment suppose that Meade had, as he claimed, shaken his pursuer off.

The rattle of the street door proclaimed the approach of the awful majesty of the law – except that to Willard, at least, the new arrival looked more like a Coney Island clown on vacation. A short, round, roly-poly pudding of a man, Derby hat askew and face reddening with the exertions of running, announced himself with the startling words: 'Anyone got a drink? Whiskey for preference.' Puzzled by the cool response he went on, 'Ain't this the Mich Much?'

'No, bud, it ain't', said Shout Porter, icily. 'This is The Tavern, and what makes you think we got liquor on these premises?'

'Always had under the old management,' came the hurt response. 'Used to end up here reg'lar as a clock after a hard day's work.'

'Same management,' said Shout, puzzled, 'different name.'

At that moment the proprietor came in from the back, threw up his arms in welcome and cried out with obvious relief. 'Polly, we meet again – you been vacationing or something? What'll it be, bourbon or Scotch?'

"Polly" Goldberg looked the twin of Izzy Einstein, New York's favorite headline-hitting Prohibition agent, but he worked on quite different lines. Where Izzy never took a bribe, and was continually devising new schemes to trap unwary bartenders whether he was on or off duty, Polly had his friends and liked his whiskey. Today had been typical. The office had received an anonymous letter of complaint from an outraged housewife about the grocery store and Polly had been sent to investigate.

"The man at the Harlem groceries store charged me two dollars for a can of tomatoes," ran the letter, *"and when I got it home I found there was nothing in it but a lot of nasty-smelling water. My husband he grabbed it and ran out of the house and I ain't seen him since. I want you to arrest that storekeeper."*

Polly, entirely unprejudiced when it came to liquor, had various friends on Chicago's South Side, but he had never heard of the Harlem Groceries. The letter suited his schedule perfectly. It was long overdue for his work sheet to show a seizure in this region of the city. He visited the store and waited his turn in a long line of impatient customers (some of whom did buy groceries). Looking every inch the small-time Jewish shopkeeper, which he had indeed been before joining the service, he did not attract attention and quickly discovered that the overpriced "deluxe" $4.00 Boston Baked Bean cans contained half a pint of whiskey and the expensive $2.00 cans of tomatoes contained gin. He had bought a sample of each, phoned into headquarters with a message to raid the address and knocked off for the day.

Now he was relaxing in the back office along with the proprietor of "The Tavern" who was a very relieved man. Thanks to Polly Goldberg, the old Mich Much had been quite untroubled by Prohibition enforcement, having been chosen from the start by that excellent agent as his watering hole. But then he had gone sick with a long illness and another agent had been assigned to the area. Hence the change of name and the misleading claims as to new management. With Polly back on duty the proprietor felt he could breath again and was soon regaling his old friend accordingly.

* * * * *

Three months later, and The Tavern found itself going through yet another facelift and name change. This time, Polly Goldberg's removal from the scene had been permanent. He reminded his superiors of Izzy Einstein every time he submitted his reports to head office. Furthermore, the Chicago press were tumbling to the fact that they had an Izzy look-alike on their patch and were beginning to build up the story. Polly had no desire for star status; all he wanted was a monthly paycheck and a friendly bar in each of his sections. His boss thought otherwise. 'Mr Goldberg,' he had said at their last meeting, 'the Agency is not a vaudeville act and its agents are not or should not be public figures. To protect the dignity of the service, I must ask that you hand in your badge.'

Polly's feelings were hurt – but not for long. He walked into another job more or less immediately. However, his successor in the Agency had ambitions "to clean out the South Side bath tub" and The Tavern went out of business for a month or so while it once again redesigned its identity. Renaming themselves The Tavern Wagon, Shout and the boys went on the road and, thanks to contacts with the likes of pianist Jimmy Yancey, picked up the occasional prestigious and highly paid booking on the high society, country house circuit.

So it was that, one July night, Willard found himself playing opposite Louis Armstrong for a dazzling party at the Davenport mansion outside Chicago. Armstrong was back from a year in New York and was standing in as trumpet with Doc Cook's outfit, the other band engaged for the evening. Yancey himself and his recently-acquired wife, Estella (known to one and all as "Mamma Yancey"), had been hired as feature vocal team, since Jimmy could still promote himself on the society circuit with stories of his pre-war European tour and how he had even played by royal command before the King of England.

Willard and Shout, waiting for their cue to take over from Doc Cook, were sharing a drink with Mary Porter, just at this moment ignoring Meade, hoping to make him jealous of Willard. In fact, Lewis was finding that life went much more smoothly without the attentions of the moral Mary, while she was becoming fonder of the Kentuckian than she had intended. She knew there was bad blood between her family and his; just how bad she would discover when her father learnt of her liaison with the old enemy.

Across the crowded dance floor, a white couple had evidently caught sight of Shout and his party and the man, grinning broadly, was navigating his partner in their direction. She was pretty in the conventional manner, with quick, intelligent eyes, bobbed blonde hair, rather more bosom than was fashionable but with the correct "tubular" legs emerging from a knee-length tubular frock and clad in off-pink silk stockings and strap over court shoes. The man wore uniform tuxedo and black tie, central parting plastered down with brilliantine. A little above average height he immediately caught people's attention with his protruding ears and small black toothbrush mustache.

Willard looked at the girl with approval and unconsciously straightened his tie. At his side, Mary gave her a hostile inspection. Just then, Doc Cook and the boys struck up again and Mary, with a curt 'Time for that dance you've been promising me all evening', whisked Willard off under the newcomer's nose.

At the end of the evening Jimmie Noone, the clarinet with the Cook outfit, drove them all back into town. Shout Porter, who had watched his sister's manoeuvring of Willard out of contact with the blonde with high amusement, reported the gist of his chat with the white couple, which the other two had missed.

The man, it emerged, was Leon "Bix" Beiderbecke: ex-college boy, brilliant on the trumpet and one-time leader of his own group, The Wolverines. The girl was a New York friend of the Davenports and a regular house guest of theirs. She had met Bix some three years' back at a Chicago Symphony concert in Ravinia Park. Beiderbecke, still at college, was already making a stir in the jazz world with The Wolverines but had gone along to the concert to please his parents, visiting from Iowa. The girl, at that time an exclusive devotee of the concert classics, was there for the music. Getting to know Bix had got her converted to his kind of music and got her to know the kind of people who played it.

What the two of them now wanted to know was if Shout Porter would play at a big society wedding in September. The bride-to-be was the blonde's friend, Barbara van Manders and the gig would be at the van Manders mansion just outside New York. A white outfit based on members of Nick LaRocca's Original Dixieland Jazz Band was booked and Bix had been roped in as fixer to recruit a black combo to play opposite them. The blonde had told the van Manders bride that Chicago music really should be represented if the occasion was to have true style. Last summer, she had heard Louis Armstrong playing a one-night stand with Fletcher Henderson at the Beaux Arts, Broadway and she had heard that Armstrong was from Chicago. According to Bix, Shout Porter was up there with the big league in the Windy City – would he take the job?

The answer had been a civilized 'No' on his own account but, Shout suggested, why not ask Willard – his brilliant new arrival. Shout had a lot of time for Bix and admired the man's music, but his attitudes to the white world in general were still in trauma following his mother's death. Before that time he could mix in any company as an uncomplicated, professional musician. But the riot had changed everything. Anger and hurt were still posted as twin border guards against too many frontier crossings into the world of fraternization. Just this evening, grabbing a snack at the buffet table, he had heard one flapper saying to another, as she drew herself away from him: 'Isn't it just *too* delicious my dear, to think we're as good as rubbing shoulders with Negroes!' He had no wish to find himself part of a piquant color contrast in the décor of a fashionable society occasion.

'I know Bix isn't like that,' he was saying to Willard, 'but now I can't fully trust even good white friends. Still, life must go on, they always say, and for a young guy this gig on the New York circuit could open all sorts of possibilities. So what do you think of the idea?'

'Fabulous, man!' came the unhesitating reply.

'Well, OK then. But just two pieces of advice. Get yourself a trumpet, cornet players don't generally make star grade these days, and keep your distance socially.'

'Mind you do, too,' muttered Mary, glowering from the other corner seat. Unfortunately from her point of view, Willard was bubbling with excitement at the prospect of the new departure opening up for his career.

'In any case,' Shout was saying, as if reading his thoughts, 'you think the boys on the wagon can get along without me even for a single gig?'

The men laughed, as Noones swung the car into the street where Shout and Willard had their apartment. Having deposited them, Jimmy, who reckoned he had a chance with Mary, happily drove her back to the family home where she kept house for Old Man Porter. As always he was sleeping fitfully, awaiting the click of the door. Mary, for her part, silent in the back of the automobile, was quite unconscious of the fact she was methodically grinding her teeth, as if sharpening them in preparation for a fight. In her mind's eye she could see the she-wolves prowling the streets of New York, ready to make a meal of, as she now realized, "her Willard".

* * * * *

A week later the Porters, father and daughter, were sharing their evening meal with Shout, Willard and Meade Lewis. The last two, like all visitors had to sooner or later, were paying for their supper as audience to a political tirade from the son of the house.

'But the African Communist League,' he was saying, 'is a central part of the work, Pa. President General Garvey has said that we must redeem Africa from the stain of colonialism, for all Africans. He says that the Negroes of the United States, after all the largest community of Africans abroad, must take the lead. According to Mr DuBois, the Negro people have their own unique mission to contribute to civilization and it is the duty of the American Negro to maintain our race identity until this mission can be achieved. In *my* view, some of us ought to be prepared to go to Africa because General Garvey is right when he says that without Africa the Negro cause is doomed.'

'So I've got to up sticks and head out for Africa, because some upstart agitator says so!" fumed Daniel. 'No thanks, son! I've traveled a hard and bloody road, but at last I know where my head's at on this continent. Besides, ain't your precious President General doing time in the penitentiary?!'

Shout angrily scraped back his chair. Since Marcus Garvey's conviction in February, he had been less and less the musician and more and more the politician. He strolled angrily up and down the confined space of the old family room, fuming and punching the air – much to the amusement of Meade Lewis.

The meal was by way of being a farewell party for Willard and he was less amused by his friend's preoccupation. In a few days' time he was scheduled for a gig in New York, supposedly arranged by Bix Beiderbecke. But he barely knew the white musician and had not seen him since the session at the Davenport place with The Tavern Wagon. According to Shout, he had been impressed by Willard's playing then, but that was more than he had said. Now, he said Willard was to go along as agreed and things "would be fine so long as he just kept that horn blowin'". But Willard couldn't shake off his businessman's background so easily. Burney Brock, his father's cautious salesman, held that word-of-mouth orders on anything important were useless. 'A thing ain't settled until it's fixed,' he would say, and by "fixed" he meant a signature. Willard hardly expected a signature, but a call in confirmation would be welcome. Just now, though, Shout was on another planet.

'Shit, Pa,' he exploded – the first time he had sworn at his father. 'That wasn't justice. That was a fix by a bunch of Uncle Toms, shaking hands with whitey.'

'Is that so?' Daniel Porter responded, coolly. 'Using the mails to defraud was the message we got in the union. An' don't let me hear you swearing at your father, boy!'

'Boy!' Shout Porter bit back the tears. He was a man of thirty-five but, to his parent, like sons the world over, he was still a child. "Boy". As long as he lived, a man's sons seemed like children to him. But in the world as created for the African

American, a father could not address his son with the most natural term in a family vocabulary, without seeming to collaborate in oppression. He shook his head angrily; shook the tears from his eyes; shook the passion from his voice.

'"*Marcus Garvey's offence*",' he resumed in a matter-of-fact tone, quoting the movement's classic pamphlet, "*was to threaten the white supremacists and their black bourgeois lackeys, thanks to his success in mobilizing the Negro masses.*" They had to put him away, Pa, don't you see?'

Dan Porter ignored the plea for acceptance in his son's words. He had heard the quotation marks just as if he'd read the pamphlet – which, Shout would have been surprised to learn, he actually had. He had not been impressed.'Marcus Garvey,' he responded sardonically, 'set up an outfit he called the Black Star Line Steamship Company, to give a triangular passage between Africa, the West Indies and the United States of America. This he advertised through the mails and, sure, he got a good response. "Mobilized", you might say, some $350,000. But no one got any liner service I heard tell of. Four vessels commissioned but they all foundered. Damn amateur!'

'Pure libel, Pa,' Mary interrupted coolly and then broke into a smile. 'They should've had a couple of black admirals up to your standard!'

But her father was not to be deflected.

'Libel? Mebbe, though I've heard better. The point is, the man hadn't kept any books and all the money was gone...'

'To serve the cause, Pa; to serve the cause. Any African American who wanted to could have shared the achievement. What about that industrial commercial mission they sent to Liberia? Invited you to be a member, didn't they?'

'Anyone could share – who paid. As for that mission!' Dan spat in the fire with disgust, something else Willard had never seen before in this household. 'Technicians they called themselves, fifteen in all. What a team, what a crew! 'Bout the only decent thing I ever heard about the whole Garvey movement was the Black Cross Nurses our Mary set up for them here in this neighbourhood.'

He held up his hand to ward off the protest.

'OK son, OK. It wasn't all bad. The man had ideas and I guess he did have inspiration, too – inspired some good people too, in fact. But in my opinion he just didn't have what it takes get to this Black American nation of ours off its knees.'

Throughout this harangue, Meade Lewis had been becoming increasingly restive and Willard, too, was beginning to tire of this latest in the family's increasingly frequent disputes. A glance of understanding passed between the two and they slipped out on the pretext of shopping for a pack of cigarettes. The Porter family nodded absent-mindedly, before returning to their domestic psychology, dressed up in the language of politics.

'Some farewell party for you,' grinned Lewis. 'Let's go to The Tavern and do it properly.' Just now the place, no doubt due for another change of name, was hosting Carol Dickerson and his band so that the Wagoners had the night off, and could combine a serious night's drinking with checking out the opposition.

Later, much later, that night, when Willard finally made his way back to the apartment he was sharing with Shout Porter, his friend, who had only just returned from what he termed the family "debate", apologized for their boring bad manners. He then added, 'Because I reckon you should know something my Pa said after you'd left: "Maybe that bastard Willard Stone Senior had the right of it. Maybe money is all that counts, no matter how you get it… so long as you know what to do with it."'

But Willard Junior was barely listening. If old Dan Porter had not told his son what the old feud was about, it was not for him to do so. One day, Shout would surely discover how things stood – that his father believed that their family had been defrauded by "that bastard". And Mary, she too would find out in due course. A frown crossed his face… why should this matter so much to him? As he drifted off into sleep, it was to the music of Dickerson and his men in his mind's ear. That was the sort of thing he was going to go for…

CHAPTER NINETEEN

Marble Halls and High Hat

'I dreamt that I dwelt in marble halls, with vassals and serfs at my side.'

It was a sweet, accurate voice and hit the notes bang center, which was more than most amateurs could manage, Willard noted with approval, and its clear tones cut through the pandemonium of splashes, shrieks of delight and barks of male courtship echoing up from the pool. What was more, the girl could accompany herself on the piano. Willard's dark head, chin on clamped hands, cuffs emerging from the arms of his dinner jacket, stretched along the top of the solid balcony barrier, was effectively invisible from below while the lights in the musicians gallery were dimmed down.

Willard had opted out of the drinks interval, twenty minutes in which the band fortified themselves on carefully rationed and not top-quality bootleg Scotch and bourbon in the landing area at the back of the gallery. It was not part of Mr van Manders' plan that the shapely, well-nourished and largely unclothed white flesh of his daughter and her friends should be casually ogled by the "jass" musicians he had engaged for the evening – fashionable and talented as such a band might be.

And it was no part of Willard's plan to ogle the girls. It was the place that fascinated him. He was distinctly pleased that

Shout Porter had stayed on with the Tavern in Chicago and suggested to Beiderbecke that he should take Willard in his place. The puritanical Shout would no doubt have preached the pleasure out of this fairyland world with a sermon on the evils of white exploitation and social injustice.

Trained by his father from an early age to estimate the size of a premises with a view to assessing its lighting requirements, Willard did his best to look upon the van Manders' swimming hall – it was the only word that fitted the place – as he would have a church meeting room. His first difficulty was that it was probably four times bigger than any such room with which he was acquainted. He estimated the overall length at some 120 feet and the width of the central area to be ninety feet. The entire pool could be seen as a sixty-foot square central area with two extensions north and south, so to speak, about thirty foot long and forty foot wide.

Wherever you looked there were vivid aquamarine blue tiles. In the north and south bays the ten-foot walkway skirting the water on three sides was in this same vivid blue. So were the heavy Egyptian-style buttresses edged in gilding which rose up to the roof beams glazed with the same material. The wall panels and the immense roof continued the vibrant color theme. Willard guessed that the entire vast basin was lined with the same costly tiles – the water was of a deep, vibrant blue that had nothing to do with mother nature and which reflected the golden globes of standard electric lamps, spaced at ten-foot intervals around the water's edge. Behind these, in special wall niches, stood strange life-sized statues of human bodies with animal heads. And now he noticed that the four "panels" at either end of the hall were in fact large, arched windows and as he watched, exterior lights blazed up to reveal swaying trees behind the swaying dancers on the dance floor. The band had taken up the music.

'Looks as though Arlene and Michael have finally left.'

Willard, who until this moment had thought himself to be alone, turned with a start to see the pianist singer at his elbow watching, like him fascinated, the scene below.

'The idea is that years back, in old Mother Russia, the serfs came out with flaming torches to light the way for the sleigh taking the newly weds to the bridal pavilion. Said to be an old family tradition. You can believe that if you like! Me, I doubt whether the van Manders, mother or father, ever got nearer to Russia than a "White Hannaka" in Amsterdam.'

Willard, who knew about "red" and "white" Russia but nothing about Hannaka, nevertheless guessed that something smart was being said and edged away from the girl in discomfort. In his own encounter with the world so far, "smart" was almost invariably something hurtful to someone and, which was worse, something meant to be hurtful. He recognized her now as the girl, Beiderbecke's girl, Mary Porter had danced him away from back in Chicago. To his surprise he found himself feeling grateful to that puritanical little lady.

The mansion in which the wedding party was being held dwarfed the Davenports' and would have put to shame most but the largest of Europe's royal palaces. The gallery in the swimming pool, this evening reserved for the band, held an eight-foot Bechstein grand piano as a permanent (and, given the humidity, a rapidly deteriorating) fixture and was large enough in addition to accommodate a twenty-four piece orchestra to provide the musical accompaniment to the unique entertainments which Mrs van Manders, a pioneer in her own way, had made her hobby and which she called "aquatic eurhythmics". Once a month, a team of expert swimmers assembled at one end of the vast hall-like bath while a select party of society guests sipped cocktails at tables on the marble tiling at the other end and the Albany Polyphonic Players provided "a tasteful and dramatic medley of classical favorites devised by Euphemia van Manders".

At a signal from the lady in question, the swimmers would plunge into the water and thread their way through a program of formation swimming which, whatever its aesthetic qualities may have been, was surely, Willard hoped, more decorous than the goings on in the swimming pool this evening.

Both in its scale and in its décor, the place was a worthy setting for a Roman orgy. The cocktail area had been extended to a sizeable dance floor by boarding over the water to a distance of twenty feet or so, the full width of the forty-foot pool, on scaffolding poles lodged in sockets built into the floor of the pool at its construction. Even though the music had for the moment stopped, scantily-clad or bathing-costumed figures were still swaying dreamily to the imagined rhythms of the dance and from time to time plunging into or being plunged in the cool blue depths to the accompaniment of shrieks of delight.

The gallery stretched back far enough not only so that the seated musicians might not peek over the balustrade but also to spare the prejudiced guests among the wedding party being incommoded by ocular evidence that the fabulous music they were dancing to was largely the work of black musicians – though organized, of course, by Leon Bismark Beiderbecke.

He it was who had welcomed Willard and his band when their antique 1907 Oldsmobile pulled up in a cloud of dust outside the servants' entrance to the van Manders mansion at the beginning of the evening. Resplendent in tuxedo, trumpet in hand as his badge as a musician, his self-introduction 'call me "Bix"' set the tone for a memorable session. Willard had little experience, as yet, of recording studios but he knew that many in the North as well as in the South practised segregation of the races. Beiderbecke's genuine color blindness in the world of music was as things should be, but by no means as they often were. White musicians were eager to learn from the black masters of their art but not many thought that fraternization was part of the deal.

Fraternization was certainly not part of the script Mr van Manders had envisaged when he had agreed to Beiderbecke setting up the music for his daughter's wedding. So Bix was not actually playing alongside Willard and his band. Nevertheless he made regular visits up to the gallery during the course of the evening – 'for any help you guys might need from a conductor,' he joked. The day they needed a conductor would be the day they drew their pension but they appreciated the gesture of solidarity among musicians.

On the other hand, Willard wondered why his girlfriend would come up to "slum it", so to speak.

'You come up to see Bix?' he asked.

'Hell no, he's drinking with the boys, same as he always is when he's not playing. No, I came up to see this,' she gestured towards the scene below them. 'Sensational, isn't it?'

'Sure is.'

'Soon as I heard the music I realized there must be a gallery and that would be the place to see the action from. Course, you can't see the band from downstairs – that would *never* do. Bix told me you were from the South so you would understand *real* good.'

The stress showed she considered things were far from ideal in the North and Willard gave a non-committal grunt. He heartily agreed and could have explained that, to some extent, given the odd set-up in Johnstoneville, he preferred the uncomplicated prejudice of Southern society. But he was hardly accustomed to talking on terms of social equality with white women and despised himself for it.

'What part of the South?'

'Kentucky.'

Willard permitted himself the one word and pulled back from the balcony barrier. He noticed the trombonist come over and glance curiously in their direction. Why didn't the girl go back where she "belonged"? She'd have to soon anyway. Bix didn't allow visitors when a band was playing. But she was not to be discouraged.

'Charming people the van Manders, that's where Barbara gets it from. But they hardly move with the times. Barbara says they would have made Ham travel steerage in the Ark… ' She stopped and turned to look at him face on, as if the serious conversation was about to begin. Or as if she had just had an important idea. In fact, all she said was: 'Kentucky… "Land of the tree and home of the grave" don't they say?'

He cracked a cool grin; he'd hear it before and it wasn't bad. But she'd got it wrong.

'No, I think that's supposed to be Mississippi. Kentucky's kind of frontier territory you might say. My grandpa fought for the North.'

'Did he now?' The voice was Beiderbecke's. 'Well let's hear you play for it now, good and loud. OK, honey, you can trot along now, we're getting back to work.'

Bix calmly brought the party back to order and Willard did not mind in the least. He guessed he knew which way the conversation was heading and he had no interest in covering a white woman's guilt by collaborating in an "objective" discussion of a subject that could not be discussed objectively. The band were all back in their seats, though, Willard noted, all had a drink parked by their chairs.

'I'll go when I'm good and ready,' replied Honey, with an impatient toss of her head.

'You'll go now,' said Bix, with the good-natured authority of someone who knows he does not have to argue to enforce a ruling. 'If not for me, then for Colonel Harry van Manders. Barbara saw you slip away up here and sent me a message to remind you that she had "given Daddy a promise there would be no fraternization".'

The pretty eyes clouded.

'That's true, she did… OK, Bix. Bye bye, Mr Frontiersman.

Say, why don't you give us a chorus from "Lift Every Voice and Sing"?' And with a swish of the pleated tennis skirt, she was gone.

'What's that?' asked Willard.

Beiderbecke stopped in the act of raising his trumpet to signal the start of the next band number.

'What's what?!' The question was delivered in a rising tone of incredulity.

'You mean you've never heard of "Lift Every Voice and Sing"!'

He leant forward for his voice to carry to the piano where Meade Lewis, having restrained his natural boogie style so far, was showing signs of distinct promise as a band pianist.

'Luxe,' called out Beiderbecke, 'you care to start us in on "Lift Every Voice and Sing"? There's a guy here need his education supplemented. You listen along, Willard, and come in when you reckon you can put in some dirt.'

In fact Willard, on trumpet now, played like a man inspired. For him, J. Rosamond Johnson's famous song, known at that time in some circles as "the Negro National Anthem", was a rousing and inspirational melody. More importantly, it convinced him that pride in his color was not an attitude or a pose to be adopted in self-conscious defiance, but rather it was a statement that represented nothing more nor less than the truth. In more practical terms, the evening itself changed the whole course of Will's life – it gave him bandleader status.

As the musicians left the gallery at the end of the session, on their way to take up their places in the breakfast room, Bix found his girlfriend waiting for him at the foot of the stairs. She insisted on a proper introduction to the new trumpet player. She hazarded the opinion that his performance in "Lift Every Voice…"was the hottest thing heard in town since Sissle and Blake hit the Harlem Opera House and that show, she added for the benefit of the van Manders, had been segregated.

'Moreover,' Bix Beiderbecke remarked with a grin to Willard, 'that was the first time a white audience saw people of color wearing tuxedos – had a quite shocking impact on all right thinking people, I've been told!'

But the girlfriend was not to be deflected. The questions came in a flood. How long was this wonder man staying in New York? Had he a band of his own? When was he going to form one? Would he promise her the launch date? She would host a special party at her parents' place on Long Island. Astounded, Willard fielded the barrage as best he could while Bix stood by, a flicker of a grin puckering his lips. What with his center-parted hair plastered down with brilliantine, his immaculate tuxedo and pixy face, he looked like a high-class contact man in a fairyland employment agency.

For it certainly was a fairyland, so far as Willard was concerned. It was barely two years since he had left home, he had achieved a solid reputation in Chicago and now he looked like becoming the latest fad with New York's smart set. It was twenty-four hours and more since his head had touched a pillow. But the last thing Willard Stone had in mind just at the present was sleep. What to do?

'Breakfast, and a big one. Then we'll take ourselves off to the theater on 63rd Street.' Will knew nothing about any theater but the first part of the prescription matched his intentions perfectly. And it was easy to fulfil. Keen to see the black musicians off the premises as soon as might be, "The Colonel", who kept clear of his daughter's parties while they were in full spate but liked to check the debris when things had cooled down, with forced good nature ordered the butler to arrange "that special breakfast for the musicians, somewhere they can be at their ease".

So, while the "Dixieland Boys" were breakfasting along with the white guests in the spacious breakfast room, Bix and his friends were accommodated in the kitchens, where the table was usually laid for the family's servants. The Scottish-born butler greeted Bix with a brief inclination of the head, as he indicated the trays and serving platters and cutlery. He said nothing as he took his leave, having no intention of conversing with the son of first generation German immigrants.

While the band laid into eggs, bacon, sausages, hash browns, chops, muffins and limitless coffee, Bix kept up a stream of comments on the music, jokes and general chatter until the cornet, weary of the smokescreen, broke in.

'No sweat, Bix, we're all grown men. We know what's the score. So, Mr White Moneybags wants to feed his black musicians along where he keeps his black servants – so what's new? So, pass that plate of muffins and let's do what the man said: let's be at our ease; let's eat!'

'But why 63rd Street?' Willard was saying. While the rest of the band had gone back the way they had come, he was being driven into town seated next to Beiderbecke in a flash, old-fashioned European type of car called, Bix had proudly announced, a Prince Henry Vauxhall Tourer, built for a German prince apparently, sometime in the years before the war. To Willard's eyes it looked more like an outsized basinet with a klaxon.

'Because Josephine Baker is in rehearsal there, should be a good enough reason. More to the point, because you're looking for a band and I reckon there's bound to be a few guys hoping for a few vacancies who should be worth giving a try.'

Willard's only association with the fabulous Miss Baker was a set of photographs of her in that Sissle and Blake show *Chocolate Dandies* that had hit Broadway the year before. Fortunately, Mary had not been around in The Tavern the day Wonder Mason showed them round the band. Willard liked Porter's sister well enough, but he sometimes felt that her concern for his morals was over done. Yes, he sure was glad she hadn't seen those pictures and would not be among those present when he met the ravishing new star of the musical theater.

'Not that you'll get to meet her.'

Beiderbecke dashed his hopes.

'The 63rd was where they opened New York with *Shuffle Along* you know. *Chocolate Dandies* was good, but they're looking for something to break that *Shuffle* record. But things aren't going too smooth, I hear. Baker's got some big-time slinky glamour acts. The idea is to send up that Dutch woman spy, Mata Hari – played the Germans for suckers and then got war secrets from them. Trouble is, Baker's a comedy dancer just now. Sure she's got the body for slinks but she keeps breaking down laughing and can't take the stuff seriously, you see. Anything can set her off and Blake's show director won't let anyone speak to her. If you want my opinion, the show will never open.' Willard, barely into his teens when the Great War ended, knew little about it and cared less. He wasn't even sure he'd ever heard of Mata Hari. More important was the prospect of finding musicians who might be willing to work with him. The fabulous Pops Foster was, at that time, working as bassist in the theater orchestra, though Will did not imagine that such a star would work for an unknown. But there again he had a privileged opening into the country mansion circuit – very fashionable and very well paid.

'What's more, you are paid on the actual night and what's even more,' Bix had reminded him, 'the booze is generally the real McCoy.'

By the time they had found a parking lot which met Beiderbeke's stringent security requirements for his treasured Vauxhall, it was getting close to midday and they had a ten-minute walk to the theater.

'No sweat, as our friend the cornet would no doubt observe, I doubt they'll be stopping for lunch today.'

But when the two friends eventually did gain admission to

the auditorium, Bix pointing out to the surly doorman that since it was a black company, a black man could presumably watch rehearsals, the show was clearly not in rehearsal. The chorus, singers and dancers, men mostly in Fair Isle pullovers and slacks, the women mostly in leotards and dancing pumps, were draped here and there over stage props or hunkered down on the floor, talking in a kind of subdued roar punctuated by the occasional squeak of surprise at some improbable yarn or choice piece of gossip.

To Willard's disappointment, Josephine Baker was nowhere to be seen. As he and Beiderbeke moved quietly down the carpeted side aisle, their ears hardly credited the dialogue now in progress between stage and house. From behind the footlights, an elegantly distraught African American ('show director,' whispered Bix to Will) was pleading with a notably less elegant, twenty-pound heavier and mustachioed, starch-collared and florid-complexioned Anglo-Saxon American vibrating near to apoplexy in the third row of the stalls. Willard turned his attention to what was going on.

'… withdraw my money.'

'But Mr Madison… '

'Young man, there are no buts here. Four years back, I came to this theater, after much heart-searching and also, I might say, after careful scrutiny of reports concerning the presentation, with my wife, my daughter and… and… in the gallery you understand… our housekeeper, to enjoy the popular show *Shuffle Along*…'

'A very successful show which I'm sure we shall equal… ' The director was winding his hands round each other like a cringing store clerk seeing a wealthy customer on the verge of deciding against a massive purchase. 'A really successful show and this one too… ' He squirmed ingratiatingly. He despised himself for what he was doing but he did not know what else he should be doing to keep this absurd but very rich sponsor behind the show.

As far as he could understand it, the complaint was that the word "damn" had been used in an exchange scripted between two of the leading characters. Apparently the sponsor had agreed to fund the show on the guarantee that "loose language of no kind whatever" would feature in the dialogue.

'But the word does not appear in the script, Sir, it was just a mistake by the actor, just an actor's mistake.' The director sighed with relief, thinking he had removed the difficulty. In fact, it soon appeared that he could not have made a worse mistake.

'I see.' The sponsor's voice had gone dangerously quiet. 'I see. Well, that is conclusive. I had thought to change my mind if the writer would agree to remove the word. But if members of your cast guard their tongues so loosely as to swear "by mistake" then there is clearly no guarantee you can offer as to the script's decency that will serve. From tomorrow you will have to find your people's wages out of your own pocket... FOR I WITHDRAW MY FUNDING AS OF TONIGHT ... IS THAT CLEAR?'

The last words were delivered at a volume to ensure that not a soul in the entire theater could fail to get the message. The chattering stopped and Madison left the place in total silence followed by a hubbub of consternation from the stage. In the orchestra, the instrumentalists methodically began packing up their instruments.

'It's an ill wind, eh?' Beiderbecke commented with a wry grin as he and Willard headed towards the pit. Willard grinned back. For a new bandleader on the lookout for top-class musicians, recruiting prospects suddenly looked distinctly bright.

Next day, in the lobby of Beiderbecke's hotel – more of a rooming house, as he had explained to Willard – the two men were sharing a pot of coffee and comparing notes before Bix took himself off back to Chicago and Willard – now a fully-fledged band leader with a full complement of bandsmen – prepared for the conquest of the New York society circuit.

'Didn't Shout tell me your father's a businessman?'

'Did he?' Willard was non-committal.

'Sure he did… Well it shows!'

'Uh, huh?'

Since leaving home Willard's anger at his father had, to his surprise, softened. Willard Senior was a hard man, yes, and no one would call him the soul of honor. Yet he was honest by his own lights, he loved and cherished his wife and was loved and cherished by her – truly a woman of honor. What was more he had raised his family to a standing and prosperity achieved by very few African Americans. If his response to Bix was guarded, then it was not because of any sense of shame about his father. No, it was because he doubted whether a business background was really fitting for a "jazz" musician, as he was learning to call himself.

'How does it show?'

'Well,' Beiderbecke laughed, 'I've never seen a guy buy a band wholesale, outright off the shelf like that. Reckon you're only missin' a piano – the guy back there was on the staff of the theater, you said – and that shouldn't be too difficult.'

'But it was your idea,' Willard protested.

'Not quite that, fellah. Sure, I suggested where you could find supplies, so to speak, but I don't remember recommending bulk purchase. Don't get me wrong. All those guys are top-flight performers but I guess I thought you'd be a bit more, well, shall we say selective?'

'Bix, half those guys are in their thirties, couple of them fought in France. Me, I'm a kid as far as they're concerned. I'm honored they were willing to sign up even if it was probably because you promised I could guarantee them work…'

He paused, then, 'Hey! I suppose you really are going to see that girlfriend of yours, with all her contacts, before you go back to Chi'?'

'Sure thing. Relax! We'll get you launched. And not before

time. You ain't that young, you know. Some people might call you a late developer! Noble Sissle formed his first band when he was only sixteen and he held auditions they say!'

'Yeah? Well, Bix, that ain't my way. What with your recommendation and them playing a New York theater, I know those guys are good. Well, certainly good enough for what I need!'

A knowing smile, reminiscent of his father, what Dan Porter called "the grin of the operator", lit his young face.

'I ain't recruiting no "all stars" outfit yet awhile. The Will Stone Seven is going to have just the one star, just the one. But, by God, is that star going to be bright!'

Sadly, Willard's first venture into stardom was all too brief; the crash of Wall Street's financial markets was to see to that.

CHAPTER TWENTY

A Reconciliation

The luxurious upholstery and fittings of the Pullman saloon car offered a pretty good setting for the high life, or so thought Nat "Stride" James, resident pianist on the New York – Chicago Flyer. The scattering of passengers evidently disagreed, looking more like mourners in a chapel of rest. Here and there a solitary figure toyed with a club sandwich, but most stared morosely at the passing landscape of northern Indiana, fortified only by a glass of Prohibition beer or a Sarsaparilla. Speculators on the stock exchange, Stride supposed, for this was the year of the great Wall Street Crash.

For days now, with each new intake of passengers, despair had come seeping through the car like a fog, so that now it seemed to have infected the ivory white, baby grand piano on which Stride was required, by his contract, "to provide light musical medleys at all reasonable hours". Instead he found himself strumming a muted, lifeless version of a plantation work song his mother, a Methodist Church chorister and his first music teacher, sang when her evangelical fervor was overwhelmed by the misery of her own life.

The date was Wednesday October 30th 1929. The day before, New York's stock exchange had experienced the most devastating collapse in the whole of its history. When business closed, the ticker tape service was two and a half hours behind, so huge had been the volume of transactions.

After almost two years of rocketing prices, in mid-September the market had faltered. Professional speculators viewed these early bankruptcies as a necessary shake out of what Yale University's Professor Irving Fisher called the "lunatic fringe". But people of all kinds had taken to investing. Newspaper stories featured chauffeurs who drove with their ears laid back to catch snippets of insider information, of a private trained nurse who cleaned up $30,000 by following tips from grateful patients, and even of musicians who came out ahead of the game. Four million transactions in a day was not uncommon in New York and even sleepy exchanges like Cincinnati boomed.

Inspired by an article in the *Ladies' Home Journal* which sought to explain the workings of the market, the normally level-headed Sarah Stone had commissioned Willard Senior to place some of her personal savings with a broker on one of his visits to that city. Quoting the article's title she observed 'Everybody Ought to be Rich...' adding, 'not just husbands.' In one of his rare good moods Willard had taken the joke. The money, however, he had put in his own bank account. When from time to time Sarah asked how her investment was doing, he replied enigmatically: 'It's still there.' As September's leveling off in dealings turned into October's precipice and more and more big operators crashed, Sarah stopped her worried questioning: Willard, she reasoned, would have told her if there was any hope. On Thursday 24th, catastrophe in New York turned into panic.

The following morning at breakfast, on reading the news in the business pages, her husband quietly folded his paper, went to the business office and returned to the breakfast table with a check made out to Sarah. It represented the money she had given him all those months back with the interest added. 'Now don't you be a silly woman again,' he said. With a full heart and tears in her eyes all she could do was hug him in return.

Only Willard, thought Sarah, *could make money a true token of love, and she knew that he did love her, for all his harshness. If only*, she wished, *he would relent just a little towards young Willard,* and she sent up a special silent prayer that the boy had not put money on the market. The day he left home, five years back, he had told her: 'Don't you worry about me, Ma, musicians *can* make money. Look at Irving Berlin!' She hoped his admiration for the man and his music had lessened with time. In August this year the society pages had splashed pictures of Berlin opening dealings at the newly installed brokerage desk on the liner *Ile de France* as it cleared New York harbor on voyage for Europe. Berlin of course had made a killing. Young Will she just knew would not be so lucky.

Sarah need not have worried on that score, when it came to money Willard Junior trusted common sense rather than luck. But if he had not lost money he had, so to speak, lost customers. In five years Willard's Kentucky Barons had established themselves as the leading band on New York's society circuit. Now that circuit was in ruins as family after family was forced to cut back on expenses. Some of his erstwhile patrons, pauperized by their stock market losses, had disappeared from the New York scene entirely. His bookings diary in tatters, Willard had decided to follow suit and try his luck back in Chicago. He called a meeting of the regular members of the band to discuss plans. Most of them, New Yorkers by birth or adoption, wished him luck, but opted to stay in the city and find work where they could in the clubs of Harlem. Just Ella Clarksdale, the singer, had decided to go along with "the boss". Thus it came about that Willard was now opening the door of the Pullman saloon with one hand, while making a courtly flourish with the carry case that held his precious trumpet in the other, standing aside for his pretty companion to make her entrance.

A Mississippi girl, Ella had been nervous about the whole idea of trying for a drink in the railcar. She just did not believe they would be served and dreaded the humiliation. He dismissed her fears with more confidence than he felt. 'We're in the North, honey, and Illinois passed some civil rights legislation a while back and I do believe the railroad company is based in Chicago, and we'll be steaming into Gary right soon and from there it's just a few miles to the state line. Anyways,' he paused for breath, 'we black folks gotta fight for our rights if we're going to get 'em. So come on, girl, stiffen up that backbone.' Even so it was with some relief that he saw a fellow black face and a musician, too, at the far end of the car and he walked confidently up the swaying compartment to dump his trumpet case on the closed lid of the little piano.

Following in his wake Ella tried to hide her embarrassment, but a quick glance only confirmed her fears. In normal times there would have been an instant uproar at this breach of the color line, illegal though that line might be. Even now, there were some angry mutterings and one of the passengers, a thin-faced man who had only that moment furtively fortified his coffee from a hip flask of amber-colored and surely illegal liquid, beckoned to the car steward.

Unsuspecting, Willard, his arm round Ella's waist, started chatting to the pianist. 'Mind 'f I rest the horn on your piano – never move no place without it.' Within minutes the two musicians had established each other's professional credentials and even Ella was beginning to feel at her ease. In his mid-forties, James had, it appeared, been a name to conjure with in the Harlem of the 1910s, teaching the art of the stride piano technique to the great James P. Johnson himself.

Willard flashed a conspiratorial grin in Ella's direction. Old jazzmen down on their luck regularly claimed some pioneering achievement. Even so, this guy was good and Willard and Ella soon found themselves humming along as he played, with a few experimental riffs of their own. However, they had not come up the train for a sing-a-long and Willard was pleased to see a waiter approaching. But the man, himself a black, was accompanied by a swelling rumble of protest from the white clientele, and was clearly embarrassed.

'Excuse me, Sir, but are you and the young lady meaning to take refreshments because if so I really would be obliged if you would reconsider.'

The characterless company-speak hid the man behind his uniform, which was the way Quenlin Bentley, in his second week of duty as railroad steward, wanted things. A graduate in literature with an excellent degree from Oberlin, he was just one of thousands of qualified men forced to find "careers" in jobs which white students would not consider, except as a means of paying their way through college. Before the angry Willard had a chance to respond, the pianist intervened.

'Best do like he says, chum. I've got a job to consider here… I guess the whole car reckons you and me is buddies.'

'You mean I *cain't* get a drink here? But that's against the law in Illinois they tell me… '

'Indeed the law entitles you to order a drink, Sir,' said the steward, 'but I fear I will not be the one to serve it to you, and if I won't, I don't rightly know who will. Perhaps you'd best appeal to the conductor here.' While the dispute was developing at the piano, the conductor of the train had entered the saloon and was methodically making his way up the car. His progress was slowed considerably as each passenger added his complaint against the idea that people of color be served in "their" saloon.

By the time the man came up to the piano group, he had evidently had time to devise a course of action that might pacify his passengers while keeping his company within the law. Having checked the tickets of the two black passengers he reached across the piano for the trumpet case.

'You a musician, Sir? I thought so. Used to play mahself, when I was young.' He spoke quietly so that only the immediate group could hear him. 'Now I wonder,' he paused, 'I wonder… would you and your young friend, who I guess must be a singer, care to join Mr James here in a few numbers? I'm sure the railroad company would be happy to stand you a couple of drinks for your courtesy.'

With a wintry smile, Quenlin Bentley prepared to move up the car, happy to be leaving the scene of action. In his brief time with the company he had come to know this conductor as a man of devious intelligence, a man who should by rights be pork-barreling in Washington for some prosperous congressional district but who would be lucky to rise above his present lowly rank in the railroad hierarchy. For his part, Willard had nothing but contempt for the man.

'You mean if I collaborate in this playacting you'll let me and my friend here stay where we're legally entitled to be, and get a bite to eat and drink?'

'Not to eat, Sir. I never heard of musicians taking a meal during performance. But drink yes!'

'It's disgusting what you suggest. We could take you to law, you know?'

'Maybe, Sir, maybe,' the steward replied with weary emphasis,' but I wouldn't bank on the result. And you would surely help those of us who must continue to work on this railroad when you and the young lady have completed your travel, if you would fall in with my suggestion.'

Willard felt a tug at his sleeve and looked down into the imploring eyes of young Ella. Glowering in impotent fury he reached for the catch of the instrument case, withdrew the dazzling trumpet which was his heart's delight and with a silent apology for involving this, his noble friend, in such humiliation prepared to play his part in the charade. To retreat would, he reckoned, be a greater public humiliation for him and Ella, and would rob the pianist of the cover for his fraternization with black passengers. Once the company decided he was a troublemaker the man would be out on his ear. Suavely diplomatic, the conductor turned to the car to announce that the railroad company had pleasure in introducing two additional musicians for the entertainment of their patrons: Mr Willard Stone and Miss Ella Clarksdale of New York.

Soon the trio at the piano were in full spate and even the gray men at the tables brightened a degree. At the bar Quenlin turned to busy himself with glasses, tears welling up behind his eyes. He himself felt his spirits revived by the insistent throb of life the musicians, now lost in their art, were pulsing through the saloon car. But he despaired for his people. So generous, so gifted, so responsive in their mutual solidarity, that even when assisting in their own humiliation they could lighten the troubles of their oppressors – for him there was no other word.

The final chorus was winding up to a triumphant break on the trumpet as the saloon, halfway down the snaking line of cars, pulled slowly into Gary station. Smiling faces on the platform turned to follow the musicians' car's slowing progress. 'Say,' exclaimed a wit, 'here comes what I *call* a bandwagon!'

A little way further on, a couple of young black women murmured a heartfelt 'Yessiree!' as they pulled open a door of the now stationary train. With only a couple of pieces of light hand luggage, they plowed purposefully through the hostile and crowded cars toward the saloon. With a dramatic gesture they flung open the door. There the protest at yet two more black faces choked hesitantly when it was seen just how pretty these faces were.

Mary Porter and Jasmine Williams were homeward bound for Chicago after a visit down the line to preliminary auditions being held for the Hall Johnson Choir. Mary had to sing somewhere, it was her nature. Disenchanted with what she called the "sleazy world of speak easy and clip joint" and the hazards it could present a girl, Mary "Moral" Porter, as she was known in the clubs, had long since broken with Meade Lewis and even left Shout and his band. The success of the Kentucky Barons on the socialite circuit seemed much more elegant. But that was New York and according to the gossip Willard had a singer who suited him just fine.

The expedition to Gary had been frustrating. The assistant holding the auditions explained that Mr Johnson was a rather serious character and that he expected his choristers not only to be able to read music but to have some understanding of music theory. At this time, Hall Johnson himself was in his early forties and with a degree in music from the University of Pennsylvania. He had turned to choral conducting four years back and his ambition, so people said, was for the Hall Johnson Choir to outshine even the world-famous Fisk Singers. Unfortunately, for all her talent, Mary had never had any kind of academic training. Jasmine, pianist for her local chapel, was asked to attend a final audition with Johnson himself; Mary, to apply again when she had had some lessons in theory. Now, as the exciting strains of "King Porter Stomp" rang from the train, Mary, with a grin of appreciation for the unknown trio's choice of melody, decided that those theory lessons would have to wait awhile and that some compromise with the speak-easy world might be found after all!

When she saw who in fact was behind the trumpet and who was the vocalist, she registered astonishment and disappointment in equal intensity. To find Willard heading for Chicago was a wonderful surprise but Willard without a talented and attractive woman in tow would surely have been a better one. Still it *was* wonderful to see Willard. With her natural ebullience at full pressure, Mary Porter sailed up to the piano with a 'Hi, fellas' that had the saloon car patrons shrinking sourly back in their seats.

Equally astonished, Willard brought the chorus to an abrupt end, which Stride James camouflaged as best he could with a brilliant final flurry of extemporization.

'Mary! How yuh doin'? What yuh doin'? What's the news?'

'Since yesterday you mean? Well I guess that ole stock exchange has taken another tumble,' came the mischievous reply in her best Southern drawl. 'An' oh! I nearly forgot, some professor says things'll get better and the market may even "experience an upturn" once it really understands the "beneficial effects that the prohibition of alcoholic liquors has had on making the American worker more productive and dependable".'

All this was spoken just above conversational level and accompanied by old-fashioned "minstrel" gestures as if to mollify the white audience to this impromptu cabaret with a show of self-mockery. The tables furthest from the piano indeed could not catch everything that was said but it was obvious to all that these young black folk were getting dangerously above themselves.

'OK folks, when you've quite finished! I got work to do.' Stride James cut in on the love feast in a harsh, not over-friendly whisper. He had played along with the conductor's pretence of two unexpected guest performers for the sake of a quiet life. Sure, he'd enjoyed the session. But now the atmosphere in the saloon car was getting hostile to him as well as to them. If the newcomers carried on like this he would surely be found guilty by association and could kiss goodbye to a steady paid job just when, thanks to the tumbling stock prices, the world of work looked set on shrinking. With Christmas barely two months away a wise man left gestures and politics to others.

The pianist's voice brought Willard back to reality. He too

332

had played charades long enough. Ella wanted to get back to the safety of their seats down the train and anyhow there was Mary to talk to and catching up to do. His mind made up, he packed away his trumpet, shook hands goodbye with Stride James and, with a flourish, made a stage bow to the audience of customers and then led his little troop of ladies out of the car.

The few remaining miles into Chicago passed quickly as Mary and Willard caught up on lost time, with the others very much sidelined. Jasmine was a quiet soul by nature and Ella, it turned out, was returning to Chicago as much to track down an old boyfriend as to help Willard. They parted with general agreement to keep in touch before Willard, trumpet in one hand and traveling bag in the other, rode the "EL" back to the Porter home with Mary. Barely conscious of the depressing city-scape as it slipped by outside the window, he kept his companion enthralled with a bubbling account of the high-life world he had come to know. Responding, Mary sparked with a new intensity of life as friendship soared into the new dimension of love.

For the time being, however, returning to the Porter home very definitely meant returning to planet Earth. The grin of delight on old Dan Porter's face at seeing his daughter safe home cooled abruptly when he saw who was with her. Not that he was surprised. Like father like son, the Stones could be expected any time any place. Shout said Willard was a regular guy: *Could be* thought Dan to himself, *so why don't he mosey on out to Shout's? Better still, go back to New York? Any place so long as he don't hang about with our Mary.* Young Stone had been out of circulation for the best part of five years, but in that time, rather than settle down with some decent young guy in the neighborhood, Mary had filled her time with politics and business.

Dan blamed Elsie Marre. Just turned sixty, the dynamic old campaigner had been a regular visitor to Chicago ever since the fateful events of 1919; in part to check that Dan was keeping up his union work begun in the aftermath of Harriet's death, in part because she saw Mary as a promising recruit to "the cause". For her part, Mary had been infected by the evangelical fervor of the old warrior, to the despair of the local boys.

And when she was not at rallies or meetings she was busy building the old Farmerson shop back to profitability. She was now a prosperous lady thanks to the handsome profit sharing scheme Dan had agreed, but he had not meant any part of her wealth should be married into the Stone family resources! Dan was proud of his daughter as a businesswoman. She had helped make Porter's the largest hardware business on the South Side. Even so, a girl should get married, when she found the right guy!

Very much to her own surprise, Mary found herself coming round to the same view. Although she had only known Willard for a few months before he left for New York, and although she had enjoyed every moment of her life in politics, the sight of Willard in the saloon car that afternoon had triggered the immediate realization that she had been in love with the guy for the past five years. All that remained to do was to convince Willard that he needed Mary Porter as a wife and persuade her father to accept her marriage into the hated family of Stone.

Mary had no doubt that Willard loved her. How could she be so crazy about the guy if he did not? But the sparkle in her eyes dimmed as she looked into the future and saw the heartache and family feuding that must surely result when her father heard of the match. This afternoon he was being coldly polite, but she abandoned any idea that they might offer Willard the sleeping couch for his first night in Chicago or even have him stay to supper.

Instead she walked round with him to Ma Blossom's rooming house in the next street and had a quiet word with that good old friend to make sure that corned beef hash, Willard's favorite, was on the menu. It was an excellent hash, but Willard barely noticed. He was too busy writing a new project into his schedule, along with house hunting and job hunting... wife hunting.

Next day, Thursday, with Shout's help, he found himself a decent enough two-room apartment and that weekend, taking advantage of the fact that Shout's Sunday meeting had been cancelled, cornered him to talk what their fathers would call "job opportunities".

'How's the scene, man?'

'Market ain't so bad,' came the reply. 'Good hood money round the clubs. Mind you, some of the names the white guys take'd make you wonder if the hoods were *playin'* in the clubs. Fellah called Mugsy somethin' sounds more like one of Al Capone's soldiers than a musician.'

'Any good, any competition you think?'

'Sure, they're competition. Whitey likes the idea of whites playin' black man's music. Some of 'em ain't bad, too. Young guy on clarinet turned up at the Mich Much other night, name of Ben Goodman, offered to play along. Said his parents want him to go straight... y'know Mozart an' all that jazz?'

Shout grinned at his own feeble joke.

'I saw Bix two years back in New York. He was talking about a recording session. Didn't come off though – the recording studios wouldn't cross the color line so Bix dropped the whole idea. Heard tell he was working in Chicago now.'

Shout paused, he was bored with the idea of yet another conversation heading back to the color line. This was the first real "crack" on music he'd had for a long time. These days his life seemed to be all politics. Abruptly he switched direction.

'Everyone's out for new sounds these days. Heard the other day Meade Luxe Lewis, one of the sweetest boogie men you could wish to hear, was messing about with a harpsichord in some recording studio. Then there's Jimmy Noone at the Apex Club, teamed up on clarinet with alto sax and four guys on percussion. When I was a kid y'hardly heard a sax any place. The music's beginning to motor like a nervous flapper weavin' way off beam, and its getting worse. Bands are getting bigger, guys composing the stuff now... anythin' goes s'long as it's different.'

'Heh, man! That's what we call progress! Things change, things move – you gettin' old or sumpthin?'

'Could be!' Shout grinned good-naturedly 'Forty next birthday.'

'Forty!' Willard was shocked. Like modern music, time seemed to be motoring too. How could Shout Porter be an old man already? And what about him, Willard Stone, he wasn't what you'd call young any more, twenty-five and still got nowhere!

For although he had chosen the uncertain life of a musician, Willard fully shared that trait in his family's heritage that demanded its members gave shape to something it called a career. The Kentucky Barons had made him a name in New York society but he wanted something more established, more permanent, more, though he would never admit the word, respectable. Perhaps Mary's views on the floating world of the jazz musician had something to do with it, for Willard had decided that Mary had to be part of that career if it was to be worth living. This would mean war with Old Man Porter, perhaps Shout could advise on strategy. Just now, however, his ally was still bending his mind to the question of work .

'You could try Earl Hines, I guess.' While Willard appreciated the help, he was not planning to join forces with an unknown and he said so.

'Not heard of Earl Hines? You sure been out of circulation! He's big-time piano here in Chicago. Plays the Grand Terrace. Started on trumpet as a kid, they say, then moved to piano lessons with his mother. He's done the town... played with Armstrong for a time in Carol Dickerson's combo at the Sunset

Café. Then he and Louis started their own club but it didn't work and Hines got hired by Noone at the Apex... now he's got his own outfit. Could well be he'd take you on... doesn't keep trumpet players too long I hear.'

'How come that? Kinda' awkward, huh?' Willard was impressed by the musician's pedigree but he was too used to running his own show to humour an awkward boss.

'Don' reckon so, seems it's more his style of music. He plays what he calls "trumpet piano" and that makes some horn-players edgy – who's the real trumpeter in this outfit eh? Things like that. Anyways I hear he's thinking of up-sizin' his band.'

'Seems to be the fashion right now,' Willard agreed. 'Ellington's the big, big name in New York. Sounds like it could be worth going round to see Hines. Right now, I suggest we go grab a bite to eat. There's somethin' I got to talk to you about an' I talk better on a full stomach.'

Over a corned-beef hash that was not a patch on Ma Blossom's but went equally unnoticed, Willard approached the subject of him and Mary with caution. It was obvious that while Shout knew there was a feud between their fathers he did not know exactly what it was about. The time had come to tell him and the job was neither pleasant nor easy. Willard guessed that Dan had not revealed the full details to his children because he felt ashamed of allowing himself to be cheated. So far as Shout was concerned, however, Willard Senior was the only villain in the piece though his son, who for five years he had counted a friend, came a close second.

'Should have told me a long time ago...'

'Suppose I thought you knew, Shout. Didn't surprise me my dad not sayin' nothin' but I sure thought yours would've told his family. Back in '24, I was jes so glad you treated me friendly, I wasn't about to ask too many questions. Anyways, it wasn't me as cheated your pa and as soon as I found out, I confronted my pa with the evidence and got thrown out on the street for my trouble.'

Willard found himself getting angry, which was the last thing he wanted to be with Mary's brother. But it seemed unfair that he should somehow be blamed for what his father had done and for what Shout's father had not done. If Mary took the same attitude he could kiss goodbye to any hope of her becoming his wife. Somehow though, he felt sure she was a friend.

'OK, OK, so perhaps it wasn't your fault. But it's a lot to take in all at once. Yuh gotta admit. Turns out we mighta bin rich but the father of my best friend cheated us. An' now the guy wants to marry into the family!'

Suddenly, Shout Porter grinned, grinned like he used to years ago, before he "got politics", before the horrid death of Harriet. It was a smile Willard had never seen and a man he had never known, a man suddenly younger, suddenly more alive. For his part, Shout, with a silent prayer to his mother, whom he hardly remembered, and one to Harriet, whom he always thought of as mother, vowed to push along the budding romance. The spirits of the two women who presided over his life would, he knew, approve. Life must go on and love must rule life. Mary should have the man she wanted and if that man was to be Willard Stone then the Porter clan would have to stand by her.

Assured of the brother's support, Willard prepared to lay siege to the sister. There was no contest. Thanks to "Aunt" Elsie Marre, Mary knew more about the family skeletons than her brother. In any case, when it came to Romeo and Juliet she was entirely on the side of the lovers and entirely against the feuding parents. As the weeks went by and 1929 grew into 1930, she spent more time than ever away from the family home. Dread of the inevitable showdown with her father was more than half the truth, she grimly admitted to herself. But there was much to be done on the political front; of an evening, when she had the time she was to be seen more and more at the Grand Terrace, occasionally singing with the band.

The politics was a test case being brought under the Illinois civil rights legislation, which Willard had hoped to use in the railroad saloon car. Five young black women had been refused service in a downtown cafe and were suing the owners, the Windermere Hotel Group. Elsie Marre had lined up the law firms and Mary's job was to keep her briefed on developments. Daniel grumbled to Elsie about being left alone at nights, but it was an encounter at the old Mich Much which in fact decided Mary and Willard that they would have to face her father.

Willard had left Earl Hines after a few weeks and, as Shout was taking a week or two off touring the clubs of New York, he took over as lead trumpet. Leaving the club on the last Saturday night in March, Willard and Mary were stopped by a notable figure of a man. Barely five foot tall, and clad in lime green trousers topped by a largely flame-colored tartan jacket, he introduced himself as Bill Bolden, nephew of the legendary "Buddy", cornet player and railroad clerk of Atlanta, Georgia and a new fan of the Mich Much and its music. Would they meet him for lunch at a restaurant of their choosing the next day when he would have some business to propose?

It was a remarkable meal, both for the speed with which the little man ate and for the suggestion he had to make. Like his great namesake, he played cornet. He and his friends had been running an amateur club in Atlanta, Georgia so successfully that the others had decided to turn professional. The oldest of the group, Bolden shrugged with a deprecating grin at his garish young man's kit, he was not prepared to risk his regular job, but had offered to find an established professional to replace him. Visiting Chicago on family business he had heard of the reputaiton of the Mich Much and when he heard Willard on trumpet he reckoned he had found his man. He told the Chicagoan how Atlanta was the hub of black culture in the United States, he told him he would have his name on the band and half a year's money. But he also stressed that the job was to start in September.

'All very businesslike,' Shout had almost sneered when he was told about the proposal, and Willard did not argue. He was beginning to grow up in the way that meant a man could live with himself without apology to anyone. Willard Stone had "businesslike" in his background but equally he had music in his blood. A weekend in Atlanta confirmed that the proposal made artitistic as well as commercial sense – so far as anything could in these uncertain days – and Mary loved the look of Atlanta as a possible future home. All that was needed was for old Dan Porter to accept Willard Stone as his son-in-law.

He not only refused but terrified them all with the violence of his refusal. Mary tried by herself a few days after but without success. Depressed, she decided she would have to let the matter rest a while.

* * * * *

It was three months later. A brisk *rat-tat-tat* broke the stillness of the drowsy evening heat. A slow grin of contentment spread over Dan Porter's sleeping face. Bess must be chopping peppers and shallots for spicy chicken fry, his favorite. The *rat-tat-tat* repeated itself louder. The woman was surely hammering down on that chopping board. He grinned again, this time guiltily. *Guess she's in a temper 'bout Mr Stone and the patent. I tried to explain,* he thought, *invention done in company time… I'll get a raise come Christmas… Women don' understand these things. Look how mad she got when I told her off for burstin' out like that in front of the kids at The Mammoth Cave. Young Willard warn't to blame none for his dad's meanness.*

Again the *rat-tat-tat*, followed this time by an impatient

thump. The dreaming mind shifted focus. Now the sound track offered the rattle of a horse hearse and the clunk of a coffin being clumsily loaded on board. The sleeping face contorted angrily. *Guess you was right Bess an' guess I was wrong. Doctor said a few months' rest would have worked the cure. You'd be alive now if I'd had my due from that crook Willard Stone. Robbed me, then sacked me… drunk on duty!'*

The hammering was insistent now and Dan slowly emerged into consciousness. He shook his head, fuddled by the whiskey he had drunk earlier that afternoon. Coming to, he sensed the familiar loom of the furniture in the darkened room, sweltering in the heat of the Chicago summer of 1930 and not a Kentucky spring of 1880. He was not now, as he had not been then, given to heavy drinking, but when young Mary had left that stormy lunchtime he had taken a long shot of bourbon to settle his nerves. 'For the last time of asking father,' she had screamed, 'Will you or will you not agree to me and Willard Stone gettin' married?'

He felt his way across the room, marveling as he did so that his Mary, truly, had screamed. 'So old man Stone slowed your life down. Does that mean that, thanks to you, he's goin' to be able to stop mine in its tracks altogether!' Her body vibrating with fury, the hot tears streaming down her face, she had taken a step forward as if to strike him and then, flinging her arm across her face, her body swinging with the force of the gesture, she had thrown herself out of the room and seconds later shattered the street door shut behind her.

Dan had reached the living room door now and felt for the hanging pull-switch conveniently placed just to the left of the opening as one entered. The wiring was barely a year old. As long as kerosene lamps had bulked large in Porter's trading profile Dan had refused the electric, despite the fact he could well afford it and Mary, used to getting her way, had begged him to move with the times. 'Insult to the customers,' he had said. Now, jerking the cord dangerously hard and roughly twisting the door handle, he growled: 'Move with the times if you like, young lady, but don't expect my blessing on any modern kiss and make up of a marriage with the Stone family.'

The low wattage electrolier flooded the room with a gentle glow, which met the faint evening gleam from the fan-light over the street door as he entered the short hallway. The door panels shook with a tattoo of knocks, which exploded into an indignant: 'An' about time too, Dan Porter, I thought you must be dead in there.' The twilight gleam haloed the grizzled hair framed in the open doorway and the faint house light caught the blaze scar.

'Elsie Marre?' He queried, puzzled by alcohol and vague with fatigue.

'Darn tootin' sure it's Elsie Marre… who else you take me for? You drunk or sumpthin?'

Starting out in mild mockery, the second question ended on a worried tone. Mary had said nothing about drink being taken over the lunch table. At once, Elsie sensed that the figure in front of her was more a worried old man than the domestic tyrant her young friend had sobbingly described. *Old Man!* Elsie thought, grinning to herself in spite of her anger. *At sixty-two who am I to talk.*

But Elsie Marre had lived a comparatively privileged life. Tireless in her work for the cause of black women's rights, she had given her body the ideal regimen of exercise and sparing diet while the various organizations she worked for had paid the cost of decent accommodations. Nobody questioned nor needed to question the expenses claims of "Lady Blaze", but in at least one modest aspect virtue had been its own reward. Her stamina seemed inexhaustible: it was still only June but this was her third visit to Chicago, just one of a dozen cities in a territory that stretched as far south as Atlanta and as far east as New York.

Slightly stooping, Dan Porter confronted the sturdy figure of a still beautiful if now somewhat portly woman who had clearly come to do battle. About what he did not as yet know but he gave way with placatory body language as he waved her into his modest sitting room.

'Not long since you was in Chi, Elsie. It's hardly time for me to sort out that business over the Pullman sleeping car union. But it'll be ready by July as I promised.'

It would also be the last job he did in his capacity as local union liaison man for the National Urban League for the promotion of black employment. In his opinion, the League was too ready to conform to the demands of the employers and too slow to speak out about the continuing discriminations against black working conditions. In a recent speech, The League national secretary had praised the activities of the Sleeping Car porters, but when the Pullman Company had immediately sought assurances that the League did not support the union's activists, the League had written Pullman what Dan regarded as a groveling apology, and effectively disowned the speech.

He had gone along with the League's position for the sake of his friendship with Elsie, though he reckoned she had fallen to the politician's besetting temptation, expediency, and resolved to do no more "dirty work" for her. But her position had been changing, shocked by the cynicism of League officials she had withdrawn from the Pullman affair and announced her intention of relieving their agent of his distasteful job.

That was the reason why she had made this visit to Chicago. But on her way to the Porter residence, she had encountered a tearful Mary coming away from her angry confrontation with her father. Over a milkshake in a nearby soda fountain, the sobbing girl calmed herself and explained that her father was still refusing to give his blessing to the marriage. Elsie was appalled. To think that the old feud should still burn so hot in Dan's memory! She told Mary to expect to be set up in Atlanta by Christmas and herself stormed on to the Porter house.

Dan's sleepy delay in opening the door only stoked the fires of her anger and now, with a workmanlike summary and dismissal of the Pullman case, she turned to the matter in hand. By the time she had finished, Dan Porter was sobbing himself, his old head resting on the bosom of his "little friend", as he still thought of Elsie. It was this in fact that broke his opposition to his daughter's departure for a new life.

Elsie's presence brought many things up to the surface of his mind which had only ever been half guessed. He remembered how her girlhood presence in the high street store had been especially sweet to him. He remembered the suspicions his dear Bess had felt about his friendship with the "child", he reflected on how Harriet, his second wife, had been so much younger than him when he married her. Was this stubbornness of principle over a wrong now fifty years in the past just a cover for something much more wrong, much deeper and much more present? He had heard tell of such things.

Too honest for his own good, Dan Porter had let the old sense of betrayal in the simple business matter of the patent fester so long that it had come near to poisoning his soul. The moment he said "yes" to Willard and Mary the boil was lanced, the pus was drained and the poison was out.

In September they married. Willard stayed on with the Mich Much. He had already heard from Atlanta that the band there had found its new trumpet. The birth of young Daniel in May the following year more than made up for any disappointment. But Bolden's sales talk had done its stuff; Atlanta was now his objective. When he and Mary eventually set up home there, pride of place among the family photographs would be the wedding photo inscribed "*All*

344

Friends at South Side Chi September 1930". Willard and Mary, Shout and his recently acquired wife, Lindy Loo, stand sturdily cheerful either side of Grandpa Dan, his old face content at last with a life well lived and smiling a serene blessing on the future of his daughter and her husband, no longer the enemy but accepted as a son.

In *Black Destinies* Geoffrey Hindley continues Loretta Stone's account of her family saga, from the typescript she first handed over to Johnny Carman. He also follows the fortunes of the Porter family, making their mark on the musical life of Atlanta. We witness the continuing, murky ascent of S.K.L. in commerce and, alongside this, the fame won by a branch of the family in the world of philanthropy. But, we witness also the destruction of the old haven of Johnstoneville, betrayed to the machinations of an international crime syndicate. The conspiracy is unmasked by a young Stone launching his career as an investigative journalist. In the process he unravels the secret of the transformation of the Kentucky roadside house from general store to mystery mansion and plunges the dynasty into civil strife. Loretta, now a rising star in the academic firmament, eventually takes over the narrative. Like "Young Willard", she leaves home, like him she too rejects the family's capitalistic ways, but she too has a career to promote. Will Johnny Carman have a part in the new saga? Indeed, will there be room for any man at her side?